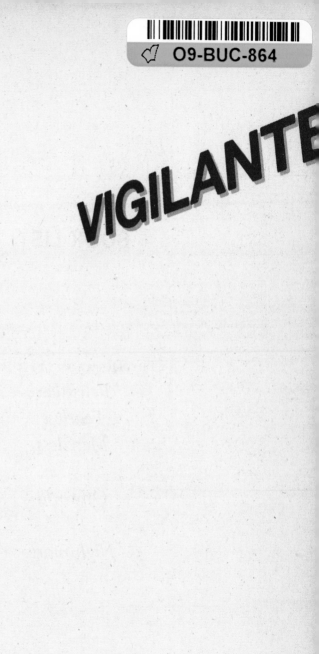

VIGILANTE

BOOK LIST

VIGILANTE

ROBIN PARRISH

◆ BETHANYHOUSE
Minneapolis, Minnesota

© 2011 by Robin Parrish

Published by Bethany House Publishers
11400 Hampshire Avenue South
Bloomington, Minnesota 55438

Bethany House Publishers is a division of
Baker Publishing Group, Grand Rapids, Michigan

Printed in the United States of America

Library of Congress Cataloging-in-Publication Data is available for this title.

11   12   13   14   15   16   17   7   6   5   4   3   2   1

For my precious, precious Emma.
You are my sunshine.

PROLOGUE

For the United States, it is a time of revolution and unrest.

Nine years ago, a long, bloody war waged on foreign soil came to a bitter end. It was a war against evils and crimes against humanity not witnessed since the reign of Adolf Hitler—evils that cut into the very soul of man.

In the years since, America has grown increasingly unstable. A faltering economy is on the brink of a second Great Depression. Despair and apathy have led to nationwide demoralization.

And once again, seizing the moment, organized crime spreads like a cancer. . . .

PART ONE

The Plan

Nolan Gray gritted his teeth and closed his eyes as the pistol was aimed at his face from just inches away. The barrel of the SIG Sauer P226 was so close, he could clearly see the tiny gold anchor engraved on its left side, designating it as a standard Navy Special Forces weapon.

Beads of sweat beneath Nolan's mop of unkempt hair gave way to droplets, and traced a path on his skin down to his eyes, nose, ears, and neck. He was waiting for the pain, knew it was coming any second, but despite his immense training and experience, it was still an incredible thing to know you're about to be shot.

Finally he blinked when the gun never went off.

"Look . . ." said Branford, the man across from him. His arm never wavered, his hand never shook. It was steady and sure, outstretched directly toward Nolan's head. Branford's crusty voice never sounded anything but confident. His comment was one of clarification.

Nolan was becoming angry, his carefully attuned discipline threatening to falter. The moment was at hand. There wasn't time for this, not now.

The light of the moon was brighter than the nearest street lamp. Nolan glanced around, the city eerily silent at this dark hour, yet he could detect a distant bicycle, a jogger—probably female, from the sound of the footfalls—and someone coughing. Sooner or later one of these passersby was going to cross his path, and he was going to lose his chance.

"*Just do it!*" insisted Nolan.

Branford's hand cinched tighter around the polymer grips of the matte black P226, so tight his knuckles showed white. Still he never quivered, the gun an immovable mass of metal that could have been grafted to his arm.

Nolan closed his eyes and braced himself again.

"This is asking an awful lot. . . ." muttered the other man.

Nolan's eyes popped open, and he choked down the outrage rising within him. "There isn't anybody else!" he said through bared teeth. "You think *Arjay* could do this?"

"And if I miss?" asked Branford, his voice the bark of a Rottweiler.

"You would never miss," Nolan said without hesitation.

"Always a first time," griped Branford with a sigh. "All right. On three. One . . ."

Nolan steeled himself one last time. He closed his eyes when Branford reached "two."

Branford squinted slightly, adjusting the angle of his weapon by the slightest degree. "Three."

The sound was swallowed by the SIG's attached silencer, but Nolan never heard a thing, even at such close range. Instead, he was on fire with a pain so intense it brought rushing back long-suppressed memories of the horrors he'd been subjected to during the war.

And just when he was about to allow himself to pass out from the powerful sensation and the crippling memories it brought, another shot rang out, and the pain became twice as searing.

He couldn't hold on any longer.

This was the end. His end.

As it should be. As it was meant to be. Nolan Gray was no more.

———

Aaron Branford stared at the man on the ground, his blood seeping into the soil. A brief examination later, he glanced around the area in every direction, careful to ensure that no one had heard the muffled shots from his sidearm.

Satisfied, Branford quickly retrieved a shoe box–sized package from a nearby bush and placed it on the ground beside Nolan's body.

As he opened the box, he pulled out a phone from his pants pocket and dialed the only number saved to the phone's memory.

He set to work on the box's many contents, placing them in the proper positions while waiting impatiently for the phone to be answered.

"Branford?" shouted a smooth voice over a pronounced clamoring of metal.

"Who else would it be, genius?" Branford growled back, peeking around the area again for unwanted eyes. "Nobody else has this number, Arjay."

On the other end of the line, Branford could hear the crackling of soldering in the background. "You were successful?" shouted Arjay over the noise.

"The trigger's been pulled," Branford said, the phone held between his ear and his shoulder as he continued to put the objects from the shoe box on the ground. "You better be on schedule."

"My work is well in hand" was Arjay's smooth reply.

A gruff "hm" was all Branford gave as a reply. "You'd best do everything you can to give him the advantage, you hear me? I've got to get off the street. Once things have simmered down, I'll check in."

There was a pause. "And then what?" asked Arjay.

Branford creased his eyebrows, his worn, leathery skin nearly cracking. "Then we begin," he replied, and snapped shut the phone.

President Thornton Hastings sat up, his mind unable to accept the information that had just been relayed to him from his bedside phone. It was 2:51 in the morning and he had the sensation that he might be stuck in a dream. But then the fog cleared and he was suddenly alert.

Quietly, so as not to awaken his wife, Glenda, he slipped out of bed and carried the pearl-colored phone to the outer room of their White House living space.

"I'm going to need you to repeat that," said Hastings into the phone.

On the other end was the voice of FBI Director Bob Yeager, speaking low and reverent, underscoring the magnitude of the tragic news he was giving to the president of the United States.

"A small explosion—maybe a couple grenades or a stick of dynamite—went off in Central Park tonight, Mr. President," said Yeager. "NYPD believes that an individual was in close proximity to the bomb when it went off—possibly holding it—because trace human remains have been recovered in the radius of the blast. I'm afraid a set of dog tags were found on the scene—tags identifying the victim as Nolan Gray."

Hastings' heart thudded heavily, his thoughts spinning. How could something like this happen? And to Nolan, of all people!

"Anyone could have been holding those tags. How certain are we that Nolan was the victim?" the president asked mechanically. He already knew the answer, but he was obligated to ask.

"It was, uh . . . I'm afraid it was a rather gruesome crime scene, sir," replied Yeager. "Blood belonging to Lieutenant Gray was found on the grass in patterns consistent with at least two gunshots, probably to the head, in addition to the wider spatter from the bomb blast.

Trace amounts of skin tissue and even some bone fragments were also found at the scene; the blood's a positive match to Lieutenant Gray, and NYPD believes the rest will be as well. The Bureau believes he may have been taken hostage by one of the New York City crime syndicates and killed in this manner as a political statement against you. Or more specifically, a warning about passing the crime bill. I'm deeply sorry, sir."

This couldn't be real. Nolan Gray was not someone you simply kidnapped or even murdered. Hastings had once witnessed Nolan single-handedly take down over a dozen enemy soldiers without benefit of a weapon.

Still, this isn't the battlefield, Hastings mused. *Nolan has been a private citizen for almost a decade now. Maybe he got soft.*

He immediately scolded himself for criticizing Nolan now that he was dead and gone. But his next thought was no better.

If someone killed Nolan as a way of hurting me . . . well, they certainly knew what they were doing.

"Did Lieutenant Gray have a next-of-kin that we should notify, sir?" asked Yeager.

"No," replied Hastings. "He was raised by his grandmother, and she died years ago—before the war."

Lieutenant Gray . . . Yeager had said. It had been quite a while since anyone had referred to Nolan by his rank. Nine years. Had it really been nine years since . . . ?

He remembered it all so vividly. It was impossible to forget. It had changed his life, just as much as it had changed Nolan's. The endless horrors of it. Everything that happened in those darkest of days was the primary reason he'd been elected president.

And now Nolan was gone. Dead. Despair seeped into Hastings' chest, but he pushed it away. There would be a time and a place for that. For now, there were more pressing matters.

"Director," said Hastings, "it is now your personal priority to find the perpetrator of this crime and bring them to justice. You have no other tasks on your agenda until the assassin is in custody. Do I make myself clear?"

"Yes, sir," he replied, though Hastings was sure he'd heard a note of hesitation in the man's voice. Hastings knew he'd set Yeager on an impossible task—bringing to justice what was probably a major crime lord—but he didn't care.

He clicked the phone off. Another thought occurred to him and he clicked it back on, dialing the White House operator.

"Get me Marcus.... I'm aware of what time it is, Sarah, just call him."

When Chief of Staff Marcus Bailey's even-toned voice answered the phone, Hastings could already tell that he wasn't going to have to deliver the news.

"You heard?" asked Hastings.

"Just," replied Bailey. The two men were so used to working closely together that they used a clipped shorthand when speaking to each other. "I just got off with Carson; he expects it to hit the press by daylight, so he's working on a statement."

That was all well and good, but it wasn't what Hastings was calling about. "I want a state burial at Arlington. Honor brigade, the works," he said.

Bailey sighed on the other end. "They'll fight it on the Hill. With the cutbacks—"

"I don't care. Can we win?" asked Hastings. He'd been anticipating this argument. Hastings himself had pushed through a budget cutback bill with nothing but his own charisma, a bill that called for all elected officials in Washington, D.C., to take a pay cut, including him. He'd stood before the entire nation at the State of the Union address and argued passionately that he couldn't ask the American people to shoulder the burden of a staggering budget deficit if their elected senators, congressmen, and president weren't willing to do their part as well. There was only a smattering of polite applause in the House that evening, but the speech drew such a flood of positive reaction from a recession-weary public that Congress had no choice but to vote in favor of the bill. But behind closed doors, even the senators and congressmen from the president's own party harbored resentment toward him for taking away a portion of their salaries and many of their benefits.

A pause. "It'll require some serious political capital, Mr. President. We'll have to call in favors, maybe even make some compromises on the crime bill."

Hastings sobered at these words. With drugs, money laundering, illegal weapons, prostitution, and human trafficking at an all-time high, his promise to make the war on organized crime a federal priority had been one of the key selling points of his election campaign. It had taken over a year to get a bill before Congress that would crack down on crime organizations, but it was currently hung up in a Senate committee comprised of many of his enemies on the Hill. The bill called for the creation of an entirely new law enforcement agency Hastings had dubbed the OCI—Organized Crime Intelligence—which would focus squarely on rooting out the sources of modern organized crime and applying new technologies and techniques to apprehending them for good.

He couldn't afford to lose the crime bill, for the sake of every person in America. But still . . . "This won't hurt the crime bill, Marcus. It'll *prove* why we need a dedicated agency to root out and destroy organized crime. Nolan Gray is—*was*—the most respected war hero of our time. Every child in America knows what he did. He was my friend. I owe him my life, many times over."

How could Nolan be dead? He hadn't spoken to the man in more than five years, but it just seemed impossible that someone with as strong a will to live as Nolan Gray could have died so suddenly, so tragically. Maybe the NYPD was wrong and the DNA analysis would prove it so. Or maybe he'd been right earlier and this was a terrible dream.

Marcus made no reply. He didn't have to. Hastings could picture the taut expression on his chief of staff's face.

"Make this happen, Marcus," he said. "Don't touch the crime bill, but do whatever it takes."

3

Nolan stirred to the sound of frantic crying.

Was he dead, and his friends and loved ones were weeping over his body? No, of course not, that couldn't be it.

He didn't have any friends or loved ones. Hadn't for years.

His head pounded, the muscles beneath his skin flared and clenched. He could feel the bandages wrapped around most of his head, although the top of his scalp down to his eyes still seemed to be free. He felt the sting of an IV in his arm, slowly dripping needed medication into his veins, dulling the pain by a few degrees.

If things had gone as they'd expected, it had probably been two or three days since Branford had shot him. Days he'd been kept completely unconscious.

Finally he opened his eyes and found himself in an apartment he didn't recognize. *Branford's place*, his mind told him. He didn't know this apartment, but it was the only place he could have been. It was dark outside, probably the middle of the night from what he could see through the window beside the bed.

The window was cracked, bringing sounds Nolan recognized from the ruined streets of New York City. Horns blaring under the fists of angry drivers. Police sirens screaming, the cars running this way and that through the streets and alleys. Raucous, high-pitched laughter from what sounded like a group of hookers, trolling the sidewalk below in a herd. Screams of the innocent. In the distance, he could even hear gunfire.

The sounds, these reviled disturbances of that which was good, made his pulse quicken. His fists clenched at his sides, involuntarily.

There was so much wrong on the other side of that window. So much pain and cruelty and wickedness. And so many others, simply standing by, watching, doing nothing. Coasting along in apathy.

He massaged his temples, pushing those thoughts aside, unable to bear following their trail any further. Very soon now, things were going to change. It would require an act of wonder, a marvel, to capture the attention of this city and change its beating heart. And a marvel was exactly what he was going to give them.

The sound of horrible moaning and weeping brought him back to the present, and Nolan sat up, his spine straight, his senses alert and focused as he listened. It was the same sound that had first roused him, and it wasn't coming from the streets below. He glanced around, searching for the source, but he was alone. So where was the wailing coming from? It was getting louder and more desperate by the minute.

"No! Barry, please don't!" someone screamed. A woman. It was a loud shout from somewhere nearby, but it was muffled, probably a few walls filtering the sound.

Adrenaline kicked in, and Nolan threw back the bed sheets and ripped the IV needle from his arm.

The woman let out another sob and this time he zeroed in on the sound. Judging by the distance, it was either next door or across the hall. Assuming there *was* a hall. He had no idea what kind of apartment building Branford lived in.

Nolan rose from the bed and threw on a T-shirt and pair of jeans that had been left for him, anything to avoid running out in nothing but boxers and blood-soaked facial bandages, looking like a crazed mummy. But then he caught a glimpse of himself in the window and realized the gauze would work to his advantage, giving him an element of surprise—and revulsion—from whoever spotted him.

Nolan's barefoot steps were fast but light as he wound out of the bedroom he'd been resting in, through a small living room and to the apartment's front door. Branford didn't seem to be home. He didn't see any weapons lying around—Branford kept a predictably spartan home—so he'd have to go without. He opened the front door and stepped out into the drab brown hall.

"I'm sorry! I'm sorry *I'm-sorry-no-don't!*" screamed the woman.

Nolan had it. It was the apartment immediately to his right. Branford's next-door neighbor.

He bounded, and in a quick, coiled motion, kicked with one bare foot. The door exploded off its hinges.

Instantly, Nolan took in the scene before him. It was the living room of a black couple who looked to be in their late fifties. The woman was facing Nolan from across the room with her hands in the air, her eyes a mess and cheeks soaked, and her form covered only in a ripped midnight-blue nightgown. There were dark bruises on her bare arms and one eye looked swollen. Her teeth were outlined in thin trails of blood.

Across from the woman, directly between her and Nolan, stood a man—her husband, he assumed. He wore a white dress shirt that spilled out over a light-brown pair of slacks that were held up with black suspenders. He was covered in sweat that soaked through his clothes, and he was aiming a shotgun at the woman. Nolan couldn't see the guy's face, but the bitter buttery aroma of whiskey that all but rolled off of him was sharp. The guy was in some kind of alcohol-fueled rage, based on his tightly wound but wobbly posture.

But he didn't seem to be very skilled with the shotgun, holding it awkwardly up high near his head, as if he were trying to stare down a scope that he didn't realize wasn't there.

What had the woman done to set her husband off this day? From what Nolan knew of human behavior, it had probably been something trivial and harmless.

Observing all of this in a fraction of a second, Nolan acted before either the man or his wife realized what was happening.

He sprang forward and slammed the flat of his hand against the left side of the shotgun's butt. The man instantly lost his clumsy hold on the weapon, which flew back into and across his face, hard, before he dropped it entirely.

Nolan used this moment of confusion to drop to the ground and sweep his leg, knocking the man's feet out from under him and sending him down onto his rear. Standing tall again, Nolan loomed over the other man, and having already grabbed the shotgun, leveled the weapon at the furious man on the ground, who was writhing, wiping blood from his forehead, and uttering obscenities.

Nolan considered his options. He couldn't have been the only person in this building to have heard the argument between these two, and the sound he made kicking the door in was even louder. For all he knew, someone may have already dialed 9-1-1.

Stupid, stupid, stupid! Acting with your heart instead of your head!
He hadn't thought, hadn't taken the time to get his bearings. He'd merely acted. And now everything he'd worked for, for years, could be jeopardized. At least his identity was well concealed thanks to the bandages.

Okay, okay. Need to control the situation, but the woman has to be the priority. She's hurt and still in danger. . . .

"You should call the police," Nolan whispered to her, never moving his eyes or the gun away from her husband.

"No, I can't, no," she replied, her voice shaking. "He's a cop. Fourteenth precinct."

Nolan felt his shoulders droop slightly. *Perfect.*

He snapped the pump under the shotgun and stared furiously into the abusive husband's face, tempted for a moment to forgo the law and finish this neat and clean, now.

"I can get you to someplace safe," Nolan said. "But what about him?"

"Just . . . don't kill him," whimpered the woman, unsteady hands up around her face. "Please don't."

Nolan thought fast. Calling the police was indeed out of the question, for the woman's sake and his own. He'd just attacked an officer of the law, a wife-beating scumbag, sure, but the police department was notoriously defensive of their own. Besides that, Nolan was officially a dead man, and couldn't afford to have any connection to this mess.

But this man was no better than a rabid dog. And solutions for dealing with rabid dogs numbered very, very few.

He saw a wood rack right by the broken front door with a trench coat hanging from it. He grabbed the coat with one hand—his other still training the gun on the man on the floor—and tossed it to the woman. She caught it and robotically put her arms into it.

Nolan looked down and felt the bile rising in his throat at this nauseating, depraved excuse for a man. There should be no such thing as abuse. No abusive husbands, no wives living in fear for months or years without end. It was wrong and he could right it.

With a snarling, upturned nostril, he flipped the shotgun around and knocked the man out with the butt of it. The action brought on a brief gasp from the man's wife, but she quickly fell silent, making no further protests.

Nolan extended his hand without looking her way. Wordlessly, blank-faced, she took it and allowed him to lead her out of her world of darkness.

Into the light.

4

After hurriedly grabbing his things from next door—most importantly his car keys—Nolan threw on some socks and shoes while the woman waited at the apartment's front door, her head bowed so far over he could see nothing but the top of her skull. Every now and then, he heard her muffled weeping. He threw on a hooded sweatshirt and wrapped a spare jacket around the shotgun to keep it out of view.

Less than two minutes later, he was leading the woman down the two flights of stairs to ground level with the hood of his jacket up around his face to conceal his bandages from the outside world. Out they walked onto the grimy street that reflected the city lights because of the steam pouring out of manholes.

This was the New York City neighborhood called Clinton. Or as it was more colorfully known thanks to its reputation as a longtime haven for organized crime, Hell's Kitchen.

Thousands of good, decent people lived in Clinton. But just as many of the wicked prowled here too, pushing drugs, recruiting gang members, pimping hookers, and worse. Much worse. An unending turf war was being waged between the good and the bad, and though their numbers were lesser, the immoral were louder, more aggressive, better armed, and ruthless. Hardly a street corner in the neighborhood didn't house some kind of corrupt, degenerate behavior.

"Disgusting . . ." he mumbled.

He noticed that the woman at his side was looking down now, with tears in her eyes.

"Oh, no—not you," he whispered to her, grimacing and scolding himself internally. "I didn't mean you. I was just . . . looking . . . at everything. . . ."

He shook his head, angry at himself. Words were not his thing.

Never turning loose his companion's hand, he raised his car keys and pushed a button until he heard the familiar *bip-boop* sound of his gray sedan. The as-nondescript-as-possible vehicle waited just across the street, and he helped the woman into the passenger seat before covertly stowing the hidden shotgun from the jacket.

Nolan quickly took his place at the wheel and started the engine, yet still the woman said not a single word to him.

She probably figured he was taking her to some kind of battered women's shelter, he decided, and was too ashamed of her situation to say anything just now. It was either that or the hospital, because she needed medical attention, but a shelter would ask fewer questions of her.

As they drove, his eyes scanned the sidewalks, alleys, and storefronts they passed. It was the middle of the night, but still there were hundreds of people out and about. They drove in silence for several minutes before Nolan noticed his new friend staring at his hands with eyes that had grown big. He followed her gaze.

"Right, yeah . . ." he said quietly, grasping for a way to explain why there were no fingernails on any of his ten fingers in a way that wouldn't give away his identity. "Uh, they were removed. A long time ago, for a . . . medical condition."

His heart sank; even he knew how ridiculous that sounded. The notion that he could have had his own fingernails removed on purpose made him seem crazy, but he couldn't risk telling her the truth.

He glanced at his fingers and had a terrible thought.

I wasn't wearing gloves! If this woman's husband—Barry, was it?— were to call his friends on the force, they would dust for prints, and . . .

And they'll find that a dead man was at that apartment tonight. You stupid idiot!!

He may not have had nails anymore, but he still had fingerprints like everyone else.

It occurred to him then that the woman had stopped crying. He could see in the corner of his eye, just beyond the edge of his hoodie, that every few seconds she would steal a glance in his direction but then quickly pretend she hadn't. Her face remained a puffy mess, but she had calmed significantly since getting in the car.

What must this woman think of him? A man whose head was covered in bloody bandages, who had no fingernails, who burst into her home uninvited and stole her away in the middle of the night. Maybe, during her years of abuse, she'd had dreams or fantasies of something exactly like this happening—a knight coming to her rescue, saving her from that hateful man she called a husband, and carting her off to somewhere she'd never have to live in fear again.

Or maybe she was wondering if she'd been kidnapped. At the very least, she had to be considering whom she could trust.

His ponderings came to a halt when she spoke, her voice registering just above a whisper.

"Thank you," she said, and he almost didn't catch it.

He glanced at her, his sharp green eyes taking her in. She was hugging her own torso, clutching the trench coat tightly around her body. Her eyes were still thick with tears, yet she stared at him without judgment or reservation. Only gratitude, and a measure of gentility.

He turned back to watch the road. "You're welcome," he answered, almost as quiet as her.

Now that she'd broken the ice, she was finding it easier to watch him. He wasn't sure how he felt about that, but ultimately decided it was beside the point. He had to drop her off somewhere. His mind ran down a list of possible destinations and settled on a home for battered women about twelve blocks away.

"Alice," the woman said, and he glanced at her again. He hadn't really expected her to say anything else. "Alice Regan."

Alice. Nice name.

From her expression, she was hoping he would reciprocate. But that wasn't possible.

She could never know. Not only for his safety, but hers as well.

Several moments passed in silence, and she must have concluded he wasn't going to speak, so she began again. Nolan wanted to be irritated that Alice kept talking to him instead of letting him strategize in silence, but there was something about her voice and her uncanny calm that he found hard to dislike.

A light ahead turned red, and he stopped the car, waiting.

"I don't know who you are, or why you . . . look like that," she said, sizing up his bandages. "But I *do* know you're a good person. And honey . . . that's everything I need to know."

He swiveled his head to look her way when he felt a cold hand on his own. She gave a weak squeeze, a very small gesture, like a mother who was proud of her son. She was smiling at him, though it was a pained smile, colored by wrinkles and blood and broken teeth. Her years of misery.

"Thank you, young man," she said quietly.

Nolan abruptly felt self-conscious. He wished that the light would hurry and change so maybe she would stop staring at him.

A bloodcurdling yell to his left took care of that. Both of them turned.

A small boy, no more than thirteen years old, was bolting down a long alley to their left. Behind him ran three huge teenagers—which Nolan could only think of as thugs, as no other term suitably described them—chasing the boy. They were laughing and pointing and shouting taunts; in their arms, one carried a Louisville Slugger baseball bat, another held a knife, and the third held a glass bottle upside down, by its neck.

Nolan shifted into Park, turned the keys, and stopped the car.

I'm being so reckless tonight. . . . He sighed.

But I won't do nothing.

He was out of his seat in a flash, with only four words for Alice: "Stay in the car."

As he ran, Nolan mashed the lock on his key ring to ensure that Alice stayed safe in the car. He never looked back, only sprinted down the alley, the wet pavement reeking of trash and urine.

His footfalls would alert the three bigger boys to his presence, sacrificing his element of surprise. It couldn't be helped; there was no time for stealth.

Weaponless and wearing nothing to protect his body—which was weakened from the ordeal of being shot—Nolan leapt into action.

His steps landed so fast and hard that the three teenagers did hear him coming, but his instincts and training kicked in, affording them no opportunity to react. The bat was removed from the first one's hand, and Nolan swung it out wide, forcing the three thugs to back up. Nolan used this opportunity to slide around and put himself between the bigger boys—who he now saw were proudly wearing gang colors—and the young one.

"Wanna get hurt?" he challenged them, holding up the bat like a Major League player. "Take one more step toward the kid."

"Looks like somebody already popped you good," teased the one who'd lost his bat, nodding at Nolan's mummy-like face. "Whatchoo hiding under there, boss? Vampire fangs?"

The other two thugs guffawed and held up their weapons a little higher, bolder. Nolan never flinched.

"Just pity," replied Nolan, "for cowards like you."

"Better watch your mouth, man!" shouted the one with the knife. "I've killed people for less than that."

"You've never killed anyone," said Nolan quietly, his gaze absorbing the three teenagers' eyes, each in turn, all of which were still too wide and eager to have ever snuffed out another's life. "You're overgrown children, picking on a boy half your size. How brave."

"Go home, tough guy," said the first one, taking a bold step forward. "Back to the hospital you crawled out of. This ain't no business of yours."

Nolan swung the bat and caught the teenager in the gut. He spun the teen around and dropped him to his knees, holding the bat up against his windpipe.

"Run," he said, glancing back at the young boy behind him, "as fast as you can."

The kid's eyes were full of fear as he seemed frozen to the spot, but finally he blinked and did as he was told.

The other two thugs advanced, but Nolan spun, tossing the first teen and the bat to the ground behind him. He carried through the motion to launch a vicious roundhouse, an action that knocked free both of the weapons that were raised to bear on him. The knife went flying, the bottle flung up against the nearest brick wall and shattered.

Nolan lunged and snatched both teenagers by the throat. His powerful fingers pinching their tracheas, he brought both of them to a sudden, painful halt. On either side of him, they went limp, struggling and dangling even though they weren't suspended in the air, unable to budge his stone-like hands from their throats.

"You came close to making a bad decision," he explained as they struggled and tried to breathe.

He turned them loose and then punched both in the stomach, sending them to the ground to join their friend. "I don't ever want to see those colors again," he said. "Go do something with your life. Something better."

All three groaned in pain and he left them to it, walking swiftly back to his car.

When he arrived, he was stunned to find that Alice was gone. At first he feared for her safety, wondering if someone had grabbed her.

Maybe her husband had woken up and acted faster than expected and the police had "rescued" her from the madman with the bandaged face.

But he saw his concerns were unfounded when he reentered the car. In his seat, she'd left a small, handwritten note that simply said, "Thank you again. I wish there were more people like you."

NATION MOURNS HERO

By Nancy Strand
Managing Editor

WASHINGTON - Lieutenant Nolan Jonathan Gray, once called "the most heroic man in the world" due to his efforts behind enemy lines during the recent war, was shot and killed last night in New York City's Central Park. Very little is currently known about the murder or the murder scene, but according to the 22nd Precinct, the FBI has taken over the investigation at the behest of President Hastings.

In honor of Lt. Gray, the President has declared today a national day of mourning, and asks that all Americans observe a moment of silence at exactly twelve noon, eastern time.

The Associated Press has reported from sources inside Washington that the President is applying every ounce of political pressure he has, to push through the paperwork for a formal state burial, despite harsh opposition on Capitol Hill, where the nation's financial crisis has forced every branch of the government to cut unnecessary costs.

The President's friendship with Lt. Gray goes back to their days in the Army, when both men served in the same unit.

CONTINUES ON **PAGE 5**

Mysterious billboards raise eyebrows

By Carter Russett
Staff Reporter

NEW YORK CITY - A series of strange billboards have appeared in major cities all over the country, yet no one can say what it is they're advertising. What's more, no one knows who paid for them.

The simple advertisements depict a white hand, over which words are printed that read, "There is a better way." The billboards contain no other information, nor have any searches for their funding proved successful.

At least 93 of these billboard ads are in use around the nation

Senate passes crime bill

By Louise Bardeau
Political Correspondent

It was nearly four in the morning when Nolan made his way through the city and arrived at home. Not Branford's apartment, but Nolan's own private quarters.

"Home" was perhaps the wrong word for it. He'd only lived there a few weeks, so it didn't feel familiar and inviting yet. And it resembled a traditional dwelling in no way whatsoever.

Branford was wide-awake and pouring over the flashing computer screens in the "Cube," as they were calling it. Arjay was nowhere to be seen, but Nolan could smell the hot metal that was evidence of his latest work, and he couldn't wait to take a look at it later.

For now, he wandered over to his new living space to give it a once-over. There were no "rooms" in this unconventional place; he and his two cohorts called them "areas" instead. His personal area was by a far wall off to his right as he entered, far enough that he could have some privacy, but not so far that it was lonely and dark. He hadn't been fond of shadowy solitary places since his captivity during the war.

In his area waited a twin bed, a reclining chair, a metal cabinet for clothes and personal effects, and a pair of old floor lamps he'd found in a Dumpster. They were broken when he found them, but Arjay rewired and upgraded them to produce brighter and more energy-efficient light. Branford and Arjay had similar areas to call their own, spread out in other parts of the platform. Arjay claimed the old women's restroom, ripped out all the plumbing, and transformed it into his own little sanctuary. Branford's space was more utilitarian, like Nolan's.

Everything appeared in order, and the bed was awfully appealing just now, but he turned and wandered through this small grotto that was, in reality, an abandoned subway platform that had been cut off from the main lines and condemned decades ago. It was centrally located underground, not far from the heart of Manhattan, and Nolan and Branford had toiled for months to remodel this musty, forgotten place to make it livable and secure. Outside access was now limited to two well-hidden entrance points, and even the huge train tunnel had been sealed by hand with dozens of layers of brick, rock, and sediment. As Branford had deemed it when they were done, "not even a cockroach could get through." Nolan prayed the old man was right about that. There had been issues of plumbing and electricity to be resolved, of course, but Arjay's engineering genius had devised solutions that were both elegant and sublime, which left no trace of their presence to the residents above.

Bathed in white and yellow cones of light that shone down from the high ceiling, in the most spacious part of the platform, was what they called the command area. The part at the far back corner was Arjay's workspace, with several stainless steel tables, which he kept spotless. Tools and instruments Nolan had never seen before nor knew what they did hung on the two corner walls. A rectangular metal crate at the front edge of Arjay's workspace bore the fruits of his labors, the latest technological marvels he would invent and present to Nolan as tools for the field.

Surrounding Arjay's workspace were a number of flat screen LCD monitors, most of which were black at the moment, and supply cabinets. Nolan walked to the space in the very center of the command area, where Branford worked. From the outside, it looked like a huge floor-to-ceiling cubicle. The Cube sat on a platform raised four inches off the cement ground, and was surrounded by what were basically prison cell bars that had been transplanted there and made into a rudimentary security system for what was inside. Arjay had added all sorts of techno skullduggery to the bars and the frames that held them, making penetrating the Cube a life-threatening undertaking.

Inside the bars, the twenty-by-twenty Cube held dozens of screens, arranged in an unorganized mishmash, overlapping one another at times and covering three of the cube's walls. A desk holding several computer keyboards and a few trackpads, mice, and other controllers sat in the center of the cube with a rugged old leather wingback chair in front of it. It was Branford's favorite chair, the one personal item he'd brought with him.

Noise from the dozens of monitors was blasting out of the Cube, so Branford didn't hear Nolan approach. All the same, Nolan knew that the old man was completely aware of his presence, thanks to the security monitors placed throughout the platform and its entry points.

"Busy night," Branford growled as Nolan stepped inside the Cube.

Nolan bristled but suppressed it. Branford had been keeping tabs on him, monitoring his activities through this complex network of surveillance taps Arjay had built them.

"You saw," he noted, watching his takedown of the three teenagers from a security camera about three stories above the action.

"Was about to erase the footage," Branford replied.

Nolan knew the man well enough to know that he was complaining for a reason.

"What's on your mind, General?"

"You took those kids down pretty hard. Seems to me that's not the image you're lookin' to project."

Nolan crossed his arms, surprised at his friend and mentor's words. "You taught me yourself that a fast takedown was the most efficient solution to any fight. 'Leave no opportunity for retaliation.'"

"You brought me into this to help you, so this is me helpin' you," retorted Branford. "You mean to attract followers to your cause, correct?"

Nolan nodded once.

"Then stop acting like the streets of this city are another battlefield for you to contain and control. People ain't gonna be inspired by someone who uses the level of brutality you displayed tonight."

Branford punctuated his words by tapping a key. The security footage vanished from the screen, permanently erased.

Nolan considered what he'd said. Branford was right. He knew it. It had always been so very easy to fall back on his training. To let instinct take over, and lose himself in the fight . . .

Branford's next words came out softly. "You still having the flashbacks?"

Nolan snapped out of his reverie. "*No*" was his forceful reply. "Inner scars fade with time just like outer ones do. That was a long time ago, and I'm only interested in the here and now."

The concerned expression, just a slight variation on his permanent frown, left Branford's face, and he went back to work.

"So what have I missed the last two days?" Nolan asked.

"Not enough," Branford replied. "You shouldn't even be on your feet, with your injuries."

"I'm antsy, General," said Nolan. "I want to get started."

"You know we're still a month away," Branford said. "And don't call me that."

It was true, Branford wasn't a general. He'd never made the rank, having been passed over time and again for promotion. He was retired now, though a decade ago he'd commanded Nolan's Army Special Forces unit in the war. Nolan wasn't entirely sure why he'd started calling Branford by that rank since they'd reconnected. Maybe it was because he felt the old man really had achieved the rank regardless of what the army said.

At last Branford craned his neck around to look at Nolan, and when he did, he suddenly stood from his chair. "Good grief, look at you. Your bandages are seeping. Come on, better change 'em before they get infected."

Nolan dutifully followed his old colleague out of the Cube and to a first aid table they'd set up just outside the command area.

As Branford set to work unwinding the endless roll of white that spiraled around Nolan's head, he smirked. "Your funeral's going to be on all the major networks in a few hours. Wouldn't want to miss that. Our glorious president is giving the eulogy."

7

I have never known anyone," said President Hastings into the lectern's microphone, "with the heart, courage, or conviction of Lieutenant Nolan Gray."

His words echoed across the field at Arlington National Cemetery, where hundreds of members of the press were in attendance, along with thousands of Americans who'd shown up to mourn Nolan's death. Dozens of cameras were trained on the small dais where Hastings stood wearing an onyx-black linen suit that his stylist had ordered specifically for the occasion. It was handmade, and like everything else about Nolan's funeral, no expense was spared.

Nolan's dog tags were clutched in Hastings' hand, held so tight that they were biting into his skin. He didn't care.

Members of Hastings' own administration made up much of the small audience that was provided with white folding chairs near the podium. A handful of foreign dignitaries had come to show their support for Nolan and what he meant to the American people. A half dozen compatriots from Nolan's time in the military were seated as honored guests—all of them owing their lives to Nolan Gray. Hastings' staff had been unable to locate anyone else who Nolan called "friend."

"It is no exaggeration to say that Lieutenant Gray was the best soldier this country has ever trained, skilled in at least nine forms of martial arts, extremely high proficiency with every weapon he got his hands on, and an uncommon focus and clarity of purpose while on the battlefield. His strength of will was unmatched, his character unequaled. There exists no official count of the number of people whose lives he saved, because that number is far greater than anyone could possibly keep track of. To watch him in battle was to stand in awe of a man doing precisely what he was put on this earth to do, and doing it with confidence and razor-sharp precision. The Army Special Forces can claim to have turned him into the perfect soldier, but those of us who served with him know the truth. He was a warrior from birth."

Hastings cleared his throat and chided himself for displaying signs of anxiety. The next topic in his speech—which he'd revised five times himself, by hand—was not the most comfortable subject to talk about. But it was impossible to honor Nolan and not get to this.

He swallowed.

"During a covert mission on enemy soil during the war, Nolan and seven other members of his unit were discovered and taken prisoner—a captivity that would last those who survived more than two years. It was a day that I will never forget, because as the whole world knows, I was one of the men taken captive alongside Lieutenant Gray.

"We were already comrades. We trusted each other, the way that men serving together on the battlefield are forced to. But it was after we were taken prisoner that we became friends. While I and others succumbed to illness, Nolan made it his mission to protect us, keep us safe. He routinely gave some of his daily rations to those of us who were sick, and regularly took on our portion of the daily punishments. The horrific events of those dark days are . . . well, they're a matter of public record."

He paused. It was the first time in his entire speech he'd gone off script, and the first time he let emotion seep through.

"The things that we endured will haunt me for the rest of my life. My body still bears the scars. My sleep still suffers from recurring nightmares. There are times when I smell something, or hear something, or my wife touches me in a certain way—unintentionally—and it comes rushing back.

"Nolan suffered the most, and so his demons in the years since the war were the worst of any of us. For two years, Lieutenant Nolan Gray fought with every ounce of his strength to keep the rest of us alive. Two years that he was subjected to the most humiliating, excruciating tortures man has ever conceived. Two years during which they broke bone after bone, removed his fingernails and toenails, branded him, drowned him, burned him, starved him, and inflicted other punishments far too repulsive to mention in a public forum. But their relentless evils only strengthened his resolve. He never broke. Never. I don't think any other man alive could have held out that long, or kept his sanity intact.

"He was a hero in every capacity of the word, even before our imprisonment. It was he who engineered the call for help that led our rescuers to our location. He never stopped believing that we would escape, that we would see better days.

"Nolan was a man of very strong faith. It was a faith he grew up with, instilled by the grandmother who raised him. He believed in the redemptive qualities of mankind, and despite all that he suffered, his faith never wavered. I have never shared his beliefs. I have seen too much of the darkness within mankind.

"But just as those years hardened my resolve, those years changed him in other ways. He became terrified of small spaces, but also couldn't bear being in large crowds. As a result, he spent the last nine years of his life—following his honorable discharge—as a nomad. I saw him only a handful of times, usually at memorial events. He regained his health and strength, but in retrospect, I wonder if he was ever the same.

"And in that way, I believe that we, the American people who showered him with praise and held parades upon his safe return to the U.S., failed him. He never asked for anything, but we should have given him more—more of the help he needed and deserved. He was my closest friend, I owe my life to him hundreds of times over, and *I* failed him.

"He is not here with us today," said Hastings, clearing his throat again and trying to ignore the burning sensation in his eyes, "but I hope that wherever he is, he can forgive us for our neglect. Because he is not forgotten. Let the bravery, compassion, and unwavering goodness of Nolan Gray *never* be forgotten."

8

Glad Arjay's not watching this," mumbled Branford as they listened to the president's speech. "He'd probably be crying."

Nolan didn't react. He tried not to talk more than necessary; moving his face made his wounds itch.

The third member of their team, who was currently back in his work area banging away on his latest piece of equipment with earbuds in each ear, was as different from the two military-bred soldiers as could be. Arjay Thale was what it said on his passport, though neither Nolan nor Branford had any idea if that was his real name. In America he was perceived as a black man, but he claimed to be of multiethnic, aristocratic European descent, and he spoke in a very formal manner as if to prove it. His words came out with inflections somewhere between Cockney and South African.

The truth was, they had no idea where Arjay hailed from, and it really didn't matter. The man was a gifted engineer and inventor, as much scientist as mechanic. Branford had found him through some underground channels and Nolan personally convinced Arjay to come on board with their mission, though that had proven a difficult task.

Arjay was a hardcore pacifist. So the only way Nolan could convince him to join their project, live in seclusion and absolute secrecy under New York City, and lend his brilliant mind to their needs, was to promise that Nolan's goals were in line with Arjay's peace-loving ways. But Nolan knew it would take a lot more than hugs and puppies to do what they were planning to do.

"Enough of this," Nolan said, tired of hearing the president praise him. Big talk seemed to be the one thing his old friend was good for these days. "Turn it off."

He turned and left Branford alone in the Cube, unconcerned about whether the general did as he asked. Arjay looked up from his work space and motioned for Nolan to join him. He wore an apparatus on his head that had two extending goggles in front of his eyes.

Without a word, Arjay pointed at the steel table in front of him. Nolan saw nothing but an empty tabletop.

"What?" he said, louder than necessary due to Arjay's earphones.

Arjay pulled the cords out of his ears and smiled. "Just there. On the surface."

"I don't see anything, Arjay," Nolan replied, his patience nonexistent. He wanted Arjay to complete his work so he could get out there on the streets and do what he was born to do. Every time he thought about having to wait around for another month, it made his skin itch on the inside until it was hard to stand still.

But Arjay was still smiling. He removed the goggles from his head and held them out.

Nolan dutifully placed the bizarre hat on his head and pulled the goggles down in front of his eyes. He was immediately disoriented, as his suspicion had been that they were night-vision or ultraviolet specs of some kind. Instead, they appeared to be ultra-high-resolution scopes that focused automatically on whatever was in front of them. It was nauseating looking at the world this way, so in an attempt to get the experience over with, he zeroed in on the steel tabletop.

Now he could see an intricate latticework of hexagonal lines, like a honeycomb that had only one paper-thin layer. He was stunned to find that something had been on the table after all.

"What is it? Is it invisible?"

"Not as such, no," said Arjay. "It's called graphene. A form of carbon discovered only a short time back. Graphene is rare, expensive in any large quantity, and must be crafted by hand. It is a time-consuming process. It is also the strongest substance known to this world—harder even than diamond, but at a minuscule fraction of the size. In its purest form, it is two-dimensional, the width of a single atom, if you can imagine—"

"Okay," Nolan interrupted. "So it's all that. Why am I looking at it?"

"Very soon it will save your life," Arjay replied. "Once I am done layering it several dozen times, I will apply it in a way that none have ever tried. I intend to weave it into the fabric of your combat fatigues."

Nolan removed the goggles and considered Arjay's words. "Are you saying this stuff that I can't even *see* with my own eyes—this is bulletproof?"

Arjay locked eyes on him knowingly. "It will stop more than bullets. Not that I would see you try it."

Nolan's eyebrows flew upward. "It's impenetrable?"

Arjay wagged his head side to side. "It is flexible enough to absorb *some* impact, but not all. It simply will not break, unless subjected to something more powerful than standard melee weapons or gunfire. High-velocity sniper fire, for example. But for hand-to-hand work, it is superior to Kevlar in every way, easily preventing penetration by point-blank gunfire or bladed weapons."

Nolan looked down at the table again. He couldn't believe it. He knew Arjay was good, but this was beyond cutting edge. He vaguely remembered hearing the term "graphene" a good while back as some kind of experimental material that might be usable and abundant ten or twenty years in the future. The fact that Arjay had managed to manufacture the stuff here and now was nothing short of miraculous.

"This is . . . it's unbelievable. I can't begin to thank you," he said.

Arjay held his eyes locked on Nolan. "There is a drawback."

"There always is," said Nolan, his enthusiasm for Arjay's work in no way diminished.

"We haven't the means to manufacture graphene easily. I have allocated the majority of my time to this, so you shall have this one wardrobe selection that's lined with graphene. But no more. And it is not everlasting. Over time, it will take damage just like anything else. After it is deteriorated beyond repair—even if that is years away—it is unlikely that we will have the resources to make more."

Nolan didn't care. It was still an additional layer of defense he hadn't been expecting to have, one that was superior in every way to anything he might face.

Branford's voice rang out from the Cube, and Nolan looked up to see the old man standing at the rear entrance. "New billboards are going up tomorrow," he reported. "Got proofs of 'em here if you wanna see."

Nolan thanked Arjay again and left him to his work. Returning to Branford, he found three screens inside the Cube had been illuminated with the light-gray billboard mockup images, which were identical to the first billboards in every way, except that the message had been changed. Where the first design had said "THERE IS A BETTER WAY," this second series of ads proclaimed "I WILL SHOW YOU A BETTER WAY."

Nolan nodded. "Looks good. Question is, will they work?"

"Already got regular coverage from every major national news outlet. Every time a new ad appears someplace, the reporters go nuts trying to track down the source. There are even some sites online that are treating it like one of those viral marketing games."

"Good," replied Nolan. The billboards were serving their purpose. After this second phase, a third and final message would be rolled out for all with eyes to see.

"Did the egghead say anything about—" Branford started.

Nolan shook his head, cutting him off. "I didn't ask."

Branford glowered. "I know you promised him he wouldn't have to make any weapons, but you've got to have *something* to defend yourself with out there! It doesn't have to be a lethal instrument, just a defensive one. And I'm not letting you go through with any of this unless you're carrying something more than body armor."

It was a bold statement, and Nolan wondered if Branford was willing to back it up. He'd never known the old man to bluff, but Branford wasn't in charge of this operation, and they all knew it. This was Nolan's project, and the buck stopped with him. Even so, Nolan had served under Branford's command for two tours of duty, and some subliminal effect of spending time with him again made Nolan feel like he was still the man's subordinate. At least a little.

"I'll ask him," Nolan replied at last. "I promise."

9

Yuri Vasko adjusted his glasses as he tread and retread over the same section of carpet, his feet every bit as angry as his head. Even the strains of Tchaikovsky's "Serenade for Strings in C Major" emerging quietly from his side-table stereo did little to cool his outrage.

He ran his misshapen right hand through what was left of his brown hair, then pocketed it and cursed the appendage for being so useless. It ached in response and he stopped pacing for a moment to take a deep breath and push away the pain. His assistant, Marko, stepped forward as if worried, but Vasko brushed the younger man away, upset he'd shown even a moment of weakness.

Three men stood in his office, on the opposite side of his desk, waiting and watching his movements: two burly gentlemen who were on his payroll, and a frightened messenger sitting on a chair between them, who'd been sent by that swine, Nimeiri.

Nimeiri had sent this very young, very dark-skinned Sudanese man on his behalf, to demand three times his usual rate for a substantial shipment of cocaine that had come into his possession.

Ninety thousand! Does he think I'm made of money?

Life was difficult enough as it was without his business associates trying to wring more money out of him for the same services they'd always provided.

It's that accursed crime bill! he thought. *They're all peeing their pants, terrified it's going to put us out of business.*

Vasko stopped his pacing to stare out the picture window behind his desk. Below, the early evening streets of Manhattan were dotted with hundreds, maybe thousands, of pedestrians. Office workers headed home. Construction workers digging up another street for no obvious reason. Families taking in the big city sights.

It was innocent and pleasant, and Vasko wondered what it would be like to be one of those people, living a simpler life as an office clerk or a retail salesperson. His wife and daughter lived a simpler life than he, as removed as he could make them from his business. But they enjoyed the luxuries they had because of what he did, which ultimately made them as far from normal as he was.

His attention was drawn to an oversized billboard being erected on the side of a high-rise across the street. At first he thought the sign was going to advertise some new Broadway show, and was about to make a mental note to remember the name, when it turned into something else altogether.

Two workers began to unroll the long digital printout that made up the sign, securing it in place on the billboard foot by foot until the complete image emerged: a slate-gray background topped by a huge hand that was completely white, with fingers stretched out. Layered over the hand was black lettering in a big blocky font.

"I WILL SHOW YOU A BETTER WAY," it proclaimed. And that was it. It offered no further details or information. Not even so much as a phone number.

Another of those signs, Vasko mused. *Ridiculous. Absurd.*

He'd followed the recent news stories about these odd billboard ads that had been popping up all over the country. Identical, every one, all bearing the same hand and the same simple message. Major news agencies had tried for weeks to track down the company or individual paying for the billboards, but they were handled through a front company that led reporters in circles, impossible to penetrate.

And what were the ads supposed to mean? "A better way"? A better way to what?

The chair holding the young man behind him creaked when he shifted his weight in it, and Vasko's thoughts came back to the here and now. He returned his attention to this messenger, this boy-man. Vasko tilted his head to one side, examining him.

"You have . . . family?" said Vasko in his thick Ukrainian accent.

The boy nodded. He couldn't have been more than twenty, Vasko thought.

"My mother, father, and sister still live in Sudan," the young man spoke up. "I work for my uncle to earn money to bring them here to live."

Vasko's eyebrows jumped slightly. "Nimeiri is your uncle?"

The young man nodded again and almost offered a smile, but seemed to think better of it. "Uncle is a very powerful man. He commands much respect. I hope to be like him someday."

Still Vasko studied the boy. "Family *is* everything. Yes? What could be more important?"

"Nothing," replied the boy, a bit uncertain that he was giving the right answer.

Vasko smiled lightly. "Nothing indeed. Absolutely nothing. Family is everything."

He turned to Marko and gave a nod so subtle that no one but he could have perceived it.

Vasko walked around his desk and bypassed the young man and the two goons, instead heading for the door at the opposite end of his office. He opened it and held it open, motioning for the three men to join him.

"Come," said Vasko. "Please, come."

He led the way to a nearby elevator and ushered Nimeiri's nephew inside, with Vasko's two men close behind. He pushed a button and they began to descend rapidly.

When the doors parted, they were on the ground level, and Vasko spoke as he wound his way through the building toward the loading dock in back.

"I want your uncle to know that I understand how important this transaction must be to him, to send his own nephew to deliver his offer," he said. "I want him to know that I value family as much as he does. You look like you haven't eaten in a week; let's get you properly fed before sending you back to your uncle."

"Thank you, sir," said the young man uncertainly as they continued to walk. "I will be sure to let him know of your kindness."

"Good," Vasko said, smiling again at the boy. He stopped at a sliding garage door that was closed. "Now let's see that your uncle gets that message."

He hit a button on the wall beside the garage door and it rolled upward to reveal the rear of a cement mixer. Vasko's two big men grabbed the boy under his arms and dragged him to the back of the heavy truck and forced open his mouth.

Nimeiri's nephew tried to scream, but it happened too fast and his yell was muffled by a rush of wet cement over his mouth, gagging him and pouring down his throat. He thrashed but Vasko's men held him firm. Tears flowed like a stream, his face turning blood red as he struggled and fought to get oxygen into his lungs until finally going limp.

Vasko motioned for the truck to power down. The young boy's eyes were still open wide, though Vasko knew he was dead. He pulled a small knife out of his pants pocket and cut off one of the dead boy's thumbs. This would be sent back to Nimeiri, along with seven of his best men, who would shoot as many people in Nimeiri's organization as it took for him to get the message.

And that message was simple: Nimeiri was out of business, effective immediately.

In the meantime, Vasko ordered the young man's body placed aboard one of the twelve cargo ships that he owned and chunked in the Atlantic, where it would rapidly sink thousands of feet to the ocean floor.

THERE IS A BETTER WAY.

NEWS

New Billboards!!!

*posted on June 13 by **Biron Sharpir** with **82 comments***

Where were you when you saw it? I was driving to work on I-95.

There's a third billboard! It looks exactly like the first two but it says, "NEW YORK CITY. JULY." (See our Gallery for the latest snapshots of the third billboard in cities across the U.S.)

Man, oh man, did my heart race when I laid eyes on this one! The first two ads were so vague—this one actually gives us a time and a place! The message is clear. *Something* is going to happen in New York City in July.

But what? The ads have gotten more specific with each new one, and I believe this latest one may be the last. Why? Let's review.

The first billboard said, "THERE IS A BETTER WAY." Completely lacking in detail. Left us with nothing but questions. What is this "better way"? A better way to *what*? To clean your teeth? File your taxes? Become a millionaire? And who's doing the talking?

Then there was the second ad: "I WILL SHOW YOU A BETTER WAY." Now we knew that not only would this "better way" be demonstrated for us, but it was coming from a single individual. "*I* will show you," it said. But we still didn't know who was sending the messages, or where or when they would reveal themselves.

Now this third billboard gives us the answers to two of those questions, with a promise of a third answer. In July, in New York City, the mystery figure behind these advertisements will be revealed, and I have to believe that he or she is going to show themselves to the world and explain what this has been about.

Of course, the billboards have been *the* topic of watercooler conversation for months now. Websites like this one have popped up with the sole purpose of finding all of the ads, determining who's behind them, and deciphering what they mean. The most popular theory is that it's just a marketing stunt for a summer movie or maybe some hot new gadget

BILLBOARD #3 SIGHTINGS CONFIRMED IN THE FOLLOWING CITIES:

Atlanta
Austin
Baltimore
Boston
Charlotte
Chicago
Cincinnati
Cleveland
Columbus
Dallas
Denver
Detroit
Honolulu
Houston
Indianapolis
Las Vegas
Los Angeles
Miami
Milwaukee
Minneapolis
Nashville
Newark
New Orleans
New York City
Orlando
Portland
Philadelphia
San Diego
Seattle
St. Louis
Tucson
Tulsa
Virginia Beach
Washington, D.C.
Wichita

Don't see your city on this list?

Email us a photo to have it added!

10

The weeks passed methodically and tediously. Ready for the rush of action, Nolan instead spent his time in training, honing his reflexes, his senses, and his skills. He worked with the new equipment Arjay was producing, learning the subtle feel of each device until it was second nature. After he awoke and before he slept each night, he spent an hour on his knees, praying in his personal living space; Branford and Arjay gave him all the room he required to prepare for what was about to begin.

The billboards had become a nationwide phenomenon; they were the water-cooler topic for many an office, and theorizing on what the signs meant—and more importantly, what was going to happen in New York come July—was virtually a national pastime.

Some in the media speculated that it could be a setup for a terrorist plot, that the terrorists might be trying to use Americans' own innate curiosity against them. But the government dismissed this, reporting that they had no intel or chatter suggesting that the terrorism threat level was any higher than normal.

By the last week of June, tens of thousands journeyed to New York City, filling hotel rooms, restaurants, cabs, and sidewalks. They came from all walks of life, all parts of the country and the world. They came to sate their curiosity and feed a growing obsession. They were compelled to witness for themselves whatever it was that the billboards promised would happen.

So when a very hot and sticky July first arrived at last, Nolan was unsurprised to see that the crowd gathered in Times Square came close to rivaling the masses that converged on the same spot every

New Year's Eve. It wasn't quite that big yet—not shoulder-to-shoulder down there. But the crowds were growing by the minute, and not just in the Square. Thousands watched Liberty Island from the edges of the Financial District, and Jersey City across the bay. Countless others stood at the foot of the Empire State Building, and filled Rockefeller Plaza. In some places, the crowds spilled out onto the streets, resulting in shouted responses from the city's infamous cab drivers.

Nolan saw all of this from his vantage point atop the tower standing at One Times Square, where he crouched at the edge of the roof and surveyed the sea of humanity far below. From there, Nolan could easily pick out the native New Yorkers bustling about, garbed in business black, not bothering to hide their frustration over the gawking tourists blocking their every move. Yokels who came to witness what would probably amount to nothing.

This slender tower, crammed into the narrow space between Seventh Avenue and Broadway, had, over the course of its history, been home to the *New York Times*, Douglas Leigh's electric billboards, industrial engineering firm Allied Chemical, an art deco restaurant, and a number of retail stores. In more recent years, it had been largely vacant, serving as nothing more than a giant canvas for a dozen or so billboards and the famous giant LED screen that tourists loved. Capping the tower was the world-famous rooftop where the ball was lowered every New Year's Eve.

It was an astonishing thing to see so many thousands of people gathered below, watching and waiting. Almost as if a parade might begin any moment, all eyes were peeled, innumerable camera lenses were pointed in all directions, and there was a loud buzz rolling like waves through the crowd. As Nolan inhaled the same air that they breathed and listened to the dull roar of their conversations, he felt the rising heat generated by so many bodies in close proximity to one another. It was intoxicating and overwhelming. He felt not unlike an ancient general watching the preparation for a battle from afar, the troops awaiting the trumpets that would signal a formal declaration of war.

If very many more were added to these numbers, Nolan decided, the city would not hold them. Some held signs and banners declaring their desire to see something happen, to witness this "better way" that Nolan's billboards had promised. Of course there were plenty of crazies milling about as well, offering everything from "free hugs" to "free sex," and suggesting that they could show the world "a better way" all by themselves.

His vision enhanced by one of Arjay's toys, Nolan spotted one group of a dozen or so marching in a picket line, complete with wood-handled signs hefted over their shoulders. He couldn't tell what they were protesting and he didn't care; as long as people lived and breathed, they would find some inane thing to boycott. He had no problem with their desire to make a difference—even if a lot of them based that desire on misguided ideals—but historically speaking, picket lines and boycotts had no lasting influence on the shape of society. They were a poor tactic, usually assembled in a last-minute panic, that at best might achieve some modest level of change. A change that always proved to be temporary.

The NYPD was woefully unprepared for this day, having underestimated how many people would venture into the city on July first, the day that the mysterious billboards spoke of. He saw only a few black-clad officers running interference between the heat of the visitors and the native New Yorkers. With so few cops and the outdoor temperature climbing, it was only a matter of time before tensions escalated. Something would happen. Someone would start something. Rule of law would collapse. Which was exactly what Nolan was waiting for.

He kept reminding himself that this was not a performance. He was not doing this for show. He intended to do something that was needed and that was *good*—but he *did* require an audience for it to have the desired impact. So he crouched at the top of the Times Square building with all of Arjay's fancy cutting-edge equipment and waited for the inevitable. Praying all the while that everything would work toward his plan.

"Got your head on straight?" said Branford through Nolan's earpiece.

Nolan knew what the general was asking. To an outsider looking in, any tactical maneuver in the field was all about physicality. Strength, speed, agility, aptitude with weaponry. But anyone who'd spent any time at all in combat knew success was primarily mental. A good soldier relied on planning, training, muscle memory, his body instinctively knowing what to do before his brain ordered it to happen. If you were distracted or overcome by unwanted emotions, you were dead.

Branford was asking if Nolan was ready. If his mind was focused and prepared to act.

"Good to go, General," he replied.

Within the hour, a pair of rival New York gangs had amassed, one group on Broadway, the other on Seventh Avenue. Arms crossing their chests, each group stood in a defiant posture, staring one another down with palpable malice.

Each group was at least twenty strong.

Forty against one, Nolan thought.

"I think it's time," said Branford.

11

Two factions were about to break into open war in Times Square, right in the midst of thousands of pedestrians. Nolan needed a closer look.

Weeks ago, he'd watched as Arjay demonstrated the custom-made eyewear that he'd designed for Nolan to use in the field.

"Slide them on, just so," Arjay had said, placing the device on Nolan's head.

They looked not entirely unlike sunglasses, with wraparound lenses that were impossible to see through from the outside. The black frames were a bit larger than normal sunglass frames, and came outfitted with some extra hardware. Custom-fit to the contours of Nolan's head, they would offer a full range of vision, including peripheral. Inside, they didn't darken the world so much as enhance it. It was like looking at a live high-definition photograph, where light colors and dark shades were both enhanced and then blended together to create a sharper contrast and a more vivid picture. He had no idea how Arjay had achieved this effect, but the clarity was at least twice that of normal human vision. He could see every crack, crevice, and pebble in his underground surroundings, and it was astonishing.

The glasses were also made to even out the luminosity of his surroundings, so that there were no dark shadows or blinding lights. Everything he looked at was seamlessly illuminated at the perfect brightness for his eyes to perceive every detail possible.

Earpieces curved down from the sides and tucked comfortably into his ears. Nolan assumed this would give him some auditory enhancements when needed, as well as keep him in touch with Branford. Then there were a few buttons on either side of the frames. On the right, two buttons allowed him to zoom in up to one hundred times magnification, and zoom back out. Arjay was explaining something about electromagnetic polarization, but Nolan wasn't listening. He was too busy examining the footprints of a mouse in the dust on the other side of the subway platform. Buttons on the left allowed him to switch to X-ray or thermal vision, which Arjay said would effectively let him see through walls.

Atop the Times Square tower, he tapped the zoom button to move in even closer. The world came alive with vivid color before him, and the situation converged into focus.

The two gangs below were both made up of pasty white men, so Nolan guessed they had to be Russians and Irishmen—likely Russian mafia and IRA, who had been fighting over inner-city territory the last few years. They'd brought tools for the fight, armed with handguns, blades, long steel pipes, brass knuckles, and more, easily visible beneath their shirts or hanging out of the back of their pants. Their faces were stoic, but their eyes, locked on their counterparts across the way, were ablaze with hatred.

Their numbers were impressive, but Nolan didn't feel threatened. These men had no training. They were thugs with guns and knives that didn't fit in their hands. Little boys pretending to be men.

His worry was for the crowd. If Nolan had known this many people would turn up in New York City just to find out what the billboards meant, he never would have placed those ads. Neutralizing the gangs didn't give him pause, but the thought of doing so in such a way that the pedestrians didn't get caught in the crossfire did. Once he laid into these guys, weapons of all kinds would appear instantly. His only option was to strike fast and hard, take them down before they could hurt anyone.

It was so hot this day, Nolan's one-of-a-kind graphene-infused combat fatigues felt like an oven, yet he could sense heat of a different kind pouring off of the gangs on the streets below. The crowds were backing away from both groups by several paces, giving them as much space as the increasingly tight confines would allow. But they hadn't withdrawn entirely, watching in abject fascination, unable to tear themselves away.

It was the train wreck principle. Morbid interest and curiosity were basic human nature. Nolan wished terribly just now that they weren't. Especially when a blood feud was sure to break out at any second, and—

Hold up.

His thoughts halted. It struck him that this situation was perfect for his needs: two rival gangs about to explode into a turf war, smack in the center of arguably the most famous street corner in the world. Between the restaurants and retail outlets lining the streets were several major news agencies. All he had to do was descend to the ground at just the right moment and save the day.

The whole world would be able to watch.

It was so perfect it could have been scripted. And Branford had casually proposed that morning that Nolan camp out at Times Square, thinking that something dangerous might inevitably occur there, what with the size of the crowds waiting for the billboards' messages to play out.

He wouldn't dare.

Would he?

"General," Nolan said into his earpiece. "Please tell me—"

"*Heads up,*" said Branford, cutting him off. "*They're on the move.*"

The question would have to wait.

He looked down over the side of the building and saw that twenty-five stories below, on the ground, the two gangs were crossing the streets to meet in the middle, right in front of the Times Square building, on the footsteps of the tiny New York Police Station positioned there.

"I need to hear what they're saying," he mumbled.

After a brief silence, Branford replied into his earpiece, "*Hold your left hand out in the direction of the gangs. Arjay says he built a sound wave amplifier into the palm of your glove. Touch the tips of your thumb and ring finger together to activate it.*"

Nolan almost laughed. "Gotta be kidding. . . ." But he did as he was told. As promised, he could immediately hear what was being said on the ground below, as long as he kept his hand trained on the right spot.

The leaders of the two gangs were arguing, chests puffed out, spitting obscenities and testosterone at each other. Nolan didn't pay much attention to the specifics of the dispute; it was something about disrespecting one another. Nolan growled. Respect. An argument, essentially, over nothing.

It felt like fingernails scraping across the chalkboard of creation. Every time he thought about it, a lead brick settled in his stomach and his head started to pulse with the earliest sign of a migraine. Something deep inside wanted to stop this kind of thing once and for all. He couldn't lose himself right now though and warded off the sickening sensations by compartmentalizing his thoughts regarding the state of the world.

But he kept his eyes peeled. It was going to happen any second now, and when it did, he had to be ready. He felt his muscles coil. He pulled out Arjay's prize toy—a contraption that looked like a sleek oversized pistol—and grasped it tight with his right hand. He threw his jacket's hood up over his head.

All right, Arjay, don't fail me now.

He heard glass shatter and looked down. Flames were rising at the base of the police station, pouring forth from two or three glass bottles that had been tossed there. He saw several guns appear and heard the screaming begin.

The gangs ran, converging on one another atop the central median in Times Square.

A blood-filled battle was seconds away from breaking out down there, and hundreds of bystanders were going to get caught in the crossfire.

Showtime.

12

Why does this look like a gun when you made so much noise about being opposed to weapons?" he'd asked Arjay several days ago, examining the all-important device that Arjay called the grappler. The younger man had produced the grappler with great flourish and fanfare, and assured Nolan that it would save his life and make his work easier, many times over.

It was jet black with a handle, barrel, and trigger much like a pistol, only it was quite a bit larger than a typical handgun, and it had a spearlike silver tip at the end of the barrel. It was heavier than a gun, too, by two or three pounds. It felt solid and powerful in Nolan's hand.

"It is not a gun," Arjay replied, "it is something better. As I would have you to be."

Arjay took the device in his own hand and pointed it at the far wall, a good two hundred feet on the opposite end of the subway platform, and tapped a small red button right where his thumb rested. Four spikes expanded outward in north, south, east, and west positions from the silver tip, forming a grappling hook. When Arjay pulled the trigger, the silver hook shot out as fast as a bullet, if not faster, and instantly found purchase on the lever that served as the handle to the men's restroom. Arjay handed Nolan the grappler and told him to pull.

Although Nolan could see no wire, he knew one had to be there because the grappler held fast in his hand, refusing to move back even an inch away from the door that was so far away. When he pressed the trigger down about halfway, the line loosened and he could move with it. When he mashed the trigger down tight, the line not only strengthened but started to recoil, and he was forced to let go of the thing lest it rip his unprepared shoulder off, winding its invisible wire back inside itself and traveling like lightning back toward the silver hook.

"Wow," he said, massaging his shoulder.

"Apologies," said Arjay, retrieving the grappler from where it had shot out of Nolan's hands. "I neglected to tell you to release the hook. Pushing that red button expands the four spikes; it also brings the spikes back in and lets you retract the entire rig in seconds."

"Got some serious velocity to it," Nolan remarked.

Arjay nodded. "Strong too. The hook will penetrate wood, brick, even concrete up to three inches thick. But be cautious. I would not have you aim it toward anything living."

"I can't see the wire. . . ." said Nolan.

"The wire is an improvement on the same fiber filament that illusionists employ when appearing to fly on stage. Less than one millimeter in thickness, yet it should support about twice your weight without strain. You have nearly a full kilometer coiled inside."

"Huh," Nolan said. "What would happen if my fingers got caught in the wire?"

Arjay eyed him sideways. "Exactly what you think would happen. Always wear your gloves."

Nolan was already thinking of the tactical uses for such a device. "Say I'm in a hurry . . . Can I use it to zip from rooftop to rooftop?"

"If you are suicidal," Arjay shot back. "Imagine holding a rope tethered to the back of a bullet train. Use the grappler horizontally and you will not have gravity to assist in controlling your trajectory. Assuming you even survived the impacts you would suffer along the way, you would acquire bruises and broken bones all over your body. It is for going up and down. Nothing else."

Nolan smiled at the memory, his thoughts lasering in on the gangs and the innocents far below, and how he was about to do everything he could to keep anyone from getting hurt, or worse. It all came down to this moment.

Nolan jumped.

Falling fast, he twisted and shot the grappler toward the very spot where he'd been standing only seconds ago. The grappler hooked instantly onto the ledge and he executed a fast but controlled descent. Finally, when he'd reached about two stories off of the ground, he mashed the red button at the back of the grappler while holding down the trigger to both release the hook and recoil the wire. Before landing, he'd already replaced the grappler to its resting place on his right hip.

His special boots absorbed most of the impact, just as Arjay had promised they would. Arjay had built shock dampeners into the boots' soles, assuring Nolan that the boots were designed to disperse the shock of a landing from even three stories up. They could handle no more than three stories, though. And they offered a kind of kinetic optimization, giving Nolan a little extra momentum in his step, so while practicing, he'd found he could actually run marginally faster while wearing them. Best of all they were lithe—light and flexible—despite their bulky appearance, lacing up to several inches above his ankles.

Arjay prided himself on thinking of everything, and the boots were no exception. The tread design, for instance, was based on the sole of a popular work boot, so anyone trying to trace Nolan would find nothing distinctive about his shoeprint.

Even though the boots absorbed the landing beautifully, Nolan let himself fall to one knee, his training taking over. He heard a handful of screams from the vast crowds on either side of the block. And then there was a cacophony of chatter, rising fast as excitement overtook the pedestrians who assumed that this was the reason they were there.

Nolan's attire no doubt helped with that assessment. Clad in loose-fitting military fatigues that were outfitted with his custom-made equipment, Nolan found it hard *not* to feel as bad to the bone as he appeared. He wore a black army-style flak jacket over black cargoes that were tucked into his black boots. At Nolan's request, Arjay had added an oversized white hood to the jacket that he could flip up to conceal his head. His special glasses removed any chance that his eyes might be visible. Only his mouth might be seen from beneath the hood, but that was a grotesque mess thanks to Branford's precision handiwork with a pistol. A single emblem marked his chest: a large white hand, matching the hand used on the billboards. His black gloves completed the ensemble.

Nolan stood and glanced both ways, finding himself exactly where he'd wanted to be: standing precisely between the rival gangs. Arjay's ingenious equipment couldn't have functioned better.

The gang members on the front lines on either side of him took a sharp step backward at his dramatic, unexpected drop from the sky. He calculated that six men could currently strike at him after taking approximately four paces toward him.

He took the first few seconds of shock on their parts to scan the crowd from behind his goggles. The zoom had been turned off, but now, swamped by so many faces, he almost wished it was still on. Thousands, maybe tens of thousands, watched him.

Nolan swallowed the rising bile in his throat. The only other time in his life when he'd been in a crowd this size was upon his return home from the war, where a ticker-tape parade was held in honor of the escaped POWs from his unit. But that was in the open-air historic streets of D.C. Here, skyscrapers boxed him in with this vast sea of people, and every single eye was fixed on him.

He took a deep breath, using calming techniques he'd been practicing for months. Placing a gloved hand inside his jacket, he gripped his sole weapon tightly and let out a slow huff of air.

13

Branford had convinced Arjay to make one defensive weapon for Nolan; Arjay had fought the idea from the beginning, but eventually the general had worn him down with concerns over Nolan's safety. Arjay agreed only on the condition that it be a nonlethal instrument. Nolan didn't let the young man know that in the right hands, even a paper clip could be lethal.

Arjay's invention was a slender metal tube, like a pipe, about a foot and a half long. There was a seam in the center that separated it into two distinct rods.

"Twist it," Arjay had explained to him, mimicking the proper motion with his hands. He twisted one hand forward and the other back, like wringing out a wash cloth.

Nolan copied the motion, and the dual tubes turned in opposite directions until they clicked and stopped. From each end shot out more metal tubes of nearly the same size, only narrower, and then another set followed, until the stick had grown to over six feet long.

Nolan whistled. "I've seen retractable staffs before, but they couldn't hold their shape in a fight. They always bent at the seams."

Arjay was unmoved by this concern. "This one will not."

Nolan held the staff in one hand, at its center, and it remained perfectly balanced, still and threatening. Impressed yet again by Arjay's skill and ingenuity, he took several steps back and sprang into action, twirling the staff in his hand like a baton. Raising it over his head, he continued twirling until he spun and jabbed the air with it. Next he swept it through the empty space around him, as if taking down multiple enemies using both ends of the staff, and then twirled it again until it landed neatly beneath one arm, tucked under his armpit.

More than satisfied, Nolan stood at ease and twisted the center rods again until it retracted down to its original length.

"Amazing," he said with sincerity. This thing was beyond flawless. It was a precision work of art.

Striding the median in Times Square, Nolan saw that everyone's attention had shifted to him. From the Irish and Russian gangs closing in on both sides to the scores of pedestrians, they all had to be wondering who he was and how he had managed to fall out of the sky right between these two warring factions.

With the full attention of the crowd, he twisted the staff until it expanded, right before their eyes. He held it under his arm and spread his legs apart in a defensive posture.

It was a very obvious threat. An unspoken invitation to attack.

"Who are you supposed to be?" spat one of them.

Nolan stood perfectly still, but his mind was whirling, his eyes quickly taking in the weapons and numbers of both gangs. He leveled his focus on the teenager near the front of the Broadway gang who'd spoken up—a pale-skinned blond boy sporting short sleeves that molded to sizable biceps underneath.

Nolan considered what his response might be to the young man's question, but it was an exercise, nothing more. He'd decided months ago that he wasn't going to speak while in his vigilante guise. For too long, people relied on empty, pointless words. And what would he say? That he was there to fix the city, eradicate immorality on her streets, and see her citizens live by their consciences? There was no explaining such things in cynical times. His billboards promised action. He needed to *show* the better way.

And yet he didn't want to come across as the cold, detached, all-business automaton either. In his bones, he had to do this. Doing nothing was making him sick. The world was a nasty place and somebody needed to take a stand, draw a line, and push back against the darkness.

He couldn't afford to not let himself *feel* things like compassion and empathy for those who were suffering. Allowing emotional responses to assimilate into his actions had been trained out of him long ago. Yet now he knew he had to find a way to integrate those feelings into his actions, or all of this was for nothing.

It was a work in progress.

Instead of speaking, he held up a single black glove with fingers stretched out wide. Chatter from the onlookers rose in volume, and Nolan knew the gesture had had the desired effect: it was the outstretched hand, just like the one on the billboards. Just like the one on his chest.

He glanced at the buildings on either side of the street and noted that at least two major networks already had cameramen who were hurriedly positioning themselves with tripods to capture what was happening.

A gunshot went off, and Nolan felt a slight thud against his rib cage, but the bullet bounced off his graphene fabric and fell to the ground. He didn't even lose his footing.

Thank you, Arjay.

As fast as he could, he rounded on the one who'd hastily pulled out the pistol and grabbed the gun by the barrel. After triggering the manual release so that the gun came apart in the gang member's hand, he knelt and swept his staff across to knock the kid's feet out from under him.

Two others rushed in from the opposite gang, but Nolan spun at the last second and whacked his staff hard enough against one's head to knock him out. Continuing the same motion, he swung around and jabbed straight into the other man's stomach, sending him to the ground, cradling his abdomen. The two men went down so fast they almost hit the ground simultaneously, ultimately toppling into each other in a heap upon the double yellow lines at the center of Seventh Street.

Nolan rose to his feet again like a bullfighter, ready and waiting to take on whoever would step up next. But he could tell something had changed in the electricity of the moment. It was worry, fear, the subtle sense that the dynamic on the battlefield had been drastically altered.

These gang members were sizing him up, knowing now that he wasn't some clown in a black combat suit. Several of them seemed to have registered that he was the source of the "better way" billboards, and were probably wondering if he was there to make an object lesson out of them.

And he was.

Another man charged him like a hungry shark, and he sidestepped the attack at the last second. He pulled up behind the burly man and yanked his wrist until it was pinned against his back. With another spin, he was kneeling on the ground in front of the man, and sending him flying over his shoulder.

The attacks didn't stop; one after another, and sometimes in pairs or more, they came at him. Again and again. Most bore knives or guns, but he disarmed each and tossed the weapons aside. He took down every last one of them, and made it look incredibly easy.

He thought his work was done when from the crowd there was a piercing scream. He looked up just as a gang member who had been hiding among the pedestrians stepped out with an AK-47 drawn and pointed at him.

Nolan raised his right hand and touched his thumb to his pinky. Another device built into his glove was activated by this gesture—a high-powered electromagnet that Arjay had somehow focused like a prism. Nolan aimed it square at the rifle, and the semi-automatic weapon was yanked violently from the gang member's hands. In a blink, Nolan was holding it up with one hand. Just like the rest, he tossed this one aside onto the small pile of weapons he'd made in front of the tiny police station.

The disarmed man was stunned but did his fellows proud by refusing to flee. Instead, he followed their example and ran straight at him, this time with a bowie knife that Nolan estimated to be at least six inches long.

Nolan stood his ground, but this time when he spun out of the way, his attacker was expecting the move and jabbed to the side with his knife. Nolan felt the knife stab at his side, yet his jacket was untouched, impenetrable to the metal blade.

He grabbed the wrist holding the knife and twisted it well beyond the average person's tolerance for pain. But still the man fought, punching at Nolan across the face and the abdomen.

Nolan hated to do it, but this guy was different, likely military trained, and wasn't going to go down easily, so he twisted the man's wrist sharply, until it snapped.

The man screamed obscenities at the sky and clutched his broken wrist, but still he fought, launching another barrage of fisticuffs with his one good hand, but it was over before it began. Nolan deflected the blows easily and then elbowed the man in the face. He joined his friends on the asphalt.

From the moment he had leapt from the top of the tower until this last man had hit the ground, less than three minutes had passed. Now he stood alone, king of the hill next to a mound of unconscious men. Like a gladiator in the Roman arena, thousands of eyes followed him, watching hungrily to see if he would kill or be merciful. The news crews were filming every second of this, and he noticed for the first time that he was being displayed on the big video screen above.

For a few seconds, nothing happened. He merely stood in a coiled silence, scanning the crowd and ready for any more late entries to come forward. If more gang members were out there, they were showing the good sense to stay away.

Then the audience seemed to realize that it was over, because as one, applause and cheers broke out. Those on the front lines of the crowd broke into a run to rush up closer to him, no doubt with endless questions on their tongues.

Nolan pulled out the grappler and fired it at the top of the Paramount Building to his left, which was taller than the Times Tower by eight stories. The hook solidified somewhere on the roof and he jumped into the air, retracting the grappler as he flew off the ground. When he approached the side of the building, he stuck out his feet and ran across the surface of it, holding onto the grappler all the way, and then he followed through on the motion by retracting the grappler at full blast until he had cleared the far corner of the building in mere seconds, and was out of sight.

14

Marko was rattling off a series of accounting numbers, a standard part of Yuri Vasko's daily routine. But for once, Vasko wasn't listening.

He leaned forward on the edge of his chair, his face glued to the flat screen television set mounted on the side wall in his office. Live news coverage was replaying footage of a brawl in Times Square from only minutes ago. It showed the mysterious figure dressed in black, who appeared as if from nowhere to defend the people from the threat of a gang war. Vasko was riveted by the images.

When the report cut back to the news anchor, Vasko hurriedly located the remote on his desk with his good hand and rewound the broadcast to watch it again.

His assistant was still talking, but Vasko finally cut him off without looking away from the TV. "How can you still be talking, Marko? *Look* at this man! The way he moves, the way he fights. His skill is without equal. . . ."

Marko, in his late thirties, with round glasses and a small mouth, glanced up from his clipboard to inspect the man on the TV screen, then dispassionately turned back to his work. "You are preoccupied with the actions of a madman?"

Very few people in his organization were allowed to speak to Vasko with such a tone of voice, but Marko's talents with numbers and figures far outweighed his social shortcomings. He was also one of Vasko's closest friends, despite the slight age gap between them, and understood him in ways that few could. Their bond was based on a common past of growing up in poverty.

"No no no. This man is no fool," Vasko replied. "He's ingenious."

"He desires fame, Yuri," Marko said with a scowl. "An unworthy act of the self-absorbed."

"How do you not see it?" Vasko leaned in further to the television footage, his enthusiasm rising. "He's executing a plan. A well-thought-out plan. The mysterious billboards. They foretold his appearance on this day. This footage is barely twenty minutes old, yet it's on every channel. He's igniting the fascination of the populace."

"A man you do not know fascinates you so completely?"

"I am fascinated with the actions of *all* men," Vasko replied. "But this one is something new. What would compel a man of such skill to rise above the law and take justice into his own hands? He's doing exactly what he promised to do: he's showing the people a better way."

"Now you sound like you admire him, Yuri," said Marko. "What is he showing them if not violence?"

Vasko finally looked up at his friend. "You miss the point. He's a gifted fighter, for certain. I've noted mastery of at least three different martial arts disciplines. But he's not showing off his skills, he's sending a message to the criminals. A very clear message. And he's doing it before the eyes of the city—the world, even, so that they will know too."

"Know what?"

"That he's come. He's here, to fight for the innocent. He will defend them and he will show them how to live. And he's not going anywhere."

Marko looked at the screen with new eyes, considering what he saw there more seriously than before. "Perhaps we should find his price. The crime bill is days away from passing, and if it goes through, we're going to need talent like his."

Vasko shook his head again. "This man is a believer. A fanatic. His confidence in his actions and motivations is absolute. He has no price."

Marko examined his boss. "Again your words betray admiration."

"*Understanding,*" Vasko corrected him. "I understand him, Marko. That is not the same as admiration. He's acting on a plan that he probably put into motion years ago, and we are witnessing just the first steps."

His vocal modulation had changed, and he knew that Marko had noticed. Instead of enthusiasm, he was now expressing distaste.

"He thinks himself righteous enough to influence the behavior of others. Probably believes he is on some kind of divine mission. He thinks the rest of this godforsaken city can be as 'good' as he is. Give him time. He will come to see things differently. 'Good' does not exist here. Not in this world. No merciful creator would cobble together a place so viciously cruel as this. No loving creator would sit by and do nothing while there is pain and suffering."

Marko said nothing, waiting for his boss to get his thoughts off of his chest.

Vasko paused the image on the screen, showing the best image of this "hero," but still his identity was well hidden. "This man thinks he is different than the rest of us. Better. He is wrong, Marko. He is no different at all."

atch me in to the police band, General. I want to hear what they're saying," said Nolan as he zipped to a lower level behind the Paramount Building and then shot the grappler to another rooftop across the way.

Arjay had been right about the grappler. It was invaluable.

Branford did as he was asked, and overlapping chatter filled Nolan's ears. Branford spoke above the din. "Near as I can tell, there's a sort of crime wave breaking out. It's like the criminals got their heads together and realized that the city is wide open for the taking, thanks to the influx of tourists all through Manhattan, and the cops having their hands too full to deal with them all. I'm hearing reports of multiple robberies-in-progress, assaults on police officers, a shootout of some kind in Harlem. . . ."

Nolan stopped listening as his soaring spirits plummeted. Of course, it was way too early to tell if his debut in Times Square had had the desired effect, but he'd never intended it to actually make the city a more dangerous place.

Well. Only one thing to do, then.

"Tell me you've already got a sim-map running," he said.

"*Grid's in place, overlaying the police reports now,*" Branford replied.

In his mind's eye, Nolan pictured one of Branford's biggest screens inside the Cube being transformed into a wire-frame map of the city, with red dots popping up one by one to illuminate locations where reported crimes were taking place right now.

"We'll take them one at a time. What am I closest to?" he asked.

———

Two minutes later, Nolan was pounding the pavement, enjoying the sensation of speed. He felt incredibly agile. Graceful, even. He was sprinting down another part of Seventh Street, away from Times Square, chasing a pair of thieves who had raided laptops and money from an accountant's office.

His quarry doubled back across Fortieth Street and ran past a tiny tchotchkes dealer, ducking into the next doorway, which led to a back staircase that went up to the second floor of the building. Not taking notice of where the stairs led, Nolan hustled to keep pace, and soon burst into the retail space that occupied several thousand square feet on the second floor.

It was an enormous comic-book store. Punk rock music blasted from speakers in the ceiling, and a dozen or so geeks milled about, filing through bagged-and-boarded collections of their favorite super-heroes' exploits.

For the first time in his life, Nolan felt conspicuous and uncomfortable, making a big entrance in his customized military garb and gadgetry. A pair of grungy slackers to his left had been having an enthusiastic discussion of some kind, gesticulating with gusto and laughing hard, but they came to a sudden stop at the sight of him. Every eye in the building turned.

And then, as if because of some unwritten geek code, they all seemed to know exactly why he was there. As one, they pointed to the far end of the room, where a spiral staircase led to the third floor.

One of them, a pale boy dressed in black with a mop of blond hair that nearly covered his eyes, muttered "bad guys" softly as he pointed.

Nolan looked up and tapped the side of his glasses until the X ray came online. He saw two human skeletons that were darting frantically right over his head, through what looked to be another retail level of the same store, trying to find a route of escape.

Nolan ran and ascended the stairs two at a time. His prey were trying to find a way out on the other side of the room, but the only door appeared to be locked. Spotting Nolan, one of them turned and grabbed a store patron by the back of his shirt and held a blade up to the kid's throat. The teenage boy was a good head and a half shorter than the two much older crooks.

"Back off, man!" the man with the blade shouted. "Somebody let us out of here! *Now!*"

With a snap of his wrist, Nolan had his staff in his hand and, in one motion, twisted and flung it, backhanded. It expanded in midair, allowing its six-foot length to catch both men across the face. Their disorientation gave Nolan all the time he needed to get a running start toward them.

The one with the knife recovered quickly, reaching out to grab the staff and preparing to use it against Nolan.

Nolan never slowed, he merely held out his right hand and activated the focused electromagnet there. The staff soared right out of the man's hand and into Nolan's, and he caught up with the two men just in time to slide down on his knees and knock both men off their feet. Spinning fast, Nolan sent a punch into one man's jaw, followed by a similar blow to the other.

He hoped he hadn't hit them too hard; Arjay had outfitted his gloves with a special chemical compound that, when electrically activated by wires embedded in the gloves, made their flexible material turn hard and solid upon impact. Arjay had set the electrical leads to activate automatically whenever Nolan made a fist. It effectively gave him a fist that was as hard as metal.

He hadn't practiced as much with the gloves as he had with the rest of his equipment—Arjay had only completed them a few days ago. His intention had been to hit these two thieves not hard enough to do any permanent damage, but enough to keep them unconscious until the authorities could arrive. At least they were still breathing, and a quick look with the X-ray setting on his glasses confirmed neither of their skulls was fractured.

As he ran back through the store, he saw that the clerk on the second floor was already on the phone with the police. He also noted that most of the patrons had gathered in a small crowd near the checkout counter, where they were talking excitedly. They froze when Nolan came into view, and the way they gaped at him with big excited eyes told him exactly what they'd been discussing.

"Bad guys?" asked the boy who'd whispered it before.

Nolan threw the kid a nod before dashing out of the store and back onto the city streets.

16

Hours passed, and Nolan stopped a bank robbery in progress and three muggings, and put an end to a violent disturbance between two women at Grand Central Station. He'd even intervened in a police car chase using his grappler on the vehicle tearing through the Fashion District, though he'd nearly popped his shoulder out of its socket in the process.

Everywhere he went, people seemed to realize who he was, or rather what he represented. He was there to show them "a better way," and they gawked as he saved the day, again and again. He'd had to quickly get used to the sound of tourists' cameras clicking in his direction. Yet he never stayed around long enough to talk. He didn't want to talk. The action was enough so long as fear didn't define their existence. If they felt peace, even for a second, he'd done his work.

It had been a very long afternoon, and although he wanted to keep going, Branford insisted that he pack it in so they could check his shoulder for injury and so Nolan could rest and refuel. Arjay was also itching to give the equipment a once-over to see how well everything was holding up. Nolan removed his goggles, grateful for the advantages they'd given him. He pulled his hood back up, keeping his disfigured face obscured.

As Nolan neared his underground home, satisfied no one was watching, he ducked through a small set of scaffolding. Behind it was a storefront, well hidden by a large renovation tarp covering the entrance and windows. He pulled back the tarp and froze.

Someone was sitting in front of the door, wearing an old fedora, a trench coat, and a dark scarf that obscured his face.

He'd considered that something like this could eventually happen: some obsessed person who was determined to find him would somehow track him back here.

But it was only his first day on the job, for crying out loud. If someone had already managed to find him, this whole thing was going to be a lot harder than he'd expected.

Then he noticed that the trench coat was dingy and frayed, the hat was smeared with grease and condiments, looking as though it had been pulled from a trash bin, and the scarf was ripped. This was no crazed fan. This was a squatter who'd located a comfy spot, oblivious to the fact that it was the entrance to Nolan's underground home.

"Get out of here," he said in his most intimidating voice, and took a threatening step forward. He thought it would be enough to deter all but the most dogged of unwanted guests.

The squatter slowly got to his feet but was moving much too slow for Nolan's liking. He didn't have time for this.

"I said *get lost!*" he thundered, stepping even closer. He winced slightly as the expansion of his chest caused his aching shoulder to flare.

His visitor unwound the scarf to reveal a familiar face. A black woman in her late fifties.

"I *am* lost," she said weakly.

"Alice!" Nolan shouted, reaching out both arms to steady her as she swayed dangerously. "What are you doing here? Are you all right? What happened?"

Her eyes, which seemed to have aged at least another ten years in the weeks since the night he saved her life, found his and were filled with sorrow and hurt. "My husband—he, he's got the police looking for me. I can't get away from them, been running for days. . . ."

"Your husband?" Nolan replied, feeling stupid. Of course, her husband had been a police officer. She told him that night. "He's not looking to reconcile," he said.

Alice shook her head, and the huge fedora flopped awkwardly to one side of her head. "I didn't know where else to go," she said through her tears.

"It's all right, you're safe. But how did you find me?" he asked. "You couldn't have followed me...."

She was evidently proud of this next part, because for a moment the tears were withdrawn and a wry smile appeared on her face. "Your white-haired friend is a very private man, but I lived next door to him for thirteen years," she explained. "All I had to do was wait outside the building and watch for him to come home. I waited a long while, but he showed up eventually, so I followed him here. Watched him go under this tarp, but the door was locked by the time I got to it. Been waiting here ever since."

"You're lucky I got to you first," he replied. "If Branford or Arjay had found you here ..."

"Who?" she said, but the strength had drained from her voice. She was so weak she was about to fall over.

He considered the options, and once again while in this frail woman's presence, found that there was only one. It took enormous effort not to betray his frustration, to find that compassion deep in himself. "I uprooted you from your home. I guess that makes me responsible for your safety. Come with me."

A metal plaque was on the brick wall next to the heavy metal door, bearing the street number of the building. Nolan took off his glove and pressed his full hand against the metal. Several clicks resounded within the metal door after a few seconds.

For the second time, Nolan took Alice Regan by the hand and led her into the light.

17

Nolan watched as Alice spun a slow circle, taking in the technological wonders of his subway platform home. It was a strange amalgam of the nearly ancient station and its musty, chipped stonework, and the bright, high-tech equipment and endless gadgetry and wires that he and his friends had installed. His thoughts went back to how difficult it had been culling this place together. And that didn't even include procuring the billboards and other advertisements all over the country. It had taken time, perseverance, and money. A *lot* of money.

"You can stay here," he said, placing his gadgets down on a steel table, one by one. "It's not the most comfortable place, but it's safe. From your husband."

She nodded wordlessly, looking around with big eyes. It was a long moment before she said anything, and he waited, allowing her to take her time to absorb.

"How do you afford all this?" she whispered, as if afraid that some Big Brother might be listening in via all the technology.

It was true, his grand plan had required one thing he didn't have enough of: funding. He had his own life savings, and a handsome chunk of money his grandmother had left him. Branford had contributed part of his personal savings as well. But all of that still wasn't nearly enough to carry out the full extent of his plan. So over a year before the two of them faked his death, Nolan had called in favors from old friends—as many as he'd dared. Soldiers he'd served with during the war, anyone who wouldn't be alive today if not for him.

It was a long list, but he'd only bothered calling the wealthy ones.

Never one for small talk, their conversations usually started with Nolan reminding his friend that they owed him their life.

"I'm calling to cash in," he would say.

"Okay . . . What can I do for you?"

"Money."

Usually there was a swallowing sound or some other twitch that Nolan could hear through the phone. "How much?" one of his new benefactors would ask.

"Lots."

This would be followed by confusion from the war buddy, along with a demand to know why Nolan was asking. "You in some kind of trouble? Can you tell me what you need money for?"

"I'm going to change things."

That was all the explanation he could afford to give. By force of personality alone, he'd managed to acquire over four million dollars to finance his plan. And all of it in cash, completely off the books.

Nolan explained to Alice how it had taken years to plan all of this out. Years in which he watched the political system, waiting and hoping that things would change for the better and this weary world would see some vestiges of real hope. When hope never came to Washington, or anywhere else, he decided he would deliver it himself. He knew it would be impossible to impact the whole world all by himself, so he created a plan that was focused on New York.

"Why New York?" she asked.

"This city is, for all intents, the de facto capital of the Western world."

There was nowhere else in the United States or the world where international politics, finances, culture, and dreams intersected in one place. And of course the people. Sixteen million residents from every corner of the world. The perfect microcosm, a model of the entire planet. The eyes of the globe were always watching New York; there was no better platform from which to send a message.

Nolan heard the familiar creak of the gate surrounding the Cube swing open and Branford's even footsteps.

"The Hand," announced the General. It was his way of welcoming Nolan back home and congratulating him on a job well done. "That's what they're calling you. This one reporter for the *Gazette* coined it."

He seemed unsurprised by their visitor, but waited in silence.

"General," Nolan began, "may I introduce—"

"Alice Regan," interrupted Branford. "Fifty-nine years old. Currently unemployed. Suffers from bursitis. Moved to New York from Atlanta twenty-six years ago so her husband, Barry, could accept a position with the NYPD. No other living family members."

Alice's eyes had gotten bigger with every word, and now looked ready to leave her head.

"I was just going to say she was your next-door neighbor," said Nolan.

Branford glanced at him. "Got her on camera when you were bringing her in. Ran her through facial recognition software, wasn't hard to access her records."

"That's . . ." said Alice, at a loss for words. "Well, that's something."

"Oh *snap*," said a voice from the dark.

"And that's Arjay," Nolan continued. Then he called out to the back corner, "Take it easy, guys. *I* brought Alice in. I helped her out a while back, but she never told anyone about me. We can trust her. She's going to stay with us for a while."

Arjay walked over to inspect the newcomer. Then he looked horrified, taking a step backward. "She's seen my face! Those of us that still *have* faces have something to lose, you know. My work here was meant to be untraceable, but *she* now knows I am connected to you. This jeopardizes everything. . . ."

"Calm down," Nolan said, in a tone that was more domineering than he intended. "I said you can trust her, and that means you can."

Arjay crossed his arms in front of his chest, a skeptical look on his face. "You are certain of this?"

Nolan glanced at her. "Yes. And if not, I'll kill her."

Alice's eyes grew huge, and it was clear she was thinking she'd made a mistake coming here.

"Kidding!" Nolan backpedaled. "I'm kidding, Alice."

Arjay retreated to his work space, but not before calling back to them, "But he could, you know. With his little toe."

Nolan turned to Branford, who gave Alice a clipped "Ma'am" and then motioned for Nolan to follow him. Something dangerous flashed in his eyes, and when they had a little space he growled, "Should we expect more tenants in the future?"

Nolan shot Branford a look of warning and lowered his voice. "There's nowhere else she can go. Put her on the street and she'll be dead within a week. Now, what were you saying about the media?"

"Uh, some members of the press are calling you 'The Hand,' and it seems to be catching on."

Nolan considered the name and shrugged mentally. *Could be worse.*

"Who *are* you people?" Alice called, as if finally finding the courage to voice the main question on her mind. "What's all this about? And why are you hiding under a hood?" she said, pointing her final question at Nolan.

Branford made to speak, but Nolan cut him off. "New York's soul is bleeding out. She's dying. This is about making the city a better place. A moral place, where the innocent aren't trampled on and the wicked don't get away with whatever they want."

Branford turned and wandered away. Nolan knew his old friend so very well. He knew that they would continue their conversation about Alice later, but for now, Branford had decided to leave before he said something inappropriate.

Nolan turned back to Alice, who'd approached. When she spoke, her voice was lowered. "Why did that man in the corner say that? That you don't have a face? Is that why you were wrapped up like a mummy . . . that night?"

Nolan sighed and closed his eyes. Slowly, he pulled back the hood of his jacket.

He'd expected her to recoil, or make a face of disgust. And he wouldn't have blamed her; even *he* didn't like looking at it.

Alice didn't blink. Instead, she smiled sweetly.

"There now," she said, nodding. "You've seen my scars and bruises, and I've seen yours."

"This is hardly *all* of my scars," he interjected.

"Mm. Well, the difference is, you saw me at my worst. I've only ever seen you at your best."

Nolan felt his cheeks burn, which he imagined had to be a disgusting display given the condition of his mangled face. His face had the appearance of having been melted and then frozen in place, while there were crisscross scars all up and down his cheeks. The scars were still red lines, having never fully regained their original color. The tissue around his eyes was drawn and narrowed, but thankfully his eyesight remained unimpaired.

He felt awkward under her gaze, suddenly aware of all his pains, particularly a searing burn in his shoulder. He rubbed at it, trying to find relief.

"Are you hurt?"

"It's nothing," Nolan replied.

Alice had already reached up to unzip his jacket. "Let me see."

He hesitated a moment but then slipped the jacket off, revealing the ribbed undershirt he wore beneath. The shirt was sleeveless, so the swelling in his shoulder was embarrassingly visible.

"You still have range of motion," she mumbled, "so it's not out. A good sprain, probably."

Her wrinkled hands came up and proved surprisingly strong at massaging the raw muscle tissue around his shoulder. She checked a number of pressure points, watching for his reaction.

"You a doctor?" asked Nolan.

She gave a brief smile as she continued to work. "I had some training, though it was a long time ago. You wouldn't know it to look at me, but once upon a time, I was an assistant virologist. Worked in a lab, studied diseases up close, looking for cures."

Nolan's eyebrows climbed his forehead. He couldn't help it; she was right that he would never have guessed.

"Why'd you quit?" he probed. "Your husband?"

She shook her head. "This was years before I met Barry. I was right out of grad school, and I never advanced past 'assistant.' "

"Why?"

"I got tired of the darkness of it all. Four years of my life, I spent eight hours a day in a full quarantine suit, working with some of the most dangerous pathogens to ever exist. It dawned on me that if I kept looking into the darkest parts of nature, that one day I would be infected by it."

Nolan stared at her. The way she looked at him, it almost made her words a warning about his own life and this path he'd chosen.

"Your shoulder will be fine in a few days. Ice will keep the swelling down. So . . . does it hurt?" she asked, studying his face now.

Nolan was glad for the change in subject, pulling his jacket back up over his shoulders. "Branford estimates 60 percent of the nerves in my face have been destroyed. My face doesn't move very much anymore, but I also don't feel much in the way of pain."

"And you look this way . . . on purpose?" she asked.

"If I didn't, you'd recognize me." Nolan nodded. "Everyone would."

Alice looked him in the eye with a sheepish smile. "I recognized your voice the first time you spoke to me, Mr. Gray."

His eyes went wide. He had no idea she knew who he really was. He suddenly felt as if his insides were a balloon that had popped.

"You were on TV all the time after the war," she explained, almost apologetic, and Nolan was suddenly very grateful he hadn't spoken in public earlier today. Alice looked uncomfortable and tried to change the subject. "Don't I remember hearing back then that you're a believer?"

He nodded, still reeling from the fact that she'd figured him out so easily. "Yeah."

She smiled. "I thought so."

"Well," Nolan echoed. "If you know who I am, and what I believe, then you must know why I'm doing this."

Alice looked at him sideways. "More or less. But why would you almost kill yourself just to hide your identity? Aren't there other ways—?"

"It's bigger than that," Nolan said softly. He crinkled his brow. "Everything about us is now governed by the information that's out there, about you. Any form of ID can be tracked, any email or social network can be traced. Hospitals, banks, creditors—all of these agencies keep ongoing records about you. I had to be erased from this flow of data. Nolan Gray had to be dead."

He looked away, almost embarrassed that she'd known who he was for weeks and never told a soul. Even after his funeral. Any concerns about trusting her were suddenly gone.

He had held on to an admittedly silly hope that his name would die when his funeral was carried out, and that no one would ever discover who he really was. Aside from Branford and Arjay, of course.

"You probably think I'm nuts," he sighed.

Alice never took her blazing eyes off of him. "I'm alive because of you. I told you that very night that that's all I need to know."

PART TWO

The Hand

18

The president of the United States wrung his hands anxiously as he waited for his turn at the podium. He never got nervous about making speeches anymore, but this day was different.

Pride swelled within him. Everything that was taking place at this ceremony was because of his resolve, his determination, his sheer nerve. The promise he'd made a decade ago to a friend was bearing fruit before his eyes.

Two weeks prior, Hastings' crime bill had finally passed both the House and the Senate. He'd lost out on a number of other legislative priorities because of Nolan Gray's expensive funeral proceedings, but the crime bill was the one pillar of his administration that he stubbornly clung to, refusing to budge even one inch. He'd taken it upon himself to appeal to the citizens of the nation to reach out to their congressmen and women and implore them to sign on with the bill; he'd spoken eloquently from the White House on national television, asking every American to call their representatives and tell them exactly how their lives had been impacted by the rising levels of crime across the nation. This kind of personal appeal was an unprecedented move for a president—asking for a direct outpouring of emotion from the people to gain momentum for a high-profile piece of legislation. It had cost him friendships and the respect of many in Washington, but his gamble worked, and members of Congress from both sides of the aisle were forced by the sheer tide of popular response to vote in favor of the bill or risk losing the support of constituents.

Years of dreaming, planning, and hard work had put the culmination of his dream at hand. He was effecting real change, pushing positive action forward. Doing the right thing. Ending the suffering caused by organized crime was what basic human decency and compassion dictated. It wasn't about some deity who was watching from afar, waiting to eagerly pass judgment while doing nothing to fix the problems of this world himself.

How often had Hastings wondered if this day would come? He'd wanted to give up so many times. Yet here he was, about to give the commencement address for the first group of agents to be accepted into the brand-new "Organized Crime Intelligence" agency. He had handpicked the OCI's no-nonsense director, Sebastian Pryce, himself. Pryce, who was currently speaking at the lectern, was a portly man with huge eyebrows, an impossibly deep voice, and a permanent scowl. The man was so rough around the edges that he nearly lacked social skills altogether, but he knew how to get things done, and he had a personal hatred for organized crime that stemmed from years of law enforcement.

Hastings peered down at the eager faces of the eight people who sat in the front row of the audience, waiting to be called to the stage in turn so Hastings could shake their hand and present them with their official OCI badge. Five men, three women. Six of them held degrees in criminology, most had started their careers as beat cops, and every one of them had years of field experience in at least one other major law enforcement agency. Each of them had gone through a rigorous new training course, after having been subjected to intense screening and review procedures where their aptitude, worldview, intelligence, morality, and dozens of other character traits had been picked apart to ensure they would be entirely beyond corruption. This was the cornerstone philosophy of the OCI; with so many of the nation's law enforcement personnel succumbing to the pressures and bribes of the Mafia, the drug cartels, the gangs, and the terrorists, it was crucial this newest department be held to the highest of standards.

At the head of the class was Jonah Janssen. Tall, broad-shouldered, and handsome, the thirty-two-year-old Janssen had graduated with honors from West Point before applying to the FBI, where he went on to lead an organized crime taskforce for four years. To many in the media, he was the face of a new breed of crime fighter: a ground pounder who was bold, adaptive, intelligent, and confident of his purpose.

Since there was so much media interest in Janssen, the OCI had already made his partner assignment known via a press release days before the ceremony was to take place. Coral Lively was a Secret Service agent of seven years who specialized in rooting out counterfeiters. Her uncanny knack for intuition and fast thinking had given her hundreds of hours in undercover work, and it made her an ideal yin to work alongside Janssen's yang, since his approach was far more traditional and straightforward. He was the logic, she was the wisdom.

The president hoped they would work well together, since they were sure to be under heavier scrutiny than any of the other agents. While the OCI agents took orders from Director Pryce, it was field agents like Janssen and Lively who would be on the front lines, leading the charge to take down organized crime once and for all.

As such, Hastings had just yesterday attended a briefing with the eight agents-elect and Director Pryce, where a number of potential targets were examined in order to determine the first priorities of the OCI. There were arguments for and against various mob bosses, drug cartels, and homeland terrorist cells. Most of the room wanted to aim straight for the top of the heap, attempting to take down the most well-known and notorious crime lords in the United States. But Hastings had offered a countering opinion. With all their necks on the line and media scrutiny at its highest, what they needed first was a victory. Take down a group with fewer numbers that would put up less of a fight than the big dogs, he'd argued, and they'd establish their reputation. Gain the people's trust, put other crime lords on notice, and start with momentum.

It was a winning choice all around, and in the end the president got his wish.

Starting that very afternoon, after the formal luncheon that would follow the ceremony, Janssen, Lively, and the six other agents would set their sights on the OCI's first major target. A small-potatoes mob boss operating out of New York City, who had a relatively minor organization but a dangerous reputation.

The name of their first target: Yuri Vasko.

19

Agnes Ellerbee tapped her pen rapidly on the long boardroom table, her agitation growing with every passing minute. The meeting room was packed today at the *Gazette*, and everyone knew why. The Hand.

Since the coming of the Internet, newspaper sales were dying off across the board. A number of competing rags had already shut down or stopped printing in order to go entirely digital with their news delivery. But the *Gazette* doggedly refused to bow to the future, even though its sales had nosedived every bit as much as the others.

That all changed when the mysterious vigilante dubbed The Hand appeared on the scene. Papers were flying off newsstands as fast as they could be printed, with obsessed natives and tourists alike desperate for any glimpse or word of The Hand's latest exploits.

Lynn Tremaine, editor in chief of the *New York Gazette*, had called an all-staff meeting this morning, and everyone was required to attend because she was not happy with the quality of coverage they were producing. The ruthless Ms. Tremaine possessed a sharp mind and an acid tongue, and every reporter in town knew it. Staying in her employ for more than two years was seen as a badge of honor by the few who managed to keep her happy that long.

Agnes had not yet achieved her two-year mark but was getting close, having managed to fly under Tremaine's radar for most of her tenure. Today's meeting was testing her patience and she toyed with throwing out her aspirations to move up at the *Gazette* because of the inanity of it all. It's not like she was well liked at the long-running news agency anyway; her lack of charm and her tall, thick build had always made her an outcast wherever she found herself.

She didn't care about that in the slightest.

"Russell, Francine, I want lifestyle pieces about residents who have been saved by The Hand," said Tremaine, handing out assignments with the finesse of a great white shark marking its next meal. "And don't give me another piece of bleeding-heart sludge. We print newspapers, not tissues."

Agnes sighed. There was an eighty-ton elephant in the middle of the room, and she couldn't believe everyone else was missing it.

"Callie, Darnell, you're on tourist duty," continued Tremaine, going around the room. "Hit the pavement and give me *balanced* pieces that give voice to both sides—Hand supporters *and* skeptics. If I want any more eyewitness accounts from Farmer Turnip and his inbred off-spring, rambling on about the 'awesomeness' of what The Hand can do, I'll turn on the TV."

Agnes cleared her throat. She couldn't take it anymore. "I'm sorry, can I ask a stupidly obvious question?"

"Ellerbee," Tremaine sighed, "when have you asked any other kind?"

"Why are we focusing so much on public reactions to The Hand, instead of going after the man himself?" Agnes asked, undaunted by her boss's insult. "He's a flesh-and-blood human being with a real name, and yet *no one* is asking what that name is."

Tremaine extended a single eyebrow upward, and Agnes knew she'd hit paydirt.

"Who is this man? What's his story? Why is he doing this?" she went on, pressing her advantage. "I say we do some good old-fashioned investigative journalism and find out."

The boss sat back in her seat, pondering this behind her dark, calculating eyes. "You want to expose him," she said.

Agnes wanted that exact thing, but decided to employ a little diplomacy. "I want to *introduce* him. To the world. He's captured the public's imagination in a big way; don't you think we should know if he's *worthy* of all the attention and accolades? Now . . . imagine the *Gazette* being the first to bring this information to light."

Tremaine did not speak immediately, but Agnes recognized that a spark of interest had been lit, because she was sitting up straight while gazing at a nondescript spot on the conference table. "All right," she finally said. "I'll allow you to pursue this. But I want regular updates on your progress. And if I find that you're not making any, you'll be writing obits till you retire."

"I'll find him," Agnes replied with a rush of adrenaline. "That's a promise."

20

Remind me again," said Alice, watching over Branford's shoulder as the tiny camera mounted on Nolan's special glasses gave them a live view of what he was seeing and doing. "Is this phase two now, or phase three?"

Branford didn't look up, though he hadn't noticed her enter his cube. "Two," he replied, "which means he's engaged in more proactive, offensive maneuvers against specific targets. Stopping crime before it can happen. But he'll get back to that later. . . . He's dealing with a hostage crisis at the moment."

On the screen, Nolan was using his grappler to scale the side of a glass-sided skyscraper a few blocks west of Wall Street. Some disgruntled office worker there had been laid off from his company after thirteen years of employment. Apparently the company's refusal to reward his loyalty had driven him to snap, because he was standing in his boss's corner office on the thirty-ninth floor, a bomb-covered vest over his chest, aiming a pair of submachine guns at his former boss and the support staff. The crazed man had holed himself up with his hostages, barricading the door. He'd already shot a pair of building security officers who'd tried to talk him down.

Alice was glued to the screen, her lips moving quietly as she prayed for Nolan's safety and success. It had become her ritual over the last month, every time he went out. This was terribly dangerous work he was doing, and after all he'd done for her, she couldn't help feeling like a mother hen to him, and to a lesser extent, to Branford and Arjay as well.

Those two had taken their time in coming to accept her presence, but after the first couple of weeks, they seemed to get used to her. She was already fond of both of them and deeply impressed with the work they did, though she made no secret of the fact that she worried about how far outside of the law they were operating.

She gave little thought to her husband or how long she would have to live there in the underground "home." It was enough for her that she was safe. So she had decided early on that she would busy herself contributing to this work of theirs. Her medical skills had already been useful many times over, but she hated having nothing to do when Nolan had no scrapes or cuts to patch up. She was devoid of anything that might be of any use in field operations, but she was an excellent cook and she suspected it had been her culinary skills that had finally won over Branford and Arjay.

As she watched, Nolan did the impossible. He was running up the side of the building, holding tight to that grappler gun thing of his, and it was a very disorienting sensation to see it happening from his point of view. It was as if the world had been set on its ear, and the vertical side of the skyscraper was now the ground. Now and then Nolan took a fleeting glance at the world around him, and the dizzying sight of New York City's towering edifices from this amazing perspective made her gasp.

"How is he going to stop the hostage taker?" Alice asked while swallowing the sick feeling in the pit of her stomach.

Branford glanced up at her for the first time, a moderately bemused look on his face, though she wasn't sure if he was puzzled by the question or its answer. "He never tells me. I'm not even sure *he* knows until he does it."

They both turned back to the screen and watched as Nolan crouched to his knees; he'd arrived. As he leaned in close to the reflective glass to get a look inside, Alice could see that he'd stopped just shy of the thirty-ninth floor and was peeking up over the bottom edge of the corner office's window. Nolan tapped the side of his glasses and the view turned to a dark blue shade, showing the people inside as human-shaped outlines of bright red. She could make out the hostage taker standing over the five hostages. They cowered on the floor with his two Uzis trained on them.

Touching his thumb to his ring finger, Nolan placed his gloved palm up against the glass, and speakers inside Branford's area played the same enhanced audio that Nolan was hearing through his headphones.

The hostage taker's voice was immediately heard, talking to one of his hostages. "*You think I care about your family?*" he screamed, placing the muzzle of his rifle up against the man's head. "*Don't you get it? This office wouldn't even be here without me, and you gutted me! My whole life was poured into this place, and if I'm going down, I'm taking all of you with me.*"

Branford spoke up. "He'll never negotiate. He's going to kill the hostages and then himself."

"*Agreed,*" Nolan replied. "*Is the building secure?*"

"Negative," said Branford. "Police aren't far—maybe three minutes out. The other tenants in the building don't even know what's happening yet."

"*What are you thinking, General?*" Nolan asked.

Branford sighed. "That five hostages are an acceptable loss if it means a nut job doesn't blow a whole building apart."

Alice's ears burned red. She reached down and snatched the headset off of Branford's skull. "*Give* me that!" she hissed, putting the earpiece up to her ear and swatting Branford's hand away when he tried to take the headset back. "Now, you listen. There is no such thing as an 'acceptable loss.' You hear me? Those people aren't dispensable soldiers who signed up for danger. They're regular folks, with families and jobs and lives, and you are *going* to help them, just like you helped me."

She all but threw the headset back at Branford, but not before she heard a soft but conviction-filled "*Copy that*" from Nolan over the speakers.

Already Nolan was switching off the temperature-based setting of his goggles and springing into action. Releasing some of the coil from his grappler, he rappelled quickly down to the thirty-eighth floor and slammed his steel-hard fist into the glass while releasing the catch on the grappler. It recoiled instantly while Nolan tumbled to the floor and then continued the roll to stand on his feet.

"Stairwell's near the center of the floor," said Branford, still eyeing Alice warily as if she might grab some other piece of equipment without warning. Only then did Alice notice that Branford had pulled up a blueprint of the building's layout. She wondered how in the world Nolan and his friends had access to such information—not to mention virtually every security camera in the city—and made a mental note to ask him about it later.

Ignoring the shocked gasps and stares from people in the spacious meeting room he'd leapt into, Nolan ran out, through a receptionist's area and past a large space with cubicles on both sides. Alice wished she could get a better look at the people he was running past, but Nolan never stopped or even slowed. Right where Branford said it would be, he found the stairwell and darted up it to the thirty-ninth floor.

"But won't that man know he's coming?" Alice asked. "Didn't he hear the glass break?"

Branford never moved his eyes from the screen. "Just watch."

Of course, she thought. *Of course the man heard it. Which Nolan knew would be the case long before he broke the glass.*

She had come to learn pretty fast that these were the rules by which Nolan lived. She sometimes heard him muttering them under his breath: control the environment, account for all parameters, stay one step ahead, and adapt as the situation changes. His training had taught him how to know exactly when and how an enemy was going to strike so that he could have a countermove ready before the attack came. If he lost focus for even a millisecond, he would be vulnerable. But she knew he was far too good at this to ever lose focus.

When Nolan reached the top of the stairs, he switched to X-ray and spun in a circle. The floor was empty—probably on the orders of the hostage taker—save for the crazed man and his captives in the far corner. But the one skeleton that was standing was walking away from the window now and toward the outer office.

"Police have entered the building and are on their way up," Bradford hissed.

Nolan burst into the open and quickly ducked for cover behind a cubicle. The gunman's skeleton appeared from the corner office and his head turned, scanning the area. His head stopped in the direction of the stairwell and remained there for a long moment.

"He must've left the door ajar," Branford whispered.

The man took a step backward and then looked again around the office, a large, open space filled with dozens of cubicles. The partitions didn't reach all the way to the floor, so he dropped to his knees and looked under them, searching for the intruder's feet. But Nolan suspended himself atop a U-shaped desk so that he was visible from neither above nor below the thin partition walls.

The gunman held up both of his weapons and, with a roar, pulled their triggers. A rainstorm of bullets showered the room as he spun in place, and Nolan flinched at the impacts of several bullets that hit him but couldn't penetrate his graphene-infused clothes.

The gunman's skeleton spun to return to the corner office—no doubt to fortify himself against the intruder—and Nolan was already moving.

At a dead sprint, Nolan reached the hostage taker in seconds. While running, he'd retrieved his staff and extended it, so that when he caught up to the man, he swept it into the backs of the man's knees, causing him to buckle. The man's trigger fingers tensed involuntarily and shot round after round wildly into the walls and the ceiling. He scrambled back to his feet, but Nolan was far too quick.

Nolan stretched out his gloved hand and tapped his thumb to pinky. The electromagnet was activated, one Uzi flew from the man's hand until Nolan grabbed it out of the air, and then he nabbed the second one. It was so fast the man had no idea what was happening until it was too late. Nolan stepped forward and landed a rock-hard fist against the man's jaw followed by an uppercut beneath his chin, and the guy actually lifted several inches off the ground before going down hard, unconscious. Nolan ejected the guns' magazines, pocketed them, and then tossed the useless stocks on the ground beside the crumpled man.

"Hold it right there!" shouted a nearby voice, and Nolan heard the hammer pull back on at least half a dozen police-issue nine-millimeter semiautomatics.

21

Branford wiped gathering sweat from his forehead that was threatening to douse his eyes as he watched the events playing out on his screens.

Nolan didn't stop to count the number of policemen who had spilled out of the stairwell. He ran as shots were fired, and another tiny but powerful impact jabbed into his thigh. He raced into the corner office, locking the door behind him. He ran to the room's center, grabbed the oversized desk, and dragged it quickly to the door to serve as a makeshift barricade.

"Get out of there!" Branford roared.

Nolan looked about, taking in his surroundings and by extension, his options. The five hostages were still kneeling on the floor up against a side wall, and with a wave of his hand, Nolan ordered them to stay put.

He ran over to the corner plate-glass window and looked out at the city. But he'd no sooner arrived there than his view was obstructed by a police helicopter that dropped into position and hovered right before him.

"Open this door!" shouted a policeman out in the hall.

Behind him, Branford heard the sounds of whispering. He figured Alice must be praying again. She seemed to do that a lot.

Branford had no interest in prayers, instead scanning the building blueprints again, looking for options to feed to Nolan. All the while, he glanced back and forth to the primary monitor that relayed Nolan's point of view. Nolan's eyes were trained on the helicopter and the two men who sat in the open cargo area, rifle sights focused on the glass window.

Angry pounding came from the office door, and then the thin

door was cracked open and an arm pushed through, blindly searching for the doorknob.

Nolan backed up five paces and then ran flat out toward the window and the helicopter waiting thirty feet beyond it.

The glass shattered in an explosion of shards and Nolan plunged, first out and then down. Branford couldn't believe his eyes as the picture swiveled from showing the ground rushing toward Nolan to the helicopter rushing away. Nolan's grappler came into view in a flash and suddenly Nolan was no longer falling. He'd stopped in midair, the hook of the grappler having punched through the floor of the chopper.

The pilot responded to his jump by pulling the helicopter away from the building, taking Nolan along for the ride. Seventy-five feet below, he dangled, clutching the grappler with both hands. Nolan built up momentum when the helicopter swerved away from the skyscraper and used it to swing toward another building close by that had a roofline only twenty feet or so below his current elevation.

Branford held his breath as the helicopter glided above the second building and Nolan retracted the grappler at just the right moment to fall onto the rooftop and into a rolling stop.

On solid footing again, Nolan ran for cover, dropping down from the opposite side of the rooftop, beyond where the helicopter could see, and found his footing on a lower ledge.

Conversationally, as if nothing had just happened, Nolan said, *"Okay, then. I'm going to reconnoiter that warehouse on the Lower West Side we talked about. I'll check in when I get there."*

And with that, he was off on his next task.

Branford took off his own headset and dropped it on the table before him. He leaned back in his seat, closed his eyes, and shook his head slowly. He had to take a few deep breaths to shake off the death-defying escape that Nolan had regarded as just another day at the office.

I am way too old for this. . . .

When he opened his eyes, he found Alice still staring at the computer monitor, frozen in place with both hands over her mouth.

"It's okay," he told her. "Don't worry, he's fine."

Alice dropped her hands. "I'll never get used to this."

"I still haven't," Branford said, rubbing the cobwebs out of his eyes, "and I've commanded men in two wars. But he thrives on this."

Alice shook her head. "Are all soldiers trained to do the things he can do?"

Branford sat back in his seat but turned to face her, letting his attention wander from his screens for the first time in hours. "Nolan's unlike any other soldier I've ever served with. He's had training in every form of combat that our armed forces teach. If he were from a different time, he'd be a ninja or a samurai or something. He was born for the fight."

"He's not superhuman," observed Alice. "Everybody has limits."

"Nolan's the best physical specimen humanity has to offer. And that's not an easy thing for an old war horse like me to say. When he was training for the Army Special Forces, every time his drill instructors thought they'd found his limits, he'd prove them wrong. He excelled at every discipline. Survival. Sharpshooting. Martial arts. Heavy artillery. Bladed weapons. Hand-to-hand. It was as if every one of these skills had been created solely for him. He broke records. He could adapt and improvise in the heat of the moment like no other. All forms of combat boil down to one thing: will. And Nolan had the strongest will power of anyone I've ever met. He's absolutely *bent* on making this 'better world' of his, and if it were anyone else, I'd balk. But he stands a real chance of pulling it off."

"You don't have to convince me that he's one of a kind," said Alice, looking back over at the computer that was showing Nolan's point of view as he made his way across the city. "I just hope he knows he's not indestructible."

Branford paused. "A buddy of mine, one of Nolan's instructors in firearms proficiency, once said something that's always stuck with me. He said that maybe once in every five to ten generations does a soldier like Nolan come along. He's one in a billion. The way that Mozart played music or Van Gogh painted—that's what it was like watching Nolan go about the art of war."

Alice paused. " 'Was.' You keep saying he 'was' . . ."

Branford scowled but said nothing.

"What really happened to him?" she asked, her voice dropping in volume. "During the war. What did they do to him?"

Branford shook his head. It was a long moment before he responded, and even then he wouldn't look her in the eye. "Stuff I can't put words to. Way beyond torture. Beyond indecency. They were kept naked and treated like animals. They were abused . . . and violated . . ." Branford lost his train of thought, realizing he'd likely said too much.

Alice was quiet for a moment. "And the president too? How was someone who'd been through that kind of thing ever deemed fit to serve in public office? If it was as bad as you say, wouldn't those men have been driven to madness?"

"Officially," Branford explained, "the tortures they suffered were never that bad. The captives testified in their debriefings that it never went beyond beatings, electrocution, starvation. But off the record, we all knew the truth. They were my men, all of them. I could see it in their eyes. They were alive, but there was no life left in them. They had been stripped of their humanity and reduced to something else. Something hollow. It was a long time before most of them healed, though Nolan and Hastings seemed to recover faster than the others. It was like they were both more *driven* than the rest. . . ."

Alice was silent for a moment as Branford went about returning to his normal surveillance of city police bands and random switching between views from various street cameras at New York's most populous intersections. He also pulled up his city grid and checked for any major emergencies, of which thankfully there were none at the moment.

"Ask you something else?" said Alice.

"Mm," he grumbled, a dispassionate yes.

"Why are you helping him?"

Branford stopped what he was doing and turned to her.

"This isn't your crusade, any more than it's mine," she said. "It's his. I know you two have this history, but you retired years ago, right? So why do this?"

Branford felt the muscles in his neck tense, clenching slightly.

She wasn't wrong. This entire plot was Nolan's brainchild. Unofficially, Nolan was in charge, because he was the one who was going to be putting himself out there, and Branford and Arjay worked for *him*. But since Branford was there to strategize, direct, and oversee Nolan's actions in the field, it sometimes proved an uneasy tension between their respective authority.

Still, there was no one else on the planet Nolan would have chosen to be at his side for what they were doing, and Branford knew it. And there was no one else in the world Branford would have agreed to help.

He frowned, searching for the words. "That young man is the most talented soldier I've ever seen. Talent like that isn't supposed to be wasted. When I saw that he was determined to go through with this plan of his . . . I knew he would need somebody watching his back. Keep him from getting himself killed. That's why I'm here. I'm doing this to keep him alive," Branford said and remembered the day, twelve months ago in Cancun, when he'd been convinced to do that very thing.

22

It was miserably sticky that day in Mexico. Branford would always remember the smell of sweat carried by the air.

Neither man had bothered to offer a greeting when Nolan approached Branford's table and sat down. That's just how it was for men who'd fought together for so long. There were no hellos or good-byes. There was only the current situation.

"You wanna tell me how you found me?" growled Branford.

"I *know* you," Nolan replied, quickly adding, "sir."

Branford frowned, letting out a sound between a snarl and a *hmph.* "Always *were* good at finding things . . ." he mumbled. "Heard you got religion after the war."

"Nah, I always had it."

"Good for you," said Branford without enthusiasm. "You go to church too?"

"Now and then. Still not big on crowds. Or small spaces."

Branford gave a conciliatory nod, Nolan's history coming back to him in a burst. He tried a different tack. "I'm impressed you could hold on to any kind of beliefs after . . . well, after what happened to you."

"What happened *strengthened* my faith."

"What're you doing here, Lieutenant?" Branford asked.

"I need your help," Nolan said. "New mission."

Branford, staring off into nothing, eyed him for a moment before speaking. "Not interested."

"I can pay you," Nolan replied.

"As if *you* have money."

"I have some."

"Don't need money. Don't need anything. Now go on, get back to your fame and your Jesus and leave me alone."

Nolan stood. "If that's what you want, sir."

He had turned to walk away when Branford said, "Oh, for crying out loud . . . What's the target?"

Nolan sat back down, seemingly steeling himself. This was the hard part. "Multiple targets."

Branford raised his eyebrows in an unspoken question.

"Immorality. Pain. Cruelty. Suffering. Apathy. In a word: evil."

From anyone else it would've sounded absurd. From Nolan, those words almost became actual enemies. Almost.

"Those ain't things you can destroy with weapons," said Branford.

"No, sir," Nolan replied. "But if you can change *them*, even on a small scale, then it might send a message to the rest of the world. And this message will be sent from New York City."

Branford almost frowned, but instead crinkled his eyebrows up. "I've never known you to do anything you weren't completely serious about. And I've never seen you fail. At anything. But what you're talking about . . . it can't be done. One man can't change an entire city, much less the world."

"I don't believe that," said Nolan, coming alive with confidence and drive. He leaned in to the table. "My grandmother taught me the difference between right and wrong. *You* taught me that distinguishing the two isn't hard. Everybody learns these things at some point. It's not a puzzle. It's the most obvious thing in the world. But people have lost faith and they need a reminder. They need something to rally around. A symbol. I'm going to give them one."

Branford shrugged. Idealism was never his thing. Objective and engagement. Battlefield terms, that's how he approached life.

"How's that going to work?" he eventually asked. "You gonna fight the good fight by destroying the wicked?"

"I'm going to push back evil by doing good," said Nolan. "I'm not naïve. I know how the world works. This has to be done just right, with intricate planning and focused intention. It's a war to be waged on two fronts. We draw a line against evil and don't let it cross. We cut off the criminals' supply lines and expose their biggest players as the dangers to society that they are. That's the first front. The second is inside the hearts and minds of the public. That's a battleground of words, ideas, emotions—a war that's fought by giving everybody the one thing they want most: hope. A symbol of hope to get behind, and bring them together. The way to make a change is to lead by example."

Branford studied him at length. "You've given this a lot of thought."

"I had plenty of time to think about it," Nolan replied. "I made a promise to a friend that I would find a way to make a difference. Look, I know it's probably impossible, but I *have* to do this. To not at least try . . . would be worse than dying."

That was another reference Branford wouldn't dispute. Whether he knew about the promise or not, Branford certainly knew about Nolan's experiences behind enemy lines during the second half of the war.

Most of his fellow hostages succumbed to death long before their captivity ended.

"You and I have never talked about that" was Branford's cautious reply. "What you went through. Do we need to?"

Nolan crossed his arms, leaned back against his chair, and searched the ceiling. "No, sir."

"You sure about that?" Branford pressed. "Because the things you were put through, that does stuff to a man—"

"Sir," Nolan said, swiveling to meet his eyes. "This subject is one you may respectfully consider off-limits."

Branford didn't argue. He was hardly the person anyone would or should choose to talk to about their personal demons.

"There's one thing I need to know," he said, softly so that only the two of them would hear. "Just one, and we'll never talk about it again."

Nolan met his gaze, his tics so subtle that Branford doubted anyone else would have been able to tell just how annoyed the younger man was. "What?" he asked, in a voice that was almost a dare.

"This plan of yours. Are you doing it because of what was done to you, back then?"

Nolan's expression never changed. "Does it matter?"

With that, he got up from the table and walked away, leaving Branford to consider his decision.

In the end, he was forced to concede the point. Nolan was already committed to this path. And his reasons why weren't going to change a thing.

KIM: Welcome back to "Walk the Talk." I'm Tony Kim, and today, we're going to do something a little different on the show. I have a special guest in the studio today—Biblical scholar Dr. Robert Sussex of Liberty University—who's here to discuss the topic on everyone's minds: The Hand. Dr. Sussex, welcome to the show, and please give us your take.

SUSSEX: Thank you so much for having me, Tony. Right off the bat, I have to say that the first question that comes to my mind about The Hand is whether or not he's a believer in Jesus Christ.

KIM: It's a valid question. Anyone who's been to The Hand's website knows that this "better way" he espouses looks a lot like Christianity. He holds in high regard principles like forgiveness, charity, and the Golden Rule.

SUSSEX: Indeed. And we as believers are required to consider how we should respond to The Hand and his activities. His goals are unquestionably good, and the positive effects of having him act as protector over our city are obvious. But what of his tactics? He's demonstrated impressive combat skills, and a willingness to intervene violently, if necessary.

KIM: Now correct me if I'm wrong, but wasn't Moses commanded to dole out punishments to lawbreakers that fit the severity of their crimes? An eye for an eye? Under that point of view, violence can be pretty easily justified. Example: If someone attacks you or breaks into your home, you have the right to defend yourself by any means necessary.

SUSSEX: Yet in the New Testament, Jesus told us to turn the other cheek.

KIM: Right. I know a lot of Christians who have trouble reconciling those two commandments.

SUSSEX: And this is not the only example of inconsistency within the Word when it comes to violence and conflict. Proverbs says that "a soft answer turneth away wrath." Yet Jesus was remarkably wrathful when he tore through the vendors' stalls at the Temple. What are we, as Christians, to do in the face of crime and corruption? Do we turn the other cheek? Or do we become enraged at the injustice of it and act, the way Jesus did at the Temple? And for that matter, is it ever acceptable to take the law into one's own hands?

KIM: It might be an easier issue to wrap our heads around if we knew The Hand's true identity, and had some measure of his character and personal beliefs. But we haven't got a clue who he is. He could be anyone -- your friend, a loved one, the random person you pass on the street. For all our listeners know, he could even be you, Dr. Sussex, or me.

-- TRANSCRIPT ENDS --

23

Her chin held as high as she dared, Agnes entered Big Al's Bar as casually as possible. The place was dark and her eyes didn't adjust immediately. As was the custom in motorcyclist-favored bars, every patron looked up at the brightness pouring in through the front door as she walked inside.

Her greatest fear was that the people would start laughing the minute she walked in. She was hardly tiny or frail. At six foot three and broad-shouldered, she had played basketball and soccer in high school and later in college, and had even considered pursuing a career in sports back then. But she'd put that aside because another path called to her.

Having been the frequent practical-joke target of the popular kids in school because of her atypical size, Agnes had turned her attention to a profession that would allow her to speak her mind without fear: writing. Through the pen, she could be the one to paint a target on the backs of those who truly deserved it, and she relished any chance to show the public that nobody was perfect.

Instead of laughter, she drew a few raised eyebrows but otherwise blank expressions as she briskly marched up to the bartender in her pinstripe gray pantsuit. It was all an adventure to post about later online.

"What'll you have?" asked the white-haired man behind the bar, who was missing several teeth but had replaced a few of them with gold.

"I'm looking for Tommy," she said.

"Never heard of him," replied the barkeep, though he kept his poker face trained on her.

Agnes frowned. She'd hoped it wouldn't come to this—that this man Tommy might be more professional than this—but she supposed that anyone who ran a business out of a motorcycle bar was probably not one to welcome unwanted solicitors.

Reluctantly, she pulled a folded-up hundred dollar bill out of her pocket and passed it to the bartender, as discreetly as possible.

He unfolded it and examined it closely, even scanning it with a special light to prove it wasn't a fake. When he was satisfied, he nodded toward a solid oak door at the very back of the bar. "Through there," he said.

She didn't bother to thank the old man; her money was all the gratitude she could afford to give. When she reached the heavy oak door, she knocked on it twice.

"Yeah?" called out a voice from inside.

"Tommy Serra? I'm in need of your services."

The door cracked open two inches, but Agnes could see little more than darkness beyond it.

"You a cop?" asked Tommy from inside.

"Do I look like a cop?"

"You don't look much like a biker," Tommy replied.

"And you don't look like you've seen anything outside this room since you were potty-trained," she fired back, her blood pressure rising. "Relax, man-child. I can pay you well, and what I'm asking you to do isn't even illegal."

After a beat, the door was shut and latches and chains were undone from the inside. Finally the door opened and Tommy stood before her. He looked like he was barely out of his teens, clad in baggy clothes and sporting unkempt black hair, with dark circles under his beady eyes. He lived in a small space so dark it could only be described as a cave. She supposed it had been some kind of storage closet before he moved in. He nodded for her to enter, and then shut and locked the door behind her.

There were some offensive odors in this strange small room, not a single extra chair, and hardly enough room for her to stand. Tommy took his place at the large desk up against the right-side wall, and quickly looked back and forth between his three giant-screened computer monitors situated side-by-side.

Agnes wasn't sure if she should wait for him to finish whatever he was doing or if he was merely waiting for her to tell him what she wanted. Either way, she was tiring of him already and decided to cut to the chase.

She pulled a legal-sized envelope out of her carryall and dropped it on Tommy's desk. He swiveled to glance at it, and then he stopped his typing and opened it quickly, like a hungry animal smelling meat.

Several dozen photos slid out, and he shuffled through them quickly. "The Hand. Been watching this guy. Been to his website? He's getting incredible traffic. I'm amazed it hasn't crashed."

"That's virtually every photo that's been taken of him," Agnes explained.

Tommy kept shuffling. "He's pretty camera shy. Not a single shot of his face."

She nodded. "Exactly. But if you look closely, you can see little bits here and there. Tiny parts of his face that peek through from under that hood—mostly his chin and jowls. No one's gotten a real clear look at him, several of these shots are blurry. But I hear you're good at 3-D rendering, among your other—"

"You want me to map each of these bits of his face onto a 3-D model, and see how much of the puzzle can be pieced together," Tommy assessed.

"How long will it take?"

"Three days, maybe four."

She handed him a business card and ten one-hundred dollar bills. "Make it two. And call me the minute it's done."

Without stopping to find out if this price was agreeable to him, or to see if he wanted to negotiate a particular rate, she closed her bag, turned on one heel, unlocked his heavy oak door, and marched out.

24

It was after eight o'clock in the evening when Nolan wearily returned to his underground home after a very long day. There had been four crimes in progress to attend to, in between which he'd turned his focus to his ongoing efforts to uncover deeper, systemic examples of crime.

With Branford's help, he'd managed to turn up evidence of corruption in the mayor's administration and had snuck into the man's office to leave behind a digital disk drive containing all of the incriminating information he had amassed.

That was just his morning. His afternoon had consisted of rounding up a number of pimps in Hell's Kitchen and seeing to it that they were put out of business for good, and the prostitutes in their employ given second chances at a better life. These kinds of missions required more finesse and planning on his part; since he could never use his voice, he had to work closely with Branford to place the dominos *just so*, so that elements fell perfectly into place. Such as luring the police to local "establishments" under the pretense of trying to catch Nolan himself, or arranging for representatives from charity organizations and churches to appear on the scene just as the prostitutes found themselves without employment and in need of guidance. Only a few of them would choose to take this opportunity to change their ways, of course, but every single one Nolan counted as a victory.

With a soreness that ached through muscle, ligament, and bone, he removed his flak jacket and hung it on the stone wall on a hook that had been placed beside the main entrance. On the other side of the entrance was a whiteboard that he'd hung himself, and he grabbed the black marker hanging underneath and added another line to the ongoing tally. The board told him that this had been day forty-eight. Almost seven weeks since Times Square.

So tired he just wanted some quiet time to himself, he slipped away to his bunk where he could address today's cuts and scrapes, alone. No need to bother Alice.

Five minutes later, he realized he should've known better, when Alice appeared with a smile and wordlessly handed him a tray filled with home cooking. Nolan accepted the food gratefully and said a soft "Thank you, ma'am" as she nodded and left him in peace. He grabbed a TV remote and flipped on the small box he'd installed near his bed, while he ate.

As he chewed a bite and stretched his sore shoulder, the TV came on, landing on a cable news network where a roundtable discussion filled the screen. According to the graphics, today's guests were a theological scholar and a well-known pastor. Their topic was The Hand. Which wasn't surprising—The Hand had been the media's favorite topic for weeks. The debate was already in progress, but Nolan paused his eating for a moment to listen.

The scholar carefully adjusted his glasses. "This mystery man's intentions seem noble enough, certainly, and I applaud them, but human beings are inherently incapable of being good on our own. This is the very reason that the Son of God was sent to redeem the world. Any attempts to 'be good' or 'do good' on this man's own—and even inspire others to do the same—are futile."

The moderator opened his mouth and turned to the pastor, but didn't get the chance to speak. The pastor jumped in immediately. "So are you saying we shouldn't bother helping our neighbor, lifting up the downtrodden, defending the weak, or being kind to one another? When was it that those things—the very types of things that Jesus himself 'led by example' by doing—became futile?"

The scholar rebutted immediately. "Acts of kindness are always good, and are to be encouraged. And if that were all that this 'Hand' fellow was interested in doing—showing people how to treat one another—then that would be perfectly fine. But he's making such a grand show of his efforts that I get the sense his endgame is something much bigger than he's let on, and I think you would agree. He wants to change New York City—it says so on his website—but that's a change that takes place in the heart."

"Again," replied the pastor, "I have to wonder, what's so wrong with wanting to make a better place for people to live? Even if his influence never spreads beyond a few, if he keeps one hurting girl from becoming a prostitute, or one kid from throwing his life away by taking part in a robbery, then I say more power to him. Change starts from within, absolutely, but it spreads to our actions, and the more of these kinds of charitable life-saving actions the world sees with its own eyes, the more they will *see* the gospel message itself—and not just hear it or read about it. For that reason alone, The Hand gets my full support and a standing ovation."

To demonstrate his sincerity, the pastor leapt to his feet and began to clap. Others in the studio audience quickly joined in, and as the camera panned around, Nolan could see that everyone in the entire room was on his feet, applauding.

The moderator quickly regained control of the broadcast by latching onto the pastor's last words. "Clearly The Hand has support from people of all backgrounds and belief systems. I've noticed a number of religious news agencies with headlines that label him 'The Hand of God,' suggesting that he's doing the very work of God himself. Here's a question for our guests. In The Hand's case, does might make right?"

His thoughts consumed with these words and opinions, Nolan turned off the television and forgot about his food.

25

I'm not trying to be the second coming, people! Nolan thought. *There's only one Jesus, and he did what no human ever can. I'm just trying to instigate some social change, remind people of the Golden Rule. Sure, I'm doing it on a big stage, but—*

He blinked. Alice was standing behind the television, watching him.

"Food's getting cold," she said softly.

He looked down at his plate and saw that it was no longer steaming. "Sorry," he said.

"Saw you favoring that shoulder," she said. "Let me take a look."

Nolan hesitated. "It's fine. It'll be fine, really."

"Let me check to be sure," Alice replied, averting her eyes. "I need to feel useful."

Still Nolan paused. It wasn't that he didn't want her to be his nurse. She'd already proven herself qualified. He just wasn't used to letting anyone see what was under his clothes.

Mostly to avoid hurting her feelings, he finally conceded. Without a word, he turned his back to her and pulled his shirt off over his head. He closed his eyes, waiting for the inevitable.

"Sweet Moses . . ." Alice whispered, sounding as if something had knocked the wind out of her. "I'm so sorry," she backpedaled. "I just . . . I didn't think."

"You didn't know," Nolan reminded her. "No one does."

His upper body showcased his strapping, chiseled musculature. But it was also covered in countless scars bearing witness to the terrible things he'd suffered during the war. There were narrow streaks of dark pink skin all over, evidence of whippings and cuts. Huge raised areas on his back and shoulders where the skin had grown back after being violently ripped off. Countless tiny spots in his forearms where he'd been stuck with needles. Perfectly straight incisions in his abdomen with stitching holes on either side, where he'd been surgically mutilated, without the mercies of anesthesia. There were bullet wounds, melted skin where he'd been burned, and even a few skin grafts.

After she'd had a minute to gather herself, Alice grasped his arm and examined it as he rotated it as far as he could. She said nothing, focusing on the workings of his shoulder by turning it this way and that. But every few seconds, she sniffled. At one point, she let go of him, and Nolan was sure she was wiping her eyes.

"You were right," she said, her voice just above a whisper. "You'll be fine."

With that, she turned to go, walking away in stunned silence.

Nolan quickly pulled his shirt back on. There was never a good time for what he needed to tell her, so he said, "Oh, before I forget . . ." as casually as he could muster. "I believe your husband *is* still looking for you. I'd hoped that if you laid low for a while, the police would get preoccupied with me and some of the heat you were feeling would die down. But it hasn't. I'm sorry. It looks like you're stuck here for the duration."

Alice turned and offered a tight almost-smile. "It's not so bad here. I'm safe. I'm alive. And I get to see you do the things you do, firsthand. Now, why don't you tell me why you were so far away a while ago, before I walked over. What's on your mind? I'm a great listener—I can listen with the best of them."

Nolan tried to offer his own smile in return, but his face wouldn't move, and besides, it wouldn't have been sincere. "I was just . . . Do people really think that stuff about me? That I'm trying to be the new Jesus or something?"

She shrugged and sat down at the foot of the bed. "At my church, we're taught to 'be Jesus to the world.' Seems to me that's exactly what you've been doing. Though I don't recall Jesus using a big metal stick."

Nolan gave a halfhearted smile. "Am I crazy for thinking I can actually change the entire city—and maybe even beyond?"

Alice considered this. "I've always found that if a man wants something bad enough, he'll find a way to get it. And I think you're the most determined man I've ever met."

"You think I'm a fool," Nolan said quietly.

She frowned. "You're only a fool for thinking that. You saved my life, and you've saved hundreds of others too. There's nothing foolish about that."

"But . . . ?"

"I worry for you. I can't help it. You're out there every day, and I'm afraid that one of these times you won't come back. You face down the entire city, telling people they need to change and here's how to do it. The city might not be interested. You've thrown yourself into the spotlight, and people are fickle. Today they love you. Tomorrow they may call for your execution."

Nolan grimaced. But he couldn't lie to her.

"You think I'm not afraid?" he said in a small voice. "I'm scared to death."

"Then tell me *why*," she said slowly, emphatically, appealing to him with the fundamental question he knew she'd been wondering since they first met.

Nolan turned inward, searching for some way to explain, and let out a long breath. He started to speak twice but stopped both times before finally finding a place to begin.

"Words are hard for me sometimes," he apologized. "During the war, we had a guy in our unit named Darren. Good guy, loved his wife, and had three kids between six and twelve years old. Showed me photos of his kids once, and he was right there in every picture with them, grinning ear to ear. Just crazy over them. He was in the reserves and called to active duty. Good soldier, dependable, honorable. I was leading a small group of men on a transfer assignment, delivering a handful of prisoners to HQ for questioning.

"We were ambushed by two dozen tangos. They got shots off before we had time to react, and Darren took one to the neck. We were pinned down for twelve minutes before we finally took them out. By the time it was over, Darren had bled out. Dead before we could get him to a medic. All I could think of for weeks was how that night, somebody somewhere had to tell Darren's six-year-old daughter that she would never see her daddy again. That's hard enough for an adult to deal with, but a child, who doesn't understand things? I heard a few years ago that little girl has been to see lots of psychologists because she never feels safe."

Nolan watched as Alice studied him. She'd never seen him talk this much before, and she was fully engrossed in his words.

"Got a friend from high school, Samantha. Ran into her a couple years back over lunch. She looked nothing like I remembered. Sam told me how she'd married the man of her dreams after school, and they'd spent a few happy years together. But then finances got tight and he started to change. Everything became her fault. He threatened to kill her, he punched her and roughed her up.

"One day when he wasn't home, Sam found a shoebox that had a loaded gun inside, along with wire, a hammer, and some matches. She freaked out but couldn't let on that she knew. They stopped sleeping in the same bed together, and she would lock her bedroom door at night, but she woke up one time in the middle of the night to see him standing over her bed, watching her sleep with a crazed look in his eyes. The next day he punched her in the head so hard that even now she still struggles with severe migraines.

"She finally found her courage and called the police. She got a restraining order against him and they divorced, but for years, he terrorized her. He would ride past her home when she was outside and stare at her with that same look in his eyes. He's tried to break in to the house a few times, he's followed her family around and threatened them. And when Sam tried to prosecute him for violating the restraining order—wouldn't you know it? His little brother was a hotshot lawyer whom he'd helped put through law school, so that debt was repaid by bringing this powerful law firm down on her. They postponed court dates time after time, and used every dirty tactic in the book to discredit her and ensure that her husband got everything, without having to pay her a dime out of all the money he'd hid from her. It was years before she was able to pick up the pieces of her life, but she's skinny and frail now, and she's still afraid to leave the house."

Nolan looked down, weariness and sadness creeping across his features. "These stories aren't the exception. They're the norm. Violence is everywhere." Nolan's temper grew in intensity, frustration. "It's not right. This ain't how the world should be. It's an evil place, and it's mired in sin and pain and destruction. And it *shouldn't be*. The world is broken, and maybe I *am* crazy, but I'm going out there every day, charging into the fires of hell, because I have to *do something*."

Alice was silent, and he found her gaze uncomfortable. He looked away. "You still think I'm crazy."

Alice looked at him, those wise eyes of hers not blinking. "I was thinking you're a lot better with words than you think you are. And I was thinking that anybody else would have quit long before now. You are exactly the right person in the right place at the right time. Don't ever let anybody tell you different."

26

Gallons of adrenaline coursed with every beat of Coral Lively's heart as she fought the jittery excitement of launching the OCI's first major field op. The streets of New York were unusually brisk, with strong winds gusting up against the dirty windows of the old storefront where the task force had stationed itself.

Across the street and one block down sat the five-story office building of Yuri Vasko, local crime lord and first target of Organized Crime Intelligence.

Coral listened as her brawny partner, Jonah Janssen, spoke over a secured line with the president himself. She had stationed herself right beside Jonah for this extraordinary moment for which they had all waited so long. Here, tonight, they would declare war on crime, and their first strike would be heard from the halls of Congress to the lowest slums of America.

"Yes, sir," said Jonah. "We're all deeply honored to be a part of this, sir."

Coral held up her wrist and pointed at it with her other hand, reminding her partner of the time. He nodded.

"Sir, the hour has arrived, and I formally request the order to proceed."

Coral took a deep breath and checked the rounds in her Sigma 9mm for the fourth time to ensure she had at least four magazines clipped to her black field vest.

"Yes, sir, we are one hundred percent certain," said Jonah. "No, sir, we are clear on the ramifications. The trail has led us here, and we have verified intel from a delivery man that the target himself is in his office as we speak. We will never be in a better position to strike against Yuri Vasko than we are at this moment."

Coral was surprised at how Jonah spoke so boldly and directly to the president, but knew that it was his boldness, precision, and determination that were the very qualities the president admired in him.

Jonah closed his eyes for a moment, celebrating victory, and she knew that they were to proceed. While Jonah offered final salutations to the president, she turned to address the other six operatives who were milling about nearby, prepping for the mission.

"We have a green light. The president has granted us discretionary powers to apprehend the target by any means necessary and remove any obstacles that stand in our way," said Coral. "Ladies and gentlemen, lock and load."

Jonah hung up the phone and looked around at the room, his eyes blazing. He would take point, there was no debate over that. And Coral would have his back.

"Here we go," he said.

———

The team started by picking the lock of a back door on the ground floor, right by an old loading dock. Fanning out in pairs, they secured the bottom level with silenced weapons, sneaking up from behind and dropping the six guards stationed on this level with silenced bullets to the head.

They worked their way up, floor by floor, in a similar fashion. By the time they neared the fourth floor, their presence had been detected, and stealth was out the window. Coral nodded at Agent Niñez, who pulled out a detonator and pushed the trigger. At the fuse box two levels down, a small fragment of C4 was set to flash, and immediately the entire building fell dark.

Jonah gave the signal for them to pop the gas grenades, and a half dozen of the small canisters were tossed in every direction as they emerged on the fourth floor, gas masks now covering their faces. Night vision goggles helped them see the ten or more guards who were scattered about this spacious floor, bent over coughing or already on the ground. They were neutralized; time to move on.

Coral's heart leapt as she knew this was it. The top floor was next, and with it, Vasko.

The group rushed up the final flight of stairs and Jonah signaled for their live grenades to be pulled. The time for subtlety was over; they were going in hot, as they must, knowing that this floor would be the most well guarded. From here Vasko ruled his little empire, and his office would be in the area farthest from the stairs or the elevator, with all of his remaining men standing between him and capture.

It didn't matter. Coral knew it, she could feel it. They had momentum on their side. They'd cleared the bottom four floors of the building much faster than she'd thought possible, and she felt unstoppable. She knew the others were feeling it too.

Jonah reared back and kicked open the stairwell door, after which Coral and the others all tossed live grenades in varying directions through the open doorway. After the blasts, the team rushed forward as one, guns raised to just below eye level.

One of the grenades had caught fire to a rug not far from the stairwell and kicked up a lot of particulates in the air, making visibility nearly impossible, even with night vision. An agent near the back of the line shot off a round, and a silhouetted figure in a suit went down, a high-powered assault rifle falling from his grasp. The floor was eerily silent for a good twenty seconds, and Coral began wondering if she'd been wrong about Vasko's distribution of men throughout the building. Maybe there wouldn't be that much to stand between them and their target after all.

Two more figures appeared, and she and Jonah each shot one between the eyes. Pushing ever forward, Coral noted that this guard she'd just shot was a woman, a small pistol still in her lifeless hand as she bled all over the floor.

Whatever. Good for Vasko for hiring from both sides of the gender pool. But too bad for the woman for picking such a poor boss.

As they spread out to clear the remaining guards and make for Vasko's office, which they knew to be heavily fortified from the inside, the smell of smoke grew stronger.

The fire was spreading. No time. The whole place would be burning in minutes.

She followed Jonah through a spacious open foyer with an

expensive seating arrangement of sofas and leather chairs. A woven rug that looked to be the genuine Persian article took up most of the floor, covering weathered hardwood.

As they were about to pass out of the room on the far side, Coral glanced down at an end table near the doorway and saw a large photo frame on it holding pictures arranged in a collage. Most of them were pictures of Vasko and what must have been his reclusive wife and daughter, whom Vasko was notorious for keeping far away from his business.

Coral turned to follow Jonah but something stopped her. The woman in the photos, smiling alongside her husband. She . . . she looked like the woman Coral had just shot, only seconds ago.

A mistress? Vasko was having an affair with one of his guards? That didn't make sense; his daughter was right there in the pictures too.

No . . .

Despite the rising heat and growing flames, fingers of ice reached down through her insides and nearly caused her to lose her footing.

No, no, no!

She looked around this grand room with new eyes—this vast open area with a big skylight up above that wasn't a foyer at all.

"Where's Vasko hiding?" Jonah hissed from up ahead. "He's here somewhere!"

"He's in his office," Coral replied, her voice dead and devoid of urgency.

Jonah noted the change in her demeanor and ducked back into the great room to see what was wrong.

Coral had dropped her gun on the ground and was walking slowly, sickeningly back out to the first hallway, where the two figures she and Jonah had killed were sprawled across the hardwood floor.

Only they weren't guards. They were the woman and the young girl from the picture frame. Both dead, with single leaking bullet wounds piercing their foreheads.

As the roar of the flames grew louder, she felt the entirety of the earth crash around her, dragging her down to the floor with it.

Jonah ran up next to her.

"We're in the wrong building," she said.

27

The blaze of the building far below flickered brilliantly in Nolan's goggles.

Why would they set the building on fire? He could discern no tactical advantage to such an action. The building's occupants hadn't put up so much of a fight that smoking them out would be necessary.

He was perched high above this mystery building the OCI had chosen to raid and watched what he could see of their field operation through the big skylight in the building's roof. He was crouching more than ten stories above the other building's roof, and across the street, on the edge of a skyscraper's roof, his glasses allowing him exceptional vision even through the smoke.

Branford had picked up radio chatter earlier in the evening about something big going on in this part of town tonight—most of it orders going out to local PD to stay clear of the area. It was mere curiosity that landed him there, where he could observe what he quickly pieced together had to be the anticipated first field operation of the Organized Crime Intelligence in action. He'd just seen headlines a day or two ago promising that a "swift, decisive first action" would be undertaken by the new agency in "a matter of days."

But Branford was unable to turn up any information about this building. Whatever it was, someone had gone to a lot of trouble to keep it anonymous, because it wasn't listed with any government or real estate agency. He couldn't even find records on who paid the building's power bill. The data was either nonexistent or very well hidden.

From what Nolan could tell, the OCI's operation wasn't going well. Their entrance looked solid, and the X-ray option in his glasses allowed him to follow their movements through the old brick building. He had no idea why they'd chosen this location, or who their intended target was. But he could tell from the start that this wasn't the home of a big Mafia don or a drug cartel. Nor was it some drug flophouse. It looked like a well-appointed apartment, one of thousands in the city.

Then the grenades exploded and the shooting began. The blast was loud enough that he could hear it from his position, and the tinny pops of the guns were just within his range as well.

The group of OCI agents appeared efficient, he had to give them that. Within seconds, the eight of them were the only people still standing in the building.

"*Huh,*" said Branford in his ear. "*They're calling for ambulance and rescue assistance. Guess they couldn't handle the job after all.*"

Nolan creased his brow. He could see what he believed to be all eight OCI agents still moving, so it didn't look like they had suffered any casualties. Then he noticed that the fire was spreading through the wooden floors and support beams, threatening to consume the whole building.

"No, the building's going to go," Nolan said suddenly. "They have to get out of there!"

Without another word, he rose to his feet and dove from his perch, his hand already firing the grappler behind him. He didn't spin to look and aim this time. He had learned that the grappler always managed to land true and find something to hold on to.

As he fell, he quickly switched to thermal imaging and counted the number of live bodies still inside the building. It looked to be over twenty total, scattered about the various floors. And with the way the inferno was spreading, he doubted the fire department would make it in time.

He released and retracted the grappler's hook just above the penthouse skylight, allowing himself to burst through and shatter the glass on his way down.

A woman—one of the OCI agents—was kneeling over a pair of bodies in the hallway just outside the big room, and when she heard the glass shatter, she spun automatically in place, her hands reaching for a gun. But oddly, there was no gun where she expected it to be, so she merely stared at him for a moment. Her eyes were distant, empty, her cheeks wet.

Something about this woman was awfully hard to turn away from. He knew he needed to head off and try to help evacuate the survivors before the building collapsed, but the woman on the floor was just so sad. He was compelled to reach out to her, speak to her or offer her . . . something.

As he took a few steps closer, he spotted her black Sig on the floor nearby. He smoothly knelt down and picked it up as he kept moving toward her, and he was quite certain she hadn't seen him do it. She was too involved in her grief.

Was that what it was? Grief? She must've been mourning a fellow agent, he decided. But when he drew near, he saw that one of the victims on the ground was no soldier or field agent; she was a girl of maybe fifteen or sixteen years old. Lovely jet black shoulder-length hair. Stylish clothes. There were braces on her teeth.

She was an ordinary girl, and yet this female OCI agent was weeping over her as if she'd just lost her own sister or daughter.

The building let out a loud shudder as the weight-bearing beams and posts struggled to hold together. Dark gray smoke was growing thicker with every passing moment.

Nolan was just about to put his hand on the woman's shoulder when a voice brought him up short.

"Get away from her!" shouted a man from behind.

Instinct kicking in, Nolan spun in place and stepped into a defensive position. Staring him down with another Sigma 9mm drawn was a tall, beefy man wearing the same black field ensemble as the grieving woman.

The big man raised his gun an inch higher and seemed to be seriously considering pulling the trigger. Nolan stuck out his hand and was about to trigger the electromagnet when a quieter voice spoke.

"Leave him alone," said the woman who knelt over the body. Nolan was surprised when she looked up not at him but at the other man. He looked back at her incredulous, unable to process what she was saying.

Nolan remained poised, ready to defend himself, even though the other man finally gave in and holstered his weapon.

A wood beam over one corner of the room broke clean in half, red embers exploding from the fracture.

The man seemed to make a quick decision and marched forward to grab the female agent by one arm. She didn't budge at first, but he was too strong for her to fend him off indefinitely, and finally she allowed him to pull her to her feet and then back toward the stairwell. She threw Nolan one last glance as she disappeared from sight.

When they were gone, even though he was keenly aware of the collapsing building around him and that he had only seconds to spare, he zeroed in his goggles onto a good clear view of the face of the dead girl at his feet.

"Run facial recognition," he asked.

"*Already on it,*" Branford replied.

Nolan was examining the gunshot wound to the girl's forehead when he sensed another presence around him. The roar of the flames had made it impossible to hear his approach, but he caught a glimpse of motion in his enhanced peripheral vision. Instinct took over, and Nolan snatched the Sig he'd picked up moments ago and spun. Something big and heavy connected first, crashing into his head and causing Nolan to lose hold of the gun.

"*What did you do?!*" screamed the other man in a thick accent that Nolan's brain registered as Eastern European.

Nolan came terribly close to losing consciousness, finding himself disoriented and sprawled out face first on the floor with stars in front of his eyes. A few feet away, he saw the wooden plank that had been used like a bat against his head. He also spotted the Sigma to his right, resting on the ground.

Get up, he commanded himself. *Get up!*

"*Nolan!*" thundered Branford in his earpiece. "Nolan, *do you read me?!*"

He had to get the gun back, there was no choice. Whoever this man was, he was trying to kill him, and getting his hand around the pistol's grip was a matter of survival.

Far slower than he desired, he watched his own arm reach out feebly toward the gun, but his head swam sickeningly with the effort, making him wonder just how hard the plank had slammed into him. The Sig felt miles away from his grasp, just as it felt that time had slowed to a near standstill. As if watching everything play out from a distance, he saw the other man—a short, dark-haired balding man with a gimp hand, a tailored suit, and an expression of unrestrained wrath—reach down with his good hand and easily pick up the gun. The man was shaking with rage, tears streaming down his face.

"Nolan!" shouted Branford, the old man sounding more frantic than Nolan could ever remember hearing before.

Nolan was fading, his vision awash in blurry orange flames and his eyes and throat burning from the thickening smoke. Blackness seeped inward from the periphery of his sight and threatened to blind him completely.

The last thing he saw was the other man point the pistol at him and pull the trigger.

28

Arjay, man the Cube!" shouted Branford, bursting from his caged work space and taking charge with a tone that left no room for argument. "Nolan's glasses are still transmitting imagery of that building burning down around him, but he's not moving and he won't answer me. I've got to get down there."

Arjay's face drew taut. "What happened? Is he alive?"

"I don't know!" Branford roared. "Just get in there!"

Arjay gave a nod and ducked inside the Cube.

Branford was at the subway station's primary exit in seconds, his car keys in hand. He was tucking an earpiece into his ear when he realized someone was keeping pace with him from just behind as he entered the stairwell.

"You're driving," said Alice, her face hardened and grim as she climbed the stairs. She carried a plastic case holding first aid supplies.

At the top of the stairs he stopped. "You're not going, and I don't have time to argue!"

"He's hurt," she said, holding her ground. "No offense, Aaron, but I've seen your skills as a medic. You need me."

Branford swore to himself. She was right, and he really didn't have time to argue. The burning building wasn't far, but he'd still be lucky to make it there before the fire department, which was almost certainly on its way already.

And Alice had called him by his first name. It made him blink. No one had called him Aaron in a very long time. When she'd said it, it felt like being slapped across the back of the head.

"There'll be cops," he pointed out, walking again, heading outside. "Aren't they still looking for you?"

"You going to take him to the hospital?" she retorted.

"Fine," he growled at her angrily. "But if you can't keep up, I can't wait for you."

He led the way to his car, where it sat parallel parked on the street.

———

Branford's car was a '57 Hudson Hornet that drove with the finesse of a World War II tank—sluggish to gain speed, even harder to bring to a halt. Alice feared for her life every time Branford rounded a corner.

But much more than herself, she feared for Nolan.

"Don't let him die, don't let him die...." was her whispered prayer as she white-knuckled her seat.

This couldn't be happening.

God had a plan for Nolan. Of this she was utterly certain. After all that he'd suffered during the war—and survived—God wouldn't let his life end now. Not like this. He couldn't have made it through all of that for nothing. He was the hero that the people of New York had prayed and hoped for, and he still had so much good to do.

He couldn't die. Not now.

Branford barreled through a left-hand turn onto a one-way street, and for a second she thought one side of the car had lifted up off the ground. She looked at Branford in alarm, but he ignored her, his attention focused on the road.

"Please, God, don't let him die...." she whispered.

Branford threw her an annoyed glance, but she never stopped praying.

———

Minutes later, they arrived at the scene of mass chaos. A pair of fire trucks and one police car were already there, but there would be more on the way. Pedestrians lined the sidewalks, watching the action unfold, and there were a half dozen people coming and going from inside the building.

The entire building belched black smoke that streamed into the sky—a sight that brought back unwelcome memories for many New Yorkers of one fateful historic day.

The fire trucks were spraying water into the first floor of the building, trying to get the fire under control before the building came down. Too many people now crowded the area, but the lone policeman on the scene couldn't do much about it.

Making matters worse, the burning edifice was situated on a street corner and surrounded by much larger and taller buildings, giving it a claustrophobic, walled-in feeling. Most of the smoke was going straight up because there wasn't much of anywhere else it could go.

It was a circus, and Branford couldn't believe he was about to walk into it.

Hadn't he left this sort of thing behind long ago?

Alice started directly toward the building, but he grabbed her by the arm and steered her around the back of the nearest building so they could come at it from the rear.

As promised, Branford didn't wait for Alice to keep up, but she did fine on her own. They'd parked two blocks from the site and within just a few minutes they'd ducked around the burning building to an old alleyway that was too narrow to fit any vehicles. He was relieved to spot a window that looked big enough to squeeze through. He pushed past Alice and snatched a large steel trash can from the other side of the alley, pushing it under the window so he could climb atop it.

Looking away from the window, he reared back and threw his elbow into the glass. It shattered, but black smoke immediately began to pour out of the opening.

He was wondering if they would be able to breathe through the thick smoke long enough to get to Nolan up on the top floor, when Alice produced a pair of surgical masks from the first aid kit and handed one to him.

"It won't last long against this," she said, nodding at the smoke.

Branford nodded his thanks and began to climb inside. When he was halfway through, he reached out and helped Alice up onto the trash can so she could follow.

They slid down to the wet concrete floor inside the building, and Branford decided that maybe having Alice along was an okay idea after all.

———

Any concerns they had about reaching Nolan undetected were swiftly erased by the smoke making it all but impossible to see anything. The entire bottom floor lay drenched by the water the fire fighters had sprayed inside; the good news was that the ground floor was no longer burning. But the smoke waited everywhere, and it took a painfully long time for them to feel their way around the outer wall until they reached the stairs. Once they began to ascend, visibility worsened with every step. A fireman nearly ran Alice over coming down as they rounded one set of stairs, but his vision was no better.

"Chief's ordered everybody out!" he shouted. "It's going to collapse any minute!"

Branford cleared his throat. "The chief just sent us up to make sure no one else was inside!" he shouted, besting the fireman's authoritative tone with his angriest drill sergeant bark.

Branford couldn't see the fireman, so he had no way of reading him, of knowing if he was buying it or not.

"Call the chief on your radio if you want, to confirm, but we don't have time to argue!" yelled Branford over the fire.

"Just hurry it up!" replied the fireman, and he was on his way.

They continued to climb, and after a moment, Alice complimented Branford on his ruse. "That was impressive."

"Started my career in law enforcement," Branford mentioned. "The mentality's not that different from the military." He wasn't one for talking about the past—and his life hadn't been nearly as interesting as Nolan's—so he decided that that was all the explanation he'd offer.

At last they reached the top floor, and both of them were winded and starting to feel the effects of the smoke. Branford led them into the big central room with the broken skylight. He felt the crunch of glass and debris beneath his shoes, though he couldn't hear it over the din of the burning building.

"*Nolan!*" Branford shouted.

The blaze all but encircled the entire room, and most of the furniture and the expensive rug on the floor were consumed as well. The man who'd attacked Nolan was nowhere to be found, and Branford saw no sign of the teenage girl either.

"Help me out here, Arjay," he said. "I can barely see my own feet! Can you describe anything that Nolan's close to?"

"*He's behind a broken chair with, I believe, green upholstery,*" replied Arjay in his ear.

"Copy that." Branford canvassed the area, peering carefully through the smoke and taking steps cautiously to avoid the spreading fire and any dangers they couldn't see.

"There!" he shouted, pointing, and he and Alice ran to the spot.

It was indeed a carved wooden chair with dark green fabric. Branford knelt down to scan the ground up close. He found a gloved human hand sticking out from under a sofa, atop which was an enormous support beam that had collapsed diagonally from one corner of the room.

The top of the wooden beam, touching the ceiling, was on fire, and the flames were slowly moving down toward the floor. The giant thing looked like it weighed half a ton, but Branford never hesitated. He crawled underneath an open section between the beam and the floor. On all fours, he put his back up against it.

"When I heave," he shouted to Alice, "you pull him out as fast as you can!"

Using the adrenaline coursing through his veins, he flexed and strained with all his strength pushing against the ground. It felt like the heavy beam moved less than an inch, but he held on as long as he could, grimacing and holding his breath. He tried counting the seconds to help him focus, but it didn't work.

By the time he reached four, Branford was already feeling wobbly, and he knew he wouldn't be able to do this more than another few seconds. The intense heat from the fire, the scarce oxygen . . . He couldn't last—

"Got him!" shouted Alice, and Branford collapsed with a groan. The beam settled with a crack, and he crawled out from under it backward to see that the flames had nearly reached his back.

When he was out and could turn around, he found Alice already inspecting Nolan for damage.

"Good strong pulse," she said, her voice loud enough to rise above the racket. "Looks like the bullet bounced off his hood without penetrating it, but it hit him like a hammer to the head. He's out cold."

"The shot was fired from point-blank range," confirmed Branford, remembering the sight of it from watching through Nolan's goggles. Seeing the crazed man with the gun point it directly at the camera was something he wouldn't forget anytime soon. The man's face had been blood red, his eyes filled with so much pain and hate . . .

Another thought occurred to him, and he glanced around at the floor. But there was no sign of the gun.

Another beam collapsed, this time on the other side of the room, sending wild embers scattering across the floor.

"I don't think I can carry him," said Branford wearily. "I'm weak and shaky now."

Alice frowned, examining Nolan again. "His legs don't look like they took any damage," she muttered. She searched through the medical kit for a moment, retrieved a tiny vial, and held it under his nose.

The smelling salts did their work, forcing Nolan to twitch himself awake to escape from the powerful odor. When he fully came to, he started violently with wide eyes and looked up at Alice in shock.

"What are you doing here?" he asked. Then he spotted Branford standing above him.

"Can you walk?" asked Alice.

Nolan willed himself to his feet, swaying wildly but refusing to yield. "Take these, General. Use the night vision," he said to Branford, handing the old man his goggles. "Lead the way."

29

Are you feeling all right?" asked Alice when Nolan awoke the next morning in his own bed. He was still wearing his clothes from last night, and Alice sat next to the bed, reading a book and watching over him.

No, he was not all right. From what he could feel, he knew he had a concussion from the two blows to the head, and he had a strong urge to cough, tasting the burnt tang of smoke in his throat. Smoke inhalation, no doubt.

But it was more than that. As his memories of the previous night came back in a rush, he suddenly felt a strong need to punch something. He would have preferred to pummel the face of the person who'd signed off on that botched operation. But since that wasn't going to happen, he made a mental appointment with the professional-grade punching bag in his small training area off beyond his bunk as soon as he'd gotten some answers.

He stood up, and Alice immediately rushed to his side.

"Stop!" she cried. "Lie back down! You've got to take it easy for at least—"

"No, no way, I can't," he said, brushing off her words as if they were meaningless.

Alice continued to protest while Nolan massaged his aching temples and walked unsteadily toward the Cube. When Alice saw that he wasn't going to listen, she came up beside him and offered herself as something he could lean on to steady himself.

"You are *the* most stubborn person . . ." she grumbled.

"Tell me what happened back there," he said, walking inside the Cube. "Tell me what those people died for."

Branford glanced up without expression, as if he'd been expecting Nolan to walk in at any moment. Alice remained at his side, while Arjay was in his corner working as usual, though when he saw Nolan, he put his tools down and came nearer.

"That *was* the OCI, right?" Nolan asked.

"Nobody's saying," replied Branford. "The major news networks have barely mentioned the fire; that's not big news these days. Seems pretty clear-cut though."

"Their actions were owed to poor intelligence?" suggested Arjay.

"That, or they just made a bad call," Branford said.

"Could it have been an honest mistake?" asked Alice.

"No," declared Nolan, thinking back on the woman he saw kneeling over the two female dead bodies. "They were arrogant. Thought they couldn't make a wrong move."

Branford was pensive. "Soon as word gets out, the OCI's days are numbered. Unless they try to bury it."

Nolan frowned. "Thor would never do that."

The room fell silent as everyone was suddenly reminded of Nolan's close friendship with Thornton Hastings, the president of the United States. The world leader who currently believed that Nolan was dead, just as everyone else did.

"Perhaps he is no longer the man you knew," suggested Arjay.

Nolan considered this, but only for a moment. "The things that . . . when we were taken captive, we were put through, I mean we saw . . . atrocities. Brutality. We vowed that if we ever escaped from that hell, we would do whatever it took to make the world a place where things like that never happen. We were brothers, and we promised each other. He would never go back on that."

"How can you be certain?" asked Arjay.

"Because *I* haven't."

The room was quiet again. Nolan knew that Branford especially was probably absorbing this little snippet about his time in captivity. No one knew the horrific things they'd seen and been subjected to back then—not the full extent of it. Much of it was just too awful to speak of or put into an official report. And until now, no one on earth knew that he and Hastings had made this vow to each other.

"All the same," said Branford, breaking the silence at last, "I'd feel better if we put up something on the website, made a brief statement. Just to beat them to the punch, in case some zealous White House aide decides to shift the blame in our direction."

Months ago, even before Times Square, Arjay had volunteered to build Nolan a website at thereisabetterway.com. It would be a place where Nolan could address public concerns without having to use his real voice, as well as a rallying point in cyberspace for all of Nolan's activities. Arjay had gotten so into it that he was now maintaining a mailing list that he used to send out daily recommendations of things that anyone could do to help their fellow man and make New York City a better place—or really, any part of the world—on behalf of The Hand.

Nolan wasn't pleased, but he conceded. "Fine. Just keep it brief and don't point any fingers."

" 'Grief fills the heart as condolences are sent out to the victims of the tragic events that took place last night in Manhattan, and their families. . . .' " mumbled Arjay to himself, composing out loud. He turned and left for his workspace, continuing to mutter.

"What about the man that attacked me?" asked Nolan, turning back to Branford.

Branford nodded gravely. "That's probably the most troubling part of the whole thing."

30

Branford ran his hands over the keys and called up a recording of everything Nolan's glasses had recorded that night. It took just a few seconds of scanning to reach the moment Nolan had referred to, when the mystery man arrived on the scene. Branford showed the results of the facial recognition program, declaring that the guy's name was Yuri Vasko.

"Who is he?" Nolan asked.

Branford pulled up an FBI dossier on Yuri Vasko and magnified it on one of his screens. "Small time crime lord. Ukrainian national, immigrated to the U.S. with a few others some fifteen years ago. Operates in downtown Manhattan, but runs a pretty small empire compared to most of the others. Got a hand in a bunch of different pots—everything from drugs to extortion. His FBI file says he has a natural talent for profiling his enemies, understanding them inside and out."

Another few keystrokes, and photos of Vasko were on the main screen. Nolan's eyes lit up. "That's the woman and the teenager I saw. They were killed in the raid."

"Vasko's wife and kid," said Branford with a bit of hesitancy. A murder in the family of any crime lord would require an answer of blood vengeance.

"Look there," said Nolan, pointing to a smaller detail on the screen. "He was known to be Russian Mafia before moving to the U.S."

"Maybe he still is," suggested Branford. "Or maybe he's doing his own thing now."

The Russian Mafia was a relatively new subset of organized crime, birthed at the end of the Cold War. It began with former Soviet soldiers and KGB agents who acted as war profiteers and black marketers during the reign of Communism. When that ended, some turned mercenary for hire while others joined together under a single umbrella that now operated very similarly to the American Mafia.

"Oh my word," said Alice, speaking up for the first time. She pointed to a different screen, where pages were scrolling up from Vasko's FBI profile. "That just said he likes to kill his enemies by forcing them to swallow and choke on wet cement. He dumps the bodies in the ocean."

Nolan's eyebrows went up, but he said nothing.

"So he's dirty, he's ruthless, and he's intelligent," said Branford, summing it up. "He follows his own set of rules, and murder doesn't bother him. His FBI profile says that someday he could be the most dangerous crime boss since Al Capone."

"This is the guy that thinks I murdered his family," said Nolan.

Branford nodded. "You've just made a blood enemy of one of the most dangerous men in the country."

Nolan shook his head. "If he's a crime lord, then he was already my enemy."

He glanced over at Alice, saw that her expression was severe. "What? Do you know this guy?"

"I think I've been here long enough. How is it that you have access to all this information?" she asked, her eyes pouring over the various screens that surrounded them.

Nolan glanced at the old man. "The uplink."

Branford frowned and sighed. "She knows everything else."

Nolan had designed the surveillance cube himself. The idea was that it would be tied into an advanced surveillance computer that was equipped to coordinate live satellite feeds, traffic copters, unmanned drones, and any home or business security cameras that the authorities could override and look through themselves. The system was set up and in place, per Nolan's specific instructions, long before his debut in Times Square, but it was just a shell without any data pumping through it.

About two weeks before the events in Times Square, he'd explained to Branford how he was going to pull off linking their hardware to existing surveillance software and systems—the kind of stuff that no one but the government owned. As with everything else, he'd figured out how he was going to accomplish this years in advance.

As he'd told Branford that day, his plan was to piggyback onto government surveillance systems, giving unlimited access to the most secure systems in the country.

When he explained it to Branford, Nolan had to fight the urge to grin; he was particularly proud of this part. "Remember Marty?"

Branford's eyebrows knotted. "Martinez? That runt that got assigned to my unit during our second tour?"

Nolan nodded. "Care to guess where he works now?" He paused for effect. "CIA. Covert Surveillance division."

Branford let out a long breath, understanding now but not entirely on board. "Kid could barely walk in a straight line, much less fire a weapon; he was a liability to the entire unit. And I was hard on him for it. Why would he help us?"

"I saved his life," Nolan said. "Twice."

So Nolan had called up his old friend, later that same day.

"All I'm asking for is remote piggyback access to the mainframe, and that you put in some masking subroutines to make it so no one can tell we're accessing it," Nolan said into the small satellite phone Arjay had programmed for him to route through an endless loop of towers and servers, putting its calls beyond anyone's ability to trace.

" 'All you're asking for ... ' " On the other end of the line, Martinez swore. "As if that's some small thing. You're asking for a lot more than that and you know it!" he hissed. Nolan imagined the short, skinny man, suit and tie, sitting in his closed-door office and trying to remain casual to passersby while the very conversation he was having was a betrayal to his oath as a CIA officer.

Martinez was probably sweating, a thought that gave Nolan an odd sense of amusement.

"This is treason," Martinez whispered. "If anyone found out, I'd be in front of the firing squad! And do I even want to know how you managed to *fake your own death*?"

"No," Nolan replied, "but if I pulled that off, then that should tell you how far I'm willing to go to protect the uplink—and your involvement."

There was silence on the other end of the line.

Nolan hardened. "You owe me, Marty. This is me cashing in."

As he finished his story, Alice screwed up her brow.

"You don't approve," he suggested, surprised to find himself bothered by the thought.

"I'm not overjoyed," she told him. "But that's not what I'm thinking."

He regarded her. "What, then?"

Alice locked those piercing eyes of hers on his. "The way you all talk about this stuff. It's so cold. Your determination to keep going, even though you're hurt . . . It's all a big military operation to you. You can't stop until the job is done. Everything in life can't be defined in military terms, you know."

Nolan was taken aback by this. It was a notion that had never occurred to him. Just one reply came to mind; it was the only answer he had. "I'm a soldier, Alice. It's all I know."

Her expression became hard as she pointed at the exit. "Those people out there on the streets that you're so eager to help? They don't need a soldier. They need a hero."

Botched anti-crime op leads to tragedy

By Anne Schneider
Local Correspondent

NEW YORK CITY - Businessman Yuri Vasko became the victim of a horrific tragedy last night, when a raid on his home by the newly-anointed Organized Crime Intelligence agency ended in disaster. For years, Mr. Vasko has been a suspected local crime lord, though he has repeatedly denied such allegations.

Vasko's wife Lilya, 43, and his daughter Olena, 15, were declared dead on the scene after a powerful fire decimated the New York City penthouse where they lived. Mr. Vasko is said to have discovered their bodies himself upon arriving home from work to find the entire building ablaze.

When reached for comment, Mr. Vasko replied, "Like most other Americans, I have watched in recent weeks as President Hastings assembled his 'Organized Crime Intelligence' with the hope that he would be able to do something to turn things around for this city, and this nation. Unfortunately, this unprecedented power was deployed with arrogance and blind force. Today, the two most beautiful people in my world have been taken from me. My greatest hope has become a nightmare."

"Clearly, the President believes that Gestapo tactics are the way to overturn this city's criminal element! But my loss today has proven his tactics are no different from those he seeks to combat. I wouldn't be surprised to find that a certain local vigilante is on the President's payroll."

There is no evidence to suggest that The Hand might secretly be working for the OCI, yet Mr. Vasko was adamant that the OCI had help when it attacked his home without cause or provocation.

An unnamed White House source refuted any connection between The Hand and the OCI, and stressed that there is an ongoing investigation into Mr. Vasko's ties to organized crime. He also confirmed that an intense investigation has been launched to determine what went wrong during last night's raid, and even suggested that the OCI may be the victim of false accusation. "For all any of us know, this 'Hand' character may be responsible for killing all of those people, instead of the OCI —an agency comprised of several highly-decorated law enforcement professionals. Doesn't The Hand say something on that website of his about taking down powerful criminals?"

How did this happen?" demanded President Hastings from the head of the table, slamming a single fist onto the hard surface to punctuate his words.

His underlings—Chief of Staff Marcus Bailey, OCI Director Sebastian Pryce, OCI Agents Janssen and Lively, and a few others—were seated around an oval table made of dark walnut. The black walls and dark light in this underground room at the White House allowed them to see the big screens surrounding the room with greater clarity, but it only fed Hastings' feelings of anger and gloom.

Jonah Janssen was the first to speak up. "Sir, we have reason to believe that the informants who provided the intel that led us to Vasko's home were on the payroll of a rival crime syndicate in New York."

"What?" said Hastings, leaning forward and not believing what he'd heard.

"Our intelligence about Vasko's operation," said Director Pryce, a dour, overweight man with tiny eyes, pencil-thin lips, and a thick goatee, "came from a combination of four spoken testimonies given to the OCI. The physical location of Vasko's headquarters is a closely guarded secret inside his organization. The individuals who gave us information presented intel that we triple and quadruple checked. But this morning, one of our informants confessed, under duress, to having been paid to give us false data."

"I see," said the president. "So not only is the OCI a colossal failure, it's incompetent as well."

"Now, hold on," said Pryce. "The lives that were lost in this operation were far from innocent. At minimum, they were known associates to the work of Yuri Vasko. For all we know, they may have had a firmer hand in his business than is widely assumed. I think 'failure' is far too harsh a word to characterize this operation, Mr. President."

"Too harsh, Director?" chimed in Marcus Bailey, Hastings' right-hand man, who was seated directly across the table from Pryce. "If it wasn't a failure, then what would you call it?"

"It was a perfectly executed undertaking that unfortunately was based on compromised intelligence," said Pryce.

"Don't you mean *un*intelligence?" Marcus shot back.

"Gentlemen," said Hastings. "The bottom line is that everything we've worked for is over. The OCI cannot possibly survive this disaster."

"Sir, if I may?" said Jonah Janssen, rising from his seat. Hastings noticed that Janssen tossed the briefest of glances at his partner, Coral Lively, who hadn't said one word since taking her seat. Hastings understood why; he'd read her report and knew that her partner had pulled the trigger that killed fifteen-year-old Olena Vasko. Lively herself had shot and killed Lilya Vasko, Olena's mother and Yuri's wife. As her partner stood from the table to move toward its head, she cast her numb gaze in the opposite direction, at nothing in particular.

"I believe that last night has presented us with a unique opportunity," said Agent Janssen.

"Son, this administration does not want to hear the phrase 'cover-up,' " said a very bitter Marcus. "That's not how we do things."

Pryce shook his head. "A cover-up would be pointless; the destruction of Vasko's home is a matter of public record, with hundreds of eyewitnesses."

Hastings wondered if he'd made the right choice in his appointment of OCI director. Pryce had fit the profile perfectly, with a long background as an assistant director at the CIA and a history of fighting organized crime. But Hastings didn't like the way Pryce had struck down any thoughts of lying about what had happened; he'd objected not because it was wrong, but because it was logistically impossible.

The room turned back to Janssen, who touched the enormous

monitor behind the president's seat. Hastings had no idea what his confident young agent was up to, but he didn't like the photograph that came up on the screen.

"I'm sure everyone in this room is familiar with the New York–based vigilante known as The Hand," Janssen said, nodding at the larger-than-life close-up on The Hand's hood-covered head. "He showed up at Vasko's home last night."

"Why?" asked the president, eyeing the photo carefully. "What was he doing there?"

Hastings had followed the headlines about this enigmatic individual and was impressed by his accomplishments. Not only had he pulled off some extraordinary feats, but he'd displayed some fine detective work as well. Just last week, The Hand had tracked down and brought to justice a serial killer guilty of thirteen vicious murders. The culprit had eluded the NYPD for months. And hadn't he heard something recently about a Mafia-backed business in Clinton that The Hand had shut down?

"We're not entirely certain, sir," replied Janssen, glancing again at Agent Lively. "We suspect he may have been conducting surveillance on our field op. Maybe he hoped to take credit for our success, but changed his mind after . . . well, after what happened."

"Why would he need to take credit for OCI operations when he has so many successes of his own already on record?" Hastings asked rhetorically. It was a ridiculous notion.

"As I said, sir, we believe that his presence last night presents an opportunity. A chance to kill two birds with one stone."

Hastings could guess the direction this was heading. But he decided to hear the man out. "Go on."

"The Hand is a vigilante. His activities—however noble in their intent, however commendable in their success—are illegal by definition. Americans do not take the law into their own hands. Not ever. He's a wild card, Mr. President, and we have no idea to whom or what he's ultimately loyal. As long as he's allowed to continue his actions, organizations like the OCI are at risk. How can we conduct operations when we can't keep this man from interfering? And consider this. It's no secret that he's extremely popular among New Yorkers, and his notoriety is on the rise across the nation. What happens when his influence and fame become so great that they overshadow your administration? With all due respect, the nation is being held together by a thread as it is."

Marcus made a show of rolling his eyes. "You're reaching, Agent Janssen. If you think pinning the blame for your blunder on some misguided vigilante is all it'll take to save the OCI from extinction, you're living in a fantasy world. Besides, this Hand character is a mild curiosity at best, a novelty. He'll be old news within a month."

"What if you're wrong about that?" Janssen challenged the chief of staff, but then turned to Hastings. "Sir, we have an obligation to stop him before he gets someone hurt or killed. Not to mention our larger responsibility to end the reign of this nation's crime regime. No one feels the weight of what happened last night more than Agent Lively and I, and we grieve for the lives that were lost, but one mistake cannot be allowed to prevent this agency from fighting and winning this war. If the OCI goes out of business, then the United States government is telling the cartels and the terrorists that it's open season to drag this country into chaos and devastation."

Hastings was silent as all eyes fell on him. In the course of one briefing, his opinion had changed about several of the people in the room.

He hated that Janssen was right. The fight against crime was bigger than one mistake, and millions of Americans were counting on them to bring an end to the corruption, violence, and death. He had been elected on that very promise. Whoever this Hand guy was, even though he was operating outside of the law, he was doing real *good* in a part of the nation that needed all the good it could get. He didn't deserve to take the fall for the mistakes of the people in this room.

But Hastings had learned—as all presidents do—not long after taking the oath of office, that the choices his job required were never, ever easy.

32

Agnes Ellerbee was sitting at her desk, scanning a collection of old Special Forces records, hoping she might come across a candidate whose build and abilities might line up with her mysterious quarry, when her phone vibrated inside her purse.

No one else in the office heard it; they were too busy following the TV reports about last night's incendiary raid on a New York crime boss by the OCI. Lynn Tremaine stood in the center of the office and barked out orders about what angles of the story to cover and who would be covering it. Agnes's name was never called.

She didn't mind. The number on her ringing phone was unknown, but being a reporter, she couldn't afford not to answer it. You never knew when an anonymous tip might come in or a source might be trying to reach out to the media. Granted, the chances of someone like that calling her, of all people, were slim, when there were much more famous and respected reporters out there to choose from.

But she could dream.

"Ellerbee," she said into the receiver.

"It's Tommy," said the caller in a terse, urgent tone. It took a few seconds for her to put it together. "You need to get down here."

The hacker!

She dropped her voice to a conspiratorial whisper so that none of her colleagues in the office could hear. "Do you have it? Did you get his face? Do you know what he looks like?"

"There wasn't enough to go on to put his whole face together," Tommy replied. "But I have something you're going to want to see."

Agnes dropped the phone into her carryall and darted for the exit.

Out of breath, Agnes raced into the bar and didn't bother stopping to see what the reaction to her presence was this time. She raced to the tiny back room that Tommy Serra called home and banged on the door.

"Who is it?" Tommy called out.

"It's the Easter bunny," Agnes replied, impatient and gulping deep lungfuls of air.

Tommy flung the door open and she stepped quickly inside.

Without a word, he returned to his desk chair and entered a series of keystrokes. The center screen on his panel went black and then the wireframe shape of a human head appeared there, rotating slowly. But it was just an outline. It had no skin or features, nothing to identify it.

With a few more keystrokes, Tommy input the sum total of his work on the photos Agnes had given him, and the bottommost portion of the face was filled in with skin textures that had been lifted from the photos and wrapped around the 3-D model. It wasn't much—just the bottom inch or so of the man's face and the top of his neck. His chin was almost completely filled in, but there were tiny blank spots here and there where Tommy hadn't found a photograph to fill it in.

"That's all you could get?" Agnes asked, unable to hide her disappointment.

"From the pics, yeah," said Tommy. "But then I applied this algorithm I've been working on that extrapolates the most probable data for the empty spaces and fills them in with what they look like. And . . . there." Tommy tapped a single key and suddenly the empty spaces were filled in on the wireframe model, along with another inch or so of skin above the part that was already there.

Agnes leaned in. Now she was intrigued. "What is that?" she asked, pointing at something on the face.

Tommy shook his head. "Can't be sure . . . But to me it looks like a scar. And this is one over here, too," he added, pointing to a second scar. Both of them extended up into the parts of the face that weren't filled in, but what they could see definitely looked like mangled skin that had been damaged beyond repair, with some hasty stitching to sew up the flesh wounds.

Agnes took in a sharp breath, then let it out slowly. "He's . . . disfigured."

Her mind spun with thoughts, mostly about how this drastically reduced the number of potential candidates. Because how many people could there be in the world who had faces mangled so badly? A few hundred? A few thousand? Even at that, she could further narrow down the list by including only those who were highly trained at hand-to-hand combat. Maybe she could even find someone who was equally skilled and could tell her which martial arts disciplines The Hand used. . . .

Her thoughts returned to the present when she saw that Tommy was staring at her.

"Can you get me a—"

"—a copy?" he finished for her, holding up a tiny data card. "Includes both versions."

She accepted the item and then got out her wallet to give the young man any amount of money he wanted. However much it would cost her—even if she had to take out a second mortgage—she didn't care. Tommy Serra had been worth every penny.

33

Yuri Vasko's dead hand rested on his desk, and his eyes fell on it and would not move.

Marko stood close, as ever, prepared to obey his master's every command, but more interested in their profits than all other concerns. He might as well have been incorporeal as far as Vasko was concerned. Vasko cared no more about money at this moment than he did any of the other random thoughts that came to mind.

The hour was late, the sun nearing the bottom of the big picture window behind him, causing his own frame to cast a long shadow over his desk and the floor beyond. Any other day, he would be preparing to head home right now.

Today, there was no home. No one was waiting to welcome him, to shower him with daughterly affection in that special manner that Olena possessed. No beloved wife to talk to, dine with, take long walks with, or make love to. They were gone. He'd carried them both from the fire himself, refusing the police their autopsy examination. Their bodies had been so badly burned in the fire, he'd had them both secretly cremated this afternoon.

Turned to nothing but ash.

How could they be dead?

Without them, what did he have left? What was his purpose?

Was it his business? He was good at what he did but he would gladly trade it all to hold his wife and daughter again. They were his world, and the world was hollow without them. A lonely, empty place that was offensive and alien.

How Vasko wished that he could have died with them!

No. He had to put such thoughts aside. They would not serve him.

Marko was babbling something about believing one or more of his rivals to be responsible for this tragedy. Vasko didn't hear him.

He had to decide what to do now. Yes, that was important. It would make Marko happy to see him get back to work. But why did he care about making Marko happy? The man was a sycophant who secretly siphoned a fraction of Vasko's income for himself. Vasko had known for years, but Marko was so good at keeping the books—and keeping the company's nose clean—that he would be impossible to replace. Besides, with their shared heritage, Marko was the closest thing he had to a friend in this world.

The man who stole from him was his only real friend. What a sad commentary on his life this was. But it was what it was: his life.

Vasko pounced; rocketing to his feet, he upturned his massive walnut desk with an animal's furious roar. He looked up at the ceiling and howled a scream that was like nothing that had ever escaped from his throat before. Its volume and rage surprised even him.

"Yuri!" said Marko.

"Shut up," Vasko cut him off, plopping back down in his seat again, his manner suddenly calm. "I'm thinking."

My life.

That was what triggered the outburst. Those two words. He knew Marko was looking at him in fear, the way one looks at a madman. But he didn't care. The very notion of thinking any longer about his life as if it were something normal, something everyday, was insulting on a primal level. It was an affront to his wife and daughter—two glorious, beautiful women who'd lost their lives to an end that was not of their own making.

His life was not his life. Not anymore. Without the ones he loved, it no longer made sense to him. There was nowhere for him to go should he leave this office. This place was all he had left. What would the world have him do now, if he was no longer truly alive?

He cared nothing for his business. Not now. It was a means to an end, a way of providing the ones he loved with contentment, safety, and peace. Now it may as well have been as dead as the lifeless fingers on his ruined hand. As dead as . . .

No!

He burst from his chair, ready to howl once more, but stopped. His thoughts had been circling one lone notion all day, but he kept pushing it aside, kept turning back to the grief of losing his dearest ones.

No more. There was another emotion clawing to the surface, one far more powerful than sorrow, and he would take refuge inside it.

Vasko turned, stepped up to the window.

"I know you're out there," he said softly. He stretched his arms open wide, and when next he spoke, his voice carried a hollow-throated thunder. "I know you want me! So come on, then! Let's have it!"

This city worshiped The Hand. Even the media loved him. They called him "The Hand of God," "The Hand of Life." The city's "champion" and "rescuer." The man had saved countless lives. But he didn't save Lilya and Olena. For all Vasko knew, he was their murderer. He knew the OCI had raided his home. This was something he'd learned soon after the slaughter. And he knew he had made things easy on them by removing his loved ones' bodies after the attack; had their bodies been found there by the police, the OCI would have been skewered by the press. But as it was, the bodies of more than a dozen of his men had been found at the scene. That would have to do. The OCI would get their due in time.

For now, he was more interested in another. When Vasko had found his home on fire, the OCI was gone. But *he* was there, standing over his daughter's body holding a gun—a gun which he'd this morning matched to the bullet that killed Olena.

The Hand had never murdered before—at least, that anyone knew of. Why had the man come after him and his family? There was only one reason that made sense: Yuri was a warning to every other crime boss on his to-do list. *Get out of this business, or your loved ones pay the price.*

Vasko looked down at his own black sickly hand. It was a thing of death.

The Hand of Life.

The hand of death.

Plans took shape in his mind before he'd consciously decided to formulate them. This business of his, this company—it had always been a means to an end. If that end was gone, if he no longer had any life within him, then he would see the business become a means to a new end.

Vasko took a step closer to the window, so close he saw his breath condense on the glass, and he scanned the city. That man was out there right now, not dead as he'd initially hoped from that gunshot to the head, but recovering from his encounter with Vasko. Or maybe he was back on his feet already, somewhere on the streets or the rooftops, saving someone's life or stopping a robbery or tracking down some heinous criminal.

Vasko's plans would take time to see to fruition. Meticulous, elaborate plotting would be required to countermove against the intricate plans of the The Hand, as he had told Marko not that long ago. It was all the better this way; it would keep Vasko going, giving him the purpose he needed.

His new trade was the business of hate.

34

It was after nine in the evening as Nolan ran along the tracks of the F line, under southeast Brooklyn. The F train had just passed by as he pressed himself up against the stone wall, and he took off running after it, grappler in hand.

A bomb threat had been called in at Coney Island amusement park just under an hour ago. The NYPD had done a once-over of the premises after ordering a full evacuation of the park and found nothing. But Branford intercepted a Hazmat call from the Bureau office in New York that had picked up a spike in radiation somewhere on Coney Island.

And anything big enough to register a radiation spike was big enough to affect the entire city, and beyond. The Hazmat Unit was still half an hour out, and the radiation levels were rising. All three of his friends had protested, but Nolan argued that New York might not have that much time left. So he went.

Arjay had warned him against firing the grappler to grab onto objects in motion. If the vehicle was going fast enough and he managed to hold onto the grappler, the resulting action could rip his arms off. Arjay had said this without a trace of humor, so Nolan knew it must be true, even though the scenario brought to mind cartoonish images. So he was running at a dead sprint, speeding along at his fastest possible rate, pushed a bit further by his marvelous shock-absorbing boots. Still, the train was far ahead and getting farther by the second.

Not daring to stop running, he aimed the grappler and fired. He was already retracting it before he heard the loud metal clap that signaled contact. He jumped from the ground as high as he could, to avoid being dragged, but landed back on the ground anyway. Landing on his feet, he immediately leapt into the air again, and this time the grappler pulled him all the way to the rear of the subway car, where he saw that it had punctured straight through the metal wall.

He rode the back of the train for five minutes, standing on the tiny platform there, until it finally came to rest a few miles out from the Coney Island stop. No trains were allowed to get any closer to the area affected by the bomb threat. A quick grapple up a manhole pipe leading to the surface, and he was on the streets under the cover of night. He would have to hoof it the rest of the way.

He'd never been there before, though he recalled wanting to come at some point in his childhood. Every surface, every stretch of asphalt, was steeped in a history that one could smell and touch. The place was a relic of a forgotten era of American youth and optimism.

Nolan ran through the empty streets, scanning all directions with his enhanced vision. Police barricades blocked the major thoroughfares, but they were easy enough to avoid since the officers on the scene had their hands full with straggling pedestrians who refused to leave.

"*Take Twelfth Street, head for the beach.*" Branford's voice came over the radio so tense it sounded like the old man was out of breath.

Nolan followed his instructions and found himself at Deno's Wonder Wheel Amusement Park. "Can you narrow it down for me?" he asked between shallow breaths.

"*It's hard to say,*" replied Branford. "*On the Hazmat map . . . I think it's somewhere between the big wheel and the Cyclone—the roller coaster.*"

You "think"? Nolan wanted to ask, but bit his tongue.

Okay, okay, Nolan. Think. Calm down and think.

The big wheel was to his immediate left, towering over the horizon. A chain-link fence stood in his way, but it was easy to scale. Up and over and a quick dash, and he was at the foot of the enormous Ferris wheel. The historic white wooden roller coaster called the Cyclone stood proudly not far off to the east. A number of attractions were situated in between, including a merry-go-round, a Tilt-a-Whirl, a few smaller kiddie coasters, and a vertical lift ride that gave a bird's-eye view of the park from way up in the sky. There were enough vendors and nooks and crannies in between all that to require hours of searching. All of it had been abandoned, of course, due to the evacuation. None of the rides or attractions were on, nor were any of the park's lights.

"Does Arjay have anything in his bag of tricks that might help me find this thing?" he asked with the sudden thought.

There was a pause before Branford answered, "*He says the X-ray option on your specs will detect forms of radiation, but that this could lead you astray, since lots of ordinary things give off radiation. He also says the radiation source won't be very bright until you're right on top of it.*"

"I'll take it," said Nolan. Anything to narrow it down.

He tapped the X-ray option on the side of his glasses. The world went black-and-white, and he saw a number of items in his immediate vicinity that shone brighter than the rest. The first turned out to be a group of ceramic toilets in a public restroom, the second a big bunch of bananas inside a vending shack.

The third bright X-ray light led him to a pickup truck parked on West Tenth Street, just beside the Cyclone.

"*Careful,*" said Branford in his ear.

"This is it," he said, sprinting for the truck. "I know it."

The glasses led him to the floorboard of the truck, which he could only reach after breaking out a side window. There he found a shoebox that glowed brighter than anything he'd seen yet. Cautiously, he opened the top and found himself staring into the sun.

He ripped off the glasses and stared at the small black device inside the box. It was a pipe of some kind, but it was warm to the touch.

"*What is it?*" Branford asked.

"Some kind of dirty bomb, I think," he replied. "But I don't see a timer."

"*Then it has to be on a remote,*" Branford said, his terse words coming out in a rush.

"I remember reading somewhere that bombers that use remote

triggers usually station themselves close enough to see the detonation with their own eyes."

"*Where did you read that?*" asked Branford.

"Eh, I'm lying. Saw it in a movie."

He picked up his glasses and switched to the thermal camera. Climbing atop the truck's cab, he spun in place and scanned the area. Nothing. He removed the glasses again and pocketed them.

"General, what do I do with this thing?" he asked, climbing down from the truck. "I don't think I can disarm it. For all we know, it could be rigged to blow if I tamper with it."

"*Hand it over to the police?*" Branford suggested. "*Alice's husband works in a Clinton precinct; unlikely that he'd have the Brooklyn cops on his side. Or you could leave it for the Hazmat team. They should be able to find it as fast as you did.*"

Nolan was about to reply when the words caught in his throat.

Something flashed in the corner of his eye. It was fast and faint, but he saw a reflected light glimmer high overhead in the circular car that went up and down the vertical lift tower.

The tower that was extended halfway to the top.

After the park had been evacuated and closed.

If someone was inside that thing keeping an eye on the bomb, they already knew that Nolan had found it. The bomber's finger was probably on the trigger right now, about to press it.

There was no time. He whipped out the grappler, took aim at the tower, and fired. In less than a second, he was zipping through the air, and just as he reached the tower car, he went through the glass side, steel fist first, following through the motion to land on the narrow floor inside and roll to his feet.

A teenage boy was squatting on the floor, less than three feet from where he'd landed. The boy was holding a homemade device with an antenna, but Nolan's sudden entrance seemed to have startled him so badly that he passed out.

Moments later, Nolan was applying a wrap of chain-link fence around the unconscious boy, latching him to the tower's base. The bomb and its detonator, sitting on the ground not far from the tower, were already waiting for Hazmat to arrive.

He had just locked the fence together when he sprang to his feet.

What was that?

He spun in place, his eyebrows knit together as he scanned his surroundings. He hadn't heard or seen anything. Maybe it was some cumulative effect of his diverse training, or a forgotten instinct he didn't even have a name for.

But he could have sworn . . .

"General, pull up a live satellite view of the area," he said.

He heard the tapping of computer keys in his earpiece. "*What am I looking for?*"

Nolan's eyes danced across the landscape, his skin tingling. "I don't know. Probably nothing."

A moment passed, and still Nolan found himself alert and ready to pounce, like a guard dog that smelled something funny.

"*I'm not seeing any movement,*" Branford said. "*Nothing looks out of place.*"

The Ferris wheel.

He turned and looked up at the massive, ancient park ride. But there was nothing. Everything was perfectly still.

Scowling, he forced himself to relax. "Forget it," he said. "I'm heading home."

35

Nolan heard muttering coming from the Cube as he entered. It was three hours later when he finally made it back home, having dealt with a few minor disturbances between Coney Island and Manhattan. But he expected that the others would still be inside the Cube, no doubt following the police reports about what had happened, and waiting to fill him in on the boy and his troubled life that had led to his building his own dirty bomb. And how a teenage kid could even get his hands on radioactive materials.

"Unbelievable," said Branford's voice as Nolan drew nearer.

"Going to get himself killed," Alice added. "Do they know it's a man? It could be a woman."

"Who now?" Nolan asked as he walked inside.

Branford thumbed toward the screen they were all looking at. Nolan saw a recorded TV news report about what looked like someone in a homemade costume that was meant to look like Nolan's own black combat fatigues. But it was a poor imitation—just a black sweat suit complete with a sewn-on white hood. Nolan didn't recognize the costume-wearer's surroundings.

"Is this for real?" he asked.

" 'Fraid so," said Branford. "Got yourself some bona fide hero worship."

Nolan peeled off his gloves and jacket, listening carefully as the reporter on the screen explained that the footage had been shot in Chicago, where what they called a "Hand copycat" was shown standing on a rooftop. According to the report, a bunch of people thought he was a crazy person about to commit suicide by jumping, when he let loose a banner that fluttered down the side of the building and proclaimed in enormous hand-written lettering, "I will show you a better way!"

The footage cut to a different shot where this would-be vigilante was seen running wildly through the streets. Another shot showed him helping an elderly woman pick up the contents of her burst bag of groceries and carrying them to her home for her.

Nolan actually smiled. "I hoped this might happen," he said.

"You expected people to pretend to be you?" asked Arjay.

Still smiling, Nolan replied, "I hoped that others might follow my example. I didn't think anyone would dress like me, but I always knew I wouldn't be able to change things by myself. From the start, if this was ever going to work, there would have to be others who would take up the charge."

"But is that a good idea?" asked Alice, ever the voice of concern. "This man doesn't look like he has any of your training or skills. Won't he get hurt? Or worse?"

"Eh," said Nolan. "Looks like all he's doing is good deeds. As long as he leaves the crime fighting to the professionals, I say this world needs all the acts of kindness it can get."

"I still don't understand why we can't use all this goodwill to accept donations," said Arjay, not quite under his breath.

For weeks, he'd been nagging Nolan about an inquiry he received daily on the website: people wanted to know how to make monetary donations to The Hand's cause. And Nolan's answer had always been the same. They were to refuse all offers of help.

Nolan felt his ire rise at Arjay broaching this subject once again—a subject he'd intended to be closed after the last time it came up.

"It wouldn't be the worst thing," Branford chimed in. "I know how you feel about it, but our resources *are* going to run out eventually. If people want to help us keep doing what we're doing, why not let them?"

Nolan's ears burned red, and he fought the urge to shout. Instead, he spoke slowly and emphatically. "Do you not understand the tightrope we're walking? People are so cynical. . . . It's not even about what we do or don't do. It's about what people *think*. I can't afford to dip one single toe into morally ambiguous waters. If we accept donations, then someone out there will accuse me of doing this whole thing just to get rich. The *second* somebody suggests that, this is over. An accusation is all it takes these days for the people to find you guilty."

The room fell silent at Nolan's sobering words. He knew he was right, and his friends knew it too.

There was no need to say anything else. He changed the subject. "Tell me about the bomber."

Everyone fell silent. Branford warned him that it was the kind of story he didn't want to hear. Nolan demanded they tell it anyway, and Branford read the police report that had been filed just a short while ago.

The kid's name was Nicky Solomon, and he was, as Nolan expected, the product of a troubled home life. His parents had divorced a year ago, when Nicky was just fourteen. But when the police went to his home after his arrest tonight to deliver the news to his mother, they found her dead, shot by a gun that the killer had then turned on himself.

And the killer was Nicky's father.

Both bodies had been lifeless for more than twenty-four hours by the time they were found. A husband's crime of passion, that led to a son's crime of desperation, of attention-seeking, alone-and-mad-at-the-world rage. Nicky's mother, it turned out, was a part-time nurse, and the police were quickly able to determine that the material inside the pipe bomb had come from the hospital's radiology department. The boy had been exposed to near-lethal amounts of radiation while building his makeshift pipe bomb using instructions from the Internet. If he managed to recover, he would have health issues for the rest of his life. Not to mention a criminal record with a terrorist-level offense.

It was yet another sad story in this broken world that would never have a happy ending.

Nolan left his cohorts inside the Cube and walked out, but not toward his bunk. Not toward anywhere, really. Just a private spot where he could process this without everyone watching him. The world had grown a little darker tonight, and he needed to escape the black hollow pit that he felt himself teetering toward.

———

The next morning, as Nolan was eating breakfast, he felt someone's eyes on him, and he knew whom those eyes belonged to without having to look.

"How do I fight that?" he said quietly, picking up their conversation where they'd left it the night before. "How do I fight something that could cause a normal, average teenage boy to turn into a mass murderer?"

Alice's hand landed on his shoulder. "I don't know," she said softly, honestly.

She circled around to look at him head-on, and her eyes were filled with sadness and concern. "The war that was waged over that boy took place inside him. In his heart, and his mind. In his very soul."

He looked up at her. "How do I fight that war? How do I impact the human soul?"

She smiled, but there was no humor in her. "Outside of prayer, there's only one way to reach the soul, and you already know what it is."

Nolan looked down at the table. For the first time in a very long time—since as far back as his time in captivity—he felt his eyes burn with moisture. "I can't just *love* this city into becoming a better place."

She closed her eyes. Sighed. "I know. You're a man of action. But you and I both know that the illness of the soul has already been addressed, through the sacrifice of someone a lot more than human, two thousand years ago. You can't improve on what he did."

Nolan looked up, eyes wide, almost hurt. "I'm not trying to! Are you—Look, I'm not trying to *replace* . . . *him*! I wouldn't—I mean, I could *never*, not even a little . . ."

"Easy," Alice said. "I know why you do this. I've seen your heart. But there are some things that simply aren't up to you to fix. You're still approaching this tactically. But it's not a military operation, remember?"

Nolan looked down. Alice wanted him to *feel* more. To connect with the people he saved, to let his emotions out. But he wasn't trained for that. He was taught to compartmentalize his feelings into a nice safe box and focus only on the job. He feared he would never know how to reconcile the mission with the emotion.

"I'm sorry," said Arjay, quietly, from behind Nolan. "I'm sorry to interrupt. But you need to see this."

The two of them followed him to the Cube, where Branford was watching a press conference taking place live at the White House. The familiar blue curtains stood just behind a young woman who was at the presidential lectern, addressing a crowded press room.

"The president is emphatic," the woman said, "that he deplores the loss of life from the events that took place at the home of Yuri Vasko last week in New York. President Hastings asked me to assure all Americans that the rumors of Organized Crime Intelligence involvement in the destruction of Mr. Vasko's home are false. The OCI is aware of Mr. Vasko's alleged involvement in illegal business practices, but the Intelligence's operations are currently being targeted at higher-profile enemies of the American people."

Nolan glanced at his friends. The president had just lied to the world about the OCI's involvement in the raid on Vasko's home. This was bad.

The young White House press spokesperson concluded her remarks and said she would take a couple of questions.

A reporter from a television network got the first question. The white-haired gentleman stood to his feet. "Can you comment on the eyewitness accounts suggesting that the vigilante known as The Hand was on the premises the night Vasko's home was destroyed?"

"Those reports are unverified," said the press secretary. "Next question."

An elderly woman from the *New York Times* stood next. "If the Organized Crime Intelligence had no involvement in the disaster that took place at Yuri Vasko's home, then do the police have any leads on who *was* responsible?"

The press secretary shook her head. "Any and all leads the police are exploring are of course confidential, lest we tip off the persons of interest. As I said in response to the last question, we have no concrete evidence as yet, but reports of a mysterious individual on the scene during the destruction of Vasko's residence *are* mounting. The president of course condemns any and all unlawful vigilantism in this nation. Regarding Mr. Vasko's home, citizens with information about the events of that night are urged to report what they know to their local police—whether it involves any rogue crime fighters taking the law into their own hands or not."

36

Ellerbee," started Lynn Tremaine. The word came out in the only tone of voice she possessed, which made Agnes think of the *mew* of a bored Cheshire cat. "Your Vasko piece was . . . adequate."

Agnes blinked and was unable to hid her surprise. Praise from Lynn Tremaine was a rare thing. At least she thought it was praise.

"How so?" she probed her boss, turning off the computer screen in front of her. She'd just noticed—to her great shock—that the number of people following her on her favorite social network had jumped to over a hundred thousand in just a few hours' time. This morning, she'd had fewer than four hundred followers.

"Apparently, it was good for the paper. Though personally, I found your use of the tragedy to launch a screed against The Hand, to cast doubt on his motives, the kind of grandstanding that gives journalism a bad name," said Tremaine. "But I was just informed that today's edition had a circulation seven times our normal volume, and reader response has been off the charts. The office switchboard has sustained a maxed-out call volume all day long."

Agnes couldn't believe it. It was true she had taken the Vasko assignment and used it toward her own ends. But she wasn't trying to denounce The Hand; she merely wanted to provide some balance to the unending praise that the rest of the media so willingly awarded him. Objectivity was the bedrock by which journalism operated, yet somehow it didn't seem to apply to The Hand because of his apparent good deeds.

"Well," she said, struggling to find an appropriate response to her boss, "that's great news. Thank you for telling me."

When Agnes turned back to her desk, Tremaine didn't move. "There's something else."

Of course. There was always something else.

Tremaine cleared her throat. "The board of directors has instructed me to give you your own weekly column. You will follow The Hand's activities and provide a different . . . *perspective* . . . from what other journalists write. Congratulations. You're getting a 15 percent raise after your fourth column is published."

Agnes was doing somersaults inside but had to try not to show it. She couldn't resist letting a gloating smile escape, though. This couldn't have possibly come at a better time, now that she was making real progress at unmasking The Hand.

Tremaine stood, scowling at her.

"I'll expect your first piece in my in-box Friday morning," said Tremaine. "Also . . . you may want to watch your back. Your article is popular because it's provocative, but it's not particularly endearing. Not to the public—or to your co-workers."

Tremaine made her exit.

Slowly, Agnes rose to her feet, just enough to look over the top edge of her cubicle. The newsroom was bustling with activity, looking just like every other day she'd worked there. The three or four dozen other employees were working at their desks or zipping about to and fro. She didn't spot a single person giving her the evil eye or wringing their hands maniacally with wicked grins on their faces, plotting her downfall.

She sat back down, relieved that her life was not in immediate danger. Suddenly, a dozen or more wadded up balls of paper were lobbed into her cubicle from all directions, and Agnes ducked. When the paper rain ended, she picked up one ball that had landed just behind her keyboard and flattened it out. In big black magic marker, a single word had been written: SELLOUT.

She balled it back up and threw it out of her cubicle in a random direction.

Whatever. She had work to do and a column to prepare. She already knew what her first column would be about: the scars on The Hand's face. But first, she would need a little more to go on. . . .

And this was just the beginning. If her job was to provoke, imagine the response when she made the world-exclusive announcement of The Hand's true identity.

————

Two hours and one bribed prison guard later, Agnes was sitting across a reinforced glass window from a man named Chas Graves. Graves was a recent addition to the inmate population, courtesy of The Hand.

And as Agnes suspected, he was only too willing to talk about what he'd seen of the crime fighter.

"His face—it was just wrong," said Graves into the phone receiver. "Like it had been through a blender."

Agnes tried to play cool her level of interest, but inside she was celebrating. "How much of his face were you able to see?" she asked into the phone.

Graves held up a hand and held his fingers apart about an inch. "His hood covers most of it. But what I saw was pretty nasty."

She nodded and noted what he'd said so she could quote him in her article. Then she pulled out her phone to update her social network status.

"So did I help you?" Graves asked. "What are you going to do with this?"

Agnes dropped her phone back inside her purse and looked up into the criminal's eyes. "I'm going to tear that hood of his off."

37

Thornton Hastings leaned back, resting his tired bones in the comfortable plush leather chair that only the president was allowed to sit in. It lived behind the enormous wooden desk that he'd picked out for himself shortly before he'd taken the oath of office.

The Oval Office was empty at this late hour save for the standard Secret Service agents stationed outside. He felt a little silly being here in his long robe and pajamas, and wasn't even sure why he'd walked all the way down here in the middle of the night. Other than his inability to sleep.

The latest edition of the *New York Gazette* was all alone on his desk, having already been read cover to cover. He picked it up again and turned it over to find the column on the bottom of page one. There it was. "The Hand That Hides the Face," by Agnes Ellerbee. A piece about the scars that some claimed were visible under The Hand's hood.

He didn't particularly like the tone of the article. It was diplomatically written to appear to showcase both Hand supporters and detractors, but he'd been in politics long enough to recognize a veiled attack. Maybe something about The Hand had gotten under this Ellerbee woman's skin. Maybe she was just using him to advance her career.

But then, if that's the case, she's not exactly alone. Is she.

Hastings knew that it wasn't like he was doing any better by this selfless hero of the people. He'd signed off on the equally passive-aggressive attack that his press secretary had fed to the media a few days ago, calling into question The Hand's character by linking him to the "mysterious" figure behind the destruction of Yuri Vasko's home. It was a calculated lie, pure and simple.

What kind of man did that make him?

He'd done it for the greater good. The OCI stood a better chance of taking down the major players in modern organized crime than any other government agency in recent memory. If the OCI was no more, millions of Americans would pay the price, suffering under the boot of mob bosses, drug cartels, even homeland terrorists.

Was one good man's reputation worth sacrificing if it meant saving countless others?

He folded up the newspaper and threw it in the garbage. After staring at it there for a moment, he searched his desk for the remote control. With a single button, a large TV appeared behind the wall to his left and swiveled to face him. Instantly it blinked to life, already tuned to a twenty-four-hour news network.

He wasn't sure whether to be surprised or not that Agnes Ellerbee was the topic of conversation among a roundtable discussion of four journalists and pundits. A heated debate was unfolding on the screen as two members of the panel ardently disapproved of Ellerbee's "attention-grabbing" work, which they said was written "solely to sell newspapers." The other two showed stronger interest in what Ellerbee had written, suggesting that a balance of skepticism and integrity was healthy for journalists—something that many members of the media seemed to have forgotten when The Hand appeared on the scene.

The show's host returned to the screen, interrupting a spirited round of discussion. "We've conducted a new poll among New Yorkers, in which the disparaging comments of Ms. Ellerbee's exposé article are the primary focal point. I'm sure it will interest all of our panelists to find out that the vast majority of those polled—89 percent—said that Ellerbee's articles had no impact on their opinion of The Hand. A separate poll indicated that The Hand still commands a positive opinion from an astounding *97 percent* of New York natives. This is effectively the same level of approval the hooded crime fighter has maintained since he initially appeared on the first of July. So it would seem that the

New York Gazette's article—as well as the implied accusations of the White House—has had no discernible effect on The Hand's popularity."

Hastings let out a short burst of air that was almost a laugh. Whoever he was, this Hand guy wasn't just bulletproof, he was scandal proof.

But he was actually relieved that the OCI's ruse had had no impact on The Hand and his standing among the people. It was proof that he should never have signed off on the idea. Trying to connect The Hand to the disaster at Vasko's house was a bad call from the start, and Hastings had felt it in his blood. He should have trusted his instincts and put a stop to it before it started. That sort of political maneuvering was not appropriate for the kind of man he was, and not for the kind of president he was elected to be.

Maybe he should take a page from The Hand's playbook and just *be good*. In every way, in everything he did. Never let anyone talk him into compromising. Not ever.

Maybe Hastings could do even better. This Hand guy had done so much for the people of New York—and the entire country, as the numerous Hand copycats popping up all over the nation were proof of—and had asked for nothing whatsoever in return. Instead of gratitude, the police and even the FBI had labeled The Hand an unlawful vigilante and were incessant in their attempts to find and stop him.

That was one thing Hastings had the power to do something about.

"A Better Way"...
To the Emergency Room?

by Antoine Atkins

NEW YORK CITY'S media darling has inspired several men and women to throw on a hooded sweatshirt and patrol the streets of their hometowns. When things went wrong, though, one of them underwent emergency surgery after a gunshot wound to the stomach.

This would-be vigilante from Akron, Ohio—his name hasn't been released by the authorities—is just one of a dozen or more copycats of the mysterious figure known as "The Hand," who see it as their mission to take up his cause and spread his "better way" outside of New York. Most of these street-level vigilantes have been involved in humanitarian efforts, such as the female Hand copycat in Lubbock, Texas, who made headlines when she ran into a burning building and single-handedly rescued a family's beloved pet collie. She's since made a number of publicized appearances at local schools, libraries, and community events, encouraging kids to read and stay off of drugs.

Lubbock's friendly masked figure is a relatively benign disciple of The Hand. But others, like the gunshot victim in Akron, may be taking their devotion too far.

Anyone who's seen footage from New York City of The Hand in action can see for themselves that this man, whoever he is, is in peak physical condition, and shows clear signs of being highly-skilled in hand-to-hand combat. The Hand's followers, for the most part, are ordinary citizens, wholly unprepared for the realities of placing themselves in the line of fire.

The man in Akron, shot while trying to intervene during a robbery at a local grocery store, remains in critical condition at the time of this writing. But his situation stands in stark contrast to The Hand himself, who sports several high-tech gadgets and an unequaled physical prowess.

The Hand's message—this "better way" business—has struck a nerve among crime-riddled middle America, where people are willing to put their lives on the line to tell the criminals and the terrorists that enough is enough. But if this New Yorker's plan always involved stirring others to follow his lead, then he should have included a warning to go with his inspirational actions:

Showing others a better way can be hazardous to your health.

38

Nolan descended the stairs into the beautiful bronze interior of Grand Central Station's main concourse. The vaulted "sky ceiling" seemed impossibly high, and the famous four-sided clock at the very center of the concourse was instantly recognizable.

He'd been there before, of course, but while he appreciated the historic architecture and grandeur of it, at any given time the big open space could be filled with so many people it was difficult to get from one spot to another. He didn't imagine he'd ever get past the claustrophobic panic that so many people in one place caused him. Another gift from his merciless captors during his overseas imprisonment.

As always, he changed the subject to compartmentalize those emotions. "Zipping around the city is quite a rush, but it's very demanding physically. Maybe I should have a motorcycle. Or a car."

He heard Branford *hmph* in his ear. *"Don't you dare tell me you want Arjay to make you a* Handmobile."

Nolan scanned the area, hoping to pass with a minimum of attention. *Not an easy thing to do when you're dressed like a battle-ready monk.*

"It'd make it a lot easier to get around New York," he replied. "Wouldn't have to constantly be hitching rides on trains and such."

"You honestly think it would be easier navigating through New York traffic?" Branford deadpanned.

Nolan smirked. "Yeah, maybe not. So where was this big 'public disturbance' you mentioned, again? Because I'm not seeing anything."

"Lower concourse," said Branford. "That's what the police dispatcher said. You'd better hurry, they're almost there."

Some kind of public demonstration had been called in to NYPD, and the caller claimed it was nearing riot proportions. Something about a union dispute with the subway drivers. They'd been delaying trains, and the natives who relied on the tightly kept schedules were growing agitated. Several people had already been trampled, and the crowd was getting angrier by the minute. The local terminal cops were horribly outnumbered.

The big staircase at the back of the hall led down to the lower terminal, and Nolan sprinted toward it as fast as he could, ignoring the stares he drew. A few flashes even went off from pedestrians with cameras, but he sped past them all.

Suddenly, he drew back and froze. He turned and looked back up at the top of the stairs, and for a second, he thought he'd caught a glimpse of someone watching him. It was an afterimage, the last moment of someone already turning away from him and then disappearing from sight.

It might have been his imagination. But it was the second time he'd felt this pair of eyes on him; the first was at Coney Island. He wanted to turn around and run back up the stairs to find his mysterious stalker, but there wasn't time. Someone was going to get killed downstairs in this angry riot if he didn't get there fast.

He'd stepped off the last stair when something jabbed him in the head from behind. His fatigues lit up and surged with electricity, and he lost consciousness.

———

Drifting in and out, Nolan caught snatches of imagery as the world passed by. He was in a subway tunnel of some kind, a smallish one that the public didn't seem to be using, in some kind of old fashioned–looking rail car. There were at least a dozen men in black suits standing around him and throughout the car.

But why was his hood still up around his face? They'd gone to all this trouble to acquire him but didn't care to find out who he was? Not that seeing his mangled face would help them all that much, but still.

The train zoomed through the narrow tunnel, but the ride didn't last long. He wanted to move, to act, to escape, but his body was tingling, nearly numb and unwilling to respond. It felt like every inch of his skin had been fried by lightning; he half expected to look down and see his body smoking from the massive current. .

He knew he'd been hit with some kind of electricity, and somewhere in his memory he had a vague recollection of Arjay saying something about how graphene was a highly conductive material. If someone had hit him with a Taser from behind, they wouldn't have realized his suit would carry the charge. Whatever it was, it had apparently knocked out his communications as well, so he was unable to hear Branford in his earpiece. Imagining the old man frantic over losing contact with him was a worrisome thought, yet one that also gave him an odd chuckle.

Now he was being carried—or rather dragged—by the arms, by a pair of large men in black suits. The others walked in tight formation behind. He wasn't in the subway anymore; he was in some kind of small underground tunnel that was just wide enough to accommodate him and his two escorts. It was decorated with sconces on the warm-colored walls, and ornate burgundy carpet.

When next he awoke he was riding in a gold-colored elevator with five of his captors. He was relieved to notice that he was regaining feeling throughout his body now, but he kept up the ruse that he was unconscious. That he could take all five of these men was not an issue. But whoever these guys were, they'd gone to a lot of trouble to abduct him—was that public disturbance at the train station even real?—and he had to at least find out why they'd done this before making his escape.

The elevator stopped and the doors opened to what looked like a hotel hallway, with numbered doors on both sides.

The other half dozen or so men joined up with the ones surrounding him, and as one, they carted him inside an empty hotel room, where they dropped him on the carpet.

Nolan dared to raise his head—lazily, to keep up the appearance of being incapacitated—to get a look around, but it was dark and without his glasses he was left staring at shadows.

He guessed they had brought him there to wait on whoever had ordered his abduction. But Nolan had no interest in such games. It was time to pounce, to turn the tables and get some answers.

As he coiled in a heap on the floor, ready to spring, a single lamp in the room was illuminated and the suits filed out without warning. Not a word was said between them; they simply moved as one to the door and exited. All but one of them—a man Nolan hadn't noticed before, who was also wearing a suit but looked decidedly different from the others.

Standing as the remaining man walked toward him from across the room, Nolan found himself staring into the face of President Thornton Hastings.

39

Nolan fought to maintain his equilibrium. He made a show of brushing himself off so that it would be clear he didn't appreciate the way he'd been treated. If Hastings wanted to meet The Hand, that was fine, but did he really have to do it like this?

Frankly, the thought of Hastings discovering his identity was of no concern; he'd always assumed that his old friend would find out the truth sooner or later.

"Hello," said Hastings, smiling. His voice was carefully modulated to sound light and jovial. "I want you to know that you're not under arrest, and you'll be free to go when we're done here. I just thought it was time you and I met. Forgive the less than cordial welcome. Our Tasers apparently interacted with your . . . costume in an unexpected way. This was the only private way that you and I—"

"Thor," said Nolan, after clearing his throat.

Just that one word escaped from his lips. Nothing more.

Hastings stopped short. His smile vanished, and he seemed to be stuck in place, unmoving, just staring. His lips slightly parted, as if words were on the tip of his tongue but couldn't find an exit from his mouth.

Nolan nodded in a mechanical way, his body still sore and weak. "It's me, Thor." He threw back the hood from around his severely damaged face, not even sure how much of it Hastings would be able to see in the room's low light.

"Nolan?" said Hastings, unable to accept what he was hearing—or seeing. "But . . . You—you're *alive*?"

"Here I thought you were smart," replied Nolan. "All this time, it never once occurred to you that it could be me under this hood."

A hand came up to Hastings' mouth, then traced upward to his hair, where it stayed. His head shook back and forth, and Nolan could tell his old friend was finding it impossible to swallow this. "It was you! All this time. It *is* you! *Of course* it's you. . . . I mean, really, who else could possibly . . . But how?"

For a long time Nolan had pondered what this conversation might be like. So far it was exactly what he'd expected. "The idea came to me during the war. Took a long time to plan it all out. The evidence at the murder scene, my dog tags, the billboards, Times Square. I've been working toward this for years."

Hastings was shaking his head again, but his hand finally fell to his side. "Why didn't you come to me? Why didn't you bring me in on this? I could have helped you."

"We both know you wouldn't have," replied Nolan, his voice even and controlled. "When we came home after the war, I watched you ride the sympathy train straight to Washington. I really hoped that you might do some good, make some real changes there, but it was clear pretty quick that you were being held back by the same bureaucracy as every other politician."

Hastings had left behind the shock of this revelation and was moving on to offended. "Nolan, do you even know *why* I entered politics? Why I wanted to be president?"

" 'Course I do. It's the same reason I'm doing *this*. If I stop, evil wins."

Their pact was forged near the end of their imprisonment together. As the days and weeks became one big blur of pain and hopelessness, their captors devised inventive new ways of trying to break their prisoners. These despicable acts were designed to rob inmates of sensory input, nutrition, dignity, and even identity. A sort of theater was held in a large room within the prison, where every day a new batch of victims was brought forward. And when he and Hastings weren't subjected to the tortures, they were made to watch as others were. Day in and day out. On and on it went.

Some time into their second year of captivity, when several of their fellow army captives had already died, Nolan and Hastings were placed in a pitch-dark, freezing-cold isolation chamber together for three straight days, and they made a promise to each other. There, in the absolute darkness, they vowed that if they ever escaped from this hell, they were going to change things for the better, so that no one else would ever have to suffer as they had.

But their promise went even deeper. They weren't out to change laws or depose wicked rulers. It was an unspoken understanding between them that their real goal was to change *people*. Change their minds and hearts, so that wickedness would never take hold of an entire society again.

"I gave you your chance," said Nolan, pushing those buried memories back where they belonged. "That's why I waited this long to begin. I only acted once it was clear that you weren't getting results. Thor, you did your best and I don't fault you for being ineffective. You're buried inside a system that's damaged beyond repair. So now it's my turn. All you have to do is stay out of my way."

Hastings turned his head up to the ceiling as if searching for the words to say, written up there. He massaged his eyes for a moment before turning back to Nolan. "I can't believe you let me think you were dead. I'm hurt by that. But I know the real reason you didn't let me in. You know I don't have your faith. It's the one thing we never could find common ground on. You're doing what you're doing because you think God will reward you with an eternity of bliss after you die. But isn't it better, isn't it nobler and more selfless, to help others because you actually *care* about the suffering of your fellow human beings?"

Nolan was fighting a rising anger. "I would think that as a politician, you of all people would know better than to try to speak a language you don't know. I'm not doing this for a reward; I'm doing it *because* I care about others—because God does too. And hey—you not sharing my beliefs doesn't invalidate them." Another thought occurred to him, and he added it before he could stop himself. "God's not responsible for what they did to us, Thor."

"He's responsible for not stopping it!" Hastings shouted back, raising his voice for the first time. "If he's real, and he's as good and loving as you say he is, then why didn't he prevent it?"

Nolan fell silent and had to look away. Unspeakable memories that he'd worked to put aside for so long were threatening to rush to the surface. He swallowed them down with everything he had. "We survived *because* God was there with us," he said, his words barely a whisper.

Hastings was breathing hot air like a bull, a war going on between his mouth and his head. "Forget the faith stuff. Do you have any idea how much your funeral cost me? And I'm not talking about money! Do you know how much I sacrificed to give you the memorial I thought you deserved?"

"Yeah, I do."

When he didn't elaborate, Hastings caught on and his gaze turned dark. "Oh, I see. You know how much heat I took for it, and you think that works to your advantage."

Nolan shrugged. "I didn't plan it that way, but it's convenient. You expose the truth about me, and the media will make you out to be the foolish president who spent taxpayer dollars burying a man who wasn't dead. Your friends on the Hill will string you up. Face it: you have a lot more to lose than I do."

Hastings closed his eyes and swallowed a very long breath. "I always knew you were methodical, and you *know* I don't disagree with what you're trying to accomplish, but you can't do it this way. You're so far outside the system, you're starting to make others believe *they* can do anything and get away with it too."

"Guilty people walk free if they have enough money, while the innocent suffer without any recourse. Your 'system' is a failure in every way. It's tired and useless, and I don't acknowledge it. I answer to a higher authority."

Hastings sighed again. "Nolan. We want the same things. I want to find a way to make them a reality just as much as you do. We're on the same side."

"Are we really?" Nolan shot back. "Do we really want the same things, like absolute truth? Because I've seen the so-called truth your administration gives the people."

Hastings put up both hands in a show of capitulation. "The Vasko thing was a mistake. It wasn't my idea—"

"Your mistake," Nolan interrupted, "was trying to pin it on me."

"Nolan . . ."

"Having the support of a politician won't help my cause," said Nolan, his manner suddenly formal. "It'll harm it. People don't trust elected officials anymore, and rightly so. They're all corrupt, all willing to do whatever it takes to get elected and stay in office. I know you're not like the rest of them, and I know you're genuinely interested in changing things from within . . . but, Thor, you're still one of them."

Hastings' frown deepened, and his tone changed. "You're not leaving me with a lot of options here. I have the power to shut you down and I'll use it if you make me."

"No you won't," Nolan said simply.

Hastings blinked and had to take a moment to regain his footing. His next words came out at a lower pitch. "There are very few people in this world who would presume to predict the actions of the president of the United States."

But Nolan shook his head, his voice full of conviction. "You won't stop me. You can't afford to. Because with all due respect, *Mr. President* . . . my approval ratings are higher than yours."

Feeling a surge of both confidence and indignation, Nolan turned his back on his oldest friend and left him in the darkened room.

40

Filled with righteous anger, Nolan barreled past hotel patrons and staff, through lush hallways and a grand foyer, until he burst through a set of glass double doors to find himself on Park Avenue. He turned around and looked up at the old concrete building to see the glittering gold letters that said this was the Waldorf-Astoria Hotel. If memory served, he was about five blocks north of Grand Central Station.

His skin no longer tingled with the aftereffects of the shock, but it had become numb in various patches across his body. He ignored it.

He was getting the usual stares and even a few cheers from pedestrians coming and going from the hotel, but he was in no mood for their blind adoration. He knew he needed to reset his earpiece and attempt to reach Branford and the others, to let them know he was okay. They were no doubt frantic by now at his lack of contact. Instead, he found himself just walking, aimlessly, for the first time in years.

Nolan didn't know whether he was going north or south, east or west, and it didn't matter. Hastings could have had people tailing him right now in unmarked cars, but this he also cared very little about. If he kept at this for very long, people would start to swarm around him, asking for his autograph or just wanting to shake his hand. News crews would soon appear with ambitious reporters trying their best to get him on camera. Some more aggressive members of the police may even try to arrest him.

None of it mattered. He just kept putting one foot in front of the other, never lifting his eyes from the pavement. Something about it felt good. A private moment of rebellion from all the rigid rules and strictures of this path he'd chosen.

Every time Nolan thought of Hastings, he felt his blood pressure rise. Was it because the man had had the gall to trick him with a false emergency and then abduct him, just to talk to him? What was Hastings expecting to get out of the conversation? Did he think he could get The Hand to join forces with the White House in the war on crime?

Seeing his old friend had brought back a rush of unexpected memories and sensations. For a moment in there, he had almost tasted the sour urine smell of the solitary confinement chamber from his captivity. He remembered the gaunt, skeletal features of Hastings' face when he became ill while they were prisoners, his sunken eyes and withdrawn cheeks. He remembered the pain. The endless, endless pain.

And it had reminded him of Hastings' stubborn refusal to believe in God. Nolan had drawn on his faith as his only source of strength during those dark days, while his friend had denounced any belief in a higher power. Nolan credited God with their survival and escape; Hastings saw their suffering as evidence of God's absence. Or worse, apathy.

The two of them had been strict in their avoidance of arguments during their captivity. Disagreeing was a luxury they couldn't indulge in; it would sap what little morale they clung to, and drain their energy.

Things were different now. They had quickly drifted apart after their escape, as the unspoken disparity between them no longer had anything keeping it in check. Without a common enemy to focus on, suddenly their differing ideological viewpoints became all-important.

Hastings was the leader of the free world. Nolan was a symbol of goodness and hope. He almost felt bad for not trying harder to rekindle the brotherly bond they'd had so long ago. They really did want the same things, and it wasn't like Nolan had gone out of his way to embrace his old friend. Hastings was right: Nolan had kept him out of this, very intentionally.

Nolan couldn't shake the guilt he felt, even though he knew his reasoning for everything he'd done, for the decisions he'd made that had gotten him to that point, were sound. He and Hastings were different.

They always would be. Even if their goal was the same, their reasons and methods would always be in direct opposition to one another.

Thor will never be my ally, he concluded sadly, and suddenly he stopped dead in his tracks.

There it was again. The sense that he was being watched.

To his immediate left was a building made of stone, four stories high. Acting on instinct, he pulled out the grappler and aimed it straight up at the roof of the stone building. He retracted it at its top speed, and in a moment, he was standing on the building's roof.

Perched less than four feet away—and taken aback by his sudden confrontation—was the last person he expected to see.

"You!" he spat. "What do *you* want?"

OCI Agent Coral Lively blanched, wilting right there in front of him. She was wearing the same gray camouflage combat fatigues that Nolan remembered from that night at Vasko's home, but had added sunglasses over her eyes. Her dark hair was pulled back in a simple ponytail.

When she couldn't manage to come up with an answer, Nolan lost his patience. "You've been following me, haven't you."

"No," she said. "Yes. Sorry, I—"

"What do you want, Agent Lively?" he said, his words a challenge.

She looked surprised, so he spoke again. "I know who you are, Coral Anne Lively. Thirty-three years old. Born in West Virginia, raised in D.C. Four years detective work with DCPD, followed by seven with the Secret Service. I looked you up."

Coral was speechless. Apparently she'd had no idea he possessed such resources.

Nolan was growing angry again. "So, you're keeping tabs on me so you and your boss can think up new lies to feed the media?"

"No," she said, finding her voice at last. "Nobody knows that I'm . . . I mean, I had no part in that decision. I filed a formal complaint—"

Nolan paused. "Really? You put on record a dissenting opinion about an executive cover-up? Well, that got you off the president's Christmas card list."

"My partner's furious with me," she went on. "But I didn't sign up to defame and deceive."

"Good for you," he said, and meant it, though he was still too angry for it to come out with sincerity. "Why are you following me?"

Coral looked away. "I don't know," she said. "I really don't. I just—I was . . . curious. About you."

Nolan tilted his head down, ensuring that his hood covered his entire face. "Who I am doesn't matter," he said. "All that matters is what I do."

"It matters *why* you do it," she countered.

"Okay, then why did you shoot Vasko's wife between the eyes?" he asked. He knew it was a cheap shot the second it passed from his lips, but she had it coming. And he was still in a foul mood.

The blood drained from Coral's cheeks, and her lips parted, but no sound escaped them. She took a step backward, and though she worked hard to fight it, Nolan was certain he saw one of her knees buckle for a fraction of a second.

He turned his back on her and pulled out the grappler. "Go home, Agent Lively. And put some thought into a new line of work."

Nolan fired the grappler and left her standing on the rooftop alone.

Vasko a hit with elite at Mayor's annual fundraiser

Keynote speaker Yuri Vasko eloquently addresses loss, grief, and healing

HASTINGS VOWS JUSTICE

President promises renewed resolve to crack down on organized crime

THE HAND DOES IT AGAIN!

NYC vigilante brings down empire of a fourth major crime boss
Popular do-gooder again proves more effective than OCI

Vasko donates $1 million to Red Cross

41

Despite noise-canceling headphones, the din of Yuri Vasko's newest toy still made his ears ache. A helicopter, previously owned by one of Vasko's rivals, hadn't been on his list of acquisitions, but when the Feds made their arrest—aided by a truckload of evidence provided by The Hand—the aircraft had become available at a bargain price.

The chopper buzzed low over the Manhattan skyline, hitting the base of the altitude requirement for privately owned flying vehicles. This was supposed to be merely a trial run around the city, a chance for Vasko to try out his new toy. The pilot—a former employee of his arrested comrade, who basically came with the chopper—had warned him how dangerous it was to risk the wrath of the FAA by narrowly skirting the legal boundaries this way. But Vasko insisted on being as close to the ground as possible, to facilitate a better view of the buildings, streets, cars, and people below.

Since the vehicle's takeoff, Vasko's eyes had never strayed once from the view out of his side window. It was remarkable. How he wished that Lilya was experiencing it with him; she would have relished the contrast of the beautiful sun rising over the man-made metropolis.

Instead, as ever, his only company was Marko, who was ignoring the view entirely and focusing instead on the accounting books he'd brought along.

"With Flanagan in jail, his people have agreed to sign on with you too," Marko said into his headset. "It's astounding, really; your manpower and income have more than quadrupled in just under a month's time, and they're still rising. There's barely anyone left—"

Marko's voice stopped. It didn't trail off or fade away, it just stopped.

Finally, Vasko thought. *He's put it together.*

Took him long enough.

"Yuri, do you realize what this means?" said Marko with a dawning awareness. "Did you know this would happen? All of the others have fallen to The Hand or the OCI, and one by one, their remnants have sided with you. With you taking on so many additional resources, and your fame rising to such a measure . . .

"There is no one in the city with the power and influence you have. You have risen to the top of the city's crime syndicate. And the public still thinks of you as a sympathetic figure. You're all but untouchable."

Vasko was expressionless, accepting this information as fact without comment. He continued to scour the streets below, searching, searching . . .

"Did you know? Did you know this would happen?" Marko asked again, in awe.

Vasko nodded, just once.

It was a victory he'd seen coming weeks ago, yet he felt no joy over it. He'd hoped to derive pleasure from this rise to power, but it felt as hollow as his own insides. Tactically, it was extraordinary how the tragic events of his life had made it possible for him to reach this point, almost overnight. Even the efforts of The Hand were working in his favor, eliminating the competition one by one and making it easier for Vasko to reach the top.

While The Hand and the OCI were busy focusing on other syndicate bosses, Vasko had quietly moved in and taken possession of their old assets, properties, and operatives. At first he had used bribes and payouts, but as the number of men pledged to his side grew, he was soon able to achieve the same results by applying threats and intimidation. Like dominoes toppling, each falling piece triggered the next until soon he'd been the only one standing.

Yet still he did not celebrate. There was no victory without Lilya at his side and Olena holding his heart.

He pulled a piece of paper out of an inside jacket pocket and handed it to Marko. "I need you to find the items on this list and purchase them. I don't care what they cost."

Marko grew agitated as he scanned the sheet of paper. "I don't even know what some of this stuff *is*, Yuri. And the rest—it won't be easy."

Vasko ignored him. Even now, his eyes remained fixed outside his window. "Once that's done, I want you to sell the building," he said into his headset.

"What building?" asked a confused Marko. "The office? *Our* office building?"

Vasko nodded once. "We're moving to someplace more central. More visible."

"*More* visible? Is that wise?"

Vasko didn't answer. He was in no mood to explain himself, and he didn't care to humor Marko's anxieties. Vasko was afraid of nothing. Not anymore. There was nothing to fear. Only something to hate.

"Where are we moving to?" Marko asked, his voice jittery with concern. "Have you already purchased this new office?"

"No, not yet," Vasko replied, continuing to inspect the city below. By all rights, it was now *his* city. He owned more of it than anyone. "But I have something in mind."

42

I've read your stuff. What have you got against this guy?" asked Danny Sze. He was a short, stocky man, dressed in a traditional white karate gi, though the belt tied around his waist was jet black with several white stripes on the ends. He sat in his office, which he'd adorned with elaborate amounts of traditional Chinese decor, all over the walls, his desk, and even the floor. His voice, however, was pure New York. And upset.

It could not have been more obvious to Agnes that he was not happy to see her. Moreover, he'd gone out of his way to make her feel unwelcome there when she'd knocked on his door and asked for a few minutes of his time. He hadn't even offered her anything to sit on when he'd returned to his own desk chair.

Agnes didn't care. She wanted to stand anyway. She liked the feeling of towering over him.

All of New York knew that she was zeroing in on The Hand's identity, and that it was only a matter of time. She'd already revealed more about the man than anyone else had even tried to, including observations about his scars, examinations of his weaponry and gadgets, and most recently, a psychological profile of the kind of person that would resort to taking the law into his own hands.

She was on the verge. She was close and everyone knew it.

"It's nothing personal," she replied. "Just doing my job."

"Your job requires that you destroy a good man?" Danny asked, crossing his arms.

Agnes had to fight the urge to roll her eyes. "I'm not trying to destroy him. I just want to understand him."

Danny continued staring at her, his eyes heavy and judgmental. He said nothing.

"Look," said Agnes, growing impatient, "I was told that if somebody wants to find out about martial arts fighting styles, nobody in town knows more than you do. I can pay you for your trouble, but if my information's incorrect—"

"The claim is accurate," he said.

"Then name your price," she replied. "I've cut together a video disc with clips of several fights The Hand has been in—"

Again Danny interrupted her. "Three weeks ago, very late at night, my sister was emptying trash into a large bin in her backyard. A pair of men grabbed her, muffled her cries, and dragged her six blocks from her home in the dead of night. They hid her beneath a patch of trees in the shadow of the Manhattan Bridge.

"After removing her wedding ring, earrings, and a gold necklace my mother had given her as a child, these men tied her to a tree and began to rip off her clothes. What they didn't know is that her nine-year-old daughter had witnessed her abduction and called the police. But the police never came. *He* did. He not only saved her life, he saved her dignity, her humanity, her peace of mind."

Danny Sze stood from his chair and looked deeply, uncomfortably into Agnes's eyes. "There's nothing you could expose, nothing you could reveal about this man's character in one of your articles, that I don't already know. I'd die before I'd help you denigrate him."

Agnes didn't flinch. She merely sighed. Unfortunately, in the last few weeks, she'd gotten used to this sort of treatment. Everyone was in love with The Hand, and everyone hated her for trying to break the magic thrall that he held over them.

"That's a great story," she said, digging into her carryall and retrieving a file folder. "But you left out a crucial detail. The abduction was retribution for your sister's teenage son—your nephew—who the day before tried to end his membership in the Flying Dragons. The Hip Sing Tong triad doesn't look kindly on such things, do they?"

"How do you know that?" Danny hissed, his demeanor suddenly dark.

"Wouldn't it be a shame," Agnes said, leaning in a hair toward Danny, "now that your nephew has decided to turn his life around and make a fresh start—wouldn't it be a shame if evidence reached the authorities of his involvement in over a dozen robberies, at least seven grand larcenies, nine felony assaults, and more counts of grand theft auto than even *I* could turn up?"

She handed Danny the file and watched as he opened it and examined the contents. After sifting through it, he finally looked back up at her, his face smoldering.

"Shall I deliver this to the local precinct, then?" she asked.

Danny muttered something under his breath in what she thought sounded like Mandarin—and given his tone of voice, she was sure he'd made a vulgar observation about her—and then said, "Give me the disc."

Twenty minutes later, Danny had finished watching the clips of The Hand fighting various enemies. He handed her a list of martial arts styles that he recognized The Hand using, which included Jujitsu, Muay Thai, Krav Maga, Silambam, Gatka, and Jogo do Pau. Several of these, he said, were martial arts that focused on the use of quarterstaffs, which wasn't surprising since that seemed to be The Hand's defensive weapon of choice.

Agnes thanked him for his help, left the file about his nephew in his possession, and left.

———

It was after eleven o'clock that night when Agnes had a sudden flash of insight while sitting at her desk. There was no one else working that late, so the place was dark except for emergency lighting and her desk lamp.

She'd been reviewing the various fighting techniques on Danny Sze's list, exploring their histories, and trying to find out who might be trained in such techniques today, when she landed on an interesting martial arts magazine article that listed most of the disciplines from Danny's list in reference to advanced combat training given to elite special forces officers in the U.S. Army.

The thought first came to her when she was pondering that along with The Hand's proclivity for anonymity and the bizarre scars that likely covered most of his face.

She'd been slumping in her chair, fighting fatigue, when a notion shot through her like a bullet. She sat straight up, rigid.

It was ridiculous, her theory. Beyond preposterous.

It couldn't possibly be true. Yet the more she tried to disprove it in her mind, the more she found that the facts supported it. It was impossible to discount, because it fit with everything she knew. It just made sense.

Agnes cupped both hands up around her nose and mouth, carefully considering the implications, the ramifications, the meaning of it. If it were somehow true . . .

But there was no *if*. She knew it was true. She felt it, with an inexplicable certainty that she knew not to doubt.

It was true. It was insane, it was impossible, and it was *true*.

She'd promised to figure it out, and she'd done it. She was the first person to solve the puzzle, and now . . . now she had to decide what to do with it.

There was only one answer, of course. She hadn't been working so hard for so long to discover The Hand's true identity only to help the man keep his secret. She had too much at stake, and landing this exclusive reveal would secure her position at the paper for years. Who knew? It might even be enough for the board to hand her Lynn Tremaine's job.

So that was it, then. She was going to do it.

Better head home and get some sleep.

She paused for a moment, logged on, and updated her status: "Tomorrow, I will tell the world who The Hand really is."

43

Again Nolan found himself running up the side of a building. It was a sticky, starless night and his grappler had taken him to the window of one particular apartment on the outskirts of Greenwich Village. It was dark inside, but thermal and night vision revealed that no one was home.

"*So we've moved on from helping people and bringing criminals to justice, and have now turned to breaking-and-entering,*" said Alice. "*I don't feel good about this.*"

Nolan was still getting used to hearing her voice in his ear. Branford and Arjay had finally given her a headset of her own.

"*It's the only tactical option,*" replied Branford's voice over the com. "*You've seen what this woman says about The Hand. If she says she knows his true identity, I think we have to take her seriously.*"

"*This Ellerbee woman,*" said Alice, "*I don't know how anyone can take her seriously. She writes the most one-sided, biased pieces of 'journalism' I've ever read. She's not reporting the news, she's spitting in its face.*"

Nolan heard the crinkling sound of newspaper and assumed that Alice and Arjay were again reading over Ellerbee's latest article—a scathing commentary on the ego required to believe you could do that which the police and the government could not.

"*Jealousy leads people to such disgusting actions,*" said Alice's disapproving voice. Nolan heard the crinkling again and figured the newspaper had just been balled. "*I have a question,*" she continued. "*So what if she knows? If she's figured out that Nolan's The Hand and tells the world . . . why does it matter? I mean, I figured it out, and it didn't change anything for me. Most of the city—most of the country—loves*

Nolan. *He's created something bigger than himself, and I don't see that being erased by his real name. Even the president knows, so it's got to come out sooner or later."*

"There is the matter of his faked death," said Arjay, who had been given his own headset as well. This used to be a two-way call, but now it was a party line. Nolan wasn't sure he liked that. But Arjay did have a point.

"I reminded Thor that it was in his best interests to keep my secret," said Nolan as he retrieved a glass-cutting knife that Arjay had made for him. "But the fact is, I've got just as much to lose as he does. If people know who I really am, their perception of me becomes tainted."

"You can't be serious," said Alice. *"You're a war hero! The most famous one there is. Your rep wouldn't take anything away from The Hand. It would probably give you even more fans."*

"That's not the point—" Branford started to explain.

But Nolan took up the explanation as he pulled out the small piece of glass he'd cut down near the bottom of the window, where the latch was. "Nolan Gray is a human, identifiable man. He's damaged, he has weaknesses and flaws. He comes with preconceived opinions. But The Hand is something better. He's a symbol. A nameless, faceless representation of an ideal."

No one said anything on the other end of the line, and Nolan assumed his point was taken. Or possibly that they were all wondering how many times he'd practiced saying that in his head.

He reached through the tiny opening he'd carved into the glass and unlocked the window. Once it had slid upward, he was able to slip inside the tiny apartment.

From the start, this whole thing had stunk of a trap. Ellerbee's bold claim to her followers that she was about to unmask him . . . It was exactly what someone would say if they wanted to lure The Hand out into the open. And it had worked.

Ellerbee's apartment was horribly unkempt. It was the residence of a person who hadn't spent any significant time there in weeks, apart from changing clothes and the occasional bite to eat. The kitchen—where he climbed in through the window—was a disgusting mess, with half-eaten food on nearly every surface.

The next room was no better. It appeared to be her bedroom, but he couldn't see the bed anywhere beneath the piles of dirty clothes. Her wardrobe closet stood wide open, but only one or two items were hanging inside.

Alice's voice came through Nolan's ear, the sound of revulsion. *"How do people live like that?"*

Nolan didn't care about her mess. He was just glad Agnes Ellerbee wasn't home.

"I don't see a desk," noted Branford. *"See if it's out—"*

His voice was cut off by a crinkling sound again, but this time Nolan knew it wasn't paper he was hearing.

"What is that?" he said over the static. "Do you hear it?"

"Yeah," Branford replied. *"They're expanding one of the tunnels about five blocks south of here. Must be generating some kind of interference."*

"In the middle of the night?" Nolan wondered.

"The tunnels tend to be in use during the day," remarked Arjay.

Nolan found the reporter's living room. Still using night vision, his muscles tensed when he saw Agnes Ellerbee slumped over on her desk, unconscious.

This was all wrong. Nolan sensed it before he knew it. Something was way, way off.

"How did she not hear you come in?" asked Alice.

There was something wet on the floor beneath the woman. Something that showed up as a bright hot white in his night vision . . .

"Is that—?" started Branford.

"Blood," confirmed Nolan, moving quickly to her side to check her pulse.

He heard Alice gasp.

It was far too late. Ellerbee's blood was running down from her lifeless neck, just beneath the chin. She was hunched over in a pose of shock, her eyes still open. Her blood was pouring down the wooden desk and pooling on the carpet below.

"This is recent," he said with alarm. "Within the hour."

Branford's voice was stern. "*Somebody's trying to frame you—get out of there!*"

Nolan shook his head, then noticed that the dead woman's laptop was missing from the desk, her Ethernet cord dangling freely with nothing to hook to. "No, it's not a frame. Somebody wanted what she knew."

"*Which means there's a murderer out there who knows who you really are,*" Branford remarked, a comment punctuated by another burst of static.

"General?" Nolan asked, when the line remained quiet after the static vanished.

"*Nolan? Do you read?*"

"Yeah, I'm here."

"*Police band's going crazy all of a sudden!*" shouted Branford, his words stilted from listening to the reports coming in on his end. "*There—there's been some kind of explosion down at the Battery. . . . This is bad. . . . They're saying there's cops down. . . .*"

"Call in an anonymous tip about the reporter," Nolan said. "I'm gone."

44

When Nolan Gray approached Battery Park at Manhattan's southern end, he ascended to the top of the high-rise at One Broadway to try and gain a view unobstructed by the clouds of dense smoke filling the area. Fire trucks, police cars, and ambulances raced by below, disappearing inside the dark cloud. The spinning red and blue lights created a surreal, pulsing strobe effect within the smoke.

Battery Park was named for the location of the first batteries of cannons to ever be placed on Manhattan Island by Dutch settlers, but tonight the fort was impossible to see, even from more than eight stories above ground. Switching his glasses to heat vision, Nolan counted over thirty prostrate bodies at varying temperatures—some cold enough to be dead—scattered throughout the immediate area surrounding Castle Clinton. Zooming in tighter he discovered some of the bodies weren't on the ground but below ground somehow.

"What's beneath the Castle?" he asked.

After a moment, Branford said in a grave tone, "*The South Street Viaduct runs right under it.*"

It took a lot to get Nolan flustered, but this news made his heart skip. The viaduct was an underground traffic tunnel, completely closed off on all sides. A perfect disaster waiting to happen.

He zoomed his goggles even further, trying to get a better view of the chaos. He couldn't wrap his mind around what he was looking at.

"*Listen, the radio's still pretty chaotic. The police were really caught off guard by all this,*" said Branford, his voice unusually hollow. "*But it sounds like some kind of shooting war took place about an hour ago between the NYPD and a large group of criminals. It didn't start there, but I think the crooks lured the cops there on purpose, stationing them-selves behind the Castle at the waterfront, because there was some kind of explosion under the Castle, and the cops were caught in it. There's an unknown number of vehicles trapped in the tunnel, too. Rescue personnel are working blind; they can't see anything down there."*

Nolan's mind was spinning fast, his breathing rapid. "This was an act of war. Somebody *attacked* the NYPD tonight. Do they have a count on the number of dead?"

"Fourteen cops and six civilians so far. More than twenty officers are unaccounted for. Hold on a second, there's some chatter. . . ." After a moment, Branford said, *"It sounds like they're having trouble getting down into the viaduct. Both ends of the tunnel are sealed off, and there's a lot of damage inside."*

That was all Nolan needed to hear. He stood to his full height. "How do I get in?"

He heard the tapping of computer keys. *"Both ends of the tunnel are completely blocked off by the police. How about this: there's a big ventilation duct about sixty meters southeast of the Castle. All roads in are closed. I don't know how to get you there."*

Nolan pulled out the grappler and triggered open the four hooks on its tip. "I do."

"No. No!" shouted Arjay into his ear. *"That vent is three hundred meters from your position, with nothing but low-hanging trees in between. Have you forgotten what I told you? Up and down only!"*

"Those people don't have time!" said Nolan, terse, immovable. "It's the only way. There's more than enough cord in the grappler to make it."

"There's nothing to stop you from dropping like a rock!" Arjay called back.

"The grappler's fast," Nolan argued, using his goggles to find the top of the ventilation shaft. It stood in the midst of a large area of green foliage. "It's crazy fast. It's got enough pull to clear the street beneath me. I'm sure I can get at least halfway there before I hit the ground, and I stand a good chance of hitting a tree. Should soften the blow. I'll try to roll or run when I reach the ground."

"*Nolan,*" fretted Alice, "*this is a really bad—*"

"Think, *man!*" said Arjay. "*You'll impale yourself on a tree branch!*"

"Not likely with this graphene armor you gave me," Nolan said, projecting confidence. More than he felt.

"*It won't keep you from breaking your—*" Arjay tried to argue, but it was too late.

Nolan had already taken aim and was firing the grappler directly at the vent cover. Allowing some slack in the line, he backed up as far as the rooftop would allow and breathed a silent prayer. Then he ran at a dead sprint for the edge. When he reached it, he did his best long-distance jump with every ounce of will he had, while releasing the grappler's trigger.

The cord caught tight the very instant he let up off the trigger, and it pulled on him at full force. It happened so fast it took Nolan's breath away, and he didn't have time to anticipate and react as it yanked him forward like a rocket. One second he was running on the roof, the next he was hurtling into a patch of trees just inside the barrier of smoke.

He did what he could to tuck and roll, but the speed of the grappler made it impossible to situate himself perfectly for his first contact with the ground. He barreled through the trees, obliterating leaves and branches with sickening cracks until finally he stopped, sprawled flat on his back, the air entirely sucked from his lungs. With a heaving gasp he tried to recover from the great shocking rush of it all. He needed air, but he found the oxygen replaced by bitter, putrid hot smoke.

He was completely disoriented by the impact, but there was no time, no time to stop and get his bearings. He had to get down inside that shaft. He ordered his body to get up, to ignore the pain and *rise.*

Right now.

"*Nolan?!*" shouted Branford. "*Nolan, do you copy? Are you hurt?*"

Nolan rolled onto his stomach and put his hands beneath him, pushing up to a crawl. He forced his mind to run through the training he'd received all those years ago for how to react in low-oxygen environments. It was a mind-over-matter thing—like everything the military had taught him—where he had to concentrate on slowing his heart rate and taking short, shallow breaths to allow the lungs to adjust to the poor air quality.

After a minute of concentrated effort, he dared risk no longer. Painfully pushing himself to his feet, he felt a number of sharp pains throughout his ribs, legs, and arms, but ignored them all. He had to get inside that tunnel. . . .

"*Nolan!*" Branford was still shouting in his ear.

"I'm here, I copy," he replied, as loud as he could manage. "I'm all right, General—"

"Nolan! *Do you read me!*" shouted Branford.

The com system was fritzing again, probably because of the smoke and interference from the dozens of rescue workers in the area. There was no time to worry about it now.

The grappler was still attached to the vent shaft, so he followed the wire to it. The vent was a few hundred feet to the south of Castle Clinton, about five feet across, and it jutted up two or three feet out of the ground. Climbing unsteadily atop the vent, Nolan balled up a fist and started pounding on the wide grate with his rock-hard glove. After several blows, it gave way and swung down open.

Nolan didn't have the strength to dive. He forced his way up and over the hole and allowed himself to fall.

45

With Branford still shouting in his ear, Nolan opened his eyes inside the South Street Viaduct and found himself in the fires of hell. Or if not hell, some nightmare that could only have been born out of that terrible place.

Illuminated only by the beams of headlights and the flicker of flames licking at a half dozen or so of the countless vehicles, Nolan surveyed the wreckage. Unbreathable smoke filled every crevice, every square inch, and it burned through Nolan's throat and lungs. The volcanic heat was nearly unbearable, and only his eyes, protected by the goggles, escaped being singed.

Nolan heard screaming and crying from all around, and switching over to X-ray vision, he found that all through the tunnel, vehicles were crashed. Rear-ended into one another, slammed into the tunnel walls, sideswiped and totaled, and twisted into unrecognizable shapes. One sports car was actually perched across the bed of a beefy pickup truck.

The X-ray also revealed the victims. They were everywhere; they surrounded him on all sides. They were pinned inside their cars, or they'd been ejected through their front windshields. Far too many of the skeletons his X-rays revealed were twisted and bent into impossible positions. Dead. So very many, dead.

He set to work at once, approaching the nearest car and using his steel fists to break its glass windows. Its roof was crushed, and a teen-age boy sat in shock at the wheel. Blood gushed down his face, and he couldn't seem to make any sounds come out of his mouth beyond panicked moans and screams. He looked up to meet Nolan's eyes, his face ghostly pale and drenched in blood and sweat. Nolan then saw that the boy's right leg was pinned and impaled by a piece of his transmission sticking up through the car's undercarriage.

Could he save this man, or was he already dead? The tactical side of his brain was telling him to triage: assess quickly, do what he could, and move on. There were others here with a chance of living, who were in danger of losing that chance if he spent too much time helping one person.

How was he to decide who lived and who died? He wasn't a doctor.

Nolan set to work. He had to get the car's door off its hinges; there was no way he could get proper leverage on the boy's leg if all he could do was stick his head in through the window. Once again he shouted into his earpiece, hoping the static had cleared. "Do you copy?!" he yelled. "I'm in the tunnel, are you reading me?"

"*Loud and clear!*" replied Branford.

Nolan had to fight the urge to swear as he tugged with all his might against the crumpled door. "Where are the paramedics?!" he screamed in a furious howl, partly over the devastation around him, and partly with his efforts to pull free the driver's side door. "It's really bad down here!"

"*They're all over the place—they're scrambling,*" said Branford. "*They're spread out, dealing with the victims on the surface. They seem to be concentrating most of their efforts on the cops that were hurt in the gunfight.*"

"We've got to get them down here!" Nolan shouted.

Sweat ran down his back, his forehead, cheeks, and nose. A hacking cough took hold of him and wouldn't let go. It was hard enough to get a lungful of air amid the smoke without all this exertion making his body's need for oxygen that much worse. But every time he thought about how impossibly hard this was, he directed his attention back to the victims, the ones truly suffering.

The stubborn door just refused to budge an inch, so he resorted to pounding the door straight down from the opening where the window had been. His rock-hard fists made this easier, and after a few minutes of bashing down the door, he finally had cleared it away enough to get at the teenager inside.

The kid let out a primal screech when Nolan reached inside and pulled him out of the car, carefully—but not slowly—pulling his leg up and over the jagged piece of metal that had skewered it. Once he was freed, the boy passed out from the pain.

Nolan threw him over one shoulder and ran back to the spot beneath the ventilation shaft.

"Arjay, how much weight will this thing hold?" he asked, whipping out the grappler.

Arjay faltered on the other end of the line. "*It . . . I'm . . . It's never been tested above three hundred—*"

"Arjay!" Nolan roared.

"*I have no idea!*" the young engineer cried.

Nolan weighed one ninety-five. This kid had to be well over a hundred pounds. Would that nearly invisible but super strong line snap?

"I need your best estimation," Nolan persisted.

Arjay cleared his throat. "*My best estimation is that the more you use it, the more it's going to be pushed beyond its limits.*"

Oh, God, please let this work. . . . he prayed.

He fired the grappler straight up until it snagged on something outside the vent. He released the trigger and up they went. If this was putting a strain on the grappler, Nolan couldn't tell. It was just as fast and powerful as ever.

In two seconds, he was at the rim of the vent, where he was met by a familiar face.

"What are *you* doing here?" he cried.

"Same thing you are!" Coral shouted, grabbing the unconscious teenager by his shoulders and helping Nolan heft him up through the vent.

The boy was out of the hole quickly, and Nolan gave a final shove as Coral pulled him over the edge and out of sight. Nolan pulled himself up further to stick his head out of the hole and gulp down a few lungfuls of air. The smoke was still thick up top, but it was considerably better than the air down in the tunnel.

He swiveled his head until he could see Coral as she was pulling the boy down to the ground and applying pressure to the gaping puncture in his leg. Blood was gushing out of the hole, and Coral produced a length of fabric which she tied around the kid's upper leg to make a tourniquet.

"Are you still following me?" Nolan shouted, his words a furious accusation.

"You think this is the time to talk about that?!" She glanced back up at him for a fraction of a second, her eyes flashing in such anger that they could have been on fire.

Nolan said nothing, preparing to lower himself back down into the tunnel.

Before he went, Coral reared back and shot him a nasty look. "But hey, if you've got this under control, I can leave."

He didn't dignify her sarcasm with a response, instead dropping back down into the tunnel to retrieve another victim.

46

Three hours.

It was three hours of the most grueling work Nolan had undertaken since the war, in the most horrific conditions imaginable. Cramped spaces, unbreathable air, scorching heat. And amid the smell of burning rubber, hot steel, and that blasted smoke, the stench of death was overwhelming.

Worse was the psychological toll. Each corpse brought to mind unwelcome memories that he had to fight against every bit as hard as he fought the pain in his body and the impossible nature of his task. He was into his second hour when rescue workers eventually found their way down into the tunnel. In the end, Nolan had single-handedly found and returned seventeen survivors and twenty-two bodies to the surface, delivering them into Coral's arms. He'd pushed on every time, doggedly returning to the dungeon-like space to continue digging.

There were so many dead. More than sixty at final count. Many of them some of New York's finest.

And why? Why would someone do this? What was any of it for, he wondered.

The media had shown up in herds, converging as close as possible to the bloodiest, goriest scenes of the attack. It was a spectacle, an off-Broadway production on a massive scale, that people would talk about for years.

He and Coral never said anything further to each other. They just continued working. Whether she was there as an officer of the law who'd just happened to be in the neighborhood, or she'd followed him there, he never got an answer to. In the end, he didn't care.

Eventually, after all the work he could do had been done, Nolan managed to locate an ambulance that wasn't in use on the western edge of the park, where he ducked inside. He helped himself to some oxygen, breathing through a clear mask.

The vehicle's driver had left the radio on, and he sat on the floor, breathing as slowly as possible, as the station cut to a live press conference at the White House, where the president was making a statement about last night's tragedy in Battery Park.

Nolan had watched his old friend closely as he rose to power and became president. Hastings was never one to wear his heart on his sleeve; he was more calculating than that, more careful with his choices of words. But this was one occasion when the president simply couldn't keep the emotion out of his voice. In his mind's eye, Nolan could see the pools of water in his friend's eyes, the uncharacteristic pallor to his cheeks.

"To the people of New York, I make a solemn pledge to discover the culprit or culprits behind this disgraceful attack, no matter who it is or where the search takes us. Be it a villain residing on our own soil or a terrorist operating elsewhere, we will find them.

"To whomever is responsible for last night's events: the blood of the NYPD and several innocent civilians is on your hands, and you will be held accountable. If you thought that an assault on the men and women sworn to keep us safe would deplete the city's manpower or undermine this great nation, you must not know us very well. Americans do not bow down to cowards. We did not start this fight, but I promise you today that we will finish it."

Nolan couldn't suppress a grim smile. These were fighting words, the very kind of passionate, fiery proclamations that had gotten Hastings elected in the first place. His zero tolerance policy for crime and his charismatic zeal had been a breath of fresh air for a nation that was tired of impotent leaders who never managed to make any real, lasting change. This was the man they'd put their faith in, and maybe this tragedy would be just the kick in the pants that Hastings needed to plow past Congress and get some things done.

"*Finally, I want to send one final message—to the individual known as The Hand,*" Hastings continued, and Nolan sat up straight as a rod, alarmed. "*There are those who have questioned your actions, your resolve, your reasons for doing what you do. Last night you answered those criticisms with your tireless, selfless work in the South Street Viaduct. You demonstrated the quality of your character beyond any doubt. On behalf of America, you have my gratitude and my respect. It would be my honor if someday we could find a common ground to build on, that we might work together to make a brighter tomorrow. God bless you, sir, and God bless America.*"

Nolan reached around and turned off the radio, sitting in silence for a very long moment. He wasn't sure what to think or feel, and was far too tired to engage in either activity.

His last contact with the others was well over an hour ago, so he was glad to hear the crackle of static in his earpiece.

"General," he said. "I'm sure you heard that, right? I'm still trying to process—"

"*I didn't call to speak to The Hand,*" said a voice in Nolan's ear that he didn't recognize. "*Take off the hood for a moment. I want to talk to Nolan Gray.*"

47

The voice on the other end of the line was male, with a heavy accent, and it bore an unmistakable tone of self-satisfaction.

"Who is this?"

The voice turned bitter, harsh. "*I am not a husband. Nor am I a father. I used to be both. But that was before you took my family from me.*"

Nolan sat up rigid but perfectly still.

It was *him*. That man at the botched OCI raid. Russian Mafia, Branford had said. What was his name . . . ?

Vasko.

"I didn't kill your family," said Nolan, bursting from the back of the ambulance and scanning the area, hoping to set eyes on the man. "They were dead before I got there."

"*In your own hand you held the gun that killed my wife. It was still warm when I knocked it out of your grasp. At least have the decency to own your actions.*"

It struck Nolan that nothing he ever said would be enough to convince Vasko that he wasn't responsible for what happened that night. He would never believe anything but what he'd seen with his own eyes.

"*You have made it your personal mission to save people, yes?*" Vasko went on. "*You are a failure, Nolan. A hypocrite. You're not better than the rest of us. You're much worse. A lying, conniving, highly functional sociopath.*"

Sounds like you're describing yourself, pal, Nolan thought. The dark night had just given way to morning, with the faintest hints of light dancing on the edge of the eastern horizon. He used his goggles to zoom and search, looking everywhere for this man who had broken into his com line.

"*Oh, I'm not in any of those buildings,*" said Vasko. "*Those glasses of yours are impressive. Everything you see—it's transmitted back here to your underground lair, yes?*"

Nolan's world stopped dead, and he felt an icy sweat pepper his forehead. His skin became damp and cold, and there was even colder blood pumping beneath it.

There was no disaster zone around him anymore, there was no sun just entering the skyline, no rescue workers or media or victims or dead bodies. There was no one but himself and this man in his ear.

This man named Vasko who was talking to him from inside the subway platform Nolan called home, right now.

This isn't happening.

And then came an even worse thought. He wouldn't have thought it possible for there to be anything worse than a Mafioso infiltrating his home when he wasn't there. But as crazy as it sounded, this hunch *felt* true. And Nolan knew to trust these kinds of feelings.

This feeling was telling him that this entire disaster at Battery Park had been orchestrated by Vasko, as a means of getting him out of the way.

The bursts of static he'd been hearing all night that started as the sound of what he thought was crumpling paper, heard over the line back inside Agnes Ellerbee's apartment. That static was Vasko, breaking in to the line and tracing it back to the subway platform.

"*Yes, I am here inside your 'lair,' Mr. Gray,*" gloated Vasko. "*Couldn't resist taking a poke around. You have some truly cutting-edge equipment here. Fabulous stuff. I may have to help myself to a few things before my men torch the place.*"

Nolan faltered for just a second. "It's not a 'lair.' It's my home."

"*Please,*" Vasko scoffed. "*You've fashioned this 'masked crusader' persona for yourself, steeped in the mythical archetypes of pulp fiction and comic book vigilantes. Of course it's a lair.*"

"Where are my people?" Nolan demanded.

"*Where else would they be? The Hand would be nothing without his loyal support staff, yes? The elderly gentleman doesn't look well at the moment; I'm afraid my men have been rather rough with him. They tried to get him to give up his passwords for your amazing surveillance network and database. You'll be happy to know he never told them, but from the looks of it, I believe his spleen has been ruptured."*

"*You leave them alone!*" Nolan shouted, not caring about who might be overhearing his voice where he paced on the edge of the park.

"*Now, the young man—he was much more helpful. He tried to be brave, but after losing a few teeth and then one of his fingers, he broke very quickly. Told us all about the wonderful contraptions he's built for you.*"

"Listen to me very carefully. You hurt my people, and this will come back on you and yours," Nolan seethed, already looking for the easiest way out of the park and back into the heart of Manhattan.

"*You do not frighten me, Mr. Gray,*" Vasko replied calmly. "*After all, I have nothing left to lose. Besides, I am one of the few who has seen the 'real' Nolan Gray.*"

"You've seen what I allowed you to see, what I've allowed the whole world to see," Nolan said, his breaths coming faster and faster now. "You have no concept of what I'm really capable of."

"*What I understand is that people do what they do because of the relationships they have. Love, hate, and the wide spectrum between. The laws of society are out the window when it comes to the people that matter to us. I wonder how far you will go, what laws you will break, to save the people that matter to you.*"

"Don't you dare—"

"*Now, I must confess,*" Vasko went on, ignoring Nolan, "*I have not yet discovered your purpose for keeping the woman here. She is too old to be your lover, and her race would indicate that she is no relative of yours. My people have not had the chance to interrogate her yet. I do not imagine you would save us the trouble?*"

"*Don't you touch her!*" Nolan screamed, spit flying from his mouth with the words. "*When I get my hands around—*"

"*There's one other thing I was calling to tell you,*" said Vasko, his tone light and conversational. It made Nolan sick to the stomach how much the man was enjoying this. "*I have lined this subway platform with dynamite, and attached those explosives to a timer. My family was found dead in a fire, and . . . well, I'm an 'eye for an eye' kind of person. Perhaps I should have mentioned it earlier: I started the timer when you and I began this conversation.*"

Nolan's heart jumped into his throat. It was sick, all of this, a demented, elaborate construction that this man had dedicated significant time and resources to. He closed his eyes and prayed a single sentence of silent prayer before asking the obvious question.

"How much time is left?" His body was wasted and all but broken, but he willed his adrenaline to flow so that he could start running. He ran north, out of the park, beyond a horde of onlookers there to see the aftermath of the tragedy, weaving through traffic and then sprinting past anyone and everyone on the sidewalk.

"*I am not an evil man, Mr. Gray,*" said Vasko. "*I had no opportunity to prevent the deaths of my loved ones, but I will give one such chance to you. If you are the glorious hero that everyone in this city believes you to be, then it should prove quite easy for you to get here before the timer stops. If your skills are up to the task, you may even be able to disarm the timer before the dynamite is set off. If not, then this time your loved ones will pay the price for your failure.*"

"*How much time?!*" Nolan repeated, already feeling winded.

"*My men and I are leaving now,*" he said. "*We are already on our way out. Your friends are here, waiting patiently for you to save them. As for the timer, the last time I looked, I believe there were less than thirteen minutes remaining. My memory is not what it used to be, though. Don't keep your friends waiting, Mr. Gray.*"

A high-pitched squeal tore through his earpiece, and he knew that Vasko would be speaking to him no more.

Over fifty blocks in thirteen minutes?!

I'll never make it!

48

Nolan tore the earpiece out of his ear and threw it down while ripping through the pedestrians gathering on the streets. His training railed against the panic that wanted to take hold of his soul.

He had to go flat-out all the way, pushing himself and his equipment like never before. He didn't dare stop or even slow down one single time.

Because he wasn't going to lose them—Branford, Arjay, Alice. They were all he had. And they were *not* going to die today.

Nolan could think of only one way of beating the deadline, just one option for navigating the city as the sun was moving up away from the horizon and scores of New Yorkers were waking up to the news of last night's disaster at the Battery. They would be coming out of their homes in droves soon, clogging the streets with their desire to gawk and gape at the remnants of Vasko's orchestrated carnage. He had to avoid them, he couldn't let them get in his way.

He checked his watch. Less than twelve minutes now, maybe eleven. It was his only option.

As he crossed Wall Street, he pulled out the grappler and shot it wildly into the sky, aiming randomly for any rooftop its hooks might find. When it latched onto something, he retracted it immediately and was pulled up to the top of a building. He hadn't been up here before, he didn't recognize it. It might have been the New York Stock Exchange building, but he didn't know for sure and didn't have time to care.

He wheezed hard as he crossed the rooftop, his lungs not at all clear of the smoke and soot he'd inhaled in the viaduct. He had to force himself not to breathe too fast, or he could pass out.

No, that wouldn't happen. He wouldn't allow it.

He focused his mind, his senses, his body. He would take this one problem at a time. Later, there would be time to address his own injuries and see about dismantling Vasko's bomb, but right now, he had to get to his friends. There was nothing else.

Nearing the far edge of this first building's roof, he held his breath as he fired the grappler again, only horizontally this time, straight out toward the roof of the tallest building on the next block. He never slowed. He jumped free of the roof just as the hook caught on its next target and began reeling him in.

This landing was much sloppier, as he first slammed against the side of the brick building about a dozen meters below the roof. Nolan ignored the pain and let the grappler reel him up to the building's ledge. He staggered onto the roof but kept running, determined not to falter, not to fail, not to stop until he was home.

Building after building, block after block, he fired, jumped, swung, and reeled himself in. Some jumps were easier than others, taking him at a better angle to tuck and roll his way to a decent landing, but even these proved a harsh challenge to his spent muscles and fatigued body.

As the minutes ticked away, he slammed into concrete walls, broke windows, crashed through miniature satellite dishes, bounced off of air-conditioning units and old brick chimneys, and stumbled across crumbling roof tiles. Encountering one particularly long, flat rooftop, he used the grappler to propel himself straight across it, trying to run with the retracting line but ultimately being dragged the last hundred meters or so, his skin burning as his clothes slid roughly across the surface.

The pain was searing, but he pushed it down every time. Not once did he allow himself to slow down. He had to keep going, no matter what.

By the time he neared the downtown neighborhood of storefronts underneath which his home and friends were waiting, he was all too aware of the agonizing, swelling pains stabbing throughout his body.

His compartmentalized mind estimated he'd suffered at least eight broken bones—a few ribs, some fingers, possibly an arm and a shoulder, and a toe or two—but he pushed on.

His speed had diminished a few blocks back. He couldn't remember exactly where, but he was limping at a half-run, half-walk now. Propelled forward by a blind, numb momentum, Nolan was a hiker caught in a blizzard, frozen and starving but determined to make it to safety. Only there would be no safety for him or his friends anymore. The sanctity of his home had been violated, his friends traumatized, and his secret was out, all by this evil man Vasko.

At last, after what felt like hours of running and jumping and crashing and being pulled along by Arjay's blessed invention, Nolan lowered himself quickly to the ground and managed to reach a marginally faster pace one last time for his final push to the subway platform. As he rounded the last corner, wobbling, blood soaking through the black linens of his combat fatigues as well as the white hood, he came into view of the perpetually-under-construction façade that served as his surface entrance to the subway.

And it still stood.

His heart felt a glimmer of hope, and he willed his body to run, to *go go go* until he reached the tarp covering the scaffolding at the front of the vacant building.

His eyes were bleary, his skin saturated with sweat and blood, as he pulled off a glove so he could place a trembling hand on the metal plate beside the door to trigger the lock.

Nolan's heart threatened to escape his chest as he descended the stairs at the back of the building, into the dark. Was it the concussion he thought he'd suffered a few minutes ago that was making everything look so dark? Or was it just the absence of light in the stairwell?

He stumbled into the heavy metal door at the bottom of the steps, expecting to spot Vasko's timer device somewhere in the open empty space at the center of the platform, waiting to be disarmed. His friends would be nearby, probably tied to chairs or posts or something.

But when he flung the door open at last, the soul-shattering sight before him did not resemble anything he expected.

The subway platform he'd come to call home was gone and again he'd entered hell. This was a place of heat and flame and darkness.

The cobwebs in his head prevented him from entirely processing his surroundings. What was this place? Had he gone down the wrong stairs?

"Nolan . . ." someone said, a faint moan.

Nolan was delirious, unable to discern whose voice had called to him, or where. It was so hot down there, and there was *stuff* everywhere. No, not stuff. Rubble. Debris. Broken bits of *everything*. It was all over. Gone. Pieces of mortar and brick and stone that had fallen from the ceiling, or been blown free of the walls. Glass and metal and wood from Arjay's work area, Branford's Cube, the living spaces, his training area.

Months ago, or maybe years, he and Branford had reinforced the old walls, ceilings, floors, and supports. And it appeared that the supports had helped. There had been no collapse or cave-in above ground. Anyone who felt the blast probably thought it was a rare New York earthquake. But his home was dead. Gutted and destroyed.

He hobbled across the cracked floor, just managing to get clear as a bowling ball–sized piece of cement broke free from the ceiling and shattered on the ground. The sound startled him, and he tripped over a piece of metal railing that had probably come from the Cube. . . .

On the ground, he spun violently as a hand wrapped around his ankle. It was a brown hand, and it was bleeding badly . . . and missing a ring finger.

Arjay. It had to be Arjay. Hadn't Vasko said he'd cut off one of Arjay's fingers? His memory was fuzzy, he couldn't recall the exact details.

Nolan was sure, however, that the heat from the piles of burning wreckage felt good to his cold, clammy skin. He knew he needed to finish what he'd come to do—whatever that was—but the heat beckoned him to sleep and he could resist it no more.

49

Nolan felt as cold as ice when he came to, and he glanced around, wondering where that wonderful heat had gone.

His senses returned to him with a jolt as he realized he was seated on the cold cement floor inside the fake storefront up above the subway platform. Someone had propped him against a side wall and tried to incline his feet atop . . . something. What were his feet resting on?

He looked down at his watch. Only minutes had passed. He'd returned from the Battery to find he was too late. *Of course* he was too late. Vasko was probably lying about how much time was left on the timer all along. Nolan was never going to make it, because Vasko wanted Nolan to feel exactly what he'd felt that day when he came home to a destroyed house and a dead family.

And it worked. Nolan had never felt so undone, so completely without solid ground to support him. Not even in the prison camps had he felt so destroyed.

He was still in shock, he could tell that much. He was bleeding from several points, including somewhere on top of his head, and his body was broken and battered. Horribly, horribly battered. He'd inflicted considerable damage to himself, and whether it was from the smoke inhalation from the viaduct or the relentless bludgeoning from his frantic race home to save his friends, he was completely trashed.

The pain came from countless points all over his body, but it had melded together and he couldn't tell one hurt from another. Trying to sort it out required too much effort. He needed to get out of there, to get to a hospital. No, that was wrong. He couldn't go to a hospital, because he was officially a dead man. He had to get patched up somehow, but he was having a hard enough time merely commanding his muscles to stretch out of this awkward position. What *was* that beneath his feet down there?

Nolan finally summoned the strength to sit up away from the wall, and his blurred eyes came into focus, resting on the makeshift footstool. He jerked his feet back when he saw it was Arjay, passed out in a heap. A washrag had been wrapped around the stub where his finger had been, and his face was swollen, bleeding, and discolored all over.

How had the two of them made it up here? Did Arjay somehow manage to drag him up the stairs before passing out? Were they the only ones to survive?

"Arjay . . ." he tried to shout, but the word came out in an anemic, breathless monotone.

The stairway door burst open and Branford appeared at the threshold, carrying Alice in his arms.

Nolan tried to shout Branford's name, but all that came out was a guttural yelp.

He tried to get to his feet to help, but found it impossible to shift his weight. He only succeeded in falling over onto his side, where he remained. Any more movement was impossible; he simply had no strength. Branford shuffled slowly over to where Nolan and Arjay lay, his face bearing very similar marks to Arjay's from Vasko's cruel interrogation. He also favored his one side as he hobbled, and Nolan's thoughts returned to Vasko's comment about Branford having a ruptured spleen. Was it true?

"Are you okay?" Nolan asked, finally getting words to emerge from his mouth but his voice no more than a whisper. "Is Arjay alive?"

Branford gave no reply beyond a deadened, weary look, and there was a lot more communicated in that look than Nolan was expecting. Branford and Arjay were down but not out. That much was immediately clear. Yet there was sorrow etched into the old man's features the likes of which Nolan had never known from him, and Nolan's breath caught in his throat. He knew that it wasn't himself or Arjay, or even their underground home that Branford was grieving.

Nolan looked up at the woman in Branford's arms, whom he was lowering slowly to the ground beside Nolan.

"She caught the worst of the blast," Branford whispered, and as she finally came to rest on the floor, Nolan saw it for the first time. An ugly, shiny piece of metal was sticking out of her side.

"No," he tried to say, but no sound came out. His throat had constricted in an instant, pools welling up in his exhausted eyes.

Nolan crawled a few inches closer to Alice, and he awkwardly lay sideways next to her.

"Alice?" he said, his voice offensively weak. Two trails of tears carved through the grime and sweat and blood that stained his face. He couldn't remember the last time he'd cried, but the tears came effortlessly now. "Alice?"

Her body lay limp on that cold floor, but then in a start, she began to cough.

When the hacking, furious coughing subsided, she took a wheezing, labored breath and opened her eyes. Her frail eyes stared into Nolan's face. She smiled as much as she was able, but even this brought a faint grimace to her pained features.

"You found it," she said with a smile, before letting out another brutal cough. "See? There it is."

"There what is?" Nolan whispered.

She placed a cold, limp hand on his chest. "Your heart. It was always here. Right here. I knew it was. I knew it."

She smiled at him again, and he tried to smile back, but his face wouldn't obey his commands. It was insisting on producing a stream of steady tears, even though he wanted it to do *anything* else.

Alice closed her eyes, and Nolan gasped.

"Alice? Alice!"

She swallowed hard, possibly the last time she would ever do so, and Nolan had a hard time focusing his eyes due to the burning sensation they produced. He worked his feeble muscles as hard as possible to take one of her hands in his, and he prayed desperately to God to spare her, to give her a miracle. To take his life instead of hers.

She deserved better than this. So much better.

Slowly, a truth came to Nolan that he'd never known until this moment: he loved her. It wasn't romantic love, nor was it the way one might feel toward a surrogate parent. Alice was something else. She was his friend. His confidante, his rudder.

Somehow, this woman he barely knew, who was never in any way a part of his grandiose plans, had become crucial to those plans. Crucial to *him*.

Breathing became harder for her, taking on a raspy edge.

Alice shook her head faintly. When she spoke, he could barely hear her. "Promise me . . . you won't . . . give up. Promise."

Nolan didn't even consider giving up. He paused not one second in his reply. "I promise. I won't give up. I'll make a difference."

She smiled. "Say it . . . one more time."

"I promise," he whispered. "I'm not giving up. No matter what."

She closed her eyes, and Nolan held her hand until long after her soul departed the earth.

50

One week later, the bones and flesh of Alice Regan were lowered into the ground at a private graveside service at Brookville Cemetery. Located in the rural neighborhood of Glen Head, east of Manhattan Island, Brookville was a lovely graveyard park situated in a heavily wooded area, far from the overpopulated parts of New York City.

Nolan's body was wrapped in bandages, casts, and braces, but he refused a wheelchair, insisting on walking across the cemetery's rolling hills under his own power. Arjay was able to walk without hobbling, but Branford had to use a cane to avoid putting too much strain on his abdomen. The emergency surgery to remove his spleen had come not a minute too soon. Both men still sported black eyes, cut lips, and faces covered in other bruises. Arjay's hand was wrapped in gauze to cover the wound where his finger had been severed by Vasko.

No one blamed Arjay for succumbing to Vasko's torture. Withstanding such methods of interrogation was not something he was trained for, and even with the very best training, many soldiers eventually gave in and told their captors whatever they wanted to know. And it wasn't like anything Arjay had told them had contributed to their losses. Vasko would have torched their home regardless.

The climate had changed with the arrival of autumn, and a welcome breeze blew gently across the green grass. The cloudless sky delivered warm sunlight onto the graveyard.

From their vantage point several hundred feet across the cemetery, hidden within the greenery, the three men watched the funeral in silence. There were fewer than ten people in attendance under the tiny green tent, Alice's drunk, abusive husband among them. Nolan had no idea who any of the others were. Maybe sisters, or other extended family.

After the funeral ended and the officials lowered the casket into the ground, Nolan, Branford, and Arjay waited until the other mourners left. Then they finally made their way across the open field to stand before Alice's headstone.

Nolan wanted to kneel before the grave, but couldn't get down on one knee. He didn't know what to say, or what to feel. His tears had dried up days ago.

The other two men took turns paying their respects. It was Branford who finally broke the long silence.

"It's over, isn't it?" he said quietly.

"Vasko won," Arjay confirmed.

But Nolan was surprised to hear his friends talk this way. "It's not over. Not remotely."

Branford and Arjay exchanged a glance. "How are we to carry on?" asked Arjay.

"I promised her I wouldn't give up," Nolan said. "And I promised Thor."

"Our resources are wiped out," Branford said, defeat emanating from his every word and gesture. "We lost everything."

"But we haven't lost ourselves," Nolan replied. "We switch tactics. We go underground."

Branford shook his head wearily, and Nolan realized the general had already given up. He'd never seen Branford give up at anything before, and it incensed him that the old man decided to do it now, of all times.

"I think," said Branford, "it's time we realized that maybe the people of New York don't want what we're offering them. Maybe they're just not willing to change."

Fury rose up in Nolan faster than he'd ever experienced in his life. They'd lost everything and Alice was dead, but it couldn't be for nothing. He would not allow that.

His face was red and he was nearly shouting when he replied, "If people aren't willing to change by themselves . . . then I'll *make* them change."

PART THREE

The War

51

Good morning, New York! Today is November 14. I'm Jackie Turner and I want to welcome you to today's special broadcast. We're coming to you live from the gleaming new office building constructed at the heart of Times Square. Our guest today is the man who built this amazing tower, a man who needs no introduction to the people of New York: Yuri Vasko. Welcome, Mr. Vasko."

Vasko sat patiently in his chair opposite Jackie Turner, co-host of a local New York City morning show, with his legs crossed at the knee. The show was being filmed on location inside Vasko's spacious new office in the brand new One Times Square building.

"Thank you for having me, Jackie," he replied, striking a gracious, humble tone yet refusing to smile. He was also very careful to be sure that his gimp hand was visible on camera at all times. "It's a great pleasure to be here today."

"Well, as you at home can see, we're inside the penthouse office of the new One Times Square building. Mr. Vasko, please tell our viewers why you bought this property and why you've changed it so drastically."

"Of course," he replied. "I think my story has been told so many times now, you'll forgive me if I don't relive it again. But after the tragic events that claimed the life of my wife and daughter, I turned my back on my old life and devoted myself completely to humanitarian efforts." His expression carried just the right mix of somber regret for his past and pious humility regarding his future plans. It was a finely tuned performance, one he'd been practicing for days.

"I knew very soon after turning my life around that I would need a central location from which to operate. So I chose the most central location to New York I could think of. The whole world knows this place—they look to it on New Year's Eve. I had no desire to destroy this glorious landmark, but I needed a building that would send a clear message—"

"Clear is right!" laughed Jackie, interrupting her guest with typical morning show–host exuberance. "I don't know if this is obvious to our viewers at home, but One Times Square is now completely transparent, covered on all four sides with floor-to-ceiling glass. It's a beautiful, brightly lit pillar the same size and footprint as the original building. Why the big change?"

Vasko cleared his throat, swallowing his irritation at being interrupted. He couldn't afford to let his temper out; this was too important an occasion. "The new One Times Square is more than a building. It's a beacon of hope and refuge. In these troubled times, I wanted New Yorkers to know that there's someone here for them in their time of need—someone with nothing to hide."

"You're referring, of course, to the dramatic rise in crime in the months following the tragedy at Battery Park."

"Indeed. It changed everything, yes? Hardly a day goes by when we do not wake up in the morning, look out the window, and see the haze of smoke rising over our city—evidence of the latest skirmish between the Organized Crime Intelligence and the criminals. New York has become a war zone, and despite the government's relentless efforts, that does not look to change anytime soon. And as for the city's 'great protector,' The Hand—well, he seems to have vanished entirely. Perhaps he realized he was in over his head."

This was, like everything else, a veiled message. Nolan Gray hadn't been seen or heard from in his 'Hand' persona since Battery Park. Whether he was even still alive was something Vasko hadn't been able to determine despite a massive, personally funded manhunt. In his heart, Vasko knew Nolan Gray was still alive. Felt it. But the man's absence and the deaths of so many members of the NYPD at Battery Park had created a vacuum of power that Vasko's soldiers and enforcers had found easy to fill.

It was the greatest of ironies: Vasko had built an office space from which to rule over his criminal empire, yet from the outside, it appeared to be a haven for those who were suffering due to their oppression by that very empire. Marko had been baffled by Vasko's insistence that the building be made of glass on all four sides—until he discovered how willing Americans were to part with their money in the name of "helping others."

"New York needs a bright, shining light of safety and hope for the future. I have built that for them. Anyone in need is welcome to enter these walls. My new humanitarian foundation is ready and able to help in any way we can—be it foodstuffs, medical supplies, job placement, or financial aid."

"May I ask how you lost the use of your right hand?" asked Jackie in her most compassionate tone. "That's one aspect of your story I don't recall ever hearing before."

Vasko had to work hard not to frown. This was a part of his past he was none too eager to relive. "Well. My childhood was very difficult. I was raised by my father, and most of my memories of him are of the back of his hand. This injury was inflicted when I was eighteen years old. My father was a blacksmith by trade, and on this day, he flew into one of his rages and tried to shove me up against a red-hot handsaw he had standing up against his anvil. I stopped the fall by bracing myself with this hand—on the hot metal of the saw. That was the last time I ever saw him. As soon as I was well enough to leave the hospital, I gathered my closest friends—including the woman who would become my wife, Lilya—and fled to America."

Jackie sat back in her chair and took a breath. Vasko could see in the woman's body language that the tone of the live interview was about to take a turn.

"Your story is very inspiring, Mr. Vasko. Not many men would have the courage to escape, or the strength of will to endure such a difficult upbringing. But I have to ask: what do you say to the White House's accusations that you're secretly funding the city's upswing in criminal activity—that this glass building and your nonprofit foundation are nothing but a façade to hide your true purpose?"

It was irritating that he'd been misinformed. Marko had assured him that this particular news network would be the one most likely to soft-pedal him, to portray him as the sympathetic, grieving family man instead of the mob boss. It was the reason he'd agreed to do this interview in the first place.

But instead of allowing his frustration to show, Vasko came the closest to smiling he had yet. "I say, 'Look around you.' Does this look like a house of crime or terror to you? This is a place of optimism and charity. We hide nothing within these walls. Because we have nothing to hide."

This journalist wasn't going to give up that easily. "So you've completely severed your ties, then, with organized crime?"

Vasko paused, to give the impression that he was saddened by the accusation. "The past is the past, Jackie. In Ukraine, I was born into poverty and raised by a cruel father, but these things do not make me who I am today. Today, I am a new man. A man of peace. And I think the people of this city are more interested in the present and the future. The future holds big things for us, very big things. In fact, if I may, I would like to take this opportunity to make an announcement to the people of New York."

Jackie's eyebrows went up. "By all means."

"Well, I know that life has become difficult for so very many. Businesses are closing, jobs are being lost, people are being shot and killed every day in our streets. I have heard the reports that many New Yorkers are packing their belongings in order to move someplace safer, someplace that offers more opportunities. To them I say: *Please stay*. There is no other place in the world like New York City. Those of us who live here are family. And you do not abandon your family when it needs you most."

He paused for dramatic effect, but his interviewer thought he'd stopped altogether. "You said there was an announcement?"

"Yes," Vasko replied. "I want all of New York—and the entire world—to know that despite all that we have lost and all that we continue to suffer, *we are still here*, and we believe in what is good and right. To that end, this morning I spoke with the mayor and volunteered this building for use as the location once more of the ball drop on New Year's Eve. So, my neighbors, tell your friends and loved ones to join us in Times Square on December thirty-first for the celebration of a lifetime. New Year's Eve is officially on."

52

Thornton Hastings shook his head in disbelief.

He was behind his desk in the Oval Office, accompanied by OCI Director Sebastian Pryce and Chief of Staff Marcus Bailey, both of whom sat across the desk from him. This was their custom, a daily ritual the three of them had begun weeks ago, so that Hastings' two comrades could bring him up to speed on the latest happenings in the war on crime and the state of the nation.

Right now, all three men faced the television on the side wall, watching their biggest enemy flaunt his power in their faces. Yuri Vasko was a genius—Hastings had to give him that—but he was an awfully arrogant one. Having just announced that he'd convinced the mayor of New York to go forward with its annual New Year's Eve celebration, he would once again be heralded as "the only person doing anything to help us" by the vocal malcontents of the metropolis. This, despite the fact that every other major holiday tradition in New York—the Macy's Thanksgiving Day Parade, the lighting of the Christmas tree at Rockefeller Center, and so on—had been canceled due to the wildly dangerous conditions of the city streets.

"What's he really up to?" the president mused.

His two compatriots turned back around to face him. Marcus spoke first.

"Just watching him talk makes me want to punch something. It's the usual posturing, Mr. President, another distraction to cover his illegal practices."

Hastings glanced at Pryce. "Is that all it is?"

The heavy man leaned back in his seat. "We have no intel to suggest otherwise. But I'll have my analysts monitor the chatter for any key words related to New Year's Eve. If he's planning something, we'll know about it far in advance."

Just this once, time might actually be on their side, Hastings mused. It was only the middle of November, which gave them about six weeks until New Year's Eve.

His analysts . . . Hastings pondered. Only a few months ago, Pryce's entire organization was comprised of just a handful of people. Now . . .

"How many agents are currently on your team, Director?" he asked.

Pryce's expression, as always, remained unchanged. The man would be stoic, grim, and dispassionate to his dying breath. "We're over a hundred twenty strong. Mostly field agents, but I have a dozen or so analysts I co-opted from the CIA to help with this sort of thing."

A hundred twenty. Pretty remarkable, it was. Battery Park had been the catalyst. After the tragedy, Pryce had asked Congress for major new funding for the OCI and had gotten his request. He'd then launched a massive recruiting effort to build an army for fighting this new war that was being waged on American soil.

"And how big is Yuri Vasko's operation?" the president asked.

"It's impossible to be certain," replied Pryce. "But we believe there are more than a thousand individuals working in his organization. Those are the links we've verified. Likely there are countless others."

Hastings shook his head again. "How did this happen? Did *we* give Vasko this power?"

"The Hand is more to blame than anyone, sir," said Marcus. "He created a vacuum of power that Vasko stepped in to fill."

"By our best estimation," Pryce noted, "Vasko now owns or holds sway over at least 55 percent of New York City's businesses. And that doesn't include the real estate he owns. He's landlord to more than a third of the city. It's all handled under the table, through front companies, of course, so people don't know he's the one fleecing them while also pretending to offer them aid from inside his big glass office."

Hastings felt so helpless. This was not how he'd imagined the war on crime going. Vasko was gaining more ground with each passing day, and it seemed that every action he and his people undertook to counter Vasko only worked to the man's advantage.

"Mr. President," said Marcus, sitting up straight in his seat, "may I be frank?"

Hastings eyed his friend with complete attention. "Always."

"New York is monopolizing our resources and policies, with no tangible results. There are other parts of the nation where we may be able to create a turnaround in the crime rate. I'm sorry to say it, but I believe it's time for the OCI to move on."

Hastings didn't hesitate. "No," he said, his voice soft and distant.

"Sir?" said Marcus.

"We're not giving up on New York."

"Sir, the city is lost," Marcus stated flatly.

Hastings glanced at Pryce to gauge his reaction, but it was, as ever, unreadable.

"Marcus," said Hastings, "are you suggesting we abandon the people of New York to Yuri Vasko? Admit defeat, tuck tail, and run?"

"No one wants to see that happen, sir," replied Marcus. "But pragmatically, I believe it may be time for us to cut our losses. The rest of the country is being ignored because all of our assets are being directed at this one city. And as for the people of New York, many of them are already leaving for safer places to live. More will follow."

Hastings looked to Pryce. "Director?"

"It is not in my nature to concede defeat. Ever."

Marcus tried to hide his frustration that Pryce wasn't backing him up, but Hastings could read his friend too well.

"I can't give up on New York," the president said, his tone decisive. "Too many people are suffering there, and we have a responsibility to help them."

Marcus frowned and leaned back in his seat, crossing his arms over his chest. "It's just too bad The Hand gave up," he muttered.

"He didn't." Hastings turned to look out the big window behind his desk. "He would never," he said quietly.

I know better than any man alive . . . Nolan Gray doesn't know how to give up.

But where was he?

53

Nolan just wanted to hit something, or someone.

This whole town had gone mad, and more than anything, he wanted to pummel something with his bare hands.

He'd landed in the middle of a showdown between a pair of police officers and a trio of mob hit men, taking place in broad daylight, smack dab in the center of a residential street in SoHo. Guns had been drawn and ammo exhausted as each side hid behind their respective vehicles—a standard black-and-white police car and a nondescript black van.

Nolan had no idea what the mob guys had done to draw an attack by the NYPD, but there was no shortage of possibilities. The last of the fall leaves were being swept up and around the two sides, while Nolan could see no one else up or down the street. His thoughts were consumed with the policemen, who were both kneeling on the ground trying to stem their own bleeding. One tried hopelessly to stop a pulsing wound in his leg, while the other had a hand to his side, where his uniform was red and wet.

Both groups seemed to be debating what to do next when Nolan dropped down behind Vasko's men from a rooftop above.

The hit men seemed to recoil slightly at his appearance, and then recognition washed over them. As one, they lunged in his direction, but he was ready. Staff extending as they reached him, he flipped sideways and head over heels, his feet hitting one of the men, and the staff catching the other two. When he landed on his own feet, the three mob men were on the ground.

"Pull 'em!" shouted one of the men, and all of them produced hand

ROBIN PARRISH

grenades from inside their coats. The pins were still in the grenades, but the men were all too ready to yank them out.

Nolan froze, waiting for them to make a move.

Slowly, the three of them rose to their feet.

"Hey, hero," said one of them—the tallest and burliest of the group. "What do you want more? To help the good guys . . . or stop the bad guys?"

Right on cue, the three men pulled out the pins and lobbed their grenades in the direction of the two cops. One of the grenades went up and over the van and the police car, and two were rolled under the vehicles.

No!

His first thought was to get to the policemen and try to shield them with his bulletproof fatigues, but during the millisecond he was considering this, one of the mob men slid in behind him and grabbed him in a stranglehold from behind.

The man had a remarkably solid arm and Nolan felt his air and blood flow cut off immediately. Reacting on instinct, he dropped to the ground and threw his attacker over his shoulder. But the man clung to his neck with an iron grip and returned the favor, flipping Nolan over as well.

The grenades went off with a powerful explosion that shook the neighborhood and blew Nolan and his three adversaries back away from the van by a good ten feet or more. Oxygen rushed back into his system when his back hit the sidewalk, and then he was in motion, powering himself on rage alone.

The staff had fallen from his hands during the scuffle, so he activated the electromagnet to draw it instantly back to him. With a vicious twist, he brought it around hard and fast against one of the men's heads, knocking him out while opening a brutal gash across his forehead. A second man was already rushing him for a tackle, but Nolan brought one of his steel-hard fists around and bashed the guy in the ear.

Before he could regroup to see where the third man was, the guy tackled him. Nolan hit the ground even harder than before, the back of his head smacking on the concrete sidewalk. The guy laid into him hard, pounding his face with both fists, his expression full of unbridled malice.

A shotgun round was fired, and the man flew backward from the shot. The second man reappeared and attempted one last attack, a flurry of blows against Nolan's abdomen.

But Nolan's face was hot, his body nearly convulsing from the wrath and contempt that raced through him. With a snarl of rage, he backhanded the man so hard the assailant's body spun along the ground before collapsing in a heap.

Nolan jumped up from the ground with a single thought: who had fired the shotgun?

The answer waited partway down the block on his left, standing there with a large shotgun still raised and ready to fire.

Coral Lively approached slowly.

Together they stared at the wreckage the grenades had torn through the police car and the officers. Nolan, unable to control himself, screamed at the sky.

This wasn't how it was supposed to work. Everything was so much harder than before. The truth was, he'd been back on the job for over two weeks, but no matter how hard he tried to do something big enough to announce his return, nobody in New York was watching.

"*Why didn't they call for backup?!*" cried Nolan, angry at himself and the whole world.

"There isn't any," Coral slowly replied, watching him. "NYPD is spread so thin they can't even respond to 9-1-1 calls. The OCI is doing what we can to help, but . . ."

Her voice trailed off as he turned to acknowledge her for the first time. He was glad his hood was covering most of his face. But hers looked much the way he remembered it. Her customary ponytail was in place, and she wore standard black riot gear, complete with bulletproof armor. The letters *OCI* were emblazoned in white across her uniform's torso.

"You all right?" she asked, sizing him up. He knew the question was not directed at his emotional state.

"They couldn't have taken me," he said, stating this as fact without a hint of ego.

"Of course not," Coral said, her voice sounding guarded but sincere.

There wasn't anything more he could do here. Coral worked with the OCI; she would inform NYPD of the men whose lives had been lost. The men whose lives had been *taken* by a group of hired guns on the payroll of Yuri Vasko.

He needed to check in with Branford and let him know he was alive. But he didn't want to talk on the radio in front of Coral Lively. She already knew too much about him as it was.

Nolan walked back around to the three unconscious mobsters on the ground and searched the pockets of the nearest one.

While searching, he noticed for the first time that Coral had crossed her arms and seemed to be waiting. She watched him patiently.

"What?" he finally asked.

"Are you kidding?!" she shouted over the sound of the burning vehicles. "You were the only source of light this city had to look to, but you disappeared for more than two months while New York turned into hell. And you're really not going to at least tell me what happened after Battery Park? What happened to your one-man revolution? *Where have you been?!*"

Nolan was certain that steam must be pouring off of his skin in this cold morning air. He didn't want to answer her; he didn't owe her or anyone else an explanation. Still, there was something to be said for the fact that she worked for the OCI yet had never ratted him out to her co-workers. And she was one of the few people in this world to ever have helped him while expecting nothing in return.

"I was in a hell all my own," he said quietly. "It took me this long to get out."

"If you needed help—"

"I didn't," he said, cutting her off.

She frowned. "I was going to say you should have contacted the president. He offered to help you in any way he could. Said it on live television. And if the president of the United States can't do anything to help you, no one can."

Nolan faltered for a moment. "I don't want his help."

Her face posed the unspoken question.

"It's complicated, okay?" He sighed and tried a different tack. "Look, it's a big city. If you want to play vigilante during your off hours, I can't stop you. There's more than enough messed up stuff to deal with for the both of us."

She seemed to deflate a bit. "All right."

Noticing her disappointment, Nolan's shoulders drooped and he rolled his eyes. "Thank you. For your help," he said grudgingly. "Just . . . don't ever follow me again."

54

It was early evening by the time Nolan rendezvoused with Branford and Arjay.

After grappling up to a peaked rooftop five stories high, he ran across the center beam of this and several other buildings toward the pickup point they'd prearranged in Chelsea.

Today he'd saved a small family from an apartment fire that the NYFD couldn't get to until nothing but cinders remained, stopped a desperate man from robbing a small grocer, and most dangerous of all, he'd intervened when Vasko's enforcers tried to execute the owner of a local hardware store who refused to accept their "protection." It was the most eventful day he'd had yet since returning to the field.

No, don't call it that, he thought. *She wanted me to stop talking about things in military terms. . . .*

The chilly city streets were all but silent. The whole world seemed to be holed up inside, behind locked doors, where it was safer and warmer. At any moment, a fight between the mob and the cops or the OCI could erupt almost anywhere, even in a neighborhood as mild-mannered as Chelsea.

But for now at least, all was hushed. He slowed his progress and took a moment to savor the quiet. These simple respites gave him a chance to think, pray, and keep focused.

His wounds and broken bones had healed, though it had been a punishing recovery. And not just for him; both of his friends had suffered plenty of breaks and bruises, but the worst of it was the permanent damage. Branford was down a spleen and moved much slower than he used to, while Arjay was still trying to adjust to life with nine fingers instead of ten. At least the two of them still officially existed, so they had no trouble procuring treatment at a local hospital, though they'd had to fib about how they received their injuries. Nolan's recovery had taken place almost entirely under his own ministrations, inside the trio's new home.

"Home" was a stupid word for it. It felt no more like a home than a place of confinement. And Nolan certainly knew the difference.

Returning to the here and now, he grappled quickly down the side of the last structure on his route—an ancient parking deck—to meet his waiting friends. With senses always attuned to his surroundings, he was satisfied no one was watching. He turned the key that rested on a simple chain around his neck and ducked through the narrow door.

The old Class A motor home Arjay had rescued from an impound lot didn't so much drive through New York as *lurch*. It was a beat-up relic of another era, but a week after the events at Battery Park, this beast had been Arjay's solution to their need for a new home. Its greatest asset was that it allowed them to stay mobile. It was also an effective disguise; it may have been a significant downgrade from their old digs, but it was the last place anyone would expect The Hand to call home.

And besides, it was all they could muster. Once their injuries mended enough to regroup, the three of them had worked for weeks to retrofit the RV, turning thirty-six feet into a livable, workable solution to their needs that maximized space in every way. They had outfitted it to serve as both a home and a base of operations with what remaining supplies they had. Most of their funds and all of their resources had been tied up in the subway station, and although Arjay had managed to salvage a few pieces of his equipment and a few computers with burn marks on their cases, Nolan and his friends all saw this vehicle as a pale shadow of what once was.

For Nolan, it was a means to an end. The RV would have to do. The city still needed him, and he would soldier on. Soldiering was what he did best.

Inside, he removed his hooded jacket and hung it on a hook by the door. His uniform was no longer the pristine garment it had once been—the result of his efforts in the South Street Viaduct and his frantic trip across the city's rooftops to save his friends. It was frayed at most of its edges and even had a couple of small holes, and there were patches of crusty amber blood that refused to come out. As Arjay had predicted, the material was incredibly sturdy, but not indestructible. His personal gear had fared better; every piece remained intact. Even the grappler had held together despite the punishment he put it through that day. It whined a bit when he retracted it, but that was its only sign of damage.

The interior of the RV had two narrow beds on either side, which flipped to double as workstation tables. Branford was seated at one of these, puttering on a laptop, when Nolan entered. Arjay typically sat at the other, repairing and maintaining Nolan's equipment or assisting Branford however he could. Tonight, Arjay was up front at the wheel. No more than two of them ever slept at a time, so two beds were all they required. A pair of railed curtains could be pulled around to cover both bunks, allowing a degree of privacy. There was a modest bathroom at the vehicle's rear, but it had a full shower. A tiny kitchenette and dining table were behind the driver's seat.

The most notable change for all three of them graced the driver's-side wall. It was covered by an enormous hand-drawn map of Yuri Vasko's organization that displayed the names and statistics of the man's operatives, supply lines, known storage facilities, and other important data, along with straight lines indicating how each piece of this infrastructure was connected. Every person who worked for Vasko, every piece of real estate he owned, every business owner who'd been coerced into working for him against his will. This project had consumed Nolan's time during his physical recovery.

Vasko had forced them to completely alter their operating focus and methods. When not out helping the people of New York, Nolan meant to take down Vasko's entire syndicate, regardless of how long it took. If he had to, he would tear it apart one piece at a time.

At least they didn't have to worry about the NYPD pursuing them anymore. The president himself had called off the attack dogs after Battery Park, and the police department had its hands full with other matters these days anyway.

When he shut the door behind him, Branford and Arjay were ready to assault him with questions about his day. They still had audio communications—tuned to a rotating frequency algorithm that Arjay had designed and implemented to keep unwanted ears from listening in—but the big visual displays of the Cube were a thing of the past. Branford's laptop let him use readily available Internet maps and floor plans and other public resources to help with Nolan's work on the ground. They could do little more.

As Nolan filled them in on his day's events, he worked hard to ignore the fleeting glances that Branford and Arjay sent each other when they thought he wasn't looking. Their ongoing concern for his mental health and overall well-being was cute, but the delicate treatment was wearing very thin.

"I, uh . . ." faltered Branford when Nolan had finished talking, "I have some news. You won't like it." He punctuated this with a quick look at Arjay.

He tapped a key on his laptop and spun it so Nolan could see. On the screen was a headline from the *Times'* website, declaring that three men involved in a "small altercation" with the police had been released on bail, just a couple of hours ago. The article included three of the tiniest mug shots Nolan had ever seen, but it was enough. He recognized them as the men who'd killed the two cops in SoHo that morning.

55

I don't believe it," said Nolan, quickly scanning the contents of the article. Justice for two dead cops apparently meant tiny bails set by a crooked judge. Nolan closed his eyes, swallowed, and tasted bile.

He kept his eyes closed until his emotions were buried down deep where they belonged. The way Branford and Arjay were staring at him made him blink. He saw pity on their faces.

"Will you two please stop that?" he said, his temper rising so fast it startled even him. But he felt no desire to apologize just now. He got back to the matter at hand before either of them could reply. "Do we know who paid their bail?"

Branford nodded, and Nolan didn't really care how they'd managed to come by such information. "The release forms were signed by Marko Ostrovsky."

Nolan recognized that name but wasn't sure how. He craned his neck to examine the data map on the wall. Marko Ostrovsky was near the very top of the map, just beneath Vasko's name. This guy was Vasko's right-hand man, and in fine print beneath his name were details about how the two of them had been friends since childhood and had escaped equally abusive homes in the Ukraine together as young men. He wasn't just a close associate of Vasko's; he was practically a younger sibling.

Nolan's mind was spinning rapidly, but he paused, returning to his friends. They both looked so very tired. Neither of them complained. They were always ready to help, but he knew that things were wearing on them. Maybe even more than they were wearing on him. Their difficult conditions. Lack of quality sleep. Fear for their lives in this new world order in New York.

Nolan was conditioned for hardship. At times, he even used it as fuel to push himself. Branford was pushing seventy and was many years removed from that sort of thing. Arjay was no more a soldier than he was an opera singer.

Feeling a sudden wave of guilt, he stood. "I'm taking the next shift. You're both exhausted. I want you to get some rest."

Branford's argument was immediate. "You need sleep as much as we do. You won't be any good out there on the streets in the morning if you don't get any rest tonight."

Nolan forced a smile for his friend's benefit. "I just spent two months resting enough for a lifetime. You sleep."

———

When Branford was snoring loudly and Arjay was mumbling in his sleep, Nolan took the RV's wheel and forced the old beast to life. As he drove, he reached into his pants pocket and pulled out a business card he'd found while searching Vasko's man that morning in SoHo.

Nearly half an hour later, he parked in a small lot just beneath the northern end of the Brooklyn Bridge, not far from the river's edge. Bulldozers, earth movers, and other pieces of construction equipment were parked nearby, as well as a pair of motor homes. The RV looked like just another trailer being used during the day as a makeshift office.

Satisfied that his friends were deeply asleep and as safe as possible, hidden under the mammoth steel bridge, he slipped out of the vehicle and set off into the night.

Just two blocks away, he made his way to the roof of a six-story L-shaped hotel facing the river. At the southwest corner of the rooftop was a complex rig comprised of solar panels, ventilation ducts, and four massive air-conditioning units. In the center of all the machinery was an empty space that was completely sealed off from prying eyes. The only access was to tightrope walk across the upper edge of two huge solar panels and then drop down into the four-by-four open spot, which was completely surrounded by metal siding from the air-conditioners.

This was where, three weeks ago, Nolan had gone to great lengths to hide a large green army duffel bag. Its existence and contents—and three other bags just like it, hidden elsewhere across New York—he'd kept secret from his friends. He wasn't intentionally keeping them in the dark. But he had to protect them.

He couldn't lose anyone else.

———

Using the grappler, with the duffel bag slung across his back, Nolan worked his way to the Lower East Side. As he entered the neighborhood, most of the buildings became single-story structures, which slowed his progress.

Eventually he located the address written on the business card in his pocket. It led to a small gas station and body shop on a residential road a few blocks south of the Williamsburg Bridge. The building was covered in grime and appeared to have been closed and abandoned for several years. It was a blight upon the quaint surrounding area.

Under cover of night, he swiftly circled the building without a sound until he reached the back door. A tiny diamond-shaped window was inset, and a light glowed from inside. To its right were two huge garage doors, used by the body shop.

Risking a quick peek, he got a glimpse of three men sitting around a small table in the center of the garage. He took note of the building's layout, including every way in or out. And he saw that lining the walls were small boxes marked "Medical Supplies," which he suspected were filled with illegal drugs or weapons or maybe even counterfeit money.

With absolute clarity of purpose, he retrieved several items from the duffel bag slung across his back.

Tools in hand, Nolan went to work.

56

Five minutes later, when Nolan had complete control over the environment, he was ready to move.

The three Mafioso sat around a square card table, inspecting or counting small stacks of cash that Nolan suspected to be counterfeit. Nolan knew it was them, even from his vantage point, suspended near the ceiling atop a tall cabinet. The one with the gash across his head from Nolan's staff had a large gauze pad taped to his forehead. Another wore a small silver brace over his broken nose. The third had a bandage covering one of his ears.

There was no doubt. These were the men who'd escaped justice.

With a silent breath, he held two large black guns—one in each hand—and dropped from his perch. He landed on their table, squashing it with a loud crash and sending the fake money flying.

He rose to his full height as the three men fell backward onto their backs and struggled to get their bearings. But when Nolan commanded them to stop, they froze in place, noticing the two guns he was pointing at them. Nolan watched them carefully for any sign of movement.

When he was sure he had their attention, he stunned them by pulling the triggers on both guns without another word uttered.

Instead of bullets, liquid sprayed out of the two water guns and he took a few seconds to fully drench all three of them. He watched with satisfaction as they realized he hadn't squirted them with water. Their noses were upturned, there were grimaces etched on their faces, and their eyes burned red.

Nolan dropped the two plastic weapons on the ground and pulled out a cigarette lighter, flicking it on.

The men drew perfectly still once again, this time out of sharp fear. They were soaked in gasoline, and Nolan was holding a flame. He toyed with the lighter, playfully passing it back and forth between his fingers and waving it dangerously close to the puddle on the ground where the gasoline that dripped from their hair, skin, and clothes was pooling.

"I drop this," he intoned with a low voice, "and the flames will cover your bodies faster than the human brain is capable of processing the pain from the nerve endings in your skin. Less than one second later, white-hot fire will coat every inch of your bodies. Your hair will be burned away. Your chance of survival with burns so severe is extremely small, and I promise you, gentlemen, should you manage to live through the experience, you'll spend every last second wishing you hadn't."

The three men exchanged nervous glances but didn't dare stir a single inch. They watched as Nolan knelt to address them on eye level, bringing the cigarette lighter's flame that much closer to them.

"The three of you," he went on with what he hoped was an intense, maddening calm, "should consider yourselves in my custody. Since the judicial system failed to bring you to justice, I've made my own arrangements. In two hours, you'll be passengers onboard the freighter *Calcutta* when it casts off from Port Jersey bound for Sierra Leone. Your trip is one way, and if you don't stay put when you get there . . . I'll finish what I started. Understand?"

The smallest of the three men was the first to respond. Rather than using his voice, he nodded nervously.

"Up," Nolan said.

When the mobsters got to their feet and started filing out through the back door by Nolan's command, they stepped across a wide puddle just outside the door. A puddle so wide, in fact, that it stretched around the building and was being fed by a liquid that was dripping from the outside walls. Gasoline.

When they were clear, Nolan knelt on one knee next to the building and touched the gasoline with his lighter. Pulling up beside his prisoners, he said, "Closed for demolition," and led them away.

The small gas station burned for the next four hours, until it and everything inside was completely consumed.

———

Judge Herbert Jacobs' eyes snapped open when he felt a warm hand cover his mouth. His head was slumped toward his bedside table and the clock glowed green. It was 4:19.

A shadowy figure loomed over him in the dark, the silhouette of a pistol pointed straight at him.

"I know Yuri Vasko coerced you into setting bail for his three men this afternoon," said a gruff voice. "Don't waste time denying it. Whatever he offered you in exchange, you're going to return it. You're going to tell him that you'll never do what he asks of you again. From now on, you work solely for the good of the people of New York."

He felt the gun's muzzle bury itself against his left temple. The hand moved from his mouth.

"He'll kill me!" the judge whispered, in a panic. "He'll kill my whole family!"

The shadow shook its head. "It's a matter of public record that you presided over that bail hearing this afternoon. If you turn up dead or missing, Vasko will be the first, most obvious suspect. And that's not the kind of publicity he wants."

The judge considered this. He couldn't keep his twitchy eyes from repeatedly falling on the gun.

"If I still refuse?" he asked. "Will *you* kill me?"

"There are things worse than death," said the voice. "I'm familiar with every one of them."

57

Thornton Hastings felt more hopeless than he had in a long time.

Yuri Vasko's power and holdings were expanding every day. Hastings' Organized Crime Intelligence agency had grown as well, but gained no ground on the front lines of this war—New York City. There had been some minor progress in other branches of the OCI, thanks to agents stationed in New Orleans, Detroit, and Pittsburgh. But in New York, nothing they hurled at Vasko made a dent in his armor.

Two nights ago, his top OCI agents had made a raid on a restaurant owned by Vasko, which they believed housed an armory of weapons far too powerful to be available to the public.

But like so many times before, the intel was proven false. Not only was the raid a waste of time, it nearly caused an international incident. The Czech ambassador to the United Nations was dining there along with half a dozen friends, and he seemed to think that the raid was a political move directed at him. The restaurant was a personal favorite of his, and he made a statement to the media about the "careless and dangerous manner in which the OCI operates."

Today, Marcus Bailey showed up for their morning briefing alone. Director Pryce, he said, was still trying to deal with the Czech government's embarrassment over their ambassador being "harassed in public by the fascist American gestapo."

As if all this wasn't enough, Hastings was dealing with a nasty case of the flu. His body ached all over and longed for rest, but he insisted on working—over his doctor's strong objections.

It was his custom to glance over several news sites first thing in the morning. Marcus was used to this and knew his boss well enough to know that he was capable of multitasking. So he began going over the latest happenings in the war on crime while Hastings' eyes remained glued to the crime blotter of the *New York Gazette*.

Two minutes later Hastings started and involuntarily leapt to his feet.

Reading the reports was a ritual he'd started to remind himself of how bad the problem was in New York. Listing after listing of assault, robbery, and worse filled the pages of the blotter. Today, though, deep in the listings was a small note about an abandoned gas station that had been burned down just last night. The article mentioned that this particular gas station was long suspected to be a secret organized crime facility where counterfeit money was printed. An accelerant was used and the fire department suspected arson.

Only these days, that formula didn't add up. Nobody targeted known mob houses. Everything was Vasko's. And yet here, someone had burned one of the man's buildings to the ground.

It was Nolan. It had to be. He was alive! He was back.

Whatever the reason for his disappearance, it no longer mattered. The Hand was back on the job. Knowing Nolan, he'd probably been trying to get the city's attention for days, maybe even weeks, but it wasn't easy to stand in front of gathered crowds as a symbol of hope when there *were* no crowds.

Hastings actually smiled. Maybe hope hadn't abandoned him just yet.

"Mr. President?"

Hastings had almost forgotten Marcus was in the room with him. Seated across the desk, his chief of staff was staring at him with alarm, watching carefully as the president grinned.

Hastings hesitated, his thoughts spinning fast. His cheeks burned and his muscles felt weak.

"Sir?" Marcus said. "Are you feeling all right?"

He wasn't sure at first if he'd just had a brilliant idea or if the flu meds he was on were messing with his judgment. Either way, he made a radical decision on the spot. There were few people in this world he trusted more than Marcus Bailey. He returned to his seat.

"It's Nolan Gray," said Hastings softly, as if they might be overheard outside the office. "He's not dead. I'm sorry for not telling you sooner. Nolan is The Hand. And I think he's back in the game."

Marcus leaned back in his seat and examined the ceiling with the color draining from his face. "And you know this how?"

"Right now, a hunch. But trust me, it's him."

Marcus closed his eyes and uttered a word under his breath that was most disrespectful to the Oval Office.

Hastings immediately felt guilty. "I didn't know he was alive when we held his funeral, if that's what you're worried about."

Marcus watched his boss carefully, his lips pressed into a thin line. Hastings watched as his chief of staff's decorum was restored in mere seconds. He straightened his tie and let out a very long breath.

"I understand how difficult this secret must have been to keep. And I appreciate your confiding in me, Mr. President," said Marcus. "Rest assured it will not leave this office. If people found out that you eulogized a man who wasn't dead . . ."

Hastings paused, feeling his temperature spike, and cold chills quickly gave way to cold sweats. He hugged himself and rubbed his own arms, trying not to shiver. "No. That's just it, Marcus. That's why I'm telling you this now. I *want* you to leak this."

Marcus's restraint vanished. He looked as if the president had just grown a rhinoceros horn on his forehead. And then just as quickly, his expression relaxed a little. "You think people will rally around him if they know who he really is."

"The Hand is a vigilante," replied Hastings, his decision feeling more and more right with every second that passed. "But Nolan Gray is a national treasure. He was a hero before he was The Hand. The people of New York deserve to know who's out there fighting for them."

Marcus nodded, but then his expression turned somber. "Sir, I'm sure you don't need me to tell you that this is political suicide. Your adversaries on the Hill have been looking for something just like this to undermine your moral authority."

Hastings smiled despite his sadness. "The lives of the people of New York are more important than my political career. If sacrificing my second term will save them . . . so be it. We're losing this war, Marcus. I don't think we can win without The Hand, and Nolan's work is meaningless without popular support."

"He's just one man," Marcus said. "Is it realistic to think that he can succeed where many have failed? How can this one man turn the tide?"

"Nolan's more than a man," Hastings replied, suddenly feeling fatigued. "We need to remind people that this is the land of the free and the home of the brave. It's not owned by thugs and criminals like Yuri Vasko. If anyone can turn things around, it's Nolan."

"Very well, then," Marcus said, rising to his feet. "I'll see to it right away."

"And Marcus, don't let the trail for this lead back to the White House. Make something up. Who was that reporter that was always trying to figure out The Hand's identity?"

"Ellerbee. At the *Gazette*. We could say that . . . I don't know, maybe a backup of her files was found . . . on an anonymous server by a computer hacker."

Hastings nodded. "Yeah, yeah. That's good. Go with that."

Marcus hesitated before exiting the room. "What are you going to do?"

"Nolan is going to know that this came from us. From *me*. In doing this, I'm sending him a message—one I should have sent a lot sooner. I just hope that he understands it."

"What message?"

Hastings looked Marcus in the eye. "I've got his back. Whatever support or assistance he needs . . . he has it."

The New York Gazette

A CITY WITHOUT HOPE

By Lynn Tremaine
Editor-in-Chief

This article is dedicated to the memory of my dear friend Agnes Ellerbe, for whom I still have the utmost respect and admiration.

NEW YORK CITY - Two months have passed to the day since the tragic events at Battery Park, where more than thirty of New York's finest lost their lives, along with twenty-two civilians. Not since the galvanizing attacks of 9/11 has Manhattan fallen prey to such deadly, carefully-plotted violence. Looking back, the days before the Battery Park incident seem somehow rosier and more carefree than the dangerous times that have become our daily reality.

And still we wonder . . . Was it all planned?

Could the person responsible for the devastating events of that day have known that with so many of the city's police officers dead and many others resigning due to pressure from their loved ones, NYPD would be devastated? With the officer count dropped so low, the criminal population rose and turned Manhattan into a powder keg of violence and crime.

One faction that certainly benefitted is the organized crime unit of the federal government. Follow the attack, President Hastings's pet crime unit tripled in size with a matching increase in budget. With re-election looming, the President has doggedly refused to give up on New York City and move the OCI on to other criminal targets, despite increasing pressure from Congress. The political and personal toll this has taken on him is rumored to be causing the President physical ailments.

And where is the city's one-time savior, The Hand? As our readers know, he was last seen toiling away, rescuing survivors following the attack on Battery Park. Since then, he's disappeared completely—and just when New Yorkers need him most. Did he retire? Did he run away? Is he even still alive? And was The Hand's desertion part of some villain's master scheme?

We may never know.

One thing we do know: New York City has only one benefactor that can truly be counted on, and that is Yuri Vasko. He is a changed man. Whatever ties he may or may not have once had to organized crime have surely been severed. Having set up shop in his new, high-profile headquarters in the heart of Manhattan, Vasko's new non-profit organization was his answer to the disgusting, lawless attacks on Battery Park and the NYPD. His humanitarian aid reaches out to the victims of organized crime—including those affected by the Battery Park tragedy—and offers them anything and everything they need in these harsh, difficult times.

▌do not like being summoned," said Usko Kayone, his voice reverberating like the inside of a deep barrel in Vasko's office. He spoke with a heavy West African accent.

An unusually tall man, bald, with skin like polished charcoal, he sat across the desk from Vasko. Hailing from Namibia, he came to Vasko's attention under the highest recommendations. The man exuded an abnormal calm, and his heavy gaze was like staring into the eyes of caged panther.

"I apologize, Mr. Kayone," replied Vasko. "I meant no offense."

"Why am I here?" Kayone asked.

Vasko leaned back in his seat. "I'm looking to bring on some extra security before New Year's Eve."

Kayone's response was immediate and unenthusiastic. "You do not call me or my team because you want *security*. You call me because there is someone you want dead. Someone who will not die easily."

Vasko had to concede the point. "Is that a problem?"

"I would not be here if it was," Kayone replied. "As long as you can afford my fee, there will be no problem between us of any kind."

The office door was flung open and Marko blustered in, his chest heaving in gasps and the late afternoon sun casting his face in a deep shade of red. Vasko was furious that his friend would interrupt an important meeting such as this, and was about to berate him harshly, but the expression on Marko's face brought him up short.

"Yuri, did you hear?" said Marko, rushing to Vasko's side. "Look!" He flung a newspaper down on Vasko's clear acrylic desk.

It was a copy of the *Times* with a headline that dominated the entire top half of the front page with the words "THE HAND REVEALED?" Unfolding the paper, Vasko saw that a large blurry photo of The Hand running down a sidewalk was beside a portrait of equal size. The second image was an Army Special Forces profile photo of Lieutenant Nolan Gray.

"Hm, clever move," Vasko said, unperturbed.

"Wait, what?" asked Marko. "This was strategized? Who did it?"

"President Hastings, I would imagine," Vasko said. "He believes that this could change his fortunes, shift momentum in his favor. He thinks the people will 'see the light'—that light being Nolan Gray—and stand to fight against us."

"You don't seem terribly worried." Marko's own agitation hadn't been quelled one bit.

"This was inevitable. It had to come out sooner or later. Look here—several of our recent losses are being attributed to The Hand. That property in the Lower East Side last week . . . So he *is* back, then. This was a message. He's been trying to get my attention. He's coming for me," he mused.

Marko took a step back. "You expected this. All of it. You planned for it?"

Without a word, Vasko produced a small key and inserted it into the lock on one of his desk drawers. A fat folder was inside, and he handed it to Marko.

"The president wants the people to know who The Hand is," he said. "Fair enough. But let's ensure that they get the whole story."

Vasko watched as Marko opened the file and winced at the contents: detailed descriptions of the tortures and violations that were inflicted upon Nolan Gray during his captivity, along with a great deal of research explaining the damage that that sort of thing does to a person psychologically. He was about to tell Marko which media outlet to send the folder's contents to anonymously when his guest stood to his feet.

Vasko had almost forgotten the tall man was still there. "Forgive me, where are my manners," said Vasko.

The big man jabbed a finger down on the table, touching the newspaper photograph of Nolan Gray. "*This* is the man you would have me kill?"

"Well, yes. Is that a problem?"

Kayone turned his back on Vasko and made for the door. When it was open, he looked back and said, "I will not fight Nolan Gray. I will not kill him. Not *him*."

"I'll double your asking price," said Vasko. "Triple it. Name your fee, and I'll pay it."

His eyes taking in the state-of-the-art crystal palace Vasko had constructed, Kayone replied, "You don't have enough money." He shut the office door behind him.

59

Nolan felt disgusting. He wanted to take a shower. Or three.

He hadn't been in a dirty fight or sweating with the exertion of his task. It was where he was that made him feel revolting.

An unexpectedly brutal winter had fallen over New York the first week in December, bringing record low temperatures and a snowfall that seemed to fall from the sky on a whim and stop just as fast. Always a quick thinker, Arjay fashioned him some detachable cleats for his boots, which made life considerably easier whenever he encountered ice.

Nolan crouched on a rooftop in the Bowery in south Manhattan across the street from his target, watching for a man. Only one person remained inside the establishment across the way—the owner, a man named Nico Vinson. It was after four in the morning and no one in the Bowery seemed to be awake but Nolan and his quarry. Even the streets, which were covered in a couple of inches of snow, were void of activity.

The bright neon sign hanging fifty feet above Vinson's business was still on. Nolan kept waiting for it to go out, the signal that Vinson was preparing to go home at last.

The gaudy pink lights bore a vulgar name, declaring Nico Vinson's business to be the Bowery's one and only strip club. Nolan knew that was just the tip of what the club offered. Women had entered there and never been heard of again, a twisted place that exploited sex and poured money into Yuri Vasko's pockets. Vinson's business was a blight on the city. On Nolan's city.

The ugly neon lights finally went out and Nolan stood, switching over to night vision in the sudden dark. As expected, Nico Vinson came out the front door less than a minute after the sign was extinguished.

He was a short man with a black ponytail and a stocky build most would've found intimidating. When Vinson turned back to lock up for the night, Nolan produced a small transmitter in one hand and a button.

A shiny black Hummer parked a block up the street—with a license plate registered to Nicolas Vinson—exploded. A tiny explosive attached to the vehicle's undercarriage sent the big SUV more than three feet into the air, with bits of metal, glass, and rubber soaring in all directions.

Vinson was thrown on the ground by the blast, and when he spun in place to examine it, he gaped in horror. He recovered quickly though, fishing for the tiny Seecamp pistol Nolan knew the man concealed at all times, for self-defense. But by the time the minuscule silver gun was out in the open, Nolan had already used the grappler to lower himself quickly to the ground and run full-bore into Vinson, ramming him up against the front of his own building.

The pistol flew out of his hand and landed somewhere in the snow. Vinson swore and tossed a wild punch, but Nolan ducked, grabbed the man between the legs, and spun to slam him flat down on his back.

Vinson tried to shout, but Nolan placed a gloved hand over his mouth.

"Shut up!" he said, his voice nothing but a whisper.

Nolan pulled out his staff and without extending it, placed the baton-sized stick against the other man's larynx and pressed.

"Nicolas Carver Vinson. Seven burglaries, four years ago. Nine grand thefts auto, two months after that. Two cases of statutory rape, two years ago. Six counts of murder one, seven months ago."

Based on the bulging eyes staring at him, Nolan knew he had the man's attention now. Still he held one hand over Vinson's mouth and the other clutched around the staff that was mashing into the man's neck.

Still only whispering, Nolan spoke again. "You have one chance to tell me what I want to know. Refuse or fail, and I'll hand-deliver you to prison, right now. Along with all the evidence needed to make sure you stay there until the end of time. Got it?"

With furious eyes, Vinson nonetheless nodded his head in a curt affirmative.

"Vasko's been bringing weapons, drugs, and counterfeit money into the city for weeks. Whole crates of the stuff," Nolan said, moving his face in an inch closer and lowering his voice to an angry snarl. "Where's he storing it all?"

Nolan let up on the man's throat by a fractional amount. But instead of replying, Vinson's eyes searched the sky.

"Don't you even think about lying to me," Nolan seethed.

Vinson made eye contact, and although he was still angry, there was fear in his eyes as well. "He's got a warehouse, okay? On a pier, somewhere on the west side."

That narrowed it down a bit, but Manhattan had more than two dozen piers on its west side. Nolan supposed he would have to check them all.

Nolan didn't thank the man before him. Instead, he knocked Vinson out with a steel fist to the head and carried him across the street, where he secured him to a street lamp. Vinson stirred as Nolan finished tethering him to the lamppost. Groggy, he was still able to curse him in two languages. In reply, Nolan produced his small transmitter again.

"You're scum, Vinson," he said. "You're the scum that feeds off scum. I'm going to rid this city of you and everyone like you. And then, maybe the whole planet."

Vinson was about to come back with a retort when Nolan pressed a different button on the transmitter, and across the street, the entire club was engulfed in a spectacular explosion. It was a carefully controlled blast of C4 designed to destroy the club but do no damage to nearby buildings.

Vinson stared in horror at his former place of business before launching into a list of crude epithets for Nolan, finishing with a promise to kill him.

Nolan dropped to one knee and punched Vinson in the jaw in a sudden vicious blow.

"Tell Vasko The Hand says hi," he said, rising to his feet and firing the grappler into the air. One second later, he released the trigger and zipped away into the night.

60

Running from rooftop to rooftop, Nolan felt better than he had in months. Destroying that strip club had done wonders for him. Places like that shouldn't be allowed to exist. Razing it was good, it was *right*. Jesus himself had destroyed the vendors' stalls at the Temple, because they dishonored that holy site.

There were so many others, so many more "gentlemen's clubs" throughout New York City, and given time, he would gladly take down every single one of them. And why should he stop there? There were restaurants owned and operated by men who reported directly to Vasko. There were a handful of abortion clinics that he knew for a fact were subsidized by funding from Vasko's organization. One of the rumors going around was that the mayor himself was getting kickbacks from Vasko on a regular basis. How else could Vasko have arranged to hold his big Times Square New Year's Eve in a few weeks?

Nolan would tear down Vasko's entire organization and return the city to the people who lived here. He would give them back their home.

But for now, he required rest.

When he turned the key unlocking the RV five minutes later, he was surprised to see that both Arjay and the general were awake at that early hour. He couldn't quite wipe the smile off his face, even though he knew he needed to play it cool around them. He wasn't sure how they might react to all this. They might even accuse him of seeking revenge for Alice's death, or something similar.

Inside, both of his friends were hard at work. Branford was reclining in one of the bunks, his computer on his lap and his eyes glued to the screen. Arjay sat opposite him, tinkering with a gadget Nolan didn't recognize.

When Nolan had removed his heavy winter coat and the specialized black flak jacket he wore underneath, he plopped down in a seat next to Arjay.

"How's it going, guys?" he said, trying not to sound too chipper.

Branford cut his eyes across at Nolan and then sat up straight. He retrieved a fat newspaper and tossed it into Nolan's lap.

Nolan's heart jumped into his throat. The headline of the major papers declared the true identity of The Hand to be a very much still alive Lieutenant Nolan Gray.

Genuinely alarmed, he looked up. "How?" he asked.

Branford was scowling. "Just read."

The article explained that lost files belonging to Agnes Ellerbee of the *Gazette* had been found, and in them, evidence that Nolan was still alive and running around New York playing vigilante. Nolan was immediately suspicious of this, having a pretty good idea who was behind his being outed to the whole world.

He glanced up at his friends a few times while he was reading, but found their hardened but blank expressions impossible to read.

"Did Vasko do this?" asked Branford.

Nolan shook his head. "It's classic Thor. He's forcing my hand while simultaneously insisting that I accept his help."

"And will you?" asked Arjay.

Nolan considered the question. "Not today."

"Keep reading," said Branford.

The article went on to show correlations between The Hand's activities and known skill set, and Nolan Gray's extensive training. It ended with speculation on recent events in New York City that may have been the work of Nolan Gray—including the gas station/counterfeiting facility.

Reading this article, it finally clicked for him. He understood why his friends were being so guarded toward him just now. They knew.

"How long?" asked Arjay when Nolan put down the newspaper. "How long have you been sneaking out while we sleep?"

"It's not like that—"

"It is exactly like that!" Arjay said.

"I've made no secret of my plans to take down Vasko's operation," said Nolan, nodding at the big map on the wall. "You know he has to be put away before anyone in this city will ever feel safe again. And I'll do whatever it takes to see that happen."

"And this plan of yours . . ." said Arjay slowly, "It requires the use of *weapons*?"

"They get the job done," replied Nolan, his words sober, resigned. "And they're a lot cheaper and easier to come by than your specialized gadgetry."

Arjay didn't miss a beat. "That's because they're widely used by apes that don't care who or what they shoot at."

"Ease off, Arjay," said Branford. "Nolan's a soldier, and that's what he does. We all know this stopped being about anything but Vasko the day Alice died. But I need to know," he said, turning to Nolan, "I need to know that this is still happening for the right reasons."

"Yes," echoed Arjay. "Exactly! Thank you!"

"What do you care?" Nolan shot back at the general. "You've always said this was never your crusade. You don't share my beliefs, so why do you care what tactics I use?"

Branford faltered briefly—one of the only times Nolan had witnessed his friend at a loss for words—and Nolan immediately regretted his outburst. "My concern always," said Branford, speaking slowly and deliberately, "from minute one, is for *you.*"

Nolan sighed and found his eyes scanning the floor for nothing.

"The paper insinuates that you're responsible for half a dozen losses on Vasko's part over the last two weeks," Branford continued. "God knows *I* think he's got it coming. If he died tomorrow, I'd lead a parade. But considering . . . your past . . . I worry about where all this could take you. Didn't you start this thing so you could *help* the people of New York?"

"I *am* helping them!" shouted Nolan, unable to stop himself. "The only way New York will ever be safe again is when Yuri Vasko is out of business."

"And that's all you're looking to put an end to?" asked Arjay. "His business?"

"This is a lot bigger than just Vasko," said Branford. " 'If people won't change, I'll *make* them change.' That's what you said."

Nolan tried hard to calm his anger, but it was impossible now. A rage he didn't fully understand built up within him as he looked back and forth between his friends. "If you were so worried about my motives after Alice died, then *why did you stay*?!"

Branford's reply was even and measured. "We were *more* afraid of what you might do if we *weren't* around."

61

Nolan's shoulders sank. Did his friends really think so little of him?

He sighed. *I can't pull off the moral high ground. It's not like they were wrong. . . .*

"*Dispatch?*" squawked a voice on the police band radio. The small machine was nothing special—an over-the-counter device that they used to listen in on police chatter throughout the city. In the old days, there would have been constant radio activity with beat cops and detectives receiving orders from HQ and reporting back on their findings around the clock. These days, the NYPD was so understaffed that most precincts never had anyone on hand to work the radio.

Nolan continued to stare down his friends as the voice on the radio continued.

"*Dispatch, I got a pair of ten-forty-ones over in the Bowery. One vehicle and what looks like a night club. Going in closer to investigate, but I'm going to need a ten-fourteen.*"

Nolan knew what this call was about but said nothing. Branford grabbed a tiny book and thumbed through the pages. "Ten-fourteen is a standard fire engine. Ten-forty-one is a suspicious fire."

Arjay's ears perked up at this, and leveled his gaze on Nolan again. "How suspicious?"

"Suspicious as in probably not an accident," Branford said, closing his book and tossing it on his bunk before staring daggers into Nolan.

"It was a sex club, okay?" Nolan explained. "Those places do nothing but feed the worst—"

"Owned by Vasko, though, right?" asked Branford.

Nolan frowned. "Yeah. It was."

"*Dispatch,*" called out the officer on the radio. "*Dispatch, I think I've got a body inside this night club; moving in for a closer look.*"

Suddenly Nolan heard nothing but the pumping of his own blood like a hammer in his ears. He must've heard wrong. Or the cop was wrong. Vinson was always the last one out before he locked up for the night. There was no way there could have been anyone still in there....

Branford's eyes had grown large while Arjay looked like he was going to pass out. Nolan couldn't blame him, feeling suddenly unsteady himself.

"*That's affirmative on that body, Dispatch,*" said the cop over the radio. "*Female, early twenties, although positive ID is going to be hard. She's burned pretty bad.*"

"What have you done?" whispered Arjay, who plopped down onto the bunk opposite Branford. The young man buried his face in his hands and shook his head over and over and over.

Nolan and the general exchanged a look, and carried an entire conversation within it. Both men were in shock over the girl's death. He knew they were both wondering how Nolan could have made such an error when Nolan *never* made those kinds of mistakes. He knew they were considering the logistics of whatever rudimentary investigation the police would conduct; it wouldn't be much, with their manpower so depleted, and whatever they mustered would never be traceable back to The Hand.

Nolan knew there had been no security cameras that caught him on tape outside the club talking to Nico Vinson before he blew the place to smithereens. And he wondered who this girl had been. Was she a dancer? Was she Vinson's girlfriend? Could she have already been dead before Nolan detonated the building? Did she really and truly qualify as "innocent" if she worked at a strip club? Particularly one owned by Yuri Vasko?

These questions were doing nothing to ease Nolan's conscience. Because of him, a woman had lost her life tonight. And not because of some passive action or inaction on his part. He'd rigged that building himself to explode and then burn to the ground. He *meant* it. There was no part of it that was an accident.

Nolan had killed people before. He was one of the best killers the United States had ever trained. But until today, he'd never killed an innocent.

No. He couldn't go there. It was an accident, and he needed to put it aside. It was the only way he would be able to carry on.

But how could he possibly put *this* aside? Wouldn't that make him a terrible person, if he didn't let himself feel the remorse, the pain, the unbearable guilt?

"Mayday! Mayday! Dispatch?"

Nolan looked up in the direction of their small dining booth, something nagging him about these words. Everything was so blurry right now, every thought obscured by fog. . . . He couldn't quite figure out why this transmission had tickled something in his mind.

Branford and Arjay followed him to the booth without a word. Without making contact of any kind.

Nolan turned up the volume on the radio.

"Mayday! This is OCI Agent Lively, requesting immediate backup!"

Nolan blinked. "Hey, that's her," he said. His words sounded muffled to his ears for some reason, like he was hearing them through a wall of molasses. Blood was still rushing past his eardrums, and he could barely hear anything else.

"Her who?" asked Arjay.

Nolan merely shook his head. There was no time to explain now.

"Repeat," said the voice on the radio, *"this is OCI special task force requesting immediate assistance from any New York City officers of the law who can hear this transmission! We are pinned down inside City Hall! We have suffered heavy casualties and cannot hold this position! Does anyone read me?!"*

Nolan would have answered her, but it was a one-way radio. Instead, he blew past his two friends. "Get out of my way."

He jumped behind the RV's wheel and forced the engine to life.

62

Yuri Vasko stood alone in his office on the top floor of his glass tower, watching the first hints of daybreak on the horizon. Below, a dusting of snow covered Times Square. The streets and sidewalks were just starting to show signs of activity, signs that in an hour's time would give way to cabs, buses, bicycles, and pedestrians, all trying to navigate around one another as they hustled to work.

The world was just waking up, but Vasko had been up all night, right there in his office. He rarely felt the need for sleep anymore. Sleep was a refuge, a safe place to retreat to for rejuvenation. He had no need to retreat, and no one to share his bed with.

Bored, he used his good hand to hit the power button on the small flat-screen TV adorning one corner of his desk. Local morning show host Jackie Turner was on, showing off that dazzling white smile of hers and her incessantly chipper demeanor. He found the woman grating, but paused when she cut away to a square-jawed man who began announcing the morning's top headlines.

Had word gotten out about the OCI's disastrous defeat at City Hall? Well, it wasn't officially a defeat yet, as his soldiers were still engaging what remained of the OCI raiding party at City Hall. But he understood it was all but wrapped up, and even if the OCI were to make a miraculous turnaround at this point, they'd already suffered too many losses for this to ever be considered a victory. Besides, Vasko knew they'd come to City Hall hoping to find evidence revealing Mayor McCord to be in Vasko's pocket.

And Vasko was far too clever to leave evidence like that where anyone could find it.

Tonight had been the crowning achievement of his perfect plan. The same plan that had demoralized Nolan Gray to the point of irrelevancy. He knew now that Nolan was still out there, and that he'd declared war on Vasko's operation. But Vasko alone knew of the pain Nolan carried, the pain that was Vasko's own, which he had shared with this man. So much better than killing him was letting him live in grief, a faded glimmer of his former glory.

Nolan was special that way. Others—crime lords and enforcers— who stood in his way were simply handled. Vasko filled their gullets with concrete and tossed them into the ocean. No lingering torment. He didn't need them to suffer forever, the way The Hand had to. He simply needed them out of his way. And every time he took out a potential opponent, the message went out loud and clear to New York City's underworld: no one crosses Yuri Vasko and lives.

Now the endgame was in sight. With The Hand suffering unbearable pain and his criminal foes defeated, Vasko had only one target left.

The Organized Crime Intelligence.

He imagined President Thornton Hastings and the terrible news he would be receiving sometime this morning, about their risky raid on City Hall. The lives Hastings had lost would go a long way toward advancing Vasko's cause. He needn't kill every single member of the OCI to demoralize them, after all. All he needed was for them to lose their confidence, their sense of purpose.

A haggard-looking man's face filled the TV screen, and he turned up the volume to listen in. It appeared to be a random "man on the street" interview, where the camera focused on the interviewee while the reporter tossed questions at the man from off-camera. The man being interviewed, who showed a few days' worth of gray stubble growth, had sunken eyes and creases on his forehead and around his mouth that made him look older than Vasko believed him to be. The bright lights of the camera, which had shot this video sometime after dark, illuminated every blemish on the man's face, adding to the aging effect.

"How are you and your family surviving?" asked the female reporter from somewhere behind the camera.

The man shook his head, his skin drawn with a gloom and melancholy that seemed to have been permanently carved into his face. "We're not," the man replied. "We can't leave the house. My little girl—we're scared to send her to school. Work is so hard to find, we're scraping by on bread crumbs."

Pools collected under the man's eyes, and he looked away from the camera for a moment to pull himself together.

The interviewer pulled him back with another question. "If there was anything you might hope for, about the future, what would that be?"

The man's response was immediate, and his disposition hardened. "I can't afford to hope. Not anymore. My family couldn't survive disappointment a second time."

Vasko's cell phone vibrated, and he turned the television off. The name Oscar Pavlov was on the phone's display; Pavlov was one of his top operatives, and tonight he was commanding Vasko's men in the fight against the OCI at City Hall.

Pavlov was calling to report their success. Had to be.

"Yes?" Vasko said into the phone.

"Twenty-one of them have fallen, sir," said Pavlov. "The five remaining agents are in my custody. Do you have any use for prisoners?"

Vasko didn't even have to think. "No. No prisoners. And no survivors."

63

The northwest corner of the Potter Building on Park Row provided an unencumbered view over the trees of City Hall Park, which surrounded City Hall itself, straight into the mayor's office. That was where Coral Lively said she and several others were pinned down.

City Hall was a tall white building that looked like it belonged in D.C., with Roman columns beyond the front steps, symmetrical, arch top windows, and a huge cupola at its pinnacle.

What the OCI was doing there Nolan and his two friends found it easy to guess. The mayor was morally bankrupt, and as much a criminal as Yuri Vasko himself. Of course he'd made all the right promises and speeches to get into office three years ago, but it was sometime that first year that rumors started to spread about him taking bribes from the local crime cartels, and eventually those bribes turned into membership.

Nolan's goggles were in a pocket of his tattered jacket. Tonight, he stared down the scope of a Barrett M82 sniper rifle, taking a solid look around the spacious room. The mayor's office had two windows, but the curtains were drawn on the one on the right. The left window, however, provided a decent view of Coral's team. Nolan thought he recognized her burly partner among the five survivors being held at gunpoint, though he couldn't recall the man's name. Coral and her people were kneeling on the floor, stripped of all weaponry, hands laced behind their heads.

A raid on City Hall was unprecedented and reeked of desperation on Hastings' part. The president knew he wasn't just *losing* the war—it was all but *lost*. A successful recovery of evidence from the mayor's office might enable Hastings to depose McCord. That had to count as a victory, even if just a minor one.

In fact, this maneuver might have even been *too* desperate. . . .

Nolan had a terrible thought. What if Hastings had ordered his people to conduct this entire operation as a means of drawing Nolan out, of getting him engaged in the same battlefield as the OCI? Could he have possibly strategized this as a means of getting The Hand to join forces with the White House?

Then again, Coral had mentioned heavy casualties in her SOS, and Hastings was many things, but he would never be so cavalier about sending his people to die. He had too much respect for human life to do something like that.

Nolan's senses instantly became alert, his muscles tightening, as he watched Mayor Lewis McCord stride into his office and smile a wicked grin at the prisoners.

Nolan held out his hand and activated the sound amplifier, while continuing to peer through the rifle's lens.

"What's happening?" asked Arjay.

Tonight, in another break from standard protocol, Branford and Arjay had insisted on accompanying him into the field. Particularly when they saw the M82 that he planned to take along—the close proximity of which was making Arjay antsy. He hadn't stopped moving since they'd emerged from the building's stairs onto the roof.

"McCord just walked in," said Nolan. "He's enjoying the moment. He's mocking them. Wait a minute, wait a minute . . ."

"What?" asked Branford, his gruff voice all business. He knelt next to Nolan at the edge of the roof.

"He just ordered everyone out of the room," explained Nolan, tightening his grip on the rifle. "Vasko's men, McCord's own security. He made them leave."

"Why?" asked Arjay.

Nolan shook his head. "I can't hear what he's saying anymore. . . . He's whispering something in the ear of Coral's partner."

"Who's Coral?"

Nolan grew impatient. "The woman that called for help."

"So you know her," observed Arjay with sudden interest. "On the radio, was she calling for *you*?"

Nolan didn't answer. In truth, the thought *had* occurred to him. It wasn't like the OCI to broadcast on an open channel. They had far more high-tech equipment than that.

"I don't like this," Nolan said, focused on the scene playing out in the office. "General, am I missing something? He's got to be armed, right?"

Nolan backed away from the gun so Branford could slide into place and stare through the scope. "I see no weapon on him."

"Doesn't mean he doesn't have one," replied Nolan, resuming his position behind the scope. "He's in that room alone with the five of them, and he sent everyone else out. No way is he unarmed."

"You really willing to risk that?" asked Branford. "After what happened at that nightclub? What if McCord's trying to help them? Maybe he had a change of heart and he's whispering so his men out in the hall don't hear."

That was wrong. It felt wrong. Nolan knew it without knowing.

His response came without hesitation. "Every second I hesitate, he could pull a gun and shoot them. And they have nothing to defend themselves."

Arjay's hand massaged his forehead, and his feet paced a few strides back and forth. "Are we seriously talking about what I think we are?!" he cried. "This isn't some wartime field op where you're trying to overrun an enemy stronghold! This is *assassination*! Of the mayor of New York!"

"Please," said Nolan. "The whole city knows McCord's dirty. He was part of the mob long before Vasko took over."

"Oh, so he was on your list already, then?" asked Arjay. "You would have executed him eventually?"

"It's not an execution," chided Branford. "It's a tactical measure to save the lives of the people in that room. The rifle is muffled. If

McCord's out of the picture, Nolan may be able to zip down there and get inside that room before Vasko's men realize what happened."

Nolan glanced up at Branford. "Then we're agreed?"

Branford scowled, but nodded.

Both men looked to Arjay.

"Stuff the military speak!" said Arjay, his volume rising. "What of the moral and ethical concerns? That's always been your guiding light as The Hand. Where the cops and soldiers fight for justice, your manifesto has always been *morality*. So tell me. Is it moral to knowingly commit murder?"

Nolan pulled back from the scope to look the younger man in the eye. "Is it immoral to let five people die when I know I can prevent it?"

"And what if you're wrong?"

Nolan never flinched. "I'm not."

Arjay shook his head and threw his hands up. "You don't need my vote. Never have. Do your thing."

"You ready, General?" Nolan asked. He didn't elaborate, because he didn't have to. He knew Branford understood that he was asking the general to take over the sniper rifle after he made the shot, and cover him as he fired the grappler and got inside that office as fast as possible.

"Yeah," replied Branford. "And for what it's worth . . . I still trust you."

Nolan lined up the shot and pulled the trigger.

64

Wind whipped by Nolan's ears as he retracted the grappler and flew toward the mayor's office. The hook was fastened to the big white building's cupola. Making a fast calculation, he let up on the trigger in time to swing down and run across the building's lawn. When he neared the front wall, he squeezed the trigger again and let the retracting line pull him up the side of the building.

With a mighty windup, Nolan flew, fist first, through the glass window. It shattered on impact with a huge clamor, and Nolan swung through, retracted the grappler from the roof, and rolled across the floor, using the momentum to quickly rise to his feet. He hated that the glass had made a noise loud enough to alert Vasko's men, but he didn't have time to do this clean.

McCord's office was a spacious room with endless symbols of American democracy—flags, blue carpeting adorned with stars, chairs with bright red upholstery—and an ancient cherry desk with a burgundy wingback behind it.

The survivors had untied one another, and Coral's partner—Jonah something?—had a Smith and Wesson .45 in his hand already trained on Nolan. The mayor's body lay by the desk, his blazer flipped open revealing a hidden holster.

Nolan knew he'd been right. Mayor McCord had a gun and was about to kill the five OCI agents. Because now Jonah was pointing that same weapon straight at Nolan's head.

The thunder of pounding feet came rushing toward them from the hall. They'd definitely heard the glass shatter.

Nolan looked over Jonah's shoulder at the door that McCord had entered through. "That door locked?" he asked, cutting his eyes across to Coral.

"First thing we did, after . . ." She nodded at McCord's body.

Nolan nodded toward the broken window. Jonah was still pointing the .45 at him. "That's your way out," he said. "There are ledges and handholds. You should be able to climb down."

Coral stepped forward and put her hand on the .45, gently pushing Jonah's arms down. She took the pistol from his hands and let it hang by her side.

The thugs outside started pounding on the thick wooden door.

"Go, I'll deal with them," said Nolan, lowering his voice.

Jonah still stared Nolan down with aggressive dislike. When he spoke, he never broke eye contact. "You heard the man. We're withdrawing."

The big agent never offered any sort of gratitude for Nolan's saving their lives. Nolan didn't care; if *he* was escaping with his tail tucked between his legs, he probably wouldn't be feeling too charitable either.

One by one, the OCI agents quickly filed out of the window. The pounding on the office door became much louder. Nolan decided they were either beating it with something large, like a fire extinguisher, or they were trying to kick it down.

When only Coral and Jonah remained, Jonah motioned for her to go first.

"Go on, I'll be right behind you," said Coral.

Jonah turned to eye Nolan warily one last time before looking back at Coral. "You better be," he said, and then leapt through the window.

Once he was gone, Coral turned back to face the door and stood at Nolan's side. She popped the magazine out of the .45 to check how many rounds it had.

"What are you doing?" Nolan hissed. "Get out of here!"

"Yeah, okay," she said absently, not budging an inch. Beside Nolan, she watched as the door started to splinter and break.

When the door was breached with its first tiny hole in the wood, a soft whoosh passed their ears. Branford had just pulled the sniper rifle's trigger for the first time, and from the sound of it, the bullet had met its target.

But this merely enraged the men outside the door all the more, and apparently they teamed up to kick the door in once and for all.

Branford worked hard to pick off as many as he could, while Nolan stepped forward with his staff to take care of the rest. Coral emptied her gun into Vasko's beefy suit-and-tie-clad soldiers. The door made for an effective bottleneck, and after twenty or so had poured into the room, their bodies started to pile up in front of the door, making further entry impossible.

"That's it, let's go," said Nolan. He turned and made for the exit, with Coral at his side. She tossed the empty .45 on the floor and climbed out the window, with Nolan trailing close.

Once Nolan was out, he fired the grappler at the roof. Grabbing Coral with one arm and holding tight to the grappler with the other, he lowered the two of them quickly to the ground.

"That was an impressive kill shot," Coral noted as they started to run. They steered toward Park Row and the safety they might find beyond the park's trees.

She was talking about his sniper shot at Mayor McCord.

"You think I crossed a line?" he asked, and was surprised to find that he wanted to hear her answer.

"McCord stopped being the mayor years ago. He was a thug on a power trip, and he more than had it coming. Would've done him myself if I could've."

Nolan made no response. He didn't know what to say, though he was glad to know at least one person who wasn't judging him tonight.

"Vasko's declared war on us," said Coral, huffing hard as they rounded the corner onto the sidewalk outside the park. "On the OCI, even on the president. Vasko will be livid over this. It's not just you he hates, you know."

"It's me he's obsessed with," replied Nolan. "All the same, you might want to think about a safer line of work."

"You should consider laying low awhile yourself. Things will get a lot worse now."

She was right about that much, Nolan had to agree.

"Or contact the president," she suggested. "He seems to genuinely want to help you."

Nolan ignored this. He had no use for a politician like Hastings, old friend or not.

They crossed the street and Nolan started running toward his waiting friends at the Potter Building, but Coral abruptly stopped and grabbed him by the arm. He slowed only reluctantly.

"You really are Nolan Gray, aren't you." For a fleeting instant, her eyes danced, awestruck. She wasn't quite smiling, but nearly.

"You should go," he replied, nodding to her fellow agents, who had gathered on a street corner a few blocks away. "Take care of yourself, Agent Lively."

65

Days turned to weeks, and Vasko canceled all public appearances. He continued working in his glass building, putting on a good show for the people of New York who looked up at his office from the streets below, in search of hope. But he kept to himself and spent most of his time trying to predict Nolan Gray's next move.

He'd greatly enjoyed toying with this man that killed his family, but now that the world knew Nolan was alive, and now that Nolan had made it clear he was attempting to systematically take down Vasko's operation, Vasko found the game a lot less enjoyable. Nolan was no longer playing by the old rules, and therefore Vasko found it much harder to predict his actions.

As much as he wanted to look into Nolan's eyes as he wrapped his fingers around Nolan's throat and squeezed the life from him, he had begun to wonder of late if his actions had awakened a predator. Vasko had been so cavalier about threatening Nolan, playing with him, even outmaneuvering him. But with every stronghold of Vasko's that Nolan took down, Vasko became increasingly withdrawn and unwilling to see or talk to anyone. He puttered about in his office, often sleeping at night on a couch in the office—what little time he was able to sleep.

Vasko made an exception to his seclusion on Christmas Eve, scheduling a meeting in his office with a new group of mercenaries. He'd personally conducted hours and hours of research, interviewing the toughest, meanest, most skilled, and most ruthless guns for hire that money could buy. New Year's Eve was just days away, and he was committed to overseeing the festivities himself—even pulling the overly elaborate lever that would trigger the ball drop at midnight.

It was late in the evening on Christmas Eve when a group of five hardened mercenaries walked into his office and seated themselves without offering salutations or waiting for an invitation to sit. If you wanted someone dead, there was no one better at the job. Hardcore mercs who never let things like morals or conscience get in their way.

Their leader was a man who called himself Speck. That was all, just Speck.

Vasko rarely felt frightened or intimidated by anyone anymore, but this Speck character gave him pause. At five foot nine, he had arms the size of baked hams, both of which were covered in scars and tattoos up to his neck. This was easy to see because he wore a black muscle shirt that bore an obscene phrase about his extracurricular hobbies. He wore black pants and black leather boots that laced up almost to his knees. Speck had multiple piercings in his ears, nose, and eyebrows, and a skull tattooed on his forehead. Atop his head, his black hair was displayed in a severe crew cut.

His four friends dressed and appeared similar to their leader, though each showed off some unique properties. One had hair dyed an odd color of green, while another had two tiny horns implanted under the skin of his forehead.

"I understand that you served with the marines during the war," Vasko said, his opening greeting, since none of his guests offered to shake his hand or even volunteered their names. "And that you were dishonorably discharged. Mind if I ask why?"

When Speck talked, his voice rumbled impossibly low, like a tape recording that had been slowed down. "They said I enjoyed it too much."

As he spoke, two of his friends who were sitting on the same couch that Vasko used for sleeping suddenly whipped out nine-inch knives and began having an impromptu knife fight. Their blades clashed with such ferocity that it made a terrible racket and even threw off a spark once.

"You enjoyed being a marine too much?" asked Vasko, distracted by the two men on the couch.

"The war," said Speck. "I dug the war."

Vasko hesitated. "I see. And your friends? Did they feel similarly?"

Speck shook his head. "Not all of 'em fought in the war. But they've seen plenty of action with me."

"What kind of action would that be?" he asked, deciding it would be best to abandon chitchat.

Speck raised his head for the first time and looked Vasko in the eye, as if seeing a slow, naïve child. "We kill things. We fight dirty. And we don't care about your reasons."

Vasko almost asked what kinds of things they killed, but decided to steer the conversation back on track. "And you're willing to kill anyone? No matter the situation, or the target's identity?"

Speck looked bored, ignoring his two friends with their clanging knives, while Vasko found it almost impossible to think while they were sparring. "Rumor has it you're looking to take out Nolan Gray. We've killed plenty of people before—people, predators, vehicles, entire buildings—but we've never gone up against someone with Gray's training. That's the one reason we're here. Been a while since we had a challenging target."

Vasko cocked a single eyebrow, thinking. "The rumors are true," he confided. "So here's the million-dollar question. What makes you think you can take Nolan Gray down, when so many others have failed?"

Speck turned to look at his two knife-wielding friends. "Throw 'em!" he said.

As one, both men reared back with their knives and flung them fast through the air toward Speck, who put out both hands and caught the razor-sharp blades. Following through, he twirled them and threw them up over his head. Vasko watched in shock as Speck produced a small handgun he didn't even know the man had been carrying, and fired two shots wildly into the air. He caught the knives as they came back down, one in each hand, and handed them to Vasko.

Both of the blades had round bullet holes through them near their tips.

"Anything else you wanna ask me, Mr. Vasko?"

Vasko placed the two knives down on his desk and stared at them for a moment. Finally he lifted his face to look at his visitors.

"You're hired," he said.

66

I have good news," said Nolan, midday on the day after Christmas.

"I have bad news," replied Arjay.

Nolan had just arrived back at the RV after a busy morning, stomping his boots against the metal steps and rubbing his arms. A bitterly cold Christmas Day came and went without any major skirmishes throughout the city, and a handful of residents were taking this as a sign that it could be safe to venture out for traditional post-holiday activities like returning unwanted gifts.

So in addition to reconnaissance amid a heavy snow that refused to let up, Nolan had actually gotten to spend a little time helping innocent upstanding citizens. He'd almost forgotten what that was like. In both cases—an elderly gentleman who suffered a heart attack in a department store and needed emergency medical attention, and a little girl Nolan found playing in the snow two blocks away after she disappeared from her frantic parents' sight—the people he encountered called him by his real name. Nolan found that that felt surprisingly gratifying.

Branford glanced back and forth between both men and finally crossed his arms over his chest. He nodded at Arjay. "You go."

"We're broke," announced Arjay. "Completely, in absolute totality. As in, 'I don't know where our next meal will come from' poor."

"All right," grumbled Branford, turning to Nolan. "And you?"

"I found it," he replied.

Branford sat up straight. "Are you sure?"

"Saw it myself."

Even Arjay's eyebrows were up with excitement. For weeks, Nolan had been searching the city piers in his free time for Vasko's legendary storehouse. As the search went on, reports reached them from The Hand's website, from random conversations in public places, and from police band chatter, of just how much was stored in this vast facility—and with every report, their estimates grew. Reportedly, there were incredible caches of weapons, thousands of kilos of illegal drugs, billions in counterfeit money, and much more, all stored in this one central location. It wouldn't be Vasko's only stockpile, of course, but as his biggest and most important, his organization could become crippled without it.

The three men had agreed over a week ago that if and when they located this massive storehouse, they wouldn't bother reporting it to the police; instead, they would destroy it. While it was full of overwhelming amounts of incriminating evidence against Yuri Vasko, there were two problems. First, Vasko would have any and all paperwork connected to the storehouse assigned to one or more front companies with no official ties to his organization. And second, until Vasko was ousted and the rule of law was restored in New York, the chances of his even being so much as arrested—much less tried in a fair courtroom—were slim to none. He simply held too much power; he'd already proven time and again that he had ascended far above the law.

Another thing they'd gleaned via various sources was a fact that Nolan found deeply heartening. It came as quite a surprise to realize that most of the city's population knew the truth about Yuri Vasko. Even though he put up a great public front, and actually followed through on his promise of dispensing aid to anyone in desperate need via that glass monstrosity of his in Times Square . . . he wasn't fooling anyone. Too many had lost loved ones or lost their livelihoods to Vasko's regime, and as much as people wanted him gone, the incalculable control he wielded over New York forced her citizens into playing along with his charade. But that's all it was.

"When do we go?" asked Branford, anxious to get underway.

"A few days. We'll need to plan, and get our hands on some quality explosives. But I haven't told you everything. It gets better. This morning, I was . . . *talking* to one of Vasko's men, and he told me that somewhere in this storehouse, his boss has a secret vault that's *loaded* with cash. And I mean real cash, not the forged stuff."

"How much?" asked a suddenly excited Branford.

"Millions."

Branford closed his eyes and let out a sigh of relief. Then he smiled for the first time in weeks.

"Why is this good news?" asked Arjay.

Branford looked at him, incredulous. "Weren't you just whining about our finances a minute ago?"

Arjay looked like all the air had been squeezed from his lungs. "You cannot be serious. . . ."

Nolan sighed. "Why not? How else are we supposed to fund our cause? The people have nothing to donate, and it's not like we can take out a loan at a bank. Vasko owns all of them. This is the only way."

Branford nodded emphatically. "Absolutely. Desperate times . . ."

Arjay took a very deep breath and tried to maintain his calm, but it was a visible struggle. "First of all, why must I always be the one to point out the uncrossable line while we're happily trudging over it? And second . . . 'Why not?' Because it's *wrong*! Regardless of the situation! Some rules are never meant to be broken. Nolan, you're a Christian—or at least you *claim* to be! Stealing is addressed in one of the Ten Commandments, is it not?"

"I'm not saying I'm in love with this idea. . . ."

"*Sure* you're not," Arjay said.

Nolan swallowed his pride and didn't allow himself to ask what that was supposed to mean. He already knew, just as he knew of the war raging within Arjay's strict conscience. There was so much that Arjay wanted to say—stuff about compromise and the dangerous path it leads to, or observations about just how badly Nolan wanted to do *anything* that might hurt Vasko, even if only a little. Even if it was as petty as taking money out of his vault. But Arjay had said it all before, and his logical nature saw the futility in perpetuating the argument.

And whatever mutual concern Arjay and the general had shared when they agreed to stay on after Alice died had diminished somewhere along the way.

"Our options are limited," said Nolan. "What matters above all other concerns is that we're able to keep fighting until the battle is won."

"It's not the *only* thing that matters," mumbled Arjay. "We are talking about *blood money*. Countless people have died to grant Vasko his fortune."

"Then we're going to make it count for something better than Vasko and his sins," said Nolan.

Arjay stared them both down with eyebrows bunched and furious eyes.

Branford turned his heavy gaze on him. "Anytime you wanna leave . . . Door's right there."

"I've come this far, haven't I?" replied Arjay, sending an offended look toward the general. "I'm here until the bitter end. I just hope that's not a prophetic statement."

67

Inside a gargantuan pitch-black warehouse that occupied a pier in Chelsea, Nolan flipped a switch on one wall, and the ceiling blazed with light. He'd seen warehouses this big before, but what it contained was staggering.

Large metal containers were stacked from the floor nearly to the ceiling in the center of the warehouse. Nolan cracked one of these open and watched as submachine guns spilled out across the cold concrete floor. At the far end of the warehouse sat pallet after pallet of rubber-banded, stacked, and sealed-in-plastic-wrap piles of counterfeit money.

Closest to the three men from where they'd entered the building were thousands and thousands of small cardboard boxes, no bigger than shoe boxes. Each one was packed with vials or baggies full of cocaine, heroin, crystal meth, and other devastating drugs.

Everything there, as far as the eye could see, belonged to Yuri Vasko.

"It's like evil's own Fort Knox," whispered Arjay. "It arrests the very air from my throat."

Nolan couldn't agree more. Just standing inside that place felt wrong. Not because they were trespassing; because of the unbelievable quantities of illegal materials it housed.

"Why are you whispering?" teased Branford. "We're the only ones here."

"Was there no security system to protect all this?" Arjay asked, turning to Nolan.

Nolan shook his head. "Just a dozen or so thugs patrolling the perimeter."

Arjay turned to face him, trying but failing to hide his alarm. "Did you kill them?"

"No!" replied Nolan. "How could you—? I locked them up in this little garage out back. Look, I know I killed the mayor, and that's a big deal. But it was a special situation! And yes, we're about to steal money, but don't expect me to feel bad about that, considering who we're taking it from. Regardless, I'm not going to just *kill* people!"

"I'm sorry for the accusation." Arjay let out a long sigh and looked away. "Yet it is a troubling notion that taking lives could become an end to itself. Vasko destroyed our home. He killed Alice. It is perfectly natural to long for revenge."

"You've got to be kidding me," said Nolan, biting each word out of the air.

"We're all fighting the urge to get even, Nolan." Branford shrugged. "Frankly, I wouldn't blame you for taking out a little righteous justice on Vasko and his goons. But I know you, and that's not your way."

"I am not out for revenge," Nolan said, his voice louder than usual but not quite shouting. "We all agreed after Battery Park: Vasko has to be stopped. At any cost. We can't take him down until we remove his infrastructure and resources, or someone else will just pick up where he left off. He's going to burn the whole city down if someone doesn't stop him. And since the OCI's clearly not up to the challenge, it falls to me."

The three of them grew silent. Did his two friends really think he hadn't put any thought into this? Did they really believe that he was capable of blindly seeking revenge? Had they learned nothing from their time with him? He lived by higher ideals. He led by example. He showed people how to live a better life. He was a soldier, not an avenging crusader.

But he was of course human. The events of that dark day—including losing Alice—had changed him, every bit as much as his captivity had so many years ago. It didn't matter, though. He did not have the luxury of giving in to petty desires like payback. Especially now that everyone knew who was under The Hand's hood.

Branford looked again at the enormous room and its seemingly infinite contents. "Where do we start?"

Nolan gazed about. "Let's split—"

"No, no," said a new voice, calling out from somewhere in the warehouse. "It would make things so much simpler if you stayed together."

All three men spun, but saw no one. Nolan's body was coiled, his hand already on his retractable staff.

He knew that voice.

"Run!" he hissed, and leapt into motion.

Branford and Arjay were hot on his heels as Vasko's booming voice was heard again.

"I'm afraid there's nowhere to go, Nolan," he said. His words were being amplified somehow and echoed through the warehouse. "Forty of my best men wait outside, surrounding this place. But here, with me, I have some special guests I'm just *dying* for you to meet."

Nolan crouched behind a large pallet of gun boxes and his friends pulled up behind him. He switched to heat vision and scanned his surroundings. Vasko hadn't been bluffing; he saw a clear line of men circling the entire perimeter of the warehouse. Inside, he spotted Vasko's heat signature about two hundred yards away, on the south end of the warehouse. He wasn't alone; five men stood nearby, and Nolan could tell from their postures that they were professional killers, probably former military.

This was bad. Nolan might be able to escape these kinds of odds on his own, but not unscathed, and only if he'd come alone. His friends would be lambs to the slaughter.

"What do we do?" asked Arjay, who was breathing faster than Nolan had ever seen him.

Branford kicked open one of the gun boxes and pulled out a Remington 1100 TAC 4 semiautomatic shotgun. He grinned as he picked it up, running a firm hand over its long black barrel. "Been a long time since I've seen one of these." He retrieved a box of shells as well, and began loading the shotgun.

Nolan needed to buy some time. He had to keep Vasko talking.

"How did you know?" he called out, referring to his own attempt to destroy the storehouse tonight. An attempt that had quite spectacularly failed. "Is there really a secret vault?"

"I'd never have let you find out about it if there was," replied Vasko's magnified voice. "I've been waiting for you to try this for weeks. What took you so long? My man fed you the address days ago."

Everything felt wrong. Nolan realized that it was Vasko who was trying to keep *him* talking.

Nolan switched to X-ray and saw the skeletons of Vasko's five "guests" on the move. Their movements were smooth and fast, cat-like yet completely silent. One was in the lead, pointing with a single hand down various aisles that he wanted his men to search, while he himself seemed to be on a straight course to intercept Nolan. Whoever this guy was, he knew what he was doing.

"Get ready to move," Nolan whispered to his friends.

The odds were stacked against them, but Nolan Gray refused to lose to Yuri Vasko twice.

68

Nolan made instantaneous calculations, only barely aware of his friends and their rising anxiety levels. Arjay trembled, glancing around with a twitch, like a bird in a tree. Branford clutched his Remington with both hands like it was an old flame.

"What are we going to do?" Arjay whispered.

"Come on, Nolan," said Vasko. "Let's get on with it. I have an empire to run."

"Well, gentlemen," whispered Nolan, pulling out the grappler. "I think we're finally going to find out just how much weight this thing will hold."

He switched to X-ray again while whispering some instructions to his friends, and saw that the leader of the five-man group was almost upon them. He only needed to round the corner at the end of the aisle.

Nolan took aim at the ceiling with the grappler and fired. Retracting it only a little but holding on tight, he ran down the aisle toward the oncoming attacker and met him there just as he turned the corner, Nolan's feet ramming into his chest. The man—a bodybuilder covered in tattoos—was flung backward, but he tucked in his feet and rolled back to a standing position. Nolan followed through, rising up into the air and swinging across the warehouse, but the man he'd slammed into emptied a Jericho 9mm pistol into Nolan's armor-woven fatigues. Nolan heard the fast clicks of the Jericho being reloaded with a fresh magazine.

But Nolan had too much momentum, and with the grappler fully retracting, he swung high up toward the ceiling, right over Vasko's head.

"Shoot him!" screamed Vasko, his voice echoing throughout the warehouse. His five men fired from their various positions, their bullets causing a tremendous noise as they bounced off the metal roof.

Nolan didn't let himself reach the ceiling. Instead, firing and retracting the grappler over and over, he zipped through the vast room, staying one step ahead of the goons.

At last, Nolan retracted out of sight in a far corner, where there was too little light to be seen from ground level. He squared his shoulders and took a deep steadying breath. He would have only one shot at this. . . .

"Why have you stopped shooting?" Vasko thundered. "*Kill him! Now!*"

Seeing that his friends had come out of hiding and placed themselves in the spot he'd whispered to them about just seconds ago, Nolan kicked off from the wall and swung as fast as he could back across the room.

Arjay and Branford locked hands.

As the gunfire opened up again, Nolan swung directly toward his friends and grabbed them with his free hand. Together, the three men continued the motion, flying straight at the nearest exit.

The two extra men were heavy, and Nolan felt the strain on both his muscles and the grappler as they swung low, near the floor. But they were almost there. . . .

Something blindsided them hard from atop the crates nearby, and the three men rolled involuntarily as they crashed to the ground. Nolan was on his feet first, seeing that the man with the Jericho handgun was only inches away. He also held a twelve-inch knife, and Nolan saw that the grappler, lying useless on the ground, had had its line severed.

Branford staggered to his feet, searching for the shotgun that had flown free from his hands, as the other four men rushed toward them both. Nolan noted that they were all tattooed, pierced, and bulging with rippling muscles, just like their leader, who stood pointing his pistol at Nolan's chest. Nolan never hesitated; he spun and grabbed the gun, forcing it to one side just as it went off, missing him by a hairsbreadth. He brought a second hand in to jam it against the other man's arm, hoping to force him to turn loose of the gun, but the move was anticipated and countered with a second hand of his own. Nolan got an elbow across the face, spinning him hard down to his knees.

As Nolan shook off the powerful blow, his eyes focused on something about twenty yards away. It was the exit, the one they'd been aiming for before being cut down. And hiding in the shadows near the door was Arjay.

Nolan and his friend locked eyes for a brief moment, and Nolan could see how much fear was written across Arjay's young face. The unspoken question was there as Arjay glanced at the double doors leading out into the night. Nolan couldn't fault him for wanting to flee; he had no training for combat and would be a very easy kill for any of Vasko's men. His only chance was to run.

Discreetly, Nolan nodded. His hope was that in the commotion, Arjay would be able to duck through the doors and slip out into the night unnoticed. He would have to fend for himself against Vasko's men standing guard around the perimeter, but he stood a better chance out there than if he stayed inside with these punk-rock guerrillas.

Nolan wanted to fight, to turn the tables on these five goons as they rushed in to surround him and the general, but the little resistance he offered was purely to keep their attention off of Arjay.

He took comfort in knowing that at least one of them had escaped with his life this night.

The man with the Jericho pistol, the one who'd cut them down from the grappler, stepped forward while another approached Nolan from behind and tugged on his hood until it fell down to his shoulders.

The leader inspected Nolan's brutally scarred face with fascination. "Sloppy work" was his only comment, muttered under his breath. Nolan felt like his scars had just been appraised by an expert on the subject.

Vasko soon joined them, out of breath. He was pleased to see Nolan and Branford surrounded, their hands in the air. He watched as the mercenary leader leaned in and removed Nolan's gear, including his retractable staff, gloves, glasses, and glass-cutting knife. Nolan refused to give them the satisfaction of seeing him flinch while his precious tools were ripped from his possession.

Something cracked against the back of his head, and he was unconscious.

69

The putrid odor of smelling salts snapped Nolan from the void and he awoke violently, jerking away from the smell as hard as he could.

He had no idea how much time had passed, and had no way of telling because he was blindfolded with what felt like duct tape. A gag of cloth knotted and filled his mouth.

He was wrestled into a kneeling position, his hands tied behind his back so tightly that they'd gone numb. Some sadistic member of Vasko's crew had probably enjoyed watching them turn blue. Another rope went around his shoulders, pinning his arms to his body.

What was Vasko playing at? He could have killed Nolan while he was unconscious, so why didn't he?

Was Branford still alive, or was he similarly trussed up somewhere nearby?

Nolan tried to make a sound, to at least offer some kind of grunting indication to his friend that he was still alive. But his mouth was so full of cloth that his voice was muffled too much to be audible.

Only smell and hearing remained of his senses, and the wet rot of the river confirmed they were likely still at the docks. His hearing was filled with a loud grinding or rumbling noise, like the ignition of a race car. But he didn't feel like he was in motion. He was kneeling, and he could feel new ropes being applied liberally around his boots.

Vasko must have noticed his movements, because his duct-tape blindfold was suddenly ripped off.

Nolan blinked and looked into a bright light just overhead. It was one of the tall lamps on the edge of the pier. They hadn't gone anywhere at all—they were just outside the warehouse, but back near the road.

"I want you to see something," said Vasko. "Yes, you *will* die, quite horribly, in just minutes. I have something special in mind. But before I take your life from you just as you took everything from me, before I defeat you completely, there's one last thing I want you to see with your own eyes."

Vasko waved a hand for something to be brought to him. Nolan swallowed heavily and shivered from the biting cold as Branford was roughly pushed and pulled by Vasko's mercenaries into position about ten feet away.

Branford's face was bruised purple, with trails of blood running down both corners of his mouth, and bloody scrapes all over. His eyes were almost swollen shut. The man limped as well, barely able to stand with the help of the mercenaries holding him up.

"Before you die," said Vasko, "you're going to watch as someone you care deeply about dies right in front of you. And you are powerless to stop it."

As if to punctuate Vasko's words, whoever was tying him up produced more rope and made another tight knot just above his knees. Another rope was then pulled through the one holding his feet together and cinched through the rope around his hands, and pulled Nolan's heels until they touched his hands. He was completely immobilized, and being no longer able to kneel, he fell over onto the pier's old wooden planks.

This new ground-level perspective showed him the source of the rumbling noise he'd heard earlier. A large truck of some kind had been backed up behind Vasko and Branford, and its engine was still running.

"Don't look away now, Nolan," said Vasko. "This is the best part."

Vasko nodded to his mercs, and Branford was forced down onto his knees. With two of the muscular men holding him in place by gripping his arms on either side, the old man looked straight into Nolan's eyes. Nolan was terrified of what the general must've seen in Nolan's face; he knew he couldn't hide the pain and horror and anger that were in his heart. The fear Nolan saw in the general's eyes only heightened his own dread—he'd never seen Branford scared of anything.

The truck grew louder as some kind of tube was lowered from the back, and Branford was tipped backward so that his head was directly beneath it. The cold, white horror of understanding dawned on Nolan at last as thick, wet cement rolled down the tube toward Branford's face.

Branford fought with all his might, but Vasko brought in more men to hold him fast—while insisting that no one block Nolan's line of sight—and Vasko himself reached in to pinch Branford's nose, forcing him to open his mouth. Once that was accomplished, the cement poured down faster, much of it running down the sides of the old man's face and neck.

The general tried not to swallow, tried to spit and pull away from the cement's flow, but he was outnumbered and overpowered. The stuff soon went down his gullet, and in seconds his fight was over.

Nolan was forced to watch through eyes blurred by tears, waiting for several minutes while the cement continued to pour. As what felt like an eternity passed, the cement was allowed to begin to set.

Vasko gave the final nod. Branford's body required four of the burly men to lift, but they managed. And Nolan watched as his oldest friend was dumped over the pier's edge into the East River.

Vasko reappeared and knelt beside Nolan, examining his face. But Nolan refused to look at him.

"There," said Vasko softly. "Now you hate me. You want to kill me. Which makes us the same. The only difference between us is that I've beaten you."

Something large was dropped onto the ground behind Nolan, but he didn't bother straining to see what it was. He couldn't move an inch, and felt like he never wanted to do anything ever again. Whatever terrible death awaited him, he was ready for it. He was done. He didn't want to be in this world anymore.

"I read your debriefing from the war," said Vasko. "The classified one, not the sanitized file that's on public record. And I understand that you walked away from your experiences with an acute fear of small spaces. So when I was dreaming up ways to kill you—and I have spent many, many days doing nothing but that—exploiting that phobia rose to the top of my list."

A number of hands squeezed in beneath him and lifted him up. He was carried in his painful, awkward position and laid sideways inside what he recognized as one of the storehouse's green metal gun boxes. Secured as he was, he just fit within the box, which had been emptied out.

Vasko stood over him with a roll of duct tape in his good hand. He tore off a piece with his teeth and covered Nolan's eyes again.

"It wasn't enough for me to defeat you, you understand," said Vasko. "I needed you to feel what I felt when you took my family from me. My worst nightmare come true. And now, I'm making yours come true as well. My men are going to weld shut the lid of this box and then throw it in the river. A few tiny holes have been drilled in the box's sides so the water can enter. But it will happen slowly.

"Or with the river's water just above freezing, hypothermia could set in before you drown. Either way, I want you to feel every moment of what's about to happen, Nolan. Absorb it. Take it in. Your greatest fear is about to kill you."

Nolan heard the large green metal lid drop down onto the box. His heart rate immediately went into overdrive. Even though he couldn't see the lid being placed on top and all of the remaining light being shut out, he felt it. On the front, back, top, bottom, and both sides, he was touching the walls of this metal coffin. The walls that would never move, never open again.

Then he heard the hissing sound of a blowtorch, and he squirmed against his bonds as the lid was welded shut.

When the deed was done, he felt the box lifted unsteadily and carried to the edge of the pier.

He heard Vasko's faint voice one last time.

"I win," he said.

And the box was dropped into the river.

70

This isn't happening this isn't happening this isn't happening. . . .

Nolan fought against his ropes with every ounce of strength he had. He didn't want to die after all, especially like this. His memories of the war surged to mind as fresh as the day they began. That wretched solitary confinement chamber he was in and out of for two long years had nearly stolen his sanity from him, but if it was possible, this was worse.

God help me God help me God help me God help me!

Yuri Vasko was more wicked and twisted than Nolan had ever given him credit for, to have thought up this terrorizing demise. Not to mention what he'd done to the general . . .

Branford! Dead!

Nolan pulled and tugged at the ropes, but they were tight. The panic washed over him along with the first icy trickles of the Atlantic Ocean. Against all odds, Nolan's metal casket was somehow buoyant enough to float, but the water was coming in steadily. Very, very slowly, but steadily.

He wondered how long he had left. Minutes? Surely it wouldn't take more than an hour. Vasko wanted to prolong his suffering, that was obvious. Would he seriously let it go on for that long? What if someone spotted the floating green metal box in the river? Were Vasko and his people still on the pier, watching, or had they left? Or had Nolan floated downstream far enough that he was beyond their sight?

Can't breathe can't breathe can't breathe . . .

The water hadn't reached his face yet. He was trapped in this small space, and it required every amount of self-discipline he possessed, and every bit of training that had been hammered into him, not to hyperventilate. It felt like there was no breathable air in this little box, just him and the walls. That wouldn't do—he needed air!

Perhaps the fear wouldn't be so absolute if he wasn't blindfolded. He might even be able to peek through one of the air holes to get some idea of where he was in the river and how much longer it would be until . . .

I don't want to die! I don't! I'm not ready!

And yet he was so very tired. Somewhere, in the depths he'd never acknowledged, a part of him wanted to give in to the panic, to let it take control and drag him down into total blackout.

He didn't want to drown. He knew exactly what happened to the body, clinically speaking, when water replaced oxygen in the lungs. He knew what parts of the body shut down, in what order, and he knew that the sensations would be unbearable.

It was too much, this was too much to bear. Unquestionably alone, utterly helpless, and trapped in a space the size of a barrel. This brought to mind an image of a 1920s daredevil in a barrel going over Niagara Falls. As nonsensical as such a ridiculous thought was, it calmed him, if only for a fraction of a second.

That's good, that's good. . . . Distract yourself. . . . Calm is better than panic. . . .

He wondered idly if Coral Lively might still be shadowing his moves. For the first time, that sounded like a very appealing thing. She would know where he was, and maybe even be able to get help, fish him out, save him at the last second.

The water splashed up around his face, and he could withstand it no longer. Nolan Gray, supposedly the world's finest soldier, had reached his absolute limit.

He said good-bye to the world as he blacked out.

———

Light. It penetrated his eyelids, bright and soothing and warm. Its heat enveloped him.

Nolan slowly forced his eyes open. The light was blinding, and he knew that he was in heaven, in the awesome presence of God. He closed his eyes again, relishing the healing love of God's beautiful light of Creation.

"Ilsa! I think he's waking up!" called out a voice.

Who was Ilsa? Was that his guardian angel's name? Was he about to be formally welcomed as he walked through the pearly gates?

"Come on, son," said the voice, "open your eyes! You're going to be all right."

Nolan complied, and this time his eyes had adjusted to the daylight. He blinked hard, looking around the room. This wasn't heaven at all; this was someone's home.

He sat up sharply, but two leathery wrinkled hands on his shoulders pushed him back down onto the pillow.

"What—? Where—?" he tried to say, but his throat was severely parched and only raspy whispers emerged from his mouth.

A gray-haired gentleman in a cardigan sweater was at his side, tucking his bed sheets back in. "Take it easy now," said the old man. "You're alive, Mr. Gray."

The man's smiling wife appeared—Ilsa, he assumed—with a glass of water and a straw. The old man took it and put the straw up to Nolan's lips. He took a few small sips of the water and let it wash away the sandpaper feel that coated his throat.

"Thank you," he said, still gravelly but starting to find his voice. "Where am I? Who are you? What happened?"

"I am Rene, this is my wife, Ilsa," said the man. "You are an honored guest here in our humble home. And we had hoped you could tell *us* what happened. What do you remember?"

Nolan searched his memory. "I was sealed inside a metal box and tossed into the river."

"And you would have died there," said Rene, "if we hadn't seen those fireworks."

Ilsa nodded. "Someone must have been celebrating the New Year early," she said in a thick German accent.

Nolan put up a hand, hoping they might backtrack. "I don't understand. You pulled me out of the river?"

"My husband is a fisherman," explained Ilsa. "One of the best in the city. Owns his own fishing boat."

"I was out with my crew, about to set sail, when those red fireworks lit up the water for just a second. That's when I saw the green box. It was almost completely submerged, but we threw out a net and reeled it in. Took a few hours to get back to port and find something that could cut the thing open. Pretty shocking finding you inside, Mr. Gray."

Nolan only then realized that he wasn't wearing his graphene-woven fatigues or the hood attached to the flak jacket. "You know who I am, then."

"Of course," replied Ilsa. "Everyone does."

"It was that man Vasko, wasn't it?" asked Rene. "He did this to you."

Nolan lay back on his pillow and nodded, still astounded at the knowledge that he was alive. Then something else occurred to him, and his eyes popped open.

"How long have I been here?"

"Three days," replied Ilsa. "My husband brought you home after he found you, against the protests of his crew. They wanted to take you to the hospital, or the police. But Rene wouldn't have it. He knew who you were."

Nolan looked over at the old man. He wondered if Rene might be the same age that Branford had been . . . before . . .

"Thank you. Both of you," he said sincerely.

"You need a few more days of rest," said Ilsa. "It was quite a while before your skin—particularly your hands—got their color back. But you seem to be on the mend now."

"I'd be dead at the bottom of the river if you hadn't found me. . . ."

"It was the least we could do," replied Rene. "Our daughter owes you her life. I know she'll want to meet you. You saved her from the South Street Viaduct."

The New York Gazette

NOLAN GRAY IS THE HAND

New York's popular vigilante has returned and you won't believe who's under his hood

71

The sun was no longer shining outside the large two-paned window to the left of Nolan's bed. Morning had come, but the sun was hidden behind dark gray clouds that were dumping snow all over Manhattan.

"Mr. Gray," said Rene, after gently knocking on the bedroom door and opening it by a crack. "How are you feeling this morning?"

Nolan felt numb. Maybe even in some physiological form of shock. In every conceivable way, he felt like he was dead. His ordeal in the metal box had destroyed him. The terror of dying from solitary confinement in that tiny little coffin. The freezing cold water that soaked his clothes and his body before he was pulled out of the river. The circulation being so brutally cut off to his hands. Watching his friend die in a gruesome fashion. Knowing that the general was dead because he had chosen to help Nolan. Just like Alice.

Nolan knew he should have died in the river, and he'd begun to wish that he had.

It started with the nightmares. After Rene and Ilsa had left him alone to sleep last night, he had passed out quickly but awoken screaming less than an hour later. His two hosts had rushed to his side as he cried some gibberish about not doing it again, and they later told him it took almost ten minutes for them to get him to snap out of it. He fell asleep again and was screaming again soon after. The cycle repeated again and again, all through the night.

After the sun rose and the clouds cleared inside his head, he realized that the nightmares had been about his captivity during the war. His experience in the river had brought back all the horrors he had worked years to suppress and get past. He was again that same broken, defeated, emaciated shell of a man that had escaped all those years ago.

He feared he might never sleep through the night again.

So when Rene entered his room, asking how he was doing this morning, his thoughts were lost deep within memories of that dark, terrible place—memories he hadn't let himself dwell on in years. He felt like he was back there right now, surviving minute by minute without truly feeling alive.

"Better," he lied, forcing himself to pull back from those memories, at least for a moment. "I think I'm better today."

Rene smiled. "Good. Because I have a special surprise for you: a visitor."

The old man obviously expected this to be good news, news that would lift Nolan's spirits somehow. Really, he just wanted to be alone, but he nodded appreciatively, not wanting to be ungracious.

"Come in, dear," he called out.

A woman much younger than Rene or his wife entered the room. She couldn't have been more than thirty, diminutive in size, had dark brown hair that fell back behind her shoulders, and incessantly wrung her hands together.

Rene put his arms around the younger woman's shoulders and smiled. "This is Elise, my daughter."

Nolan didn't react immediately, because he was so lost in thought. Then it hit him: Rene had mentioned last night that his daughter had been saved by The Hand in the South Street Viaduct.

Nolan couldn't bring himself to smile. The grief and sorrow in his heart blocked out any other emotions just now. But he nodded as warmly as he could in her direction. "It's a pleasure to meet you."

Elise smiled and returned the nod, her hands still writhing. "I won't keep you. I just wanted to thank you for saving my life," she was saying. "That was . . . an amazing thing you did that day."

Nolan barely heard her, but somehow good manners emerged from him on autopilot, and he mumbled, "You're very welcome."

An awkward silence followed, which Rene quickly sensed and jumped in to fill. "Elise here has something she wishes to tell you in private. She's so quiet, you know. It's hard for her mother and I to read her sometimes. . . . I'm sorry, now I've embarrassed her. I'll just stop talking and leave you two alone."

He made a hasty exit and Elise shut the door behind him. There was a second smaller click, like a lock.

When she turned to face him, there were tears running down her face and she held a Colt Anaconda revolver tight with both of her quivering hands.

Nolan blinked. His reverie came to a crashing halt at the sight of this thin, mousy woman holding a big silver six-shooter, rounds in all six chambers.

He opened his mouth to say something, but she whispered, "Shut up," as more tears streamed down her blotchy red cheeks. She let go of the revolver with one hand and produced a pair of handcuffs. She tossed them and they landed in his lap.

"Cuff yourself to the headboard," she said softly. "Both hands."

Nolan considered attempting to disarm her, but she was a good six feet away, well outside his grasp, and the way her hands were shaking, she could easily fire off a round accidentally any second, *without* him making it worse by startling her. So he picked up the handcuffs and did as he was told; when he was done, his hands were behind his head.

"What are you doing?" asked Nolan. "What is this?"

Elise swallowed as she gripped the gun again with both hands, tight enough that it might have been the very lifeline that was keeping her alive. When she spoke, her words were still unnervingly quiet. "That day. In the tunnel. You pulled me out of a burning pickup truck. It was white. Do you remember?"

He nodded. "Yeah. I do."

"You pulled me out of it," she said, her eyes growing wide and angry. "But you left Vincent to die."

"Who's—?"

"Vincent was my boyfriend!" she said, raising her volume a notch but still keeping quiet enough to not alert anyone outside the room. "He was my everything! My parents didn't know about us, they wouldn't have approved. . . . We were going to get married! We were going to have . . ." She tried to go on, but the words caught in her throat and she couldn't hold back a bitter sob.

"I'm so sorry," said Nolan, wishing he could comfort her somehow. He remembered her truck, and it was caved in on the passenger's side where another vehicle had landed on top of it. He'd had no idea there was anyone else inside.

"*Don't* pity me!" she said, suddenly raising the gun and strengthening her grip on it. "I don't want your sympathy! I don't want anything from *you*!"

Nolan looked around the room, trying to think of anything he could say or do. Anything at all. "Are you going to kill me?" he asked. He wasn't frightened, or concerned for himself. A large part of him wished that she *would* do it.

She took a step forward and pointed the gun at his head. It shook violently from her rage and her grief. Finally it fell to her side and she dropped her head into one hand and let herself cry for a long moment.

"Why didn't you go back for him?" she whispered.

Nolan had no answer that she wanted to hear. "I didn't know," he said.

Elise snapped and brought the silver revolver around to collide with Nolan's face. He was already seeing stars when she hit him again.

"*Why?*" she screamed, no longer concerned about keeping her parents from hearing. With every word, she pounded him with the gun another time. "*Why! Didn't! You! Know!*"

Nolan thought he heard shouting outside the bedroom and fists pounding against the door, but he couldn't do anything about it. He was trying as best he could to shield his face from Elise's blows, which hadn't stopped just because she ran out of words. The gun kept knocking him back and forth, sweeping one way across his face and then the other. He saw blood stain the bedspread and realized, dazed, that he wasn't feeling enough pain.

His vision went red.

He knew he was close to passing out when the big window to his left shattered and someone screamed, "*Freeze!*"

Nolan looked up through the fog and the blood and saw someone he knew. A woman. She seemed familiar. He recognized her. But what was her name? He couldn't piece any thoughts together in the haze of the stinging pain all over his face.

"*Don't you move one muscle!*" shouted the newcomer with righteous authority. She was pointing what he recognized as a black, federal-issue Sigma 9mm at Elise.

Elise was startled by the newcomer's appearance and dropped the revolver on the ground. Immediately she burst into tears again, and Nolan saw her lost, bitter eyes move from him to the woman who'd just come to his aid.

"Uncuff him! *Now!*" yelled his rescuer.

Coral! That was her name. Coral Lively! OCI agent and moonlighting vigilante. She grabbed something off of a chair near the bed and tucked it under her arm.

Nolan felt his hands being released from the cuffs, and then Coral's arm was under one of his as she helped him up from the bed.

"Stay back!" Coral warned, and Elise withdrew, backing up to the bedroom door and making no attempt to interfere.

Coral led Nolan to the broken window, where a blast of arctic wind woke him up. With a bit of awkward help, she pushed him through it, where he landed flat on his back on what must have been at least eighteen inches of snow, because it cushioned his fall nicely. Coral jumped through the window and pulled him back up to his feet.

"Come on," she said, still holding her gun with one hand and pointing it back at the window, "I've got you now."

72

Coral supported his weight, taking Nolan to an SUV parallel-parked on the street. She helped him inside and grabbed a blanket out of the back seat; wadding it up, she gave it to him to wipe the blood from his face. Coral started the vehicle, and Nolan tossed the blanket around his shoulders and tried not to shiver.

She noticed this and wordlessly turned the heat up as she turned the SUV and roared down the snow-covered street. She was all business, her eyes darting around her mirrors to ensure they weren't being watched or followed.

Nolan glanced out his window and saw that he was still in Chelsea, not terribly far from Vasko's storehouse.

Fifteen minutes later, Coral parked the vehicle at a homeless shelter and told Nolan to put the blanket up around him to conceal his face. Carrying a large backpack, she spoke to the man at the back door and then led Nolan quickly inside, down a dingy hall, and into a small room with a bed, a nightstand, and a chair.

"Sorry about the accommodations," she said, shutting the door behind him. "But they don't ask a lot of questions here."

Nolan sat down on the bed, but nothing more. He was tired of lying down.

Coral dropped her backpack and pulled out a small first aid kit. She seated herself in the chair facing him and motioned for him to lean in close enough that she could begin stitching up the numerous cuts from the revolver's impact on his skull, forehead, nose, and cheeks.

Nolan didn't want to think about what he must look like now. With the hideous scars Branford had given him already disfiguring his face, and now at least a dozen or so cuts slicing up his skin, he figured he probably resembled Frankenstein. He was glad there was no mirror in the tiny room.

He was so lost inside his own mind that he almost forgot he had company.

Pathetic! She saved your life, she's helping you now, and she's risking everything by doing it. Don't you dare forget she's here, Nolan Gray.

He sat up at attention and truly entered the room for the first time. He looked intently upon her.

"Thank you," he said.

"Of course," she replied, continuing to work at cleaning his cuts.

"No, really. I mean it," he said, grabbing her by the arm and forcing her to stop working for a moment. "Thank you."

Coral looked into his eyes and for one moment, he saw more vulnerability in hers than he'd ever noticed before. But she snapped out of it and merely nodded.

"You followed me to the warehouse?"

She used a moist towelette to wipe the dried blood away from his wounds. "For all the good it did. Got there right as Vasko sprung his trap. He had so many men there. . . . I pulled back by a block or so and watched what happened through a sniper scope. Tried to call it in, but the police didn't answer, and my director at the OCI said our team was in the middle of an operation and couldn't be recalled. And he wasn't happy that I went AWOL for a few hours.

"When I saw what they did to you . . . I just freaked. They watched you float away for a few minutes but then left, so I ran down to the riverside and tried to reach that box. The river was carrying you downstream pretty hard, and it was all I could do to keep up. I thought it was over when I spotted that fishing boat and shot off a flare to get their attention."

Fireworks, thought Nolan. *Rene said he saw fireworks right before he found me. It was Coral's flare.*

"I'm sorry about your friend," Coral said.

He appreciated that she didn't speak of what had happened with the wet cement; he didn't need to go down that memory lane right now.

"Who was he?" she asked.

"Colonel Aaron Branford," said Nolan, looking far away. "My commanding officer during the war. When Thor and I were in the enemy prison, Branford was on the other end of the transmission I sent out that led to our rescue. He led the rescue mission himself."

Coral didn't respond to this. There was nothing to say anyway. She doubled her efforts and after ten minutes or so, declared him finished. She gave him a couple of painkillers and set her first aid kit aside, on the nightstand.

Also in her backpack was the item she'd carried under her arm from Rene's house, and he saw it was his specialized black combat fatigues. "Vasko dumped your gear in the river. But you still have this."

"Let me see that," he said, and she tossed the flak jacket to him. He found a pocket knife in the medical kit and swung open the dull blade.

Coral was still examining the pants, holding the fabric up close to her eyes. "Huh. It's not Kevlar. . . . Where'd you get this?"

"Ah, you know . . . Craigslist," he said, and she actually let out a single breath of laughter.

Carefully but forcefully, he used the knife to scratch out the white hand on his jacket. He wasn't sure what it was made of, exactly; Arjay had applied it. Screen printed, maybe. Nolan worked at it for five or ten minutes, until the logo was erased and all that remained was the black material underneath.

Done, he tossed the jacket back to her. "The Hand is dead. He died in that river."

Nolan pushed back until he was sitting on the mattress with his back against the wall. He closed his eyes and said a silent prayer, asking for forgiveness and direction, and offering gratitude that his life had been spared once more.

Coral returned to the chair and sat, patiently watching and waiting.

"She was right," Nolan said, speaking at last. His eyes searched the room.

"Who was?"

"That woman with the gun," he replied. "Her name was Elise. She said I saved her life at Battery Park, but I didn't save her fiancé. I've failed as many people as I've saved."

"That's not true," said Coral, apparently surprised.

Nolan sat up and faced her. "Branford wasn't the first friend I got killed. There was another. I also blew someone up. An innocent girl in a nightclub. I torched the place because it belonged to Vasko, not knowing there was someone still inside. She's dead because of my actions. And Elise's boyfriend couldn't have been an isolated incident. I didn't know about him—how many more are there that I don't know about?"

"Nolan, stop. You're going to make yourself crazy—"

"Nolan's dead," he said, interrupting her.

"What?"

"I killed Nolan Gray when I started all this," he replied. "Now The Hand is dead too."

For the first time, Coral's confidence appeared to waver, betraying a sliver of concern. "So who's left?"

"Just me," he said in a bleak tone of voice.

"Shut up and listen to me," she said, taking him by the hand to get his full attention. She sat forward as if to look deep into him. "Whoever you are, there are still people out there who believe in you. I'm one of them. People who believe you can give them something that no else in this city can—"

He pulled away from her grasp. "If your next word is about to be 'hope,' spare me. A friend named Alice put her hope in me, and I got her killed. I'm fresh out of hope."

I'm dead. That's all I am. I am death.

Wait a minute . . .

"Vasko thinks I'm dead, right?" he said. "He doesn't know about you or the fishing boat?"

"I have no idea. But I wouldn't think he does, no."

"What day is it?"

"The thirty-first. Tonight's New Year's Eve. Pryce has got me working Times Square, but I can't imagine why. It's not like anybody in their right mind is going to show up at such a farce. . . ."

This was it, then. The end of this year would be the end of everything.

"They'll show up," he said slowly, his mind racing. "Because most of them haven't left their homes in months and they need some release. Because they aren't in their right minds. And because they'll want to see for themselves . . . what's going to happen."

He swung around and stood up, a surge of adrenaline helping steady him. With his feet under him on solid ground, he felt something he'd been missing for several days. Purpose. Resolve. Clarity.

It was time.

Nolan turned to Coral. "Will you do something for me?"

She never hesitated. "Anything."

"I need you to get some things for me," he said. "Stuff that won't be easy to come by."

She merely nodded, as if nothing were out of the ordinary about such a request. If this concerned her, she hid it well. "What are you going to do?"

"The only thing I can do. Finish what I started."

73

At sundown, Nolan drove Coral's SUV west through Chelsea until he reached the river.

Turning parallel to the shoreline, he drove south. He stopped and pulled over when he spotted Vasko's massive storehouse through the falling snow, just two blocks away. Vasko's dozens of men were still there, black forms visible through the white haze, surrounding the building just as they had a few nights ago. Nothing else seemed to have changed. Nolan noted with disgust that the cement truck was still parked on the far side of the warehouse.

He sat back in the driver's seat and slammed his foot down on the gas, tearing through the snow on the road. When he neared the storehouse, he slammed on the brakes, sliding sideways to a stop across the street from the pier where the warehouse stood.

Vasko's men stationed on this side of the building were startled and began shouting at this unwelcome vehicle and its driver.

Nolan swiveled in his seat to grab a large object that was waiting for him in the back seat, along with a black duffel bag. He opened the vehicle's door and stepped out into the biting cold, his boots crunching the snow. He walked around to the front of the SUV so Vasko's men could get a good look at him.

They recognized him right away and raised their weapons, but Nolan ignored them. Onto his shoulder, he hefted an RPG-7, the large object he'd retrieved from the vehicle's back seat. One look at the long tube-shaped device and Vasko's men shouted in fear and ran.

Nolan took quick aim with the preloaded rocket launcher and pulled the trigger. The grenade, shaped like a thick javelin with a cone on one end, jumped free of the RPG-7 and then lit like a missile, soaring straight across the street and through the outer wall of Vasko's storehouse, where it left a hole more than two feet wide. Nolan watched until it finally hit something deep inside the warehouse and ignited. The blast tore a hole in the roof and shattered the snowy quiet of the evening. Once the explosion ended, Nolan could hear dozens of Vasko's men yelling in a panic.

Nolan knelt and unzipped the duffel bag, pulling out another grenade, indifferent to the chaos taking place across the street. He loaded the grenade and fired again.

After the second explosion, he fired again. And again.

And again.

———

The crowd in Times Square already numbered in the thousands when Vasko's phone rang. He was making an early appearance before the crowd, standing atop his glass tower at One Times Square, looking down at the masses and waving with a huge smile on his face.

When his phone vibrated a second time, it was a text message from Marko. It read simply, "CALL ME! NOW!"

"What is it, Marko?" asked Vasko after dialing Marko back. "This better be important."

"The storehouse is gone!" shouted Marko, and it registered with Vasko that he was hearing a sound like rolling thunder in the background.

"Say that again," said Vasko slowly.

"It's destroyed!" yelled Marko, more panicked than Vasko had ever heard him. "Blown up, burned to the ground! Yuri, the men are saying it was him."

Vasko froze, but kept waving and smiling to the crowd. "That's not possible, he's dead."

"I know that!" shouted Marko. "But they say he just showed up with a rocket launcher and demolished everything! I've got the rocket launcher right here—he left it on the ground."

Vasko swallowed. This couldn't be happening. It was impossible. There was no way Nolan could have survived his trip down the river.

But the destruction of the storehouse and the rocket launcher being left behind were a message. Nolan Gray was coming here. He was coming here, tonight, to end it. And he wasn't going to attack the building. He was coming for Vasko himself.

Breathing hard, he hung up on Marko and dialed the number for Speck and his team. "Get down here now. Now," he said, still waving at the crowd with a faux smile. "Nolan Gray is on his way here, and you're not to allow him to reach this roof under any circumstances. I have VIP guests coming, and . . . That's right, *kill him*. Cut him up into little pieces, tear him limb from limb, blow him up, I don't care. But leave nothing of him. I want him destroyed."

Nolan was only mildly surprised to find that the RV was still where he and his friends had left it, six blocks east of Vasko's storehouse. He was less surprised to see a light was on inside.

"Hi, Arjay," he said, opening the door.

His friend raised up and gasped. He'd been curled in a fetal position on one of the cots, wrapped in a blanket. He jumped to his feet and ran to embrace Nolan.

"You're alive!" he said. "You look terrible."

With the fresh scars from that Elise woman, and the smoke and soot from his rocket launcher, he was quite certain he *did* look awful. But he knew from Arjay's unblinking stare that the man meant more than just appearance.

Nolan was dead within, and it had to be showing on the outside. His features betrayed nothing but an expressionless distance, save for a righteous fury that rose a notch higher with every thump of his heart.

"Branford's dead," he said mechanically.

Arjay looked down. "I know. I saw . . . what they did to him. Tucked tail and ran as far as I could go after that. Not altogether brave or noble of me. I'm very sorry."

"Running was the smart move," said Nolan. "Now it's time to make another."

Nolan pushed past his friend and sat down on one of the bunks. He pulled a roll of medical tape out of his pocket and began winding white strips of it around his fingers. His eyes got lost somewhere in this, and he gazed without seeing as he wrapped his fingers one at a time, slowly, like a boxer before a big fight.

"Nolan, what's happening?" prodded Arjay. "Are you okay? What are you planning? And where's your gear? Your weapons?"

"No more weapons," said Nolan. "No gadgets, no . . . nothing. Just me. I'm the weapon now."

"But what are you—?"

"You have to go," said Nolan, his countenance dark and solid as granite. "Get as far away from me as you can."

"What?" asked Arjay. "Why?"

"If you're with me, I'll get you killed," explained Nolan, looking only at the tape as he wound it around his fingers. "Take the RV and go. Leave the city. Keep driving and don't look back. Don't ever look back."

"You're scaring me, Nolan."

Done with his work, Nolan dropped the roll of tape and stood. He looked up to face his friend. "Don't be afraid. After tonight, I promise you, no one in this city will ever have to be afraid again."

74

A ferocious blizzard raged across New York at ten o'clock as Coral Lively stationed herself inside the tall building under construction near the ball-drop site.

Under direct orders of the president himself, all OCI agents had been dispersed throughout the civilian throngs who had shown up to celebrate the New Year despite the ungodly weather. All agents except for her, whom Director Pryce had diverted to sniper duty, without offering any explanation.

As ordered, she positioned herself in what would soon be a corner office on the twenty-seventh floor. She was protected from the wind and snow yet had a straight shot down to the rooftop of 1 Times Square. She was to keep an eye on Yuri Vasko's glass tower and report any suspicious activity directly back to Pryce.

Visibility was horrendous through the billowing gusts of snow. Glancing down at the revelers partying on the street, Coral wondered how in the world they were staying warm enough to have so much fun.

She was just thankful that her assignment was protected from at least some of the elements.

Her thoughts drifted to Vasko's storehouse and the incredibly satisfying heap of ruin to which it had been reduced. She was wholly unbothered by what Nolan had done with the ordnance she'd secured for him. The world was a better place without Vasko's central storehouse in it. In one bold move, Nolan had wiped out a monumental target that the OCI had only heard rumors about. Taking it down likely would have taken weeks of planning—certainly enough time for Vasko to hear of their plans and move his stash.

Nolan's attack had done the job, but her one concern was Nolan's mental state. Had he really destroyed that warehouse because it was the right thing to do? Or did he do it . . . because it felt good?

What if he showed up here, tonight, bent on doing something dangerous and foolish?

———

At 11:24, Nolan Gray burst through the glass double doors of One Times Square.

All was dark; there were no lights on inside the building, though the outside lights from Times Square offered plenty of illumination.

There was only one reason for the lights to be off inside this place, this "beacon of hope" that was supposed to light up the city. Vasko had received his message. And he was ready.

Nolan knew exactly whom he would be facing in this building tonight, and he was looking forward to it.

Centering himself, he closed his eyes and reached out with his other senses. The slightest tick of sound. Any smell that didn't belong. The tiniest disturbance of the air. It was all there, if one knew how to detect it. Nolan let his training take over, the kill-or-be-killed instincts he'd been taught reviving once more from the part of him in which they'd been buried.

A slight gust of wind to his right. He opened his eyes and stepped back, throwing out a hand to catch his assailant by the mouth. He fish-hooked the mercenary and spun around behind him, jerking the man's head around hard to the left. Nolan knocked free a Magnum that was in the man's right hand, as the assailant threw his elbow backward into Nolan's ribs. Nolan felt a crack but dropped to the ground, holding the man in a ferocious headlock with his whole arm, cutting off his oxygen supply. The man twitched and fought, but Nolan held him there with pure strength of will until he went limp.

He freed himself of the dead man and rolled sideways on the floor, snatching the pistol that had been dropped.

He closed his eyes and listened. A tiny creak to his left—

In one move, he slipped off the gun's safety, extended it toward the sound, opened his eyes, and pulled the trigger. A second mercenary across the room, holding a pair of Uzis, slumped to the ground, the wound right between his eyes.

Instantly, a third mercenary came at him growling and charging like a beast. It was the leader, Speck, the one he'd faced at the storehouse. The man's appearance was so sudden, so close, that Nolan was on his back with Speck straddled over him before Nolan had any chance to respond. Speck still wielded his twelve-inch knife, and when he stabbed at Nolan's heart, Nolan barely had time to bring up both his hands against Speck's knife hand. It was a test of strength as the merc punched him in the face repeatedly with his free hand, but Nolan refused to budge, to let that knife come any closer.

The merc reared back with a knee and struck him hard in the groin. Nolan's face turned red as the searing pain made it hard to breathe. His arms were growing tired. The knife edged closer to his chest. . . .

Nolan freed his legs and brought them in under Speck's chest. Kicking up with both feet, he sent Speck flying backward behind him. Nolan coughed and rolled, trying to catch his breath, but by the time he was on his knees, Speck was right there again, slashing with the knife. This time it came down against his arms, his chest, his neck, as the merc systematically tried to find a weak spot. Speck glanced down and saw that Nolan's jacket didn't cover his hands, so he launched a brutal sideways slash meant to cut deep into Nolan's left wrist.

Nolan ducked at the last second but popped back up again and used the other man's own momentum against him. Nolan spun him but popped the man's knife arm with one hand slamming down and the other punching upward. The knife flew into the air and Nolan grabbed it. Speck spun again, facing him, but this time Nolan was ready and he jabbed the knife straight into Speck's chest.

Speck leaned forward and spat blood into Nolan's face, grabbing Nolan by the shoulders and grinning as death came for him.

Nolan struggled against Speck's hold but finally pulled free of him, leaving the knife stuck in his chest. Speck howled in an animalistic rally cry, and then staggered backward until he fell at last.

Three down, two to go.

———

On the eighth floor, Nolan stood over the last mercenary's body with blood covering his hands.

Nolan grabbed the guy by his shirt and suspended him above the floor as he bled all over the expensive rug in Vasko's office.

"Where's Vasko?" Nolan growled.

The man smiled at him. "Where do you think?" he said with eyes that danced.

Nolan balled up his fist and backhanded the man with it, and then flung his limp frame across the room.

75

When Nolan emerged on the roof, bloodied and sporting at least three broken bones, he saw a small group of black suits gathered near Vasko at the far edge of the building, where the huge apparatus had been erected for dropping the New Year's Eve ball.

Those were no ordinary suits. Spiral wires snaked down from the ears of the men and Nolan knew immediately who had to be there in the center of them. He glanced left and right and saw that four more suits were spread out across the roof at strategic spots.

Cheers and music from the crowd below met his ears, and he noticed that the snowfall had finally abated, though it remained dangerously frigid.

Nolan stepped out into the light, brandishing the pistol he'd taken from the first mercenary down on the ground floor. He fired five shots into the air to get their attention, and then brought the gun down with both hands to point at Yuri Vasko.

Ten pistols were trained on him at once, from all of the Secret Service agents, who wore the black suits.

"I'm not here for you, Thor!" he yelled over the din. "I only want *him*!"

Everyone seemed frozen in place, the tension of the moment wound so tight that it might explode any second. Nolan didn't bother to contemplate the damage. Vasko stared Nolan down with unbidden hatred, but no one could see Nolan return the expression with his hood up around his face.

Nolan sprinted. Shots were fired, but the bullets bounced harmlessly off his fatigues, only a few of them reaching him at all. He slammed into Vasko, tackling him to the roof, and mashed the pistol's nozzle against his forehead.

He would end this right now, before Hastings or his bodyguards had a chance to intervene.

———

Coral fought against hyperventilating. Through her scope, she watched Nolan appear on the roof with a gun. Some part of her had known it would come to this, that this had to be what Nolan had been planning that morning, but she hadn't believed in her heart that he would really do it.

But then, he *hadn't* done it. Not yet.

With sweat forming on her forehead, her finger twitched at the trigger and she nearly pulled it by accident. She let go of the handle altogether, shaking off the nerves.

She couldn't believe this was real. Was Nolan really going to kill Vasko? And with the whole world watching?

"*Agent Lively!*" shouted Director Pryce into her earpiece. "*If you have a shot,* you take it!"

Lively's instincts and reflexes kicked in. She was well trained to follow orders. Without thinking, she looked down the sights of her weapon again, her finger grazing the trigger.

But there was no way she could ever shoot Nolan. Could she? She barely knew him; he barely knew her. She didn't owe him any favors, and she had no reason to believe that he might feel the same about her. . . . Nothing at all to place such a hope on, except for a fleeting mutual gaze that they'd shared as she'd stitched up his wounds just hours ago.

That was probably her imagination more than anything else. And there was no denying that Nolan had grown increasingly erratic since the tragedy at Battery Park. What if he'd suffered a mental breakdown?

And if she had the power to stop him, but did nothing . . . ?

No, that was absurd. She looked down the sights again. Nolan wasn't crazy.

She was almost certain of it.

Almost.

———

Blood drizzled down Vasko's nose and chin from the Magnum's nozzle tearing into his forehead. Nolan was so focused on Yuri Vasko that he didn't notice that the blaring music had stopped and the massive crowd in Times Square was standing still and making no noise. They watched in silence.

"*Evac!*" shouted one of the Secret Service men behind Nolan, apparently realizing that their guns were useless against this man.

"No!" yelled Hastings, pulling free from his agents.

"Sir, we have to get you to safety—"

"*You will stand down!*" thundered Hastings with more deep-throated authority than Nolan had ever heard from him. "I am not in danger."

"Sir, my job has a very clear mandate—"

"I am the president of the United States and I'm giving you a direct order. S*tand! Down!* Back away, all of you!"

Nolan was peripherally aware of his friend taking a few steps forward, free of his circle of Secret Service bodyguards, in Nolan's direction. But he ignored this.

When he spoke, Nolan's voice quivered with rage. "For the sake of my friends—because it's what they would want—you get one chance. Confess. Turn yourself in, Vasko, right now."

Vasko never blinked, never altered his expression. His face was the epitome of hate. "I would rather die than surrender to you."

"You can't possibly imagine how much I was hoping you'd say that," Nolan growled and grabbed Vasko by the throat with his free hand. He jerked him upward while moving forward until Vasko was dangling over the edge of the roof, nothing to stop his fall but pavement.

Far below, the enormous crowd gasped in unison. But no one moved.

"Don't, Nolan," said Hastings from behind.

"What are you even doing here?" Nolan asked, tossing Vasko back onto the roof. He lifted him by the back of the collar and pressed the gun into his forehead again. Vasko was once more backed up against the edge of the roof.

"I invited myself," the president replied. "I heard about what you did to the storehouse. I know you, and I know what that means. You're here to end it. But I don't believe you really want to do this."

"*Oh, yes I do!*" seethed Nolan.

"Go ahead," said Vasko, speaking up for the first time. "It's what you've always wanted, so just do it."

If it were possible, Nolan became enraged even further, his face blood red as he rounded on Vasko. "You think I *want* any of this?!" he screamed in Vasko's face. "I didn't ask for this! I just wanted to *help* people! I wanted to make things better for them! That's all I've *ever* wanted. But you couldn't allow me to have even that much. I didn't kill your family! But you were absolutely miserable, so everyone else had to share your pain. So selfish. So full of pride."

Vasko spat in Nolan's face, and Nolan almost lost his grip on him. "*You* are determined to force your beliefs on everyone, and you call me selfish? You can't *make* me subscribe to your dogma. To my dying breath, I reject you and your 'better way'!"

"Nolan . . ." said Hastings, his voice wavering only slightly.

"*He* declared war on the U.S., Thor! On you and me and all of *them*!" cried Nolan, nodding at the silent crowd below. "How many members of your OCI are dead because of him? How many of those people down there have lost someone *all* because of *him*?"

"I know he deserves it; that's never been in question. . . ." said Hastings slowly.

"I could do it, Thor," said Nolan softly, pressing the nozzle against Vasko's head. He was barely able to keep from shaking. "You can't. *They* can't. But I can. And I *should*."

"Do it, Nolan," shouted Vasko. "Kill me!"

Nolan's face was still red and he was breathing fast as Vasko leaned in. "I could do it right here," Nolan said, "in front of all these people. I *want* to, more than I've ever wanted anything in my life. What does that say about me?"

"No." Hastings shook his head, unwilling to entertain this. "You're a good man, and you always have been. The best man I know."

"I'm a good *killer*," said Nolan, as if he hadn't heard anything the president said. "It's what I do, better than anyone can. It's what I was born to do."

———

Coral's finger touched the trigger.

"*Agent Lively, you take him out!*" yelled Pryce in her ear. "*We have to protect the president!*"

Nolan's not here for the president and you know it, you old windbag....

But what if Hastings got caught in the crossfire? What if Nolan really had lost control? This whole situation was nearing madness and getting worse by the second.

"*Agent, take that shot! That is a direct order! Or you'll stand before a court martial first thing in the morning!*"

Coral gripped the rifle and focused down the sights for the last time.

———

"Nolan, please," said Hastings, taking a step closer. "Please don't."

"Are you a man?" screamed Vasko. "Are you a soldier? You said so yourself: this is war! *Finish it!* "

"We killed a lot of people during the war, Thor. This man is more dangerous than any of them. He's the *enemy*. The one rule during war is that you kill the enemy."

"Nolan, are you really here for justice? Or for something else?"

"Don't you dare ..." seethed Nolan. "This world is cruel and hateful, and no matter how hard you try to do something *good*, there will always be people like Yuri Vasko! Why should anyone *bother* trying to make a difference? What's the point of any of it?"

Hastings was starting to breathe faster. Nolan knew his friend was growing desperate.

"Nolan, if you do this, he wins."

"If he lives, they died for nothing!"

Nolan fixed his eyes on the throng far below. So far away at this height, they were little more than large dots, but every dot held two eyes that were trained on him. So many eyes, so many lost and weary souls.

"Look at them!" Nolan shouted, nodding at the people standing shoulder-to-shoulder in Times Square. "Every one of them has lost someone. This isn't about me—it's about what this man has done to all of us!"

"Then let the legal system sort it out," said Hastings. "I will personally take him into custody right now, and you have my word—"

"*No!*" roared Nolan. "The legal system is a *joke*. It's broken, Thor, it's all broken! Good people are harassed at the pleasure of the courts to the point of losing their sanity, while scumbags like Vasko get away with anything. No! I won't let him destroy anyone else. Never again!"

Nolan hated this man with everything he was. "This is war," he whispered. "I can't let him live."

"This is not a war you'll win with a gun. Nolan, think! You used to know that, but somewhere along the way—"

Nolan pulled the trigger.

The shot rang out, echoing through Times Square. He was sure it was louder than any gunshot that had ever been fired.

Time froze. Nothing moved. No one on the roof or a single soul among the masses on the streets below.

Vasko slowly tipped toward the edge of the rooftop, teetering there for an endless moment before suddenly slipping off and plummeting to the ground below.

Hastings watched the body fall with eyes wide. He took a step back and shifted his numb expression to his friend.

Nolan looked at the gun in his hand, and the other people on the roof and the vast crowd far below all disappeared. He was alone, watching as a small whiff of smoke wisped from the end of the barrel and then dissipated in the icy atmosphere.

The gun. It was an extension of his arm, the instrument of his will. What he'd done was right. It was good, he was sure it was. It had to be done.

Another second passed and Nolan staggered, for just a moment, as if he were the one who'd been shot. He looked at the gun again, this time cold and offensive in his hand. He almost felt the burning of it in his palm. Its touch seared him.

The gun fell from his grasp and disappeared after it tumbled into the crowd below. Everything spun wildly—the world, the mass of people, the skyscrapers, even that ridiculous brightly lit ball that had touched the roof a few seconds after he pulled the gun's trigger. His knees buckled as reality twisted around him.

No! No, this was righteous! Don't you let the guilt in—it had to be done!

He swallowed hard to keep from vomiting. It felt as if the entire world were crumbling around him, and he was a tiny, inconsequential dot on the canvas of the universe. A dot who deserved to die.

Muffled voices, as if coming from a far-off distance, ordered him to put his hands up. Hastings' Secret Service agents were surrounding him, guns raised, and he watched them move as if in slow motion. Hastings was doing nothing to stop them; he merely watched in silence.

It didn't matter. Nothing mattered anymore.

He was done.

Justice prevailed.

Mission accomplished.

EPILOGUE

The next two days of Nolan Gray's life were the very worst. Despite all the horrors he'd suffered in his past, and the loved ones he'd lost along the way, he actually managed to make things even worse.

He was left completely alone in NYPD lockup—at his own request—and sequestered himself in the hell that was his mind. It was a new form of torment that he'd never before undergone, and he let it overtake him, body and soul.

It was the fate of which he was worthy. His "grand" reward.

For hours on end, the shooting replayed in his mind. It was true that he did it for the people of New York as much as for himself. But he hadn't just crossed the line by killing Yuri Vasko, he'd erased it. Nolan wasn't better than that man so consumed by evil. He *was* him.

The better way he'd promised was a lie.

Killer. Murderer.

Chief of sinners.

A police officer opened the outer door to the cellblock and stepped inside. As he was unlocking the door to Nolan's iron cubicle, Nolan snapped out of his inner anguish.

"I requested no visitors."

The officer, an NYPD sergeant, was a slightly overweight fifty-something black man. He sat down on the bench across from Nolan and stared at him. Nolan saw no judgment on the man's blank face.

"Do I look like I'm here for a visit?" the officer replied.

Nolan was so tired. So tired of everything. Why couldn't they just leave him alone? Who was this guy? What did he want?

Wait a minute. This guy sitting across from him looked vaguely familiar.

Nolan squinted, trying to read the metal name tag above the officer's badge. He couldn't quite see it from that distance.

"Regan," the man said. "Sergeant Regan."

Regan . . . ?

Alice.

"Barry Regan?" Nolan asked, feeling a rising bitterness toward this man. This abusive husband who had tormented and then hunted his wife like a predator.

Barry nodded. "That day we met . . . you busted into my home and took my wife away. I wanted to thank you."

Wait, what?

"Didn't see that coming, right?" said Barry, half a smile on his lips. "Doctors diagnosed me with a chemical deficiency. It was messing me up in the head, said it 'increased my disposition toward aggressive and violent behavior.' The man you met in my home wasn't me. Not the real me. I don't know who he was, but thank God he's gone. Doctors gave me some good meds."

Nolan blinked and let out a cautious exhale. He didn't know what to say.

"I read your statement—your debriefing or whatever," said Barry. "For what it's worth, I'm grateful for what you did for her."

"I got her killed," said Nolan, his voice thick and heavy, his eyes unable to meet Barry's.

"You helped her *live*," Barry said. "She hadn't been alive in years, because of me. She just . . . *existed.*"

Nolan certainly knew what that was like.

"Sooner or later I would have killed her," he went on. "God help me, I would have. We were told years ago that Alice couldn't have children.

Doctors said I had some kind of psychotic break or something. That was how it started. But for the short time she was with you, she was alive and she was safe. From me."

Nolan shook his head. "I'm so sorry. For your loss. The world . . . is a darker place without her in it."

"Yes, but heaven is a brighter one." Barry smiled. "And I'll see her there. I found something of hers a while back and I'd like you to have it."

As Nolan watched, Barry Regan pulled out something small and black from under his arm. Nolan hadn't even noticed he was carrying anything.

Barry got to his feet, crossed the room, and handed the small object to Nolan. "I think she'd have given it to you if she could've."

"Thank you," said Nolan, speechless. Tears came to his eyes when he realized that the small object still smelled like her.

Barry never sat back down. He stood in the doorway, allowing Nolan a moment.

"Heard a rumor that the president might pardon you."

"What?" He couldn't have heard right.

"Probably has something to do with the two or three *million* calls and emails the White House has received in the last forty-eight hours."

Again, Nolan had no idea what to say. It was too much—far too much to hope for. He didn't deserve such treatment.

"In the meantime, I'm afraid we've run into a problem. You have no valid ID. You say you're Nolan Gray, but you can't prove it. Your face is all messed up. We can't match up your prints. The perpetrator wore gloves."

"Why does that matter?" he asked. "I'm guilty. I did it. Most of the country has probably seen the footage by now."

"The video shows a nondescript man in a black hood. Could be anyone."

Nolan didn't understand where this was going. It was preposterous, though it occurred to him that without the white hand emblem, his black fatigues would appear to be nothing out of the ordinary. "So take my DNA and run a comparison."

Barry nodded patiently, expecting this argument. "Our investigators couldn't find the killer's DNA at the crime scene. Snow's melted and whatever was there is gone. Gun's gone, too. Disappeared after it fell."

"But *I* did it. *I* killed him."

Barry Regan leaned back and took a long, deep breath. "In the last forty-eight hours, more than seven thousand New Yorkers have turned themselves in, confessing to the murder of Yuri Vasko."

Nolan was sure he'd just been punched in the stomach, because there was no air in his lungs. This wasn't possible. For the second time, he was sure he'd heard Officer Regan wrong.

"That number, by the way, includes a very persistent government agent who's camped out in my office as we speak and refuses to leave until she's allowed to see you."

Had he not been so wracked by guilt and confused at what Barry was trying to say, he would have laughed at this last bit.

"NYPD's overwhelmed and understaffed," Barry said. "The paperwork alone is going to take months to sort through. Maybe years. So I suggest you retire. Find yourself someone to be with, and settle down."

Barry walked out but didn't shut the cell door.

"Wait, what are you doing?" said Nolan, rising quickly in alarm. "You're letting me get away with—"

Barry swiveled his head to look at Nolan through the bars. "You're not getting away with anything. You've been through enough, son. Whatever punishment you deserved in this life—it's already paid. Everything else is between you and God."

"But . . . you can't . . ." Nolan blustered as Barry reached the outer door. He threw out the only thing he was able to articulate. "Why are you . . ."

Barry tossed him a saddened expression, and Nolan was surprised to see a tear roll down the other man's cheek. "Because I know from personal experience what you need. And the only place you'll find it is in that book you're holding."

Nolan watched in stunned silence as Barry exited, leaving him there alone, the jail cell door still open.

In his hand rested a well-worn small black Bible.

He opened it and saw writing in the margins. It was Alice's handwriting. And it wasn't on just this page, but almost every page he turned to. This was a precious gift, one for which he was wholly unworthy.

An ancient bookmark peeked out at him, a strip of fabric woven like a tiny doily. He flipped to that page and looked down at a passage that Alice had underlined and highlighted in yellow.

Tears rolled down Nolan's cheeks, and he couldn't remember the last time that had happened. The words stepped out of the page and spoke as if they'd been written just for him. He hoped they could become true for him once more. The better way he'd lost.

I have told you these things, so that in me you may have peace. In this world you will have trouble. But take heart! I have overcome the world.

ACKNOWLEDGMENTS

To my family: my wife, Karen, my kids, Evan and Emma, my mom, my brother, Ross, his wife, Melissa, and their two girls, Kara and Kaylee, and my in-laws, Larry & Evelyn, and Karen's brother, Scott. Thank you all so, so much. I could not do what I do without your love and support.

To my friends at Bethany House Publishers, most especially my editor, David Long, who has the patience of a saint, and the incomparable Paul Higdon, whose incredible designs for my book covers have managed to blow my mind every single time. Thanks for everything. It's been a fun ride and I enjoyed every minute of it!

The crew at Alive Communications, Beth Jusino and Andrea Heinecke in particular, for their advice, help, and hard work.

To Jesus: I exist, I breathe, and I love all because of you. You are everything. I am your servant forever.

To you, dear reader: this book you are reading would not be possible without your loyalty, enthusiasm, and support. Thank you so much for taking this ride with me. Let's take another one soon!